THE SALT LINE

Books by Elizabeth Spencer

Elizabeth Spencer

THE SALT LINE

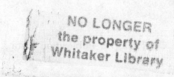
DOUBLEDAY & COMPANY, INC.
Garden City, New York

DOUBLEDAY CANADA LIMITED
Toronto, Ontario

1984

Library of Congress Cataloging in Publication Data
Spencer, Elizabeth
  THE SALT LINE

  I. Title.
PS3537.P4454S3 1984   813'.54
Library of Congress Catalog Card Number 83-45109
Canadian Cataloguing in Publication Data
Spencer, Elizabeth
  The salt line

I. Title.
PS3537.P44S34   813'.54   C83-098625-1

ISBN: 0-385-15698-7

To Joan for all her help,
and to her son,
Chris Wallman, a fine artist,
and to Tia and Peter

The author wishes to express gratitude to the Director and Corporation of Yaddo, where large portions of this book were written.

The town of Notchaki, Mississippi, lies west of Biloxi and east of Gulfport. It would have been hit by Hurricane Camille if it had really been there, but it exists, like all the characters in this book, and the island they frequently go to, only in these pages.

THE SALT LINE

part I

1

On a Monday morning in October, Arnie Carrington went into a drugstore in Gulfport, Mississippi, and saw the one person he least wanted to see. Lex Graham. Lex was not supposed to be in that area at all.

The first thing Arnie noticed was a hat. The hat was of fresh white canvas, as if just bought by someone unused to the strong sun of the Gulf Coast; it went floating as if with nothing under it, just above the stacked products at the top of the high display shelves. Something in the hat's stop-and-go motion, now turning toward a shelf, now moving on, seemed on the first instant to touch a nerve of familiarity. A clerk disappeared into the lane with the hat. Then Arnie heard a voice coming at him, around and over the air-freshener room sprays (pine, apple blossom, balsam, spice):

"Do you have any *Nox*zema?"

Nobody said it that way, the word was Noxzema. But the rich, almost Yankee roll of that classroom voice would let the world at large know that the speaker was never wrong. Others might make mistakes, but not Lex Graham.

Arnie Carrington almost said the name aloud.

But he did not. Lex and Dorothy, he thought. Arnie, stocky, could be standing yet indefinitely concealed if no one entered his aisle. The Grahams and the Carringtons, employed at the same university, had once been a foursome, "best friends." Since then? Oh, Lord! He preferred not to think of it.

He sat down on a small stepladder which had been left nearby, perhaps by the clerk now helping Lex. He leaned elbow on knee, chin on palm, and read labels from different brands of mouthwash. Maybe, he thought brightly, it wasn't Lex Graham, after all.

"Thanks so much." The hat was moving again. It proceeded toward the cashier. Arnie Carrington peered out through an ambush of toothbrushes hung from a tall rack with a multitude of little arms. The brushes were each in sanitized plastic containers pasted on cardboard, were varicolored, were soft, medium, or hard. He saw the man paying at the register, black hair sprinkled with gray showing below the band of the hat, dark blue tailored jacket, white shirt which would undoubtedly reveal a knotted scarf at the throat should he turn, white duck pants, loafers. Spying further still, Arnie saw outward through the window where a new beige Mercedes was parked horizontally with the curb. Inside, a slim woman was sitting erect, waiting. The woman's hair was streaked blond and worn in a long bob. There was also someone in the back, less clearly visible. Their child, he guessed, now grown. The man flicked through the glass door.

Eventually, Arnie Carrington got up and walked out, having forgotten what he came for. He found his own ordinary Chevrolet. A Mercedes? Lex? Full professorship had been true for a good while, a chairmanship he could believe, but even so. Still, he half remembered now, something he had heard about Lex, involving money. . . .

He saw his own large, sun-splotched hands, brushed with gold-red hair, tremble on the steering wheel. Whiskey nerves or bad memories, or both? What else was needed? There was an odd taste in his mouth.

They can't do this to me.

2

"Now there's a beauty!" said Lexington Graham at the wheel of his Mercedes. His wife Dorothy beside him and his daughter in the back seat were looking, too. He stopped the car, in which the clean antiseptic smell of Noxzema was evenly dispersed over the new leather upholstery smell beneath.

The house—white, two-story—overlooked the water of the Sound from the vantage of a rise which along that flat way was sudden and unusual. Another thing to marvel about was that it was standing at all, the 1969 hurricane having swept away all of its grander, larger neighbors. But there it was. Its outward view was unbroken. A piece of old highway, slanting up from the new, looped past the front gate. It was flanked by wind-twisted live oaks hung with moss, which were not so near the house or so large as to oppress the free and airy atmosphere around it. Two dormer windows were set in the slant of its apron roof. The front porch had been partially screened at one time, or so it would seem from its latticed facing to the left of the entrance steps; but the screens were completely gone.

On either side of this property with its few standing oaks lay desolate, weed-grown lots with broken trees or dying ones, blasted black by wind-driven sand or water laced with sand.

In some cases, all growth had been swept away, leaving nothing to see until the swamp line, itself still ragged from the catastrophe, a half-mile away. At ground level, concrete foundations or stumps of brick supports for vanished houses could occasionally be seen. Off to the left, coming almost to the smashed line of the seawall, a whole grove of live oaks was standing stone dead, their broken limbs hanging aloft by catching to one another, a family hard-hit still making its gesture.

"If the screen hadn't blown off the porch, I'd think I was dreaming it," said Dorothy Graham. "But there's bound to be something wrong, else people would still be living in it, not selling it. Do you guess the foundations got sucked out from under it and it's sitting on two splinters?"

"It may be all right. Worth investigating anyway," said Lex Graham. He was jotting down the name and number of the realtor in a small black notebook which he held on his knee.

There was a tennis court on the property; the high backstops—wire on a scaffolding of iron posts—had been left as they were. They flopped against themselves, the wire uncurled and sometimes missing, the posts sagging inward, or fallen completely. The asphalt was sprigged with weeds. Rousing from the back seat, the girl Lucinda came into the empty pause which followed her father's stowing of notebook and pen within various pockets.

"It looks so nice. Maybe they didn't leave it because of the storm. Maybe it was something else."

"Let's invent it," her father challenged.

"Somebody died and left them another house."

"In Florida."

"Long Island."

"The West Indies . . . a Jamaica house."

"Somebody died and left them a yacht. They're sailing around forever."

"Like the Czar."

"What a bore," said Dorothy, who had not joined in.

They were silent, sitting in the beautiful car.

"I'm tired," Lucinda complained, as though giving a reason for not carrying on this fantasy. They had done nothing for two days but look at houses, which all, until now, for one reason or another, were not quite the thing, damaged in some way or not even built yet. She looked out at the water. A soft late-season haze lay over the surface, as far out as could be seen, vanishing at horizon point into a mystery, tinged yellow and violet, suggesting ghost ships with happy children aboard them. No one was sailing.

Dorothy also looked outward toward the far-off west curve of the Sound. A fishing boat or two were visible out near the in-curving tip of the point, motionless. The gulls hung evenly, high up, sentinel. She did not share her thoughts. She was a woman prone to revolve between extremes of efficient work—the housewife's virtue—and seasons of reflection, which might go on, wordlessly, for hours. With women friends on the telephone or over coffee, she could release torrents of chatter, but with her family she seldom did, and was given to caustic phrases.

Lex at last turned the car back onto the highway and drove east to Gulfport again. The white of the newly built filling stations, of the line down the center of the highway, of the beach sand on their right, seemed fresh as new paper.

They ate silently together at a restaurant in the town and then took the highway inland, going home. It would seem that the very next words were Lucinda's, when they were sixty miles along the way.

"Can a house make us happy?"

The father started, half looked around, tightened his hands on the wheel, said, "When the estate was settled, I took a turn, to have something like a finer life. That can be a happy one, too. I can just see you in the house we liked, Lucy."

"Coming down the steps in my little hoop skirts," Lucinda giggled.

Her parents laughed.

"The whole Coast, the way I feel about it, is going to build up again," her father said. "These places always do, after disasters."

"It could be great," the girl admitted.

"It's great even to think of having it for you—for us," he amended, glancing at his wife. "Mother's not talking. She has a lot of work to do in a house."

"I do like the water," Dorothy said finally. She plucked at or straightened something on her stocking, at the ankle. "As for one thing or another making anybody happy—that's another thing."

"I don't follow."

She was reluctant to explain, but seemed to know she had to try. "It's nothing you can do for yourself. That's what I meant."

"Trying is all," said Lex Graham, his voice a mixture of cheer and finality, terminal to argument.

But the view he had seen, like a watery Elysium, hung steadily before his inner eye, as though he watched it already from the vantage point of the house that had so firmly refused destruction. He could go beyond professorship, assuming a new, more princely guise.

3

It was bills that worried Arnie Carrington chronically. They fell about his ears like snow. If it wasn't for taxes, it was for surveying. If it wasn't for property upkeep, it was for insurance. In one blinding hour, as he had wandered around the tumbled pathetic wreckage of the Gulf Coast, he had had his vision, and had known his calling. Something, at least, could be restored, and it was for restoring that he rose to lead the volunteers, and bought up property wherever he could find it. He had even considered the house Lex Graham had found but had no place for a residence in his scheme. On one of his properties, a row of low-rent houses smashed and derelict still, some stray dogs had camped and whelped, and when the city had removed them he was charged for the service. Signs were posted on the grounds of an old hotel he now owned: KEEP OUT, CONDEMNED, etc. But who paid for the signs?

Arnie wrote checks, he borrowed money; but mainly he thought of himself like somebody standing on the bank of a stream watching the water flow, the Money river running with its own little intimate rustle, and someday it would run dry, no matter how grand and sincere its source had been. He had his paper triumphs still, but they were long in turning into cash.

"To add to my troubles," Arnie Carrington said to his architect, Joe Yates, whom he also owed money, "this guy Graham and his family showed up down here this morning. Now I hear that he's come into a big inheritance. He's buying here."

"Never heard of him," said Yates.

"We were colleagues in the same department, up in Hartsville at the university. Up till the time I came here, four years ago."

"Nice to have neighbors," said Joe Yates.

"Nice is the last thing it is." They were sitting over coffee in a motel restaurant. "He's a guy I can do without." He gave a shudder, rabbit running over his grave. He almost looked behind him. "Everything is apt to spook me, but seeing this Graham bunch really got to me. I had an idea he was spying."

"You growing a neurosis?" Yates wanted to know.

"I haven't got time, or I might."

"You got enough worries," said Yates, among whose own worries was Arnie himself.

"It does take time to get neurotic," Arnie said. "I never thought of that. This guy Graham, though—in some ways, he's a sketch. I knew him well once; he called me his best friend. His father owned some little insurance company up in Meridian. They lived in a big old drafty house and nobody thought they had all that much money. Left close to two million after taxes, I'm told. I made a special call up to friends to find out. Seems it's all for old Lexington. There was a sister but she had died, out in Oregon. Think about year after year, all the long years since the Depression, and these little insurance policies being written, going out, enough to circle the globe twice—Negro burials, theft and accident, old maids' jewelry, fires and lightning—the worries of three or four counties in Alabama and Mississippi, all the way to Laurel, almost to the Coast, soothed and protected by Graham Coverage, Inc. Flint-fisted and Presbyterian. No outward sign of wealth. Probably ate baloney sausage, store bread, and canned beans. His son Lex always thought himself lucky to have been sent to college."

"What did he study?"

"Crazier yet. Neoclassical literature. The old man wouldn't have understood a word of it. Probably never thought to ask. Lex might have walked into the office of his major professor one day and said, 'What can I write my thesis on?' and the guy said, 'What about *The Rape of the Lock?*' So he boned his way through."

"Now he's rich."

"Rolling."

"You should have kept up the friendship; maybe you could borrow off him."

"I wasn't thinking of that," said Arnie. "Only thinking that the desert can bloom like a rose. You look out the window one morning and where there was nothing but rock and cactus, now there's a garden, all pink, white, and red, drenched in dew. I was thinking Lucky Lex."

"Did you always laugh at him?"

Arnie drained his coffee and didn't answer. He said so long and drove home. His own house, along the beach drive, up a shell road, was enveloped in shrubs and trees with untrimmed foliage so thick and close as to all but hide it from view. It might as well have been built up in a tree. Only the sheet of glass in the living room gave boldly out toward the highway, the sand beyond, and the water. So what if the Grahams come here, inheritance and all? We'll move in separate worlds. Besides, hadn't it all been just another chapter, that life up at Southern Pines University? There had been, in the course of sixty-odd years, so many chapters: wars, degrees, jobs, marriages.

He took his messages from the Ansafone. Had to renew the bank loan. Extension . . . how to get it? He lunched out of the refrigerator, standing, thought of consulting the Buddha from an Oriental garden, which the hurricane had beached up in his yard. Good on spiritual problems, but weak on profit and loss. Ask him about the Grahams, then? Say, Look here, old buddy. It's Lexington W. Graham I've just seen. He tried to kill me once.

He took a nap and wrote some letters. A thunderstorm came and went. The sky stood loftier above, he noted, going out to the post office, then to drive along the Sound again, actions that sought to leave anxiety behind.

4

Arnie had once written to an army friend who wanted to move there:

"The Gulf Coast is not what it was, nor will it ever be that way again, because of Hurricane Camille. This hurricane was the giantess to end them all. It struck in 1969, along with a tidal wave as tall as the Blue Ridge and an honor guard of eighteen tornadoes. The Coast now is nothing but the bones of itself, stripped bare. Of course, people are building back. There are new houses, subdivisions out from old towns, a lot of new motels and restaurants going up along the beach, nightclubs, shopping centers, everything except what your heart desires. Some of the old remains, looking surprised at itself, and seedy, like people after major surgery."

Had he gone on to describe his own reason for still being down that way, his latest enthusiasm, his worthy cause? How he had vowed to preserve whatever was left of the precious, languid waterfront so cherished from his youth, to restore the spirit it once had had. A resurrection of sorts—if there was any

such thing. Could it be done? Everybody said: No, resign to
change. But he thought you had to try. The day he drove out
of his property to get the Grahams off his mind, he fell to
thinking of birds and fish, who, after the disaster, had found it
only natural to return. The life struggle of the pelican, for instance, was a special cause of his; he had researched their
awkward problems and had written letters to set their case
aright. The hurricane was not their major worry. It was DDT
which had weakened them till they were unable as newborn
chicks to rise from their shells, or having accomplished that,
to spread wing and fly. But now that laws favored them, they
were increasing again, and stroked steadily in toward land, in
files, from the far Gulf water, toward pilings left standing in
lines or bunched in groups, out in the water. These were once
supports for fishing piers and docks. The pelicans perched on
top of each with their coarse wings folded, like curiously
carved statues in wood on wooden stands.

Unlike them, the gulls were beautiful and crazy. They
were numerous, vivid and swift at dawn and dusk, planing at
test pilot tilts, nose-diving for fish. At midday in the glaze of
sun, they drifted lazily up somewhere alone, a part of thought.
But sometimes, singly, they appeared unexpectedly close, like
somebody come on purpose to tell you something, thought
Arnie Carrington, observing one just landed near a waterside
restaurant and fishing pier where he had parked his car.

It's about to tell me something, a girl called Mavis Henley
thought.

She was sitting in an empty restaurant near Biloxi at two-
thirty in the afternoon, near a series of screened windows
overlooking the water. There was a pier outside, only a few
seasons old, the brown not faded out of the wood, and a small
marina which now harbored only three boats, spaced out. On

the gunwale of the nearest to her of these, the gull had perched after circling and banking and putting down its long claws. It had then looked at her, head sideways, slit eye a bright jewel glinting out its mystery in her direction.

What are you saying? What do you have to tell me? Which gull are you? Who told you what to say to me?

She eventually rose from the table, on which nothing sat but her cigarettes and empty coffee cup, to look out through the screen at it, wondering why it could give the illusion of being sent to her alone, but as she reached the window, the door at the front of the restaurant banged shut and the bird, a large, heavy-bellied boat of a creature, suddenly gave itself strong wing and rose in the updraft, vanishing into light. She was left with a feeling of emptiness and the sound of a man's footsteps approaching from behind.

The man went to the bar and sat down. When no one came out of the kitchen, she went back of the bar herself and got him what he wanted, a cold beer. When he had poured it out, he looked up at her and, she supposed, encountered the same look the gull had. It was her present dead end of a situation that made her think every crab had crawled up out of the water to reproach her, that conch shells, sighing like ghostly tides, were really whispering a personal message, that a stranger's child was going to tug at her skirt in the supermarket and tell her what to do next.

The man at the bar wore the usual stained cotton twill trousers of boating and fishing men. A pullover collarless sweatshirt, though clean, did nothing to flatter a wrinkled neck, burnt and scaly from the sun, with a few grizzled hairs around the Adam's apple, now working pistonlike on the beer. His hair, once bronze, was streaked with white bands and his yellowish eyes were examining her out of the ambush of heavy eyebrows above an untrimmed mustache.

"Met you somewhere, a few months back," he said. "I know: you were at the air force liaison bash at the Buena Vista. You and Frank Matteo, that's it."

She did not confirm or deny. She remembered going, did not remember this man, though in a blazer, shirt and tie, with a haircut, mustache trimmed, he may well have seemed distinguished, different anyway. He asked for another beer.

"I was looking for Matteo," he said.

"He's not here."

"Coming soon?"

She hesitated. "I'm not sure when. I can tell him, whatever it is. Can he call you?"

He seemed to lose the thread. "Tell you why I didn't recognize you. I thought you really looked good that night. Frank's picked him quite a gal, I thought. Now . . . you been sick or something?"

What saved her from taking what he said as a put-down was the careful, intense interest in the eyes . . . animal-colored eyes that probed through surfaces (had she seen once in a Sunday funny paper something about X-ray eyes?—she couldn't recall). At least he was seeing her. She felt herself, till then like the splattering-out of a spirit overextended, too complex, pull together, shape up, snap into place: five-feet-six, one-twenty-eight pounds, dark hair, gray eyes, a light sprinkling of around-thirty wrinkles, a way of shaking back her hair that amounted to gesture. She shook it back now.

"I haven't been too well," she admitted.

"A shame," the man said. Then he smiled at her, as though in encouragement.

A family of four trailed in, seeking food. She told them that none was served before five, and they went away.

"Do you want Frank to call you?"

"No, I wanted to talk to him personally. I've been

meaning to look him up. The fact is, we've always had a pretty good friendship. I've got this island out there in the Gulf." He pointed out the window and when she turned to look, he laughed, correcting himself. "Oh, you can't see it from here, but it's out there, take my word. I bought it from some nuns, back when my wife was living. The nuns had a retreat there, but it all got blown away in the hurricane. My wife and I, we had some good times in mind for going out there, taking friends and all."

"I've heard Frank mention it."

"In what way?"

"Oh, that if you wanted to sell he wanted to buy. Is that what you want to tell him, that you want to sell?"

"No, not that. I don't want to. I just want to keep his friendship, make him understand there's nothing personal."

"Gambling," she said, right out. "You might not want it used for that."

"I didn't say that. You did."

"I know." She let the conversation fade. "Maybe he's not coming in today. . . ."

"Oh, he's planning to come. He was meeting me." She heard her own voice. It was a statement she had to hear to believe, that she had to say in order to think it might still be true.

A young black came out from the kitchen into the bar area. He was carrying a mop.

"What time," Mavis Henley asked, "is Mr. Matteo coming in today? Did he tell you?"

"He ain't coming in," the boy said. "He gone for two, three days. He might be back Thursday. He might stay gone all weekend."

The boy did not look up as he said this; the words, as he knew very well, were insulting to Mavis Henley and he did not hesitate to deal them out, cards from a stacked deck. All around the room, above the area taken by the continuous joined line of windows—many of which were raised, the fall air not being so hot at present—enlarged photographs of Frank Matteo were framed and hanging at a forward tilt for all to see. He was flashing his white smile as he posed in his restaurant and on his pier with guests who had names of national or local prominence, or who had simply caught big fish, or who were, more simply still, stupendously (in tiny bikinis and floppy hats) female. The long black hands wrung out the mop into the bar sink. The boy began to mop the floor.

"I'm in the way," said Mavis Henley. "I guess I better move. Want another beer?"

"No, thanks."

He kept looking at her with concerned eyes, drawing tears up into her own. Her hands shook when she turned to ring up the cash. To have said that about gambling was not the right thing. But she wanted him to think she had her rights, knew Frank's business.

The man was getting up from the bar.

"You come along," he said. "If he's away, you got nowhere to go. You might as well kill an hour with me."

How could you judge about messages? Mavis Henley reflected. You could only know, seeing an envelope addressed to you, that a letter had arrived. You couldn't know what an almost-stranger's eyes were saying to you, but you could know there was something in them that might help out.

She picked up her bag and followed him.

5

That was how she happened to come wandering behind this man she hardly knew, into a patch of camellia trees, oleander bushes, sprawling azaleas, and little new pine and oak trees. There was a house among them somewhere, though hardly visible except for the roof and a second floor surrounded by screened windows, a roof beam running east and west, crowned behind like the feather on an Indian's head by a clump of longleaf pines the wind had not knocked down. Mavis Henley's sandals rustled the stiff, fallen camellia leaves. She trailed the positive step of Arnie Carrington, its slight bound holding on to a younger self. A flagstone walk wound from the shell drive to the front door, which was set in a low white Spanish arch, small windows on either side. She stepped inside.

A big living room opened off the entrance, where sofas faced each other at right angles to an empty fireplace, and a coffee table between overflowed with books and papers. At the farther end, a table with benches held a typewriter and some plants. There were bookshelves lining the back wall from floor to ceiling, all full.

He let her stand and look. The staircase had a double entrance, one from the front door, another from the hall. Its upper reach was open to view; an iron rail separated it from the room below. "I was going to seal it in," Carrington explained, "but I liked the look of it. Mounting through air, you see." He started showing her things. A framed picture of somebody historical or literary hung in the corner near some books. "Byron. Surely you know him." "Who?" The head was lifted, the hair dark and wavy; he wore a white shirt and black flowing tie.

Now he pointed out a shaggy lion skin hung up on the stairwell wall, and reminded her of the Great Danes, a matching stone pair in the front yard, and the white wrought-iron bench. This was largely, he admitted, a scavenged house. "The skin was auctioned off with a lot of other stuff in an Ocean Springs sale, but I found those dogs washed up against the side of an old bank building. One had his foot and an ear missing, but I found the ear. That bench you passed was upside down out on the beach. Somebody had left a suitcase full of baby clothes on it. People did crazy things. You weren't here then?" "No." "You saw those urns. I found them in the middle of a road to what used to be a restaurant. One had a drowned cat in it. I mean to plant some verbena."

He went on to other discoveries: a set of English bone china which had landed practically whole in a pine clump; a mounted moose head which had looked down at him out of a live oak ten miles north; golf clubs had dribbled out through a cemetery; a bayou had given him a floating soup tureen. For a while, with luck like that he had become a full-time scavenger. Upstairs he had a roomful of stuff he'd never even sorted through. When something started smelling, he threw it out. Oriental rugs, for instance. His greatest find, though, was the Buddha.

"Buddha?" she echoed. He said she would have to see. "Not that I found it so much as it found me." She felt that she was turning through a dance. She had come there to talk maybe, get a drink maybe; it had crossed her mind that fending off a pass might be required—but a lot of objects was the last thing she'd expected. Now, it seemed, a Buddha.

Out the back door, there it was. Mavis was not ready for

an Oriental bronze god eighteen feet high, more or less, sitting
cross-legged on a plant—a lotus leaf, said Carrington—with the
thick-lipped smile on its curly mouth, a soft-looking chest and
belly, and a hand raised as if about to say something—a blessing, said Carrington. Mavis sat down on the back steps. It was
a good way off, true, but just the same it seemed to be looking straight at her.

"Good God," said Mavis.

"I guess that's what it is—a good god."

"What would anybody want with the thing?"

She was thinking it was tall enough to be seen out of an
upstairs window at night, round-faced as the moon looking in.
How could you sleep a wink?

"I don't know if I did want it," said Carrington. "In fact,
I never asked myself; it just appeared. The hurricane left it.
The old lady who owned it . . . used to travel in the East, lots
of moola. Had a beautiful old home, Oriental gardens, pa-
godas, paths, lagoons, a forest of miniature trees, a lake of
lilies, black swans, a teahouse. All ripped up and gone. Same
thing with her brains. She never got right again. Died a few
months back. Her pleas were mainly about the Buddha.
'Look after it; don't let it perish.' Perish . . . she said that.
Why perish? I used to ask myself. I then got a feeling for the
word. 'Shall not perish from the earth.' It had washed up on
my property, you see, just where my house had stood. Then it
was her turn to perish. The heirs want it—it's valuable. Someday they'll sell it—but in the meantime, I'm its caretaker or it's
mine. Anyway, we've gotten friendly. For a solitary like me
and one like him, we need each other. He's not as all-wise as
he looks. He's a mixed-up kid. Don't let him scare you. He
also looks after my ducks."

"Ducks." She had passed surprise and looked where he
pointed. A low fence, beyond it a dark pond, and through

the close-set redwood-painted palings a glimpse of white moving forms.

"That's just a business deal, is what you're seeing," he told her. "An oil company here keeps testing pollution through the careful check they keep on duck livers. The pond's fed with fresh Gulf water every week. For some reason which escapes me, the white Oriental ducks were what they chose to use. The Buddha, quite likely, feels more at home with that species, and managed to get his message through. And vice versa, the ducks having methods of their own, no doubt." Standing, alert and thinking on his feet, he heard her, on the steps below him, sigh, and dropped down to sit beside her, pat her shoulder. "It's just that we live among forces; every crosscurrent in the world, if you're noticing, comes near enough to make you feel it. Don't you see it, girl?" The mosquitoes had gotten at her. Why did I do this? she wondered, slapping and scratching. He was telling how in back of the trees there, an open space lay in sunlight, thought by an almost-extinct tribe of Indians to have been a burying ground, though no mounds were visible, and personally he doubted it, but was glad when the Indians came. Meanwhile, the metal smile of the god floating out of the trees grew closer; first it seemed crooked, then straight. Like that cat—what was it?—a Cheshire cat. Call me Alice she thought, or said.

"It's Mavis, not Alice," he corrected, letting her know she'd spoken aloud. "Write me off . . . an eccentric old widower. Come on in now. Have a drink."

He shooed her in ahead of him, puffing spray from a yellow can to kill off whatever else wanted to come in. "I'll just go on now," she was saying, but he begged, smiling, the wrinkles diving and plunging all over into eyebrows, eye corners, eroded cheeks, mustache, hair. "Nothing to worry about, I'll even stop talking. I'm out of the game since my wife died, that's no lie. Just nothing doing. But I still know when a good-looking girl needs a drink. It's just for company. Come on."

Waiting on the couch, she let the familiar sounds of ice coming out of the tray, clinking into the glasses, soothe down her sensibilities. There had been a minute when she'd thought she'd had it, that things were all up for Mavis Henley. Hallucination from a gull's eye, a straight trip to a Buddha's smile, a ricochet into a duck pond. If murdered, she'd probably be buried in the Indian graveyard and forgotten. But from the kitchen, this oddball was relating cheerfully how the ducks had gotten out of their compound one rainy night, but had not strayed away. At the Buddha's base, they had huddled and there he'd found them, a full tally, looking wet, but strong and wise. He came in with sparkling glasses and, thrusting one into her hand, settled down to what he didn't have to say it was time for: the Mavis story.

He listened with great care.

She had come there from Florida, following Frank Matteo. A high school marriage hadn't worked—deserted. The hotel caterer in Palm Beach was ten years older than she and represented, of course, stability. Two children by a former marriage were his to raise and everything was all right ("Smooth if not just great," she said) until she met Frank. He was in Florida then, and went to a fortune-teller who predicted Mavis so accurately the day before they met that he knew her the minute he walked in the room where she sat. Somebody had also predicted him to her, not that it was necessary. ("He just registered, that's all.") People who gambled often went to fortune-tellers, not that Frank was so serious about it. Palm reading was common with them, so were carrying charms, reading the *I Ching*, and writing out dreams. So she had met him and they danced and, dancing, talked and met again. She got involved before she knew it ("It happened just like that") and two discoveries emerged. One: her husband had a cold, violent streak she had never known about before; and two: Frank Matteo was the one man for her. With him she learned "what love meant" for the very first time.

"What does it mean?" Carrington inquired, being curious.

She said that words wouldn't do for explaining it.

He shifted tack. "How'd you get from Florida over here?"

"Frank was coming anyway, to open up that restaurant, see how things were since the storm got cleared up. It fit in for me because I had to get away. My husband was scaring me to death. Once I thought he was going to kill me. I thought at least his children loved me. But they just got quiet and watched everything. I think they may have wanted something to happen. He was no good in bed, anyway. It took Frank to show him up. I guess he knew that. I wouldn't go back now, no matter what."

"You mean even if you split with Frank?"

"I don't want to split, but he—"

"Something happened?"

For some reason, she couldn't answer. She spilled her drink; he held her hand. Finally, she got it out. She had had the abortion three weeks ago. It was why she still looked pale, why nothing she did for herself seemed to work. He'd said to get rid of it. Yet, having done just what Frank said, she found he despised her, that every sort of happiness they'd found vanished away. Like this afternoon—he'd promised . . . then he didn't come.

"Couldn't you set him up with another fortune-teller?" Arnie asked.

At the hint he might be making light of her, she burst out crying in earnest and with such abandon that Carrington had to rescue her glass and ashtray as one takes dangerous toys from a child. His shoulder was handy for drenching. He patted and soothed. Doubtless he could have bedded her, too, but he'd told her the truth; he'd felt no stir of anything in way too long: he didn't now.

Finally, the last tear fell. She put about assembling herself, going to wash, to mend her makeup, comb her hair, settle her clothes. She came out smiling, fresh as daybreak. She sat down. "Thanks for listening, anyway. It helped a lot."

"Tell Frank something for me. You're bound to see him."

"Tell him what?"

"It's not just my island he's after. He's trying to get hold of property generally and I own some, here and there. That old hotel wreck up the road is mine, along with the grounds around it, and a little line of houses, three streets east, bashed in now, not one with a roof left or standing straight—that's all mine. Tell him I've got plans for it all, every inch. I remember this country, how it used to be. I want to sell to people with feelings like mine. But now the word's gone out that Matteo's interested, I'm the last guy anybody wants to deal with. You know why."

"If you're thinking about that murder last month, Frank had nothing to do with that."

It was the businessman fishing off Deer Point she meant, shot, drowned, and discovered floating face up and fish-nibbled at a boat dock near Ocean Springs by a crabbing child who now had his nightmares cut out for him. The deceased had put a restaurant modeled on Matteo's right down the beach. He had plans for building others at the time he went fishing, but now he would not be able to.

"I wasn't accusing Frank. It's what people think that, in this case, matters."

"Some people think he's in with the big time, but he's

not. Maybe the smaller ones, the fringes. I don't really know."

"A fringe relates to something. It's part of the cloth."

She shook her head, flinging dark hair. "Frank couldn't be much of a crook. He's got too many good points. He's so human."

"You ought to know."

She thought maybe she didn't like that either, but decided to ignore it. "Tell me all about you now, why don't you?"

It had gotten late. "Some other time, honey. I'm past the age of thinking any one story will do. I'll drive you home."

6

Returned from this not-unpleasant errand down the road, having seen her to an apartment door (not Matteo's, though he might have connections with the ownership), Arnie returned with alcohol clearing from his head but no sense of the sleepiness he had hoped for. Too much awake, instead, gears still turning fast, from this morning in the drugstore—it seemed a week ago—till this late hour. Why? He walked the shell road beside his house, and wondered what he might have answered to Mavis Henley's question.

The past was back there, certainly, as sure as the white moon was overhead, but the dimensions of it were large and problematic, even to himself. The romantic side was what she'd be listening for, would think the story was told if he said he'd had marriages, two in number, and kids, one at least, and that the last and best of the wives, hefty and white-skinned, funny and wise, had died two years ago but lived on in a sense, presiding over him. Would that do? Yes, Mavis Henley would catch on to that, all right, not thinking too far into it, not asking: If the dead live, how do they live? And where?

He would have thought the real dead were the Grahams, but there they were this morning, at the drugstore. Life was a continuation, a running stream; death was simply a rock in it, an action, a moment. But his wife Evelyn's death was a nuisance—something to get mad about. It was also a perversity: he couldn't get active because of it, not sexually. It was a bore.

Hands in pockets, he roved the shell road, sniffed the cool air, remarked how from bayous far back of the water, those swamps still ragged from the crash of hurricane, a skunk odor came drifting, riding one narrow air current, emphasizing the sweet salty stillness of the rest, the Gulf's soft breathing, season of uncertain weather now left behind. From the road came the boom of a night-traveling trailer truck, accelerating, passing, then the low swish of the tide. But the probe of headlights mysteriously lingered after the truck's sound had died away. From down the narrow, thickly fringed road, he saw the rambling of lighted shadows. He stopped still. If it's you, come walk with me. Perhaps he spoke aloud. Perhaps she might step from the trees and slip her hand in his. He turned and on the way back plucked up a toad from his path and set him down in the roadside weeds. Through the trees at his property's edge, lights low to the water and far distant glimmered, either fishing lights or stars.

But I saved lives, Mavis! Think of that.

He entered the house he and Evelyn had planned together. She had just gone up the stairs: he felt it. Okay. All right.

He went to the Ansafone and switched on a tape. "What," he said into it, "do you advise my doing about this

lovely waif of a girl who's just drifted in? No lover at the moment, needing somebody. Not what I'd call brilliant. Why
can't we make out?"

He extracted a handful of cold boiled shrimp from the refrigerator and stood eating their firm pink flesh, one by one.
His friend the architect Joe Yates had once asked him, too:
"What about your life? Where have you spent it, up to now?"
And, having had French wine at the Yateses' for dinner, he
had taken a plunge at talking about Korea, how he'd even
rescued somebody out there, but how what he mostly remembered was the racket. The cold. Carried a boy out, wounded,
with his arm shot up. Cried like a baby till he fainted. Right
now the name escaped him, drowned out of memory by the
combat noise, off to the right, the gorge booming. Left right,
left right . . . God, he was heavy, passed out. They'd written
for years, recalling the cold, the frozen ground, patches of
snow. Back to voices and small fires.

"What do you remember most vividly from your past?"
That was the girl reporter speaking, a while back; she had
tracked him down. It was college days she meant, of course;
she'd been one of his student admirers, gawking up at him in
class, writing perfect papers, now a "journalist." Idea for feature story: What ever happened to Arnie Carrington? "I remember the noise," he told her, "one long-drawn-out wrangle." Contention, disputes . . . over causes he'd thought he
could help win. Blacks enrolled at the university, scandal over
veterans' housing, Vietnam protest. Words sprouted into
banners, shouted from newspaper headlines. "You wrote
about it all for the school paper," he reminded her. "You
know as much as I." "It was you I wondered about." There
had been marches and endless meetings. He stirred restlessly.
They were sitting over coffee in his half-built house. "You
know what they said, that I was giving up a fine career for

this sort of hassle, letting down my scholarship, turning my life into one long protest. Why? they asked." "What did you answer?" "That I just had to, call it destiny, anything."

Once after a campus victory, over veterans' housing reform, he recalled, he had gone out alone and climbed the campus water tower. He had called it an impulse to look at a South Mississippi sunset that streamed with gold and scarlet banners, but he wondered now if he wasn't trying to reach some silence, a few silent moments, high on that tiny string of a ladder, mounting incredibly, higher than anyone, stopping only to experience the quiet. Up there, noise existed no longer, but only sounds from town and campus, each discrete, came floating up to him as pebbles might float down, through Gulf water.

He ate the last shrimp.

"You got a son, but where he at?" That was a black friend speaking, a woman.

"Whyn't he come and see 'bout how you are?" "He does sometimes. He's a nice boy. I had to go find him once, all mixed-up with drugs." Out in Colorado, that was. A place she, the black, might not have heard of, even. He had trailed them there, that hippie pack, wild and chummy as wolves, found them in a mountain valley at night, shrill as banshees, yelling some awful music. Had to get the boy off a mare's nest of multiplied charges, everything from car stealing to drug pushing. Out in Houston, Texas, now. "He's working out in Houston." "That ain't so far." "Guess not." Saw his mother often, Arnie less. And she—that Arkansas girl he'd treated wrong in some way—she never gave credit where credit was due. "So you saved him, so okay, so he's saved." What kind of thanks was that?

He had caught the arm of the girl reporter as she was leaving: "Wait. Say one thing." She had turned, eyes soft with

the old radiant total admiration for Carrington, the great Dr.
Carrington. "During the demonstrations, there was a plac-
ard I remember, lettered in runny blue paint, reading:
CARRINGTON CARES. . . . You have to forgive an old guy a little
pride. If you want to put that in. . . ." "I will! Yes, I will!"
And she did.

(But Lex Graham, he thought, had never cared if Carrington cared or not.)

The night streamed floating past the Buddha's face outside. I should be a Buddhist, he thought, not caring if anyone
cares. Moonlight lay on the shoulders of the stone Great
Danes; it showed that no one was sitting on the white-painted
iron bench. The toad hopped twice, out of weeds to a puff of
fallen leaves, out of leaves to ground again. Arnie went to
the corner of the living room and looked at the picture of Lord
Byron. His grant had been given and extended twice over the
last few years. *From Italy to Greece: The Last Adventure, A
Study of Byron's Final Years* by Arnold J. Carrington. "My
book," he had told Joe and Ellen Yates, "is all I really care
about. I could finish in two months, given time to concentrate." Come on, Arnie, you don't think anybody believes
you'll ever finish that book. That would be Lex Graham
speaking, of course. Absent, but that was what he would say.
Old coup-de-grâce Graham, always ready to spout unpleasant
truth. Only it wasn't truth. For he would finish it. Yes, he
would. He may have spent the publisher's advance, but he
still had the contract.

Sleepy now, switching off lights, he climbed the stair.
What was it in the poet's face he never noticed before? Now
he had it: youth. A world figure, still so young. I won't be
that again, Mavis Henley, he thought with a wince of inner
pain, then a yawn. Out with the lights. Thought of a manuscript yellowing in boxes, somewhere upstairs. Thought that

this was a day he'd sooner never have lived, now at last rounding, thank God, into the past.

7

"This house now," Lex Graham inquired, having just made an appointment for viewing it the following weekend, "have you considered the trouble a house that size might be?" Dorothy had reaffirmed it every time; she didn't mind the trouble if the interior measured up to what they wanted and the deal was a good one, the only worry being the idea of another hurricane, which, of course, no one could predict.

Housing, Dorothy had often remarked with distaste, was what they lived in. Around any university, no matter if you built it yourself, you could never escape the institutional look. She was sitting on the back steps, talking through the door, while Lex sat at the breakfast table behind her. Nothing but a cat could be seen in their redwood-fenced backyard. It belonged to a neighbor and was sunning itself in dry fall light. Lucinda was sick with a virus she had evidently caught on their Coast trip and was sleeping after the fever left her, in her pretty lacy room. Lex, as Dorothy knew, could hardly bear to be sitting in the breakfast nook with nothing to do for Lucinda. In tune with the cat, Dorothy dreamed. She saw herself in Chinese red decor, a Matisse nude in a striped chair. Years back, a man named Arnie Carrington had once helped her shed her clothes and down she'd gone for him on her own rug, as if modeled for his handling. She had barely had the sense to pull the blinds. Lex came in much later. As of now, they'd seen this house on the water. When Lex had inherited so much money, she had considered pushing for a year in the South of France, but did she want, really, to spend a year anywhere with Lex?

"I've been thinking," said Lex, "that Arnie Carrington still lives on the Coast, or did when last heard from."

"Does he?" said Dorothy.

"We won't have to bother with him, I don't suppose. What if he is there?"

"Lex," said Dorothy, turning her body half around to speak, "why shouldn't we bother with Arnie?"

"Things always get troublesome around that man," said Lex. "Not only troublesome, disturbed. We're getting a new place to make a good break from here. Going back to past connections, that's not part of the game plan, in my mind. Yet sooner or later, there he'll be—charging through every occasion, throwing weight around."

He had folded his newspaper crossways for better handling, had put on his reading glasses. One hand grasped a mug of coffee. It was a hand-painted pottery mug, but his immaculate grasp seemed to condescend to it; it was not porcelain. Lex's mouth jutted forward around the words he spoke; it encased them, a lecturer's habit, perhaps formed to make sure he was distinctly heard. He seldom smiled, but when he did only his front teeth emerged, very slightly protuberant; in upper center two crossed at the tip, giving him the look of a small forest creature. He remembered that just behind him, in their living room, which usually sat dusky behind drawn blinds, his daughter as a child of eight or nine, wearing one of her charming little nightgowns at Christmastime, had sat on the lap of Arnie Carrington, who with his wife Evelyn had been their dinner guest, and had played with his aid a toy accordion that Santa had brought her. One large red-haired hand had guided her small fingers on the keys; the other had pressed down upon her little belly. And had he not, in that very same room there at his back (empty, quiet, and formal), come in after a football game (he felt it a duty to go to one or two a year for the sake of keeping conversant) and found Arnie Carrington alone with Dorothy drinking what looked to be an innocent glass of bourbon and water? "We're drunk," Dorothy had said at once, grinning up at him. He had no reason to doubt it.

"You've still got things against him?" His wife's voice floated in through the screen. She had waited a while before she asked that, he noted, and behind the paper, he smiled his chipmunk smile. Then, never altering position or ceasing to read the news, he returned to the lecturing mouth.

"I disliked—strike it—I hated what he made of us here in the sixties. I remember President Kimball saying before he retired, 'That Carrington man made this university into his personal pipe organ, and he was forever playing on it.' "

"You don't think he did good things?"

"The few black students we have are—insignificant. They could have come in quietly a year later, after the furor was over; nobody would have had much to say. As for the other 'causes,' much the same thing was true. He—dramatized everything. Those times were ripe for that. Sure, he did some good. But making yourself into everybody's hero—that is the same as saying you really aren't one."

"You'd approve of unsung heroes?"

"I think they're the only genuine kind."

"I guess he wasn't all that modest," said Dorothy, "but I never knew he got out publicity on himself. I thought all that just happened. I felt bad when he left."

"He had to leave, to tell you the truth," said Lex, "because I personally saw to it. I got the opposition together. I suggested that petition."

"Oh." It was a small sound, flat, followed by a long silence. "I didn't know that."

He had read his paper now, sheet by sheet. He tossed it aside. "Do you think she might be awake?"

"I don't know," said Dorothy.

"I'll just have a peek." He rose to go look at Lucinda, but turned to say: "I had nothing, of course, against him personally. I never forgot for a moment that he and Evelyn were our friends."

Dorothy, her feelings numbed as her body might have been from a blow, took a bucket from near the steps and filled it at the hydrant. At the birdbath, she scraped out the fallen brown leaves and poured fresh water in, then she returned to sit for a time in her crisp brown slacks and leather sandals, forming the silent word: Arnie. She noted the curve of her instep; the dry prickle of autumn grass, often mowed, still echoed against her feet. Her hand leaned across her knee. With little else to do that morning, except stay in with her sick child while her husband taught an early class, she had whiled time away painting her nails the color of turned leaves. When her feelings woke up, would she hate or care at all?

From the inner hallway, she could hear Lex's voice. He must have found Lucinda awake in her fluffy room, head turning to him on the white embroidered pillowcase, else he would have tiptoed out again. Instead: "How's my baby feeling? How's my girl?" Dorothy could visualize her daughter's soft lovely smile.

Chased Arnie out and never mentioned it! Her feelings were waking all right—and they hated.

8

That daughter of Graham's, Arnie Carrington sat thinking. What the hell's her name? Oh—he finally had it—Lucy . . . Lucinda. . . .

"All I know of the Graham girl," he found himself saying into a quarter-inch of empty tape on his recorder, "is that her father would give her a name like Lucinda because he was an eighteenth-century man who used to keep a folio of waist-length portraits of every Belinda and Clorinda and Florinda you could think of. For his lectures, he said, but I bet he lusted privately. Flounces and ribbons and platinum perukes and little curls and beauty spots and powder. I always wondered if their underwear was clean and if they bathed enough. Cruel to ask him. Feature Lex, chasing them through woodland paths, screams and laughter, brought to earth in a haystack. Giggles. If she looks like that, then he's probably in love with her. Why keep bugging myself about those Graham crackers . . . ? Can't you tell me?" He flicked the switch, reversed the tape—his message to Evelyn, the way he talked to her now (preachers should know about this, a little buzzing wheel for the divine attention)—and catching back to the first word of this reverie, erased it. As if the clicking of the unwinding could erase knowledge, too, pulverize the solid brazen fact of her absence to faint dust.

9

"The hotel demolition has to wait," Joe Yates advised Arnie; "I can see that. But for that row of broken-in houses, if you want to make some shops there to rent, then go partners. A druggist will do for starters."

The high street-level doors of the JOE YATES, ARCHITECT office stood open on a little-used side street in Biloxi. Planes from Keesler Field, the nearby air base, made a muted drone overhead. Innocent late fall Gulf light flooded softly in.

"Things are slightly up," said Arnie. He was sitting two feet below Yates, who liked to perch on a stool as high as a flamingo's back, his thin legs wrapped backward around the legs and rungs. A mug of coffee sat beside his elbow, and he bent over drawings on a slanted board which an L-shaped steel ruler held in place. "I'm selling lots—actually selling—cash money came in. Mainly, the east lawn of the hotel property. The surveying's complete. You may have to doctor the house plans a little to suit the clientele. I'm even hoping to pay you something."

"I'd be starving if I had to live on hopes of yours," said Yates. He squinted at a line which he checked for measurements and partially erased. "You'd do well to take Matteo's money for that island. He's turning into a solid citizen, gave a boat ride and a lemonade party the other day for a cub scout troop."

"So long as he didn't drown them like puppies. Oh, I'm sure he's trying to come on decent, square, and misunderstood. But trying to rebuild the Coast makes no sense if you just let the crooks in."

"The Coast is rebuilding already. Holiday Inns and Hamburger Havens."

"I never hoped to do it all."

"I heard you'd changed your mind about Matteo. Getting in thick with the gang, I heard." He was bending forward again. He had a nose so thin at the point that when he leaned close to the sheet, the drawing pencil laid to paper seemed an extension of it.

"You mean buddying up to Mavis Henley? It's just a little friendship; she just needs cheering up. I found her looking low and lonesome down at the restaurant one day. Even having to take shit off the busboy. I think it's all up with Frank and her. But I'm not even a station stop."

"Yeah, but who're you going to tell it to and have them believe it?"

"Call her yourself, you want to start something. She might be at the available stage."

Off business, on to women. Silence. They adjourned by common consent for a beer, Yates locking up and setting the cardboard clock which hung in his doorway: DON'T GO WAY. BY 11 BACK TO STAY.

It was Yates's day for nagging. Maybe he did need to be paid. For a time, fired with Arnie's enthusiasm, he had sat up late making house plans, even drawing in landscapes, for what were white Southern houses without trees and shrubs? Then he had written out a bill and the bill was somewhere. Today Yates was remarking that, for a man who had once been a giant of his times, Arnie had sure shrunk, though he stated it amiably, working into his first beer at Friendship House, so that Arnie, not one to take offense, could only feel the touch on the scar as gentle, a soothing reminder that it was there at all. He could even talk about it.

"I gave myself to the times. When those particular times cleared up and played out, then I'd no place to belong to. There's a way of living so completely, you set fire to life, you burn it up as you go along."

"Burning bridges behind you, might be another way to put it."

"In the first place, they weren't bridges," Arnie said. "It seemed at the time that we found—that Evelyn and I found—that something needed doing and we could do it."

"Wasn't there some story I heard about your wife hiding a set of Negro twins who wanted to enroll at the university? There was a mob after them and she hid them? She kept them safe single-handed, so I heard."

"Oh my God, even to talk about it . . . I can just see her, plain as day." The way his voice, softly compelling, took up the subject of her, Yates felt that if he looked up, he would see her too. "Evelyn was bigger than life, in body and in spirit. We had the black twins at the house, to keep them safe. Evelyn stopped a whole gang of racists. I wasn't there; she was by herself. She said it wasn't all that hard. She got out the broom and held it like a baseball bat. First one to come close, she said, she'd swat hell out of him. 'A half-dozen drunk knuckleheads,' she said later. Scared? No. Evelyn even wanted to sit out the hurricane.

"Oh, we all knew it was coming. You remember. Some few little optimists kept chirping, ignorant as crickets, but the sky turned charcoal around ten A.M. I never saw a thing like that before. Still, she didn't want to move an inch. Had just been told that what she had was terminal. 'Just let me stay on right here, meet it as it comes. What better way to go than sailing off through the air, never to be seen again? The wind

might just take one push at me, come to think of it, and give
up entirely.' Evelyn wasn't exactly a sylph, so you see her
meaning; she was all solid flesh. 'You won't even have burial
expense,' was her idea. 'We're going to get you well,' I said.
She asked me not to talk like that. She was right about everything. But I couldn't walk off and leave her, and when I said
I'd sit there, get killed right along beside her if it came to that,
she wouldn't allow it.

"It's what we should have done. How decent it would
have been, to get blown and blasted off the map, hand in
hand together, or swept out to sea by the tidal wave. First, it
would have gently dandled us up high like two kids in a
swimming pool, old Daddy Death come with us out for a
swim. Sea burial . . . nothing's the matter with it; the company is as good as a Democrat could ask for. But we
couldn't resolve the quarrel: how to separate, how to die.
So we packed the car and left, just when the air was getting
gray-green and dense, thick as a hand before your face. A special kind of cold in it, heavy, the authority of whatever takes
you into death, and power, the minute before it solidified to
black. Oh God! Do you remember the moaning howl? I swear
it sounded like a voice. There was something human about it,
bigger than human, but still with that human despair. . . ."

"Take it easy, Arnie," Yates said and touched his elbow.
The wild voice stopped.

"Well, I was saying, we went away at that point, still
quarreling. It wasn't like us to do that. We both agreed to that
later."

"Hindsight," said Joe Yates. "The one thing architects
can't afford."

"Your business must have improved, after the storm."

"It's an ill wind," said Yates. "But I'm not saying I'm

glad. Just out of curiosity, who drew up your own house plans?"

"We did it together, Evelyn and I. We came back after the worst of the damage was cleared away—snakes, rats, sharks, alligators, and stray dogs—all gone back to where they belonged or burned or buried, but our house had vanished. The foundation, one garage wall, the Buddha, and some rubble. We lived in an apartment over at Ocean Springs and drew up house plans like some people play Scrabble. She liked the doctor she had, and clung to that for continuing, day at a time, the way people do."

"With memories like that, why stay? If I lost Ellen, I'd head for Florida, New Orleans, out West. Anything but here."

"Where else is she?" He struck the table. Yates looked up sharply. This solitary man—eccentric, brilliant, talked about—how little he knew him. To reminisce about a wife who'd died was one thing, fondling her lovingly in memory. But to stick around communing with the vanished spirit—could that be what Arnie was always doing? Yates looked through the window at moss-hung trees. He did not comment. Carrington, simmering back to normal, shook his large head of hair, which was once the color of the beer he drank.

Calmly, he resumed: "My memories of the Coast, you understand, go back a long way. Like most people of the state, it was my first look at the big water, a real kid's adventure to head down this way, and once seen never forgotten. If anything bugged you, head to the Coast. There was sun and peaceful sort of light, great tranquillity, a kind of inner breathing came on, the wind made the old trees whisper and stirred the long moss hanging to the ground. To open your eyes on a new day was happiness. The things I remember: 'Po'Boys and Gumbo' for twenty-five cents, 'All the Shrimp You Can Eat' for a dollar. The piers stood out in the water and ladies in their summer dresses used to sit out on them under big umbrellas, talking through the twilight. I'm keeping faith with what I remember. I'm giving it back if I can. Somewhere else, I'd do something different. But I'm not there—not somewhere else—I'm here. A guardian."

"If I could find some practical solution," Yates said, "I'd cheer you on. As it is, I don't see any."

Riding back down the highway to Yates's office only ten minutes later than the time promised on the notice, they saw a slim Chrysler Imperial glide by, its rich purple glossy in sunlight, and knew that Matteo himself had passed.

"If he's trying to keep a low profile, why the hell did he get that car?" Joe Yates wanted to know.

"It plays up his sex image," said Arnie. "Or maybe he just liked it."

"I buy the first. Women grab their groins when they see it from afar."

"The chariot of Achilles," Arnie remarked.

"Achilles," said Yates, and got mad. "Arnie, what's the kick you're really getting? I first saw you written up in a *Life* magazine article. It was when the school crisis hit the university. They spoke of you as a scholar, some sort of authority. If you want a cause, shouldn't you find one in a world like that?"

"I have to play it the way I see it," said Arnie, tired of the pounding Yates was always giving him. In a way, he agreed; Yates gave practical advice, and he was interested, genuine, and kind. But he didn't know how to go that step beyond; he never took risks for improbable truths. A Southern architect would have to be classical, Arnie reasoned, and restrained himself from snarling words.

10

Saturday night, Arnie went to find Barbra K., the mulatto woman who from time to time tried to help him out of a greater problem than Joe Yates had yet gotten wind of. He had first found her, post-hurricane, trying to exist in one of the wind-blasted little row of houses he'd bought without knowing anyone was in them, thinking, if he'd thought at all, that nobody could be in them, yet he'd gone there once at twilight, seen smoke, heard a noise, pushed through to a back room, and there she was. Two sacks of rat poison to keep them off her, cooking with oil, a pallet bed in the corner, not much else. "Who own this place now?" was all she'd asked. She was pretty, café au lait with delicate features, not exactly helpless but not very much in control either. He'd gotten that one house shored up for her, roofed it, boarded up one smashed wall. He found furniture for her because her own had floated away. He'd scavenged too much to use himself. And bedding was now hers too, and a bed to put it on, and gas radiances for the chilly weather, plus a stove with an oven. She'd done the rest, added her curtains and her throws, picked up her little cleaning jobs and the baby-care work at the day nursery, all pretty much like before, then made sure she decked herself out, robes and sandals, bracelets and lemony lotions. "You're so pretty, Barbra K.," he told her. Then (it was spring after the hurricane and he hadn't seen her for a month or so) he told her right out: Evelyn had died. She sat with him, two or three evenings, nothing to say. Just sitting, rocking now and then. Finally, he said it once more: "You're a pretty woman," but that time he tried it, moved to her, let her take him to her. The surprise came when nothing much happened.

They both worried about it. She brought gris-gris out from New Orleans. Once she spent what he'd given her on new lingerie and bought up books of hard-core photographs which they sat looking at side by side like two kids with a family album. Now she talked of an old swamp woman said to have a charm so strong it had coaxed up the last of the Confederate veterans in their retirement home at Beauvoir, where, as she knew well, Jefferson Davis had made his last home. The ones that wanted up, got up, right to the last. Arnie wondered what on earth it was. More like a scent, she said, good and strong, went right to your veins. But that there woman was a good-looking woman, back then. Now she just had straight gray hair was all, the rest of her was bent, said Barbra K., gone crooked and shriveled up. Arnie speculated that it was age that had gotten to him, too. "You ain't old," she said. "Ain't hardly fifty." "Fifty-plus," he set her right. "Ain't nothing," she said.

Barbra K. was down on the world in general, but to any one person she was good and kind. She had a beautiful ample body, narrow in the waist, the breasts still youthfully tipped forward, the beam firm and broad. Arnie would lie with her happily—naked, caressing—while she played some of her soft jazz, but of late had mainly sat shucking shrimp and sipping wine and looking at her, in some flimsy skirt and low-cut lacy blouse, or printed robe. She had one of those big straw chairs in the corner, its back opened out like a peacock's tail. She herself sat with knees carelessly apart on a small divan slipcovered in fabric stamped with rosebuds. She read mystery stories; they sat between bookends on a table with the TV. The statue of a saint with some holy water was nailed to one wall. If her ankle in its high-heeled sandal whammed his vision and braided through his senses, why couldn't he get it up? "It's something you got on your mind," said Barbra K. "I'm a bloomin' old eunuch," he grumbled. "Naw, ain't that. It's something sittin' there, don't want to move. Someday, it's gonna take wing and fly." "Thank you, Barbra K.," said Arnie, and left his twenty on the dresser.

Touch and smell and woman flesh, woman talk, was all he had to call life, sure enough, but just the same he took what comfort there was in them and, driving off into the cool of the night, he hoped she was right. The beach highway was all but empty just at this area around midnight; there were no night spots here, only residences left far up a rise of coastal ground and the highway leading on down by the beach, and just ahead a filling station, sure enough, he thought, for the motor had sputtered and, looking down, he saw the gauge pointing to lower than empty. He hoped to make it to the station. He nudged the accelerator, built up a little speed, let it coast, nudged again. He slowed to full stop just at the entrance, only a few yards from the pumps. It was then he noticed what he had not, being anxious about the gas, taken occasion to observe before. A dark sedan was parked near the pumps; it was facing toward him. The attendant was standing near the door while someone within was holding his attention so strictly, Arnie knew it was a stickup. Inside, a second man was leaning into the cash register. As he looked, he saw that the hand of the attendant, held down out of sight below the window level, was gesturing to him. Get out fast, it was saying. Leave. Go. Vanish. He got slowly out of the car. The vibes were bad. The man on the inside had come to the door, carrying a printed grocery sack. When he saw Arnie, he seemed to reach toward a gun. "Get the hell on down the road," he said. "Matteo sent me out tonight," Arnie said, walking forward. "He knows about you guys. You better hit for home." "You stay there," said the man with the bag. He was scrawny, young, in a Windbreaker and T-shirt printed with a joke only partly to be read. He went to the man in the car and spoke to him, then turned back to Arnie. "I got nothing to do with Matteo, one way or another." "It's his area," said Arnie, "and you know it." "People say that, but— Who are you?" "An interested friend." The boy looked at the grocery sack in his hand, walked over to the ledge which circled the neat ce- ment structure, and stopped at the point where the air pump was placed. He set down the bag. "Nothing but fifty dollars." Then, without a glance at Arnie or the attendant, he returned to the car and got in. "I'm gonna check you out," he said. He slammed the door. The motor started and the car backed swiftly, swirled on a long curve back into the highway, and left them, moving east.

"What in hell did you want to do that for?" the attendant asked. He went to pick up the bag. "It was too much risk. You ought to be careful. Just for fifty dollars. Those guys or some like 'em was by twice last month. I don't keep much cash after dark."

"I'm out of gas," said Arnie. "I couldn't leave so I thought I might as well get rid of them for you."

"Well, okay, you done it now."

They brought gas to the car in a bucket with a spigot and poured it in. Maybe I was proving my manhood, thought Arnie, as he drove away, no word of even grudging thanks from the station attendant. Bold hunter blasts clay pigeon; aging knight charges windmill; three rabbits down in the shooting gallery, give that gentleman a kewpie doll. Yet, he could swear it, when he stepped from the car instead of wait- ing it out, he had felt the old authentic tingle up the spine, the tightness in the shoulders, the sudden clarity of vision. He

would have been equal to so much more! He suddenly wondered about all the hero-loners of the world. Were they compelled to keep on proving it . . . in bed or out of it, on
byways and detours, back alleys and addresses found in
phone booths?

Barbra K., Barbra K.! Maybe you are right and told my
fortune. But when will the bad bird fly? You failed to tell me
that.

11

"I just came here to get a good dinner," said Arnie to Frank
Matteo, and it was Frank's restaurant and late and Frank
hardly ever showed up, at least not during the week. It would
seem he had come in from wherever he lived (some said he
had quarters above the restaurant), especially to see Arnie,
and it might be imagined that somebody in the restaurant had
even telephoned to him that Arnie was there that night.

His entry was low-key, but his presence, his alert carriage
and finely determined movement made an accumulation of itself like the widening ripple behind a smooth, high-masted
cabin schooner with its motor cut to the last notch, coming
into view with no wish of any sort, and no beauty average
enough to need thinking of, superb.

"Sit down, why don't you," Arnie, who did not like being
stood over, said.

Frank did draw back a chair and sat and everyone in the
restaurant became at once aware that they had been staring.

"Mavis was here an hour ago," said Frank. "You may have just missed her."

"I wasn't looking for her, or for anybody," Arnie said.

"She was with some guy from off a cruise ship, from the look of it. I'm glad she's keeping busy. I got too little time."

"It can be a problem," Arnie said.

"How is it you go around claiming to know me so well?"

"You're referring to the other night?" He felt silly, like an almost-grown boy caught in a kid stunt. "I was out of gas. It seemed like a way of getting rid of a couple of little punks. It was mainly a game."

"I got so little capital to use up. I'm trying to be a nice enough guy, which is what I am, or so I think of myself."

"I wasn't disputing that," said Arnie. "Not personally. I can't think what harm those little dope-starved kids could do you."

"Word could get around on me, and some might rub off on you. It just wasn't smart. I'm prejudiced against you anyway."

Mavis, thought Arnie, but all he said was, "How's that?"

"Well, you won't do any business with me, got all your property off the market is how you tell it, whenever I make an offer. What am I going to tell myself to think? Just a guy who won't add up? Don't want to?"

"I'm trying to find some answers myself. Ever think about that? Your ex-girl friend . . . she could use a few answers, too."

"So now it's my private life."

"She's pretty down is all."

Matteo, respondent to some gesture, it might be from across the restaurant, gave a nod of no meaning to Arnie, and rose.

"I can't help it about Mavis. You got to understand that. I wouldn't lie," said Matteo.

Arnie, who had gotten halfway through a good dinner (shrimp cocktail, broiled flounder, the works), wondered if he could finish the rest, knowing a girl's happiness was at the mercy of statements like that. Should he trade a little property to Matteo in exchange for a better deal for Mavis? If only things could work that way. Who knew what worked with such as Frank? What didn't work was to believe too much. Poor Mavis. She probably even said it was wonderful when Frank Matteo said, "I wouldn't lie."

12

What brings a man to look up his wife's ex-lover, if not a sense of new power that longs to try itself in every way, on this and that, to take charge? So Lex Graham felt, or thought, as he glided south of Hartsville for the fifth time in weeks, going to the Coast.

All that time, he had been maneuvering about the house. Nothing it seemed, was to be denied him along those lines. He even had luck, for the house was as sound as it looked, the owners eager to sell and living not far off, in New Orleans. The wife, her children grown, in an over-fifty period of nerves, got scared at the mention of the Coast; though they'd tried it one summer since the hurricane, they had had to pack up and leave in a few weeks. Every black cloud put her in a panic. And then, too, so many old friends had not returned, their houses destroyed, their hearts sore. "A miracle must

have spared ours," she said with a shy upward glance at Lex;
a nice, trim, aging woman, turning the diamonds on her thin
fingers. "It makes her too nervous," said her husband, "but I'd
take the chance. It'll be another century before a storm like
that—" "A miracle house," Lex was murmuring, thinking over
the new word as enhancing what he was able to do for Lucinda. It was worth the risk of future hurricanes, which
seemed to him slight.

There were times, thought Lex, traveling in his softly
glistening beige Mercedes past pasture and farm, lonely filling
station and pokey little town, when the world could be yours
if you claimed it. He meant to step right up and take. And if
the thought of Carrington was the fly in his ointment, why
then the thing to do was get it out of there. Because as sure as
anything, Dorothy was already visualizing her little scenes:
the running-into-Arnie scene—careful greetings over drinks at
a chance party, or nods at the yacht club, or glances in a restaurant. He did not intend to have it happen. He himself was
visualizing another scene entirely: himself returning from the
Coast, himself saying casually to Dorothy when presenting
her with his copy of the deed, signed and notarized, after his
greeting kiss: "You'll never guess who I rang up. Just had an
impulse to say hello. We were talking about him the other
day. Yes, Arnie Carrington!" Rug pulled from under her. She
would have had only too good an idea of what to guess from
his first word, would have already turned slate-eyed. (Hazel-
eyed people did that: blue for good times, gray for bad, and
in between a dangerous scud of green.) "Yes, sir. Carrington,
Arnold J. We had a drink, talked over old times. He's glad
we're going to have a happy retirement together." And what
she says next is up to her, he thought, though he knew well
enough at the time it had happened she had needed a lover as
much as anybody ever had, it was just the best friend part of

it that nobody, he supposed, could quite get over. Well, they'd had a go at it, and parted, and now, by God, his own terms had to be the ones that counted. So he thought, and parked his car, and went into a drugstore to a pay phone, and dialed.

But Arnie Carrington, as anyone knowing the ways of God and fate, or for that matter Arnie himself, might have predicted, was not at home. And as the deed to the house had been, because of some legal detail, delayed, Lex had to return from that one trip with nothing whatever to show for it.

Arnie, however, found a message on the Ansafone: "Lex Graham called." There on tape was that voice again, sonorous and assured, now mispronouncing his own name "Gray-am." Can't he get anything right? Arnie wondered, and the mechanism clicked off.

I be dog, he thought. Then he reflected he hadn't used a phrase like that in years. Should he take any notice? If he did, what should he say? He decided to write a note, fake and jovial. If Lex was setting up—or indicating—a disturbance in the chemical balance, he couldn't ignore it, but he could neutralize it. So he drew out paper and rolled it in his typewriter. He began to hymn away.

He congratulated Lex and Dorothy on the purchase of what, if the grapevine was correct, was a beautiful property, miraculously spared. He welcomed Lex and Dorothy as neighbors on these shores; he hoped to see Lex and Dorothy not "sometime soon" or "whenever they were on the Coast, but if possible "someday next week" and he "didn't mean maybe," he "really looked forward." There were things he "wanted to talk over" for "old times' sake," colleagues and "comrades of the sixties" that they had always been, etc. "Please believe me."

He signed with a flourish, sealed and stamped the thing

before he could stop to think, but when he did think (after the mailbox slapped shut on the letter), it was of something he had not recalled in years, something that a student of those same sixties had told him: "You know, Dr. Carrington, out there on the edge of the campus, out there that day when the demonstrations stopped about the veterans? You were climbing up the water tower and there was that dark-headed man with the glasses, that one you know—" "Professor Graham, you mean him?" "Yeah, him, and he had a gun. He pointed it at you." Carrington had never believed it. He refused to believe it. It must have been someone else. But if he did not believe it, he, at the same time, knew it was true. And all long before the football afternoon when he had come in unexpectedly and found Dorothy, bored, alone, and wanting him.

He had scarcely got home from mailing the letter when a shadow passed through, something reflected from the outside into the living room: Mavis passing the window, dropping in on him for a drink, the way she was making a habit of.

"So what am I doing to myself?" Carrington asked Mavis after a drink or two. "Setting up contact with people I don't even like anymore. Who needs it?"

"Well, you need money and you say they've got that."

"You're talking on another plane entirely. Their money is nothing to me; on second thought, it won't even be much of anything to them, unless the girl can be helped by 'advantages'—whatever the hell is meant by that."

"So why do you care one way or another?"

"Caring is not what I'm talking about. They're running me to ground is what they're doing. A brace of goddamned bloodhounds out of the past. I can do without them. Here I am, hanging upside down, blind as a bat, an old gray tough gull drifting up in the stratosphere, not even coming down

anymore to dive for fish. A turtle so old he's lost count—three
hundred years maybe—flippers like oak bark, dozing deep
down, sending up bubbles. Certain things can happen; like
hurricanes within, they just hit. After that—hell, how do I
know?—maybe I died back a while ago. Maybe I'm dreaming
all this now. But those Grahams will make me find out for
sure. It's when the past stirs that you wake. I got told off by
my architect the other day. Bankruptcy, he was saying, is just
around the corner. Do you think I care enough even to lose
sleep? Maybe I'll sell out to Frank, after all."

"You're talking that way because you don't want to face
something. I thought you cared a lot about property and all."

"I care within my dream," he said. He put his arms
around her. She wasn't all that dumb. If only he could, in that
one stubborn way, waken. Then to hell with the rest . . . the
dream itself would be complete; he could close the door on
the past. He would simply live within his vision, harder, better, finer than anybody else could live without. He pulled up
her face to him by its chin, and kissed her mouth; but though
she did not pull away, she did not really want him. As with
Barbra K. (who did), nothing really worked, and he let her go
and she didn't talk about it but just went on with what she
was thinking until he said, "Didn't you think it was time we
got closer? Was I wrong?" "I've got this thing about Frank,"
she said. "He was just so great." "By 'was' I guess you mean
he's not coming back." He hadn't yet, she admitted, but she
must be hoping still. "Then you're in your dream is all," he
said, "and that makes two of us."

"I never know what yours really is," said Mavis and,
when he didn't answer, she added: "I guess it's got something
to do with your wife."

"I guess it does," said Arnie, and thought that that was
above all why the Grahams had no right; they were going to

trespass on the very grave of his love. It belonged to them, what had happened—to him and Evelyn, exclusive owners: posted, keep out, it's ours. . . .

At some unnoticed moment, Mavis drifted off; he remembered her getting some food out for him, then he didn't see her anymore.

It was not till later on that night, when having mounted to the bedroom where he dropped his clothes in the wide-sprawled seat of a chair (one canvas piece suspended on an iron frame), and was about to lie naked on the low wide square of mattress in its pine frame and petition sleep, that a wind blew in the window past the Buddha's face, over the tops of the pines. It came out of the north and this time it was not skunk wind; it was strong and straight, no salt Gulf smell in it and no dead fish. There was a flashing of light back up that way, on the northern horizon, and the trundle of thunder, announcing a distant turmoil. He had been born and raised up there, north toward Memphis, among the old gullies and ragged bluffs, and it came to him that something Mavis had said had passed by him but was now re-echoing. The sweet inland rain hit and he went to close the window—it sprayed cold and astringent over his flesh. ". . . You need money and you say they've got that." Joe Yates had thought of it, too.

He stood looking down at the Buddha and then over the top of the redwood fence to where the ducks, usually huddled in one continuous silver-white sleeping cloud along the bank of their lagoon, had sensed the weather and taken to their hutches. "You and I," he said to the Buddha, "have got to consider ourselves at this point the world's two most impractical bastards, and if you want to keep on in that mistaken way of life, well and good, I guess it's your role. You wouldn't be you if you had to stop meditating for a while. But at present, it's a luxury I think you must agree, once you look at it in all its aspects, that I can't afford. So stop smiling now, damn it. Stop acting so goddamn superior. A little more and you'd have been a curiosity for the fish to swim around. As it is, you're probably on the way to a museum and the fine company of Egyptian mummies and hand-painted umbrella stands. Those ducks have got what sense it takes to get in out of the rain, and I have to manage too."

So that was the "why" of his letter to Lex Graham. From then on, he would be waiting for an answer.

part II

1

When Lex Graham did finally appear to Arnie Carrington, it was after the holidays were done, and a severe freeze had come and gone.

The appointment made and the hour set, Arnie waited in his living room. He looked out on the clear winter day, only partially warm, and informed with a pale sunlight which would everywhere be urging the poinsettia heads to lift again, the azalea buds to take heart, the frost-blackened camellias to put out once more. Arnie gnawed his lip and smoothed his mustache. He felt he should and must say to Lex: "Like it or not, this is my kingdom you're coming to. From Ocean Springs to Waveland. You've come to what belongs to me." It could be laughingly passed over, a remark like that, but not forgotten. It would be the sort of speech that would float echoing around the inside of a traveling Mercedes, driven by a man on private business.

But he didn't say it, or anything, being so dampened down, almost instantly, by the appearance of the man who entered; shy, wry, bitter, brilliant Lex had somewhere acquired a sense of command, much like Carrington's own in campus days of yore. Could money straighten the back and put inches on a flat chest?

Navy blue flannel blazer, smoke-gray trousers, expensive sport shoes, casually worn—here stood a new man, faintly navigational in tone, suggesting courses set and kept to. Though both of them had spruced up for the meeting, Arnie knew himself hopelessly behind; in matters of dress he had slipped beyond redemption, he could only admit. He thought of Frank Matteo, certainly no slouch, but way too flashy and given to movielike effects: silk scarves, jeweled cuff links, open silk shirts, colors of peach and pomegranate. But the region's social leaders would pounce on the new Lex and his always-fashionable wife. Appearance was artificial, but it worked, and defeated whoever didn't have it. As if a ten-pound weight were attached to his wrist, Arnie lifted his hand and, as deliberately as lighting a lamp, turned on a welcoming smile.

"Well, finally you got here, Lex. It's been forever. How are you?"

"Forever, but not a day," Lex smoothly noted, and there then was a wringing of hands.

So they stood in the living room together, in silhouette like friends, and from this attitude Arnie moved into the customary hospitalities. To turn on the gas radiance was easy, to offer a drink was automatic, to fetch one a ritual. The visitor had sat down by now and crossed his legs. In the kitchen, ice popped too quickly from the tray and went skidding over the vinyl floor. Even when gathered up and dumped in the sink, it left splinters of itself to lurk unnoticed; Arnie slipped on one and almost fell and almost spilled the drinks. Get him out of here! his nerve voices were shouting to him. He put them down, kicked ice out of his way, and strode in with a confident tread.

"So here we are! You've got to catch me up on things. How's Dorothy, and the little one—all grown up and handsome?"

"I guess I'd say pretty, not handsome. I'd be safe in saying it, you can bet."

But then he knew it was a girl, so what made a slip like that one? Nerves was what it was, but its use was clear: a corrective to a former state of close friendship, members of a foursome long since dissolved. His mistake was a way of saying that you couldn't return to things.

"Pope and Dryden still the greatest?"

"Plus Donne's satires."

"And some Milton."

"Selected passages."

They laughed and began to speak more freely, of mutual friends, changes in the campus, administrative appointments, and finally of the fact that Arnie never came up to visit anymore.

"I was given to understand," said Arnie, "that if I ever so much as drove up in that direction, a roadblock would go up on the highway to prevent my passage through the sacred region ere I could return, and a giant purifier would be sent down from Jackson to rid you of air pollutants."

"I doubt if anybody was that much against you. You've imagined it worse than it was."

"The swing back to the right," said Arnie, "left me with a chance to denounce my former errors, it is true. But did they want to tear down the decent housing for married students (which I led the drive to get), so that infants no longer had to play in a swamp and fall prey to all the diseases they might have caught only slightly quicker in Bangladesh? And did they want to deny that Negro students were at last being peacefully enrolled for reasons of merit rather than Appomattox? And did they really prefer sticking head in sand about the Vietnam war, instead of facing up to the most glaring military miscalculation in American history?"

"Who's 'they'? Some were for you, some against. The whole campus was your forum. You remember that."

"Gains were made; things happened. That was the time that was—that was the way it was then. But when the calmer days came, they wanted me to declare myself reformed from my wicked 'troublemaking.' They wanted me to recant, say I'd never meant it, Mississippi a paradise, Faulkner the world's greatest writer, every university girl a homegrown Miss America, every green halfback headed for the Sugar Bowl. No! I stayed the same as ever. Too much of the old Byron kept spurting out. So what next am I made out to be? A skirt-chaser, molester of little female students, slipping them Henry Miller to read while playing kneesie under the desk. And falling out drunk in faculty fishponds every weekend."

And sneaking off to swamp motels with my wife, Lex Graham might have said, but did not. And that petition to get me out of your sacred Eden—you signed it, too, Arnie Carrington might have said, but did not. Skidding on this sort of spilled ice, they might both have gone sprawling.

Lex Graham, like Arnie Carrington, had been born in Mississippi; but both had gone north to universities—Arnie to Cornell, Lex to Minnesota. Lex's smile showed civilized control.

"I can't discuss all that with you now. I'd just rather say it's a whole new day. I think the majority up there would feel the same, now the turmoil is over. But some were always for you, heart and soul. They would have marched after you into the Mississippi River."

"Damned good of you to say so." It was this surfacing of a wistful sweetness in cynical Lexington that could get through

to Arnie and touch him. His eyes brightened with moisture,
the way they'd been doing since his wife's death. A gentle silence fell between them during which Arnie saw out the window that Mavis had entered the drive, but noting the parked
Mercedes perhaps, was turning to walk away. She was like
one of those goddesses that popped up to urge the flagging
quest, Arnie having forgotten all about it. I guess I have to
try, he thought.

"You ought to come ride around with me, Lex. Stay over.
If you're going to live here, you've got to hear some inside stories, get involved a little. Not the rampant lion I used to be,
but I'm still operating. As usual, I'm biting off more than I can
chew. But maybe you'd be interested. . . ."

Outside, they strolled about the Buddha's base, sipping
from refilled glasses, reeking with 6-12. "It was lying in the
mud after the storm, right where the backyard used to be,
only there was nothing for the yard to be back of. The house
was gone, one garage wall left standing. I washed its dirty
ears." They spoke of ducks, about which Lex knew little.
"Feminine natures," said Arnie. "Ladies of the Methodist
choir."

"What exactly are you involved in?" Lex asked him. They
returned inside.

Lex was secretly experiencing outrage. Buddhas and Oriental ducks did not, in his mind, mix with serious plans. The
Carrington wildness; this had always baffled, discouraged, an-
gered, and—yes, in a way—criticized him. Let that wildness
get enthroned by common consent (as on the campus Arnie
had succeeded in getting it enthroned), then he (Lex) had to
turn into a critic, a foolish one, doing a fool thing himself: i.e.,
pointing a gun in secret at a man climbing a water tower to
look out in triumph on a world that lay at his feet, this man
destined not only to descend unharmed, unscathed, but also in

a matter of months to make a cuckold of him. But wildness from strength overran everything, was such a success, demonstrable. Wildness from weakness, that was different: it was knowing *that* that stopped him from shooting. Drunkenly, after this many bourbons, Lex wore the Buddha helmeted above his brow; he had taken whatever of it was a help. He sat in Arnie Carrington's living room and smiled his own personal smile of sly blandishment and cordial good fellowship. He had developed it by trial and error after he had gotten so much money. With that smile, he sat back behind his money, and no one could tell what he thought.

"Why, certainly, I'm interested. This is the area I'll soon be living in. The more I learn, the better."

"Three properties, as I said," Arnie went on. "One, an island. It may sound foolish, something that far from land, but once you know the angles, it's anything but. I'm going out there tomorrow. Oh, sure, I go anyway from time to time. There's this old shrimper I bought I make the trip in. Have to keep my postings up with the Coast Guard, the harbor master, all good friends. Weather like this, a two-hour ride at most. You'd see the Coast from a new angle, the whole sweep. You'd see the islands! Surf, birds, turtles, foam of the seas. . . . To look back on your own new house, Lex, shining there beside the water: think of it. Call up Dorothy. Say you'll stay."

To his own smile, Lex had now added the Buddha's. "You said three properties, if you recall. What about the others?"

"A lovable old monster of a ruined hotel, for one. But never mind." Arnie, as he often did, was shifting away.

Lex drank the one moderate swallow that remained in the bottom of his glass. "I don't know about tomorrow. No, it would, I think, be difficult." He rose to say goodbye, appropriate as hell, not showing his liquor.

Arnie's flight was canceled in midair. He felt like a brave hunting fowl launched, with, unbeknownst to himself, a tether tied around him. He was halted at the crest of his own rise, reduced to mumbled farewells and scratchings at his chin. Was left in the doorway to observe Lex's crisp step toward that inevitable car, that luxurious beige eminence of a thing. The cluck of the closing door detonated his true thought, which metaphysically appeared comic strip fashion above his head, set in a balloon:

"I hate your guts, can't stand you."

He waved a cordial, hypocritical hand as he felt the outburst of another balloon for a separate panel:

"Fuck off."

If only that—despite his interesting hopes, now lost—were goodbye.

Mavis Henley, coming in out of ambush from wherever the hell she had been (probably walking out on the beach), didn't help his feelings out, especially as she was all smiles. "I got a job," she burbled. "I couldn't wait to tell you."

So not back to Florida, after all. Women never gave up.

"Teaching," she said, when he asked.

"Art?" He guessed it because once over at her place he had opened what he took to be the bathroom door but had bumped instead into a whole closetful of stuff which he couldn't identify as belonging on this planet until she explained it was frames for silk screens, articles for collages, chart after chart of elbows, knees, ankles, torsos, hips, thighs, and pelvises for anatomical study. Male, predominantly; they mostly might have been Mattco, Arnie had felt, and wondered at the irony of letting fly the libido against a sketch pad, though it was an art theory as viable as any.

"It's part of domestic science at the junior college. You

didn't know, but I can sew. I studied in art school after my first marriage broke up. Graphics, cutouts, crayon, collages, watercolors, gouache, and oil—I already know just about all the requirements. All I have to learn is macramé."

"What's that?"

"You can make anything out of it, even shoes."

"Just what we need," Arnie said.

"Who was that guy? I came by earlier, but he was here. Is he the one's been bugging you?"

"He bugs me, all right. But it's nothing worth passing on to Matteo."

"You think I spy on you? You've been too good to me, Arnie. You know I know that."

"I think I'm on your true love's list of local curiosities. I think you'd do most anything to get him back. What's the guy up to, Mavis? If you think I've been so good to you, why don't you level with me? Half the Coast thinks he's with the under-world—Mafia, Syndicate, something or other. Is that so or not?"

Mavis sat down to think. She'd come in looking sharp and respectable, wearing a new gray suit and coral blouse, even a shoulder bag. She was going to make it, after all, in the efficient girl-with-a-job way known to all of female America. But pondering over a cigarette what to answer, she showed up the shallowness of all that by forgetting it, to concentrate on Frank. She said that to tell the truth, she didn't know what Frank was into. "In Florida, I thought he was one of the mob. Here, I just can't say. He wanted to operate in some of their same areas. But that man's murder off Deer Point—Frank wouldn't get mixed up in a thing like that."

"He's let it work for him. People get scared of him when they think of it."

"He can't help that. If you start saying you didn't murder somebody, how's that going to sound?"

Arnie agreed she had something there.

"It's just that— Well, people used to call him sometimes."

"People, for that matter, call me."

"So why suspect him?"

"Listen to some history: it's the one antidote to romance. The national crooks tried to buy in here, after the hurricane. The speculators came down faster than buzzards on corpses and rats out of the garbage. But things weren't ever up for grabs. You had to live here to know why. I picked up my properties from owners who'd gotten scared, maybe, but who mainly were past the prime and didn't want to rebuild. One crowd that held on to property was the old-line political bosses. They've had arrangements going back for generations: Yugoslavs, Cajuns, Poles. The shrimpers, the low-rent landlords, the little businessmen—Catholic, quiet, and strong. They knew the Coast was here to stay. So the Mafia got faced down in a way, and it looked like they decided to go respectable. Motels, restaurant properties. The low profile. Except that things go on here and there in a velvet-curtained room or two. Except that we're neighbor to Pascagoula and the shipbuilding unions. If they can get little spots here and there, like my island. . . . Well, what's the whole Southeast Coast, but a sieve for letting drugs leak through it?"

"It's going to leak through anyway," Mavis said. "How can you stop what people want to have?"

"Oh my God, that's the pits. I'm civic-minded, Mavis! I'd start a 'Save the Pelicans' campaign at the drop of a hat, but they're doing all right saving themselves. I sit twice a month with a bunch of old ladies who dye their hair blue to discuss the preservation of old homes and historic sites. A section of the local library given over to the display of Indian relics and other trashy finds was Carrington's brainchild. I even bought up that Indian graveyard—or so it's said to be—right back of the duck pond. I'm overextended, but active as hell."

"That guy that was here," Mavis remarked, "whether he bugs you or not, there was some reason he looked you up."

"It's a sort of tie he feels," said Arnie. "Old relationships —some you forget, some you can't."

"Ask him again," Mavis suddenly advised.

"Ask him what?"

"Whatever it was. He's got money. I can still smell it in the room."

"He's just an old friend. I told you that."

"He keeps coming back for something," said Mavis, to whom friendship was not a true force in life. "You ought to call him."

2

When parking his car in the motel parking lot, Lex Graham observed an ambulance with its muted yellow lights flashing softly, drawn up at the back entrance of the motel. No, said the desk clerk, no one had died, ridiculous. Somebody with acute indigestion, too much gumbo out on the pier. He handed Lex a message in a blue envelope. Outside, the ambulance met the highway with a low warning moan from the siren. The envelope, which he opened in the elevator, smelled strongly of perfume. Somebody named Doris in Room 209 would love to have a drink with him. At seven when he went out to eat, the lobby had no one in it who could possibly be Doris.

Returning, he tried to read a mystery novel by one of the better writers whom intellectuals talked about, but was not interested in the story. TV was dull. The blue notepaper scent undulated about the room and, from the highway below, passing lights recalled the ambulance. Well, should he call Room 209?

Of course, if there was a hurricane and a Buddha involved in it, it would wind up with Arnie Carrington. The one thing to bear in mind was the ducks. The hero was keeping a duck farm—white ones at that, with yellow bills and feet. Wait till he told it in Hartsville. "Carrington? He's raising ducks." "Ducks?" he could hear the colleagues, one after another, cry. "Yes, and looking pretty seedy, I'd say. Maybe if he'd taken up turkeys. . . ." He knew how to get full value out of such as that.

A knock at the door, and he jumped half out of his chair, then remembered: he had ordered ice and soda.

With the first taste of scotch sliding over his tongue, the scent soft and warm, the bite in the throat, the odor of perfume turned stale and died. Lex drank slowly, enjoying the height at which he stood dominant, looking down over the beach. The Coast spread out in glimmering points of lights below, stars above, distant fishing boats. His for the taking, in a sense: his new world. If only he would have the wisdom—as of course he would—to stay away from Arnie Carrington. No use to wonder why this was, only to know it.

Drink finished. Bath, pajamas, bed.

In pitch dark, he woke from a scrambled dream, feeling in his hand the sensation of a gun held there, a revolver. The very weight and cool texture pressed the palm of his right hand so realistically that he had to switch a light on and look twice to prove the palm empty, extended and lying upward on the spread. Back again, was all he could think. Would it never go away for good?

It was after Carrington's greatest triumph, when the veterans' housing row had made the state papers every day for two weeks. Sometimes news cropped up in the national press as well: "Quiet Scholar Turned Campus Activist," etc. . . . He was hated and criticized, editorials spat on him (conservatives); he was hailed and admired, given colorful language in descriptive articles that crooned his praises (liberals). But he was always the winner, no matter what; you had that to live with, all the time.

Then, a crisis past, the campus lay as quietly as if a hand had passed over it, smoothing its rumpled hair, or a rake had leveled scars of haste and conflict which footsteps had left on its many brown paths, and Carrington went out alone to climb unseen (or so he must have supposed) the rise of the campus toward the north and had circled the foot of the water tower to where a slender ladder ran upward.

A scarlet sunset had spread itself from one horizon to another, generous as a benediction, with the splendor of deliberate spectacle, arranged for history. The clay all around was red, bathed (not momentarily, but persistently) in this heaven-and-earth-marrying light. And there went Carrington, up the water tower.

Lex, who had driven out a country road just for a peaceful atmosphere, looked up and couldn't believe his eyes. He almost ran the car off the road. He halted and sat still, watching. Of course, Carrington would do that. Another victory to chalk up, one more wrangle over. A god, climbing toward the gods. My good friend, Lex thought, with only a touch of bitter distance. Hadn't they talked it over, he and Dorothy, Arnie and Evelyn? Hadn't they said to one another that political differences shouldn't come between friends? Think of all the good times—confidences, long evenings. Nothing could break them up. Though Lex had made it plain how he felt about it, all this hoopla which frothed up the university and made learning anything next to impossible. His idea of a college had plenty of library silences in it, an occasional frenzy over football maybe, but little else. Agitation had come to be what everybody lived for. The dean of women had turned into a camera nut, flashbulbs and speed lens always ready. "For posterity!" screamed this nice lady, hair wild-crazy in the rain, already planning her exhibition.

Upward still went Arnie Carrington, up the water tower, which reared like some abstract idea of height above the low campus. The solitary hero mounted rung by rung, Icarus and Satan and God knew who else. Not thinking anybody saw him? Suppose he fell? Suppose he'd had a drink or two? Suppose somebody took a potshot at him—anything, in overheated times, was possible; people had been shot at, on purpose, by accident, through mistaken identity, or through just happening to bump into a passing bullet. One had been a young girl, a co-ed, her cheekbone smashed, her beauty reft from her in one horrible second. Lex had a little girl, Lucinda. It shouldn't be! The thought struck with sudden passion and, shaking as though from nightmare, he looked down at his hand, grown strangely heavy, and saw a gun in it. He must have leaned over, opened the glove compartment of the car, and drawn it out. He knew now he had even aimed with it; and how the lifted sights, swinging into line with his eye, had caught the climbing figure was there in his knowledge, too. In retrospect, an echo, he heard the minute click of the safety catch removed. He reset it. Arnie, his friend Arnie, his best friend.

Vision blurring, wrist fluid, sweat drenching his shirt, staining through the light gray of his jacket, his face turned thick and dead-skinned to the touch, he let the gun fall to the floor of the car, slide senselessly over the carpeted dividing hump of the floorboard. He thought of the assassins of the great, and how they seldom missed, no matter how poor, unworthy, cheap, illiterate, low, the dropouts of the universe. He understood them, for a moment he was one of them, that shabby company—he, the reserved, reliable image of professorship. Within that perfect work, something was loose and rattling; something was roving around dangerously. He did not remember driving away, only the sight in his eyes of that figure, small now as what he had once seen in the circus as a child ("the Human Fly," they called it), mounting higher, ever higher. . . .

Home again, he went through the motions: dinner, conversation, reading, work, bath, and sleep. What was Carrington, anyway? A minor sort of hero, if that. A sham, really, a lazy scholar (rather get *engagé* than do his hard desk work on his Byron grant), a praise-seeker from the students, basking in his press notices like a movie star, full of shots of his own adrenaline—what else kept him poised above the crowds, stuck him safely to the water tower ladder, took him up, brought him down? Self-involvement, that's all. But Lex knew the target he himself had found: his own hate.

Revealed and lanced, the secret abscess poured out its contents. Lex hoped it would be emptied soon, the sooner to heal. But in the meantime, afraid of shouting out in his sleep, he went to the guest room till the spell was over.

Oswald and Graham. What was that professor doing with that big-time name? He prodded himself with ironies. But, half dreaming, he felt his eyes widen at the blue ravel of smoke from the barrel, and through it saw what it now veiled and now curled clear to expose, the fall itself, the plummeting. . . . "Oh no! NO!" "Lex! Wake up!" That was Dorothy

in her pretty nightgown and Lucinda too, in hers, running in
from being awakened by his cries. "He done et something,"
said the maid when they told it at breakfast.

Gradually, all faded. Normalized . . . that horrid invention of a word. Normalization. In his case, a pallor, a fading
scar on the psyche, a chance to return to the blessed every-
dayness of things. I had, he told himself one day in his office,
a suppressed dislike for Carrington, which has now been
wiped out. The ritual of the gun has cleansed all that. I am
free.

He almost wrote a memo to this effect, for filing away.

But what really, he thought, tossing aside the mystery
book for the third time, had "normalization" meant? People
said they wanted peace and quiet, but had only gotten restless. They developed odd ailments, drank too much, and had
car accidents. Carrington went back to Lord Byron. He was
gone for two months in Italy—Venice, Ravenna, La Spezia—
returned grave, no longer talkative. The Vietnam war went
on, but the discussions of it were repetitive. The four or five
black students, admitted with such upheaval, went dutifully
to lectures and wrote copious notes. There was nothing of any
interest going on, except, suddenly, love affairs.

Everybody was doing it. Carrington took his head out of
the library to remark that Byron had them all beat before they
started, some instinct about women—phenomenal, like absolute pitch—made him just know at a glance. Lex Graham,
working anew on the revived Carrington friendship, offered
conversational fillers about Boswell, speculations on Swift. But
were things actually going on, not just in table talk and
books? Yes, they were. Lex troubled dry old bones.

His brutish initiations; why even think of them now? The
last before Dorothy had been a library assistant at Minnesota,

where his degree was won. Slavic and flat-footed, she harbored him for a time with blowsy attractions, then scared the hell out of him by wanting to get married. When she saw the light about that, she gave him a blast of her opinion, namely, that he was no good in bed and never would be. From seductive murmurs to yells and slambangs. "Never?" It was a shame he couldn't hit back at her, but only went hangdog out into midnight snow, and eventually to a doctor, who with a thin smile stated: "Not everyone can be a sexual athlete." "I wasn't that ambitious," Lex said. "Then what," asked the doctor, "is the problem?"

So not a sexual athlete, so what? He wore heavy dark-rimmed glasses by then, making a young face older. Dorothy, when he met her that summer at a party in Memphis, looked cool. He contrasted her pleasantly to the librarian—her slim feet, high-arched in delicate sandals, her smooth hairline—groomed was the only word; the neatness so deliberate it extended even to the inside of her various handbags. Her interest, he knew, had come straight to the fore when he was introduced as "Dr. Graham," a new professor in the making. Only then did he see it for the first time: the white teeth and crinkled corners of her even smile, all for him.

"There's snow on the roof, but a fire in the furnace," some wag at the wedding had said. "Why," Lex, honeymooning with her in Bermuda, had inquired, "did he feel free to say that about you?" "Just being funny . . . I hardly know him at all," Dorothy had scarcely turned to reply. They were walking down a pretty road by the sea. On that trip, on that very walk, the deeps for him were broken and his love came out to her in a flood of words about, of all things—he was astonished—his parents. They were ugly, the way he'd had to see them. His father's false teeth floated in a stained bathroom glass; his mother never shaved her legs; they drank prune

juice for constipation; and an old aunt, who stayed with them
for months till she went off to die in a "home," talked at the
table about her piles. When they quarreled, they hid it, said
ugly hissing things. They saved everything, ate off cracked
plates with plated silver worn through to some poisonous-
looking base, never used "the good things" except for company, got a "nice" look up for church and relatives and visitors, talked about other people in an awful way. But she . . .
but Dorothy! He was free of all that now, he told her, and she
kept walking along the beautiful road by the island sea, glancing at him now and again while he talked and saying, "I see
. . . I understand." He couldn't stop. From parents he went
on, felt he could go on forever, told her one confidence after
another, stated ideas, gave shape to glowing dreams, and in a
sheltered inlet pranced about in sunlight, walked on his
hands, did somersaults and got her to photograph him, until
tired from a feat of handstands, he looked up for her ap-
plause, but found nothing but the camera resting deserted on
a rock. She had long gone and was back at the hotel, where
he found her. She was freshly bathed and was putting up her
hair to have it right for dinner. She was short with him and
said, when he caught her hand, that she had come back because she was getting tired. He wanted to hold her close, but
she withdrew her fingers from him, and turned back to pin-
ning up her hair. "So we won't be ugly people," she said,
"that's all you meant to say." No, it had been more than that,
but how to explain? He wanted to cry, but knew that would
put her off more than ever. She was withdrawn; he saw it
sadly.

Yet once at Southern Pines and into harness, he had
found her perceptive and helpful. She had made the Carrington friendship, guided them toward it. Advancing Lex might
have been her motive, for Carrington was a full professor, a

"name" scholar, head of committees, in thick with the dean. It was his wife Evelyn, said Dorothy, whom she so admired. A foursome was what they made, sharing talk, ambitions, confidence and gossip, a love of various decors, a taste for jaunts to New Orleans (and once to New York, to the theater), a liking for good food and wine. Then Carrington, as the fifties faded and the sixties grew upon them, got the bright look of the challenged; he rose to meet the times. In the moment of his rising, all was changed; like the day in Bermuda when Dorothy put the camera on the rock and walked away, nothing would come back the same again. How quickly good times were destroyed—or put behind, which was just another name for killing. Was it for this that Lex first hated Carrington, his "best friend"? He had a daughter by then, and one day when passing the busy large English office where Carrington was often to be seen, he heard that distinctively enunciated drawl, saying, "So what if it is a female? It's a wonder he could squeeze out even that." Like the sting of dry ice, the remark burned in his hearing for two days, until he finally telephoned. "Talking about you? Poor old Lex. I don't remember the conversation. Are you sure you heard it right? It certainly wasn't about you."

"Campus unrest" could end and did, but the days of the happiest friendship he could remember, Lex saw, would not return. The Carringtons now professed themselves worn out with upheavals, wanting only to be together. They turned to one another—fusing, reclusive, exclusive—as one. Evelyn and Dorothy still exchanged copious notes by telephone, but of entertaining there was only the occasional gathering, nothing intimate. The Carringtons had long ago bought a most curious house, relic of somebody's odd scheme of the twenties, just before the Crash, only one wing finished. It was down by a

lazy willow-hung creek, reached by a twisty road. Silence
came from it now. What went on there? Happiness?

Lex mentioned his thoughts on this to Dorothy, but she
gave a vague answer and changed the subject and just like
that—cold flash of moonlight on a blade not seen before, lying
in familiar grass—he caught the first glint of fear. And that
long after the gun—that deadly secret, his shame. Oh, did all
the milestones in his life have to be bad? So what was it this
time? Unfortunately, without a shred of actual proof, he
knew.

"Carrington! Carrington! Carrington!"

Did his wife chant through her orgasms what students
before her had publicly cried? Foolish, goal-less "playing
around": Lex could never bear the thought of it. He could not
bear either to open his suspicions, to hear once again the
phrase he'd come to loathe: "Poor old Lex." So his ideas
drifted around like a giant nebula in the sky of his skull—in
the mass present, in detail largely guesswork—for Carrington,
if he was having an affair, would be neat about hiding it.

Still, it was failure never to have had it out, never to have
faced them with what he suspected. What prevented him but
that guilty day of the water tower and the spectacle of sunset
which the Almighty would never have gone to the trouble to
arrange for Lexington Graham. . . .

The phone rang—not this late; impossible. Carrington was
calling, this recent Carrington with ducks and a Buddha in his
backyard, properties spoken of: a monstrous ruined hotel, a
distant island. Carrington was now the beggar, beseeching
Lex to reconsider, stay on through tomorrow, take the trip out
to the island.

I'm being petitioned, thought Lex, ironic at his own glow
of pleasure. Carrington, of course, was just after capital: Lex
had smelled it early on. And he—once the wildebeest in the

lion kingdom, long the tortoise to the hare—stood here in his high room above the Gulf, looking out, and said that: yes, if it mattered so much; why certainly, if he insisted so; as a personal favor, did he say? and obviously he could arrange it with Dorothy. "I'll just tell her there's a hitch about the deed," he soothed, frank about keeping Arnie's name out of her ears. Then he hung up and stood gazing out above the Gulf, in dimmed light to see that fine expanse of tranquil water, over which his spirit rode in Mercedes-like bliss, among silvery moonlit clouds. Oh, it was simple enough what he could do, a little thing, humble, but sufficient. He could say no to Arnie Carrington. That at least was in his power, and in a way *was* power. And he knew it.

3

"I'm just an old brown locust shell, stuck on a tree, Lex," Arnie Carrington announced next morning down on a pier in the small craft harbor. Lex had arrived at the appointed time, in tan cotton slacks looking way too new and a knotted silk scarf, dark blue, tucked into his shirt. Nothing if not well-dressed. Mackintosh and sweater, drawn from the back seat of his shimmering car, hung over his arm. "Oh, it's a great life in store for you, Lex."

Carrington vaulted into his boat, a fat-bellied old shrimper with the net masts removed, the gunnels painted red. Rocking from his weight, she made the water she rested in wash with a soft sigh. She lay as comfortably in the warm winter sun as an old dog might on a rug in a sunlit room. To

Lex, watching like a child in a kitchen where he didn't know what to do, this timeless sense came easily. (Dangerous, he thought, and stiffened.)

"Next thing you know," Arnie was shouting, and postponed the sentence to kneel in the bow, coil ropes into standing rings, return to lift down from the pier a Styrofoam cooler heavy with ice and beer, a canvas bag encasing the oddments of travel. He unlocked the narrow door that led to the pilothouse and kicked it free of the jamb. Then he was looking up and there was something coming between him and Lex, leaning down toward the boat from the pier, handing down a basket, a woman. Lex had not heard her come. She wore a loosely cut blouse, sandals, a peasant skirt, and her dark hair swung down curtainlike, blocking from his sight not only her face but Arnie's also, so that Lex saw only the hands and arms, hers to extend a basket, his to take. Prearranged. She straightened, flung her hair aside, and was, as Lex now saw instead of guessing, good-looking, sexy, what Arnie would have. Her name and his were being exchanged, but he couldn't make the words out. She said hello and left, with a wave to them both, her sandals slapping fast on the wood of the pier.

"Friend of mine. Mavis. Brought some lunch for us." Arnie held the boat close to the pier for Lex to vault in. "As I was saying, you'll next be hoarding your own fine little twin-engined launch at the yacht club docks. But for now, you must suffer with this down-at the-heels but strong and worthy character." He slapped the side of the pilothouse affectionately, like the flank of a horse. An old tan sweater, faded blue work shirt, worn chino trousers, frayed canvas shoes— what did Arnie care? "It's a great life in store for you, the way I see it. First, department head—you're in line for it, I would imagine. Then a year or so of a high administrative post, rector, vice-chancellor, something or other, then retirement. And there will be your beautiful house, waiting just for you and Dorothy and your girl, your mansion by the sea."

"As if I thought in terms like that." Lex felt the heat of anger, a tiny beginning flame which he quickly put out. Playing cool was the method.

"I'm carried away," growled Carrington and slapped his shoulder. "See my island and you'll know why. My little properties salvaged from the ruins. My heart is in them, Lex! You'll hear it all."

By then he was leaping about the boat like a jumping jack. He lifted the anchor clear on its winch, let gas into the starter mix, yanked the motor to life, and cut speech off entirely. He scurried out, cast the last rope from the pier, mounted back to the cabin, nudged the motor into a slow reversal, and steered the craft down the watery aisle between ranked rows of boats moored along the piers. Solemnly as a march, they sputtered down the distance to the end, then with a spurt of speed, a flourish of the wheel, they swung toward the open channel. The old boat seemed to feel her freedom recurring and to have for a moment what the sailboat knows even better, a single impulse with water and current, air and wind all worked to its own purpose.

Lex's busy anxieties went mercifully dead for the moment. He felt the thrill of their opening motion, saw the sweep of the wake like the parabola of a gull's flight, and thought of a skating mark on ice such as television shows often held him with, or, from a campus path in the afternoon, the sight of a jet plane rising on the wide curve of its stream. Even seediness could come to life was what he had to admit, and from its unlikely bosom he chose his moment to look back toward the shore's curve, to seek the white rise of his new home.

Barrel-chested, short-legged, looking taller than he was, Carrington stood at the wheel with his mouth working full blast, singing, it was to be supposed. It was like watching a movie before the advent of sound. Then the motor lost its sputter, cut down to a steady purr as they took direction and put on speed. Now, streaming from the pilothouse, came the loud warbling of Carrington's baritone: "You Are My Sunshine," "Home on the Range," "Basin Street Blues". . . . The pursuing gulls no doubt heard the cadence, and flapped their wings in time to it, thought Lex, and looked outward to where the winter water lay flat and rippleless, slightly hazy, sunwarmed, a dim cottony mist just above it a few yards distant, which vanished as the prow cut the peaceful surface.

Islands were rising now, at first like indentations of the horizon, then assuming individual shape and character. The gulls, hovering high, knew the islands, closing or opening distances as they chose. A string of pelicans, in configuration like the tail of a kite, beat steadily toward a knoll of land and banked, curving in unison to settle in on fishing territory, chose a given moment for folding wings. Pouches hung from their bills to dump their catch in, old ladies with their reticules. Nature's jokes, thought Lex, included Arnie Carrington, now warbling "Harvest Moon" in broad daylight. Among oyster shells on a scant slope of beach, part of an islet, a tall white heron, awkwardly alert for fish, leaned into the wind on fragile legs like ill-set bean poles. She looked up as if she knew them, saw them pass. Winter, in her pale look against the wind, recalled itself.

For now shore breath had fallen behind and they moved through the pure Gulf itself; outlines stripped by the season stood sharply visible, the water flashed up in higher play against their hull. A distant fishing boat appeared, the first in a time, two figures hunched at either end. Far off, a beach

showed the remains of a picnic: beer cans and a charred
splotch left from fire.

"Where are the shrimpers?" Lex shouted.

"Far out," Arnie waved to indicate. "Out and to the
west." Then, an hour later, it was to the southwest that he was
excitedly pointing. "There she is!" He had seen his island.

The island now rapidly drawing them toward it was like
the others only larger than most, and seemed, in the shift of
light caused perhaps by Carrington's swing to the left, to lie
under a haze of blue. Arnie cut the motor down to a sputter,
and white sand gradually extended itself before them to make
a small horizon. A deep notch appeared on their right, around
a forward spit of beach where some scrappy oaks had grown
to make a little wood, tough fighters used to wind and wreckage. The boat rounded the point and, barely powered now,
moved into a natural harbor.

Hearing surf as the motor died, Lex stood up eagerly, but
almost toppled as the boat swayed. Carrington passed insect
repellent; from beyond the trees the surf withdrew, fading.

A tapestry of mosquitoes drifted forward to meet them.
Carrington made the boat fast to a short pier. Soon they
were standing on it, carrying cooler, basket, and canvas bag,
and faced toward the island.

They had started at ten; it was now past noon. The sun
from its winter angle warmed them. The stubby oaks at this
end of the island looked dense enough to call a wood. A great
sand dune, rising up from a midpoint of the land, looked over
the wood. Lex had seen it, a landmark, on their approach, and
seen how the reach of island to the east was sandy, bare,
shell-strewn, fleeced with long grass. They were to move
through wood to beach, he guessed, by a path, but the weeds
just before them looked squashy with wet, perennially green,
the ground black and treacherous. Arnie went ahead, stepping

into weeds that nodded forward over a little-used path. He was suddenly to the waist in weeds. Lex followed. Conquistadores.

The path turned, approaching the oaks. The ground was not so spongy here. I will be taller than these trees, thought Lex, and saw their twisted branches, gray, the size of children's limbs. But they were above him, in low command, and ahead he heard, when the surf drew back, the rustle of a stream, and heard the ground suck again when Arnie stepped. "A spring?" he asked. There it came across the path, an indentation lined with rocks and shells, the rush of clear water. His eye followed it up toward the island's center, quickly lost to sight among reeds and tree roots, up toward a space suggested at its turning, where yellow flowers slanted, dry, left from autumn in this shelter, but boldly colored still. Sun was reaching in to touch them. He stopped still, head among the treetops. He saw gnats dance in sunlight, a black fist of motion. Arnie went down, sloshed through the stream and up the opposite bank, while Lex stood listening to the withdrawal of the surf so he could hear again the hidden spring. "Yes, a spring," said Arnie, looking back. "Everything's here," he added, and the surf rushed back, over his words. But it was the smell of something crushed, a wild plant stem or fungus, that pierced through the insect oil, and made Lex think of women, girls especially, their nudging odor, and that not of his present household but cousins he used to visit as a child, way out in the country, the other side of nowhere, his father said, and a spring had been there, too. His little cousin had been with him when they went to find the spring, the blond one with a cast in one blue eye, the one who had said, "When I bend over, don't look up my dress, now." "I'll turn my back," he'd said, the way his mother had told him, but then she laughed over her shoulder, "Oh, I don't *rilly* care." Face dripping with the fresh water cold as a silver knife blade, she'd tickled him and giggled, and wanted him to play a game she could teach him, but by what rules? He thought with fear of all the things they'd told him not to do.

"If you take a long enough step," Arnie was saying, "you'll clear it." The stream murmured between them. His attention returned and he smiled. When had there been a smile like that—easy, natural? Long ago, he had reached out with good faith to Arnie and Evelyn Carrington. There had been a possibility of love. He had followed it with faithful tread. How was it lost? Lex jumped toward Arnie. The canvas bag, holding a snakebite kit, a collapsible casting rod in an aluminum tube—what else?—banged against his thigh. He half slipped; Arnie caught him. They went on.

They came from the wood on the path, which now skirted the foot of the great lopsided dune. A myriad dazzle of butterflies, brown and gold, swarmed up out of nowhere. They danced around Lex's head. He saw light through them, a world of translucent amber, the dazzle of deep dimension, pulsing to its own notion. The very wings now were beating his face, soft and multiple, his cheeks, brow, even eyelids. One was wading knee-deep in his hair. When they dipped and rose, moving away as one, he was gasping. "I saw them!" Carrington was crying. "All around your head!" Lex rubbed his hand to his face as though emerging from a trance. All together, they had been like the separate parts of one creature. Cousins . . . angels . . . he seldom thought such things. But still the pressure of the wings on his flesh kept beating like a noise. They came past the dune together and walked toward the island's eastward reach, bare of trees, land risen to sun its back, whale's hump, haired with long pale grass. The surf, withdrawing, left a hush behind it, and a light, still dryness came up from the thin crust of soil, holding its own against the sea breeze. Along the slope of the earth before them, the cement foundations of a building could be seen, with a curving shell walk toward it.

"There was a chapel here," said Carrington, waving his hand. "The place was run by some nuns. They were building a retreat when the storm came. Gave it up afterward. We can sit here." He had reached the old foundations and sat down on a length of broken wall. He set basket and Styrofoam bucket down between them; the bucket lid came off with a squeak. "It's not the school cafeteria, all the better." He snapped the lid from a can of beer and passed it. "God Almighty with his powerful winds was no respecter of his servants. The nuns would make their day trips here by the boatload, I reckon, clustering around on the sand like big black birds, filing like missionaries through the wood. The Holy Ghost is a swarm of butterflies." He snapped a second can. "Happy times for the sisters. Now, swept away. After the big blow, they got discouraged. Other reasons, too. Fewer going into orders, so I've heard. Women getting less and less spiritual. Evelyn loved it here. She had a remission after the storm. A fantasy we had: the wind had drawn her trouble out, blown it clear away. No use in that. But we would come out here, middle-aged, doomed, happy, full of empty plans. All done now, no use to remember. Now I want to put a fishing lodge here. There's the natural harbor. I can rent it out. An architect —friend of mine—is drawing up the plans. A Mafia guy wants to buy. Not the deal I'd like." He pointed eastward. "Once out on that beach, a big sea turtle came up. I climbed aboard its back, Lex. I rode the bastard out to sea. I was alone, Evelyn gone. 'Take me to the deep,' I ordered and he did. Swam right out from under me." Having described a suicide attempt that failed, he drew sandwiches from the basket, bit into chicken salad, offered ham to Lex, lifted out a Thermos of coffee.

"I was sorry to hear about Evelyn," said Lex. Arnie did not reply, and he felt his own sincerity fall back upon himself. He remembered the innocence of the spring, light through the beating wings. The world, at least partly, is what we make it. He ventured further. "I want us to be friends again." The butterflies.

"Friends?" Arnie repeated, with a sudden, appraising turn of his shaggy head—unkempt and older; a wild outcast found wandering here alone might have looked the same. "So do I, Lex!" He leaped up, grasped Lex's hand and shook it, eyes flaming their strange yellow light. His grasp was rough, callused, with cracked skin. "You must understand the opportunities!" He had to shout over breaking surf.

"To hell with opportunities," said Lex, and hoped for a tidal force of understanding. "I was so lonely as a boy, and what's important now? My daughter's a treasure, but pretty girls don't stay around forever and I—" He raised shy eyes and met avidity in the yellow gaze. He was being heard, all right, his words drunk as if by a sponge, but as information only, he saw, and withdrew at once—sensible, sensitive—into silent caution. He perceived Arnie as enemy, a wearisome presence. But, in the absence of evidence to the contrary. . . .

"So you and Dorothy," said Arnie, "you never really worked it out?"

The next step, of course, had been that one. Should he go right on with it, get in up to his neck, say: Maybe she was happier with you? But there was darkness there; he had a right, at least, to normal clarity. The sea withdrew, hissing softly.

"It's peaceful here," Lex said. "Something mysterious about it. Did the nuns give it that?"

"All islands are mysterious, I guess," said Carrington. He glanced about him as though someone might be there with them. The next wave trod softly in. "Oh, to get you in on my interests here, Lex. We'd both be the better for it. Call the past shredded, ripped apart, hurricane-blasted: your choice of metaphor. We both know there was a tangle back there. But the knack of going forward from now, that's the survival route. If you retreat, even up to your ears in money, retired and neat and elegant as hell, your daughter married and moved to Kalamazoo—why, that's misery, Lex. You best involve yourself. I always had a gift for that, at least; nobody ever suggested differently. I can point to what's the vital spot like a bird dog. The mystery you mentioned—I won't hide it from you. It's Evelyn. She's out here. In spirit. Nothing sinister. Friendly as hell."

They sat eating sandwiches. A gull sailed close and tilted over them, head bent to search out what they had. It screamed. Action, Lex knew, was being pointed out, pled for. Decision, activity. He would sooner have lingered with emotions, feelings, longings he had just begun to find words for. Arnie, God knew, took feeling so for granted dozens of cousins might have gone down on their backs for him, and he would have enjoyed, forgotten them every one. In sunlight, the wind blew chill. It was, after all, winter.

In winter light, on a ruined wall on a Gulf island, Lex Graham sat tall and silent, looking out. To someone coming on the scene, he might have appeared to be controlling here— an island king. "You're asking," he said at last, "to give what I have to keep your projects going. But the ideas here, they all are yours."

"Oh, yours would be welcome. I wouldn't dictate. Working together is the only way."

"My life," said Lex, "all that's in it, or that it could ever be, cradle to grave—to you it's nothing but an episode. Why care about it? Why pretend to care?"

Arnie did not reply.

"I came all the way out here to tell you the one answer to anything you could ever ask of me. I came all this way so you'd hear me plainly, because, to tell the truth, I don't think you've ever heard me, ever really listened to what I said. I won't help you in any way. It's final."

Arnie presently got up and walked away.

Lex sat listening to the surf. The water itself, its rush and retreat, seemed to give back the hot screaming of the sixties decade, all that had made him feel out of it. So he had been true to what he felt last night, high in the motel room, overlooking the water.

Carrington sat down some distance away on a log half sunk in the sand, his head bent, his gaze gone out to sea. He seemed to have grown into the log. The shagginess of the head and mustache were intricate with growth: weeds, shells, driftwood, and dishevelment of sand. The tone was altogether earth, myriad, unfathomable. He moved once, to scratch his leg, then pulverized small chips of sandy bark from the log's back. The gesture brought life to what it touched and made that life his own. Lex, in estrangement, looked away to the east where, to his surprise, a proud silent fishing schooner, blue and dazzling white, was passing in a furrow of white foam. When he looked back, the log was empty. Did eyes play tricks? He got up and shook himself.

Lex assumed that Arnie's absence was due to nature. He went, himself, behind a wall, then strolled as far as he could to the eastern reach, saw the proud boat, a dot now, disappear, the thin trail of churned water dissolve to nothing. Alone, then: had Arnie left him there, vengeance for his refusal? The idea, which he did not really believe, nevertheless set up a groaning within him, such as one hears within a tree trunk. Dully, he noted the return of what had been absent since all the money had come to him: psychic pain. He walked inland and circled the tall dune, really only a packed drift of sand against a once-commanding tree, probably blown there by the hurricane. Branches and driftwood were laced in it, and what looked to be the side of a refrigerator, probably from a wrecked boat's galley, and the splinters of a chair. By the dune's foot, he re-entered the wood of small trees. He followed what seemed to be a path, hoping it would bring him back to the spring, which he now remembered fondly, like something out of a long-ago dream. He immediately lost direction in the thick growth. Once he stumbled over a rotted tree stump, pulverized to dust by hordes of ants, and again sank to his ankles in soggy ground, layered with thick moss and fringed with ferns. On firmer ground, he was clawed across the face by briars, and vines clung about one leg, removing his shoe which he was at some trouble to find. Then he saw what seemed to be the path again and at a little distance, just at a turning place, a naked woman with her back toward him, unmistakably his wife. "Oh, Dorothy!" He cried it at once, knowing the sight to be merely a trick of shadow, or the way a feathery bush was growing by the trail, swelling out to shape a shadow. He took the whole impression into him, even while knowing it false. A sense of her having just swum in the Gulf and now sheltering to dry herself with a towel, fit back into clothes. He saw the gleam of her thick hair, with its cosmetic streaking, the long sunken line of her spine, and again said, "Oh!" and, stepping forward (even as the configuration turned into itself only), he stumbled and fell forward, his arms stretched out.

It was difficult to scramble up. His leg at first was numb, and he was never clear whether the numbness was already occurring and had caused the fall, for it had already begun to sting like crazy, itch like fire, he couldn't tell why, but heard a scraping noise a few feet from him, to the left, and parting some tall grass, found there before him an open sunlit space with Arnie Carrington hard at work in it, clearing growth back from a flat rectangular marble slab which lay before a formal pedestal. It was astonishingly gardenlike, and Arnie's motions in clearing back what would soon obliterate it had the quality of a monkish kind of devotion, of the person who leaves off manuscript illumination or Scriptural translation in order to do his patient chores. For Evelyn? He'd said she was here—did he mean literally?

"Oh, there you are," said Arnie, looking up. "You know what this was? A shrine to St. Francis. Evelyn liked it. The statue blew away and couldn't be found. The patron saint of birds went shooting off on the wind." He dumped an armload of weeds and vines, out into the wood's edge. There went the stream Lex had sought, winding through the foot of this little civilized plot. "I thought I saw Dorothy," he said. "It was just an optical illusion."

Arnie scrubbed a sleeve across his sweating brow. "So we're all four here, you might judge," he remarked.

His work was finished. They walked back to gather up their gear, finding an easy way along the beach. But Arnie noticed that Lex looked like the wrath of God, must have wandered off into a jungle, and Lex at last admitted, limping painfully behind as they approached the boat, that something had bitten or stung or in some way attacked him when he fell —he remembered no hiss or squeak or snarl, or any animal motion, but his leg went numb and then it hurt and now the hurt was growing stronger. Arnie turned back. Lex pulled up his trouser leg. There was swelling already and a curdled mass of color—purplish-red—had commenced. Arnie knelt to look for evidence of snakebite, but found no marks of fangs. The injury simply sat there, as evident as a toad, getting worse. Lex let out a plaintive moan. His face had gone white and small, distant with strain. "Let me help you," Arnie said.

So they came painfully into the boat together. Arnie, leaned against so heavily, remembered other rescues—the soldier in Korea, the son in Colorado, episodes of other days. Well, Lex had said the truth maybe: he, too, was an episode. How much did Arnie care? Still, he was doing his best for him.

In the cabin below the pilothouse, he made Lex comfortable, put blankets around him, settled him on a bunk, soothed him with aspirin and whiskey. But what could it have been? It was as though the island itself had left its stinger in him, a venomous refusal of the Graham presence. What was this about seeing Dorothy? Evelyn was the name he mentioned now. "She's buried there—I know it," Lex mysteriously announced to him, delirious maybe. "Why not admit you've put her out there? That was her grave and you know it."

"There now," said Arnie, moving from one task to the other, mounting now to steer. The boat backed slowly off and nosed toward open water. A day not quite like any other in his life, or Lex's either, Arnie reflected, was ending in this strange way. "You'll be home soon—at the most, two hours. Poor old Lex!"

At that, the motor roared.

4

Even by morning light, the next day, nightmares which had besieged the dark hours still lingered, shadows stamped or dancing on the walls of Carrington's house. The hospital! That was what had done it, brought back all the bad times about

Evelyn. How really cheerful she had been, going in with no
help from anyone, her heels light on the steps, her smile at the
receptionist so genuine with interest the girl used to start
right in on the latest with the boyfriend. Arnie was awestruck.
"Are you just acting this way? Why don't you turn loose and
yell?" "Saving that for later, sweetheart. Hate to be a bore."
She had closed some door, he suspected, some airtight compartment. So she wasn't not letting go, she had made letting
go impossible, like falling upward, or breathing water. "Not
human," he complained. "No, humus," she said, by now in
bed, thinning knees propped up to work a crossword puzzle.
"Leafmold in five letters. Thanks." But to him, every noise
was another tick of the clock—steps in the corridor, a bus past
the window. He watched the phases of the day moon, white
as cloud, bloodless. For months after she died, he had turned
his head when he passed the hospital, pretended it did not
exist. But for Lex Graham he had finally had to return. Poor
old Lex! The phrase had been Evelyn's, but she had meant it
kindly. Hers was the law of kindness, he thought, and returned after dark alone to his house to heat some soup and
gnaw cold food, slug himself with whiskey, fall in bed. And
then her eyes returned, how they'd looked in the fatal last
moments.

He must have slept at last, but it was a shame to know
about sleep through nightmare. Strange beings wandered
through them, a life close to animals. They crowded the stair-
way, jumped away in rooms which he dreamed he wandered
to. The old lion skin on the wall then came alive and was
climbing to maul him, but when he got up, kicked it down the
stairs, and was about to slam the bedroom door, it collapsed,
and a whimpering child, a small skinny boy, ran out of it, pale
and terrified.

The sound of the whimper lingered, all morning long, or

would have if he hadn't decided to make light of it, and gone
to deck himself for what was bound to come.

He stopped by a leather shop in Biloxi and bought a
broad brown belt of the sort that young men wore, the
scrolled design, bunt with acid applied over a pattern,
suggested the flow of serpents, broken by the lozenge-shaped
faces of jaguars. He buckled it on. And saw, too, and bought,
a curious silver pendant, branches of silver forking out, join-
ing at the outer rim to form a circle. It came on a leather
thong. He hung it around his neck so that it dropped, cool
and with an assertive weight, beneath his shirt. The man who
ran the shop and made the things he sold there had lived in
Mexico, where he had picked up his designs. Carrington felt
himself painted new. Fingering the redolent leathers, sniffing
polishes and dyes of the trade, drew him toward newness,
the natural state, as he thought of it. Why bother with the refuse of the boat's wake . . . leave it to the gulls. He paid in
new bills, green as pine, and was then bold enough to go
briskly to the first pay station to make his call.

"Dorothy? It's Arnie Carrington here, calling from the
Coast."

"Not really Arnie . . . Arnie Carrington? Oh."

"Did Lex call you yet, Dorothy?"

"Not since yesterday. I was expecting him to. . . .
Why?"

So the message was his to give in its strangeness. A trip to
an island, a mysterious sting or bite, as yet unidentified;
high fever, puzzled doctors, calls to specialists, a hospital
room. . . . Could she consider coming down?

All the while, his memory was busy with the experience
of her voice, long absent from his hearing. Voices were as distinctly different as thumbprints, ready to be known as a par-
ent might know a baby's worn shoe outgrown for years. He

turned his mind around her syllables and thought of photographs of sound, its various notes weaving in and out of one
another. The crisp outer layer—deceptively businesslike—she
might have been answering the phone for some boutique
where luscious little items, expensive as hell, clicked, clucked,
and whispered together: Money and sex. All ye need to know
on earth. For never shall that marriage part: the eternal
union. He pictured her hand with slim fingers, convex, lac-
quered nails, wrist thin as a bird's.

"Something bit him . . . fever? How did he manage to
get bitten?"

There was amusement, unmistakable, in this question.
Derision of Lex. Shameful element in all that he'd shared with
her. Well, those days were done now, he firmly decided. He'd
have no further truck with all that.

"I think you ought to come," he said. "There's something
a bit uncertain about everything and doubtless he may be
needing you."

She could and would arrive by early afternoon, would go
straight to the hospital. He heard the distant cradling of the
phone. He came out of the booth and gulped down the sea-
fresh wintry day. The thought of her . . . the very idea. . . .

5

Coming to Arnie's house that day from separate directions
were Barbra K. and Mavis Henley, both by request: Arnie felt
that things had gotten rundown. His idea was that Barbra K.
should clean up everything, Mavis direct her. Mavis, who wel-

comed a Saturday occupation, brought her sketch pad along.
Most of Arnie's house, including Lord Byron, had by now
posed for her, but the Buddha was her favorite model. On the
back steps, she would sit for hours sketching him, bare feet in
leather sandals, her dark hair an uncombed thicket. By now
she was his devotee; with him her spirit grew calm as a water
lily. Only Frank Matteo could still trouble her, and she was
bringing some news of him that morning: there'd been a sort
of fight he'd had.

"A sort of fight?" Arnie repeated. Well, a nephew of his
had showed up from Texas, wanting to sing rock music at the
restaurant, but Frank didn't want that kind of emphasis, and
wouldn't let him. There had been a row—the boy was on
something, probably speed. Also, he had later tried to break
into Frank's private apartment. Frank had knocked him downstairs but was now trying to locate him to get him onto a
plane back to Texas, willing to pay the fare. There was a
bunch of small-time crooks operating on the Coast just now—
just filling station stickups and one or two cars stolen, but
Frank thought the nephew had joined up with them to spite
him. "Cautious of his reputation?" Arnie inquired. Then,
"Tell me, Mavis, why wouldn't Frank let a relative into his
apartment?"

"Oh, it's just restaurant gossip," she said, adding that she
still had a free meal ticket there. She went out to feed the
ducks, carrying their grain in a rough hemp bucket. She
moved away, down to where the small pond took a bend to
vanish among low oaks. Then there they came, beginning to
tune up with lusty quacks, heads stretched forward toward
her. She would scatter feed, hose out the hoppers, then sweep
the hutches out, no stopping her. She'd all but taken over
here. Sometimes on sunny days, she would take a deck chair

back to the Indian graveyard to sit and doze, breathing Spanish moss and ancestral spirits.

This time Arnie followed her, standing near the pond's edge just where the pipe flowed in from the Gulf; she was bending to turn it on, as the water level was low; three ducks laid their necks over her lowered arm.

"If you're taking information in, you might be letting some out."

"You mean to Frank."

"I mean in general."

"All I knew, you went out to that island. I brought you some sandwiches, so I'd have to know that."

"The guy with the Mercedes, remember? He's in the hospital with some kind of bite. Bingo. I never saw anything happen so quick like that. His wife's coming down. He just might die."

There was some knocking from the back of the house, but it was only Barbra K. "A friend of mine, this lady," he told Mavis. "Can you tell her what needs doing? She's never seen the house. There are books fallen all over the floor upstairs, and there need to be more rugs out. All those papers strewed over the downstairs table. Some vases and stuff like that might be in the spare room upstairs; I've got some rugs rolled up you can get out. If the wife comes and the daughter, say I'm at the hospital or I will be soon. We need to look good here. This wife of his, she's somebody that always has things looking right."

Then they were meeting Barbra K. He stepped back a little to say the two women's names, and watch them meet. He himself was in both their thoughts and saw them know it, noted their separate curiosities and spareness, the pace of their greeting.

"So do what you can," he said, to either, to both, and

glanced up at the great bronze spirit, then went on, thinking that it was clear that Barbra K. had wanted to remark on the newness of his Mexican medal and his leather belt, but only her eyes had said something, and that Mavis wanted to know who was involved with whom, and how, but had given nothing but a silent nod. A relief of them, a frieze, a legend of two meeting women—he kept the impression all that day, as decor to his motion.

6

Raving Lex at the hospital: Lex with a wildly fevered brow and crazy fantasies. Such as: Arnie had wiped out his wife Evelyn, had murdered her. She was buried on that island. The island secret had spoken. Arnie guessed it and had tried to kill Lex. His poisons were at the ready. Dorothy had been out there with them. Once he had glimpsed her; she had glimmered naked in the wood. She was in on it. Lex was in the way. He had money now. They would take that later.

Lex had been in somebody's way all his life. He had a choice—either be a cog in the wheel of life, or get out of the way while it turned for others. One thing certain, he could never be of any importance. Life was drawn up without him. People knew this and, knowing it, they blocked him. Ignored him. Easily. Fever pulsed around his head. Its heat blazed coronalike around his eclipsed outline. "Bitch!" he screamed at the nurse and tried to throw a glass at her. They strapped him down to keep him in bed and considered a mental clinic in Mobile.

The doctor said it was all from the fever. Meantime, he addressed questions to Arnie Carrington. Did Graham drink too much? Would he be called an alcoholic? Was he ever known to have epilepsy? Seizures? Attacks of depression? Amnesia? Manic phases?

All Arnie knew was that Lex had once tried (or so he had been told) to shoot him down from the water tower at Southern Pines University up in Hartsville, and that he could not release (or so Arnie had been told by the lady herself) his wife's sexual passion. He told the doctor neither of these things. "What bit him?" he wanted to know. The doctor was a thin, austere man with thick gray hair. "We can't say yet. Could have been some sort of scorpion, a viper, even a poison spider. Something not common in this region. Brought in in some way. Off a boat perhaps. We've sent blood, urine specimens to New Orleans for analysis. It's a troublesome case."

Arnie sighed. Lex had always, he guessed, been a troublesome case.

Lex himself, as any case at all, was at the moment hard even to locate, sinking downward as his consciousness moved to find that second Lex, the one who lived steadily on through bouts of nausea, seasickness of the tossing wave, far beneath the flailing arms of his hatreds. Down, down he sank, a boy in a green summer, nesting in a depth of summer, sick, looking out the afternoon window in the small town of his youth. The abandoned hut he dreamed of, there back of the privet hedge, nothing but the cook's cabin, empty and fallen in decay, but for him the home of little playmates, a tribe of tiny friends, eager to do his bidding. He slept.

He woke to rise moderately, calling to mind his more recent playmates, those ladies he collected, full-busted, rococo, their portraits reproduced from paintings. They rested now in secret, waiting for him between stiff flat bindings tied with satin ribbons. Down in his playroom basement—his study. The Countess of Derby, La Princesse de Talleyrand, Drouet's Du Barry, Lawrence's seductive Lady Hamilton—all were waiting. Sexy tickling little hands demure in their laps, touching the dainty collar of some impossible little dog, or holding an ornate tasseled fan. Or a scented note, perhaps, as in Fragonard's "Le Billet Doux." And oh the high platinum wigs, the black patch on the cheek, the ribbons, the bosoms! The names he gave them: Florinda, Clorinda, Belinda, etc. The great day it all started, when he had seen in an art catalog a reproduction of Boucher's "Madame de Pompadour" for sale and had ordered it sent, careful as a lover, to a false name at the post office of a neighboring town. To "Paul McLain." Madame de Pompadour had led the long procession of those to come. And him also she had led, to the little waitress in her black and white frilled apron at the motel restaurant in that very neighboring town. She too was his for the ordering, in a sense, till she had to depart at a moment's notice, leaving no message behind for Paul McLain but taking with her forever a piece of curiously carved gold jewelry—loops knotted at either end, a love knot—which he had found in a New Orleans shop and brought to her; he thought of it as floating off somewhere, among humanity, dragged along in a sluggish river. His fever, returning, heated his brow with a circlet of fire.

He seemed now to levitate. Rising above his bed like a singed Miltonic angel wandering through strange air, knowing about bad sooty things, he struggled against the bands they had tied him with while they poked and questioned. Were his ladies safe? Then he was shouting, "Leave what's mine to me, you crazy thieves!" Though robbery was not in question.

Lucinda. If only she would come and shed her quietness

round about him. A girl of eighteen, quiet? Well, she brought
an atmosphere like that, so that his needs faded just at the
thought of her, his fantasies returned to their distance. ·

The door flew wide. The entering pair were all in white.
"Lie still and rest," they said. "You've got to try not to carry
on like that. Lie still." A sting in the arm.

7

It was in the Japanese "second car" that Dorothy and Lucinda drove to the Coast to see what had happened to Lex.
Dorothy wanted first to go by Arnie's house, though the address was difficult and the house half-hidden in trees and
bushes. She had to see, she thought, and her excuse was that
he'd called her and could tell her more. She parked in the
drive, walked the twisting flagstone past urns, Great Danes,
and garden benches, heels cutting the fallen camellia leaves.
A lizard turned its head to look at her. She pressed the bell. A
woman opened to her, heavy-lidded eyes, heavy-haired, a rag-
bag of clothes hung on her. In back of her, in some shadowy
cavern of a living room—mysterious as the cave of a giant—a
smooth, soft, coffee-colored woman with a scarf around her
head looked up from dusting a table.

Mavis herself thought she might as well have opened a
fashion magazine as a door. The woman before her was trim,
drawn up, made up, intentionally produced—even to her
fingertips. She was obviously the one who went with the Mercedes; as if to prove it, wearing beige.

"Is Mr. Carrington here? Is this his house?"

"Yes, but he's at the hospital, waiting. You must be Mrs. Graham."

"Of course I'm going there. But I needed to see Mr. Carrington, too, to know, just what happened, how he is. . . ." She broke off, lips parting, vague, puzzled, anxious line between brows; there was just a glimpse of that for Mavis before the glossy product woman returned. "It's all a bit mysterious. I can't help but worry, you understand."

Dorothy kept getting the sense of herself saying the wrong thing. Who was this woman? She might have known he'd have somebody. But the Negro was a woman too. Just cleaning up? They both of them seemed proprietors, known to each other, in accord making her the intruder. Yet she had force she knew of to give out with, and so she could stand, capable, beautiful, responsible, with the authority of perfect pitch, what she had attained. How important are *you* to him? They both must have been mentally asking the same thing.

"Maybe you know something about it. Maybe, since he isn't here, you could tell me."

Now she had gotten bold enough, just by still standing there, to look over the mop of dark hair before her into the entrance hall, noting the animal skin (bear? lion?), the iron rail of the stair, a picture of gulls hung above a table.

"Oh, I wouldn't say I know anything, Mrs. Graham. I'm only a friend. I come to help out now and then." For no reason she kept explaining. "He's just got these ducks, you know—"

"Ducks!" The woman looked actually annoyed, as if ducks had been brought into things to irritate her, personally.

"The hospital, then. Just tell me the way."

"You keep on west. It's near the lighthouse. You can't miss it."

The door had finally closed.

"You ain't working?" Barbra K. asked Mavis. "You get off Saddy?"

"I work at the school now. I go up there on Saturday sometimes just to fool around in the lab, making designs, but recently I've been scared. It's just these boys, some in my class, all the time stealing stuff. Stole a lot of art supplies the other day. You seen any of them?"

"There's them kind all over the wurruld, chile," said Barbra K. She poured out coffee for both of them. They found themselves one on either side of Arnie's table.

"What you reckon is wrong with that white man?" Barbra K. asked.

"I got no idea," said Mavis. "I stay away from the islands. Even in Florida, I did. One island just off shore, a man got snakebit and died before they could get to him, just a little way off."

"There's all kinda stories down here. Man from Arkansas come to find his girl friend, ain't two weeks back. Went everywhere looking. Out to Waveland, last seen walking a long sandbar . . . gone."

"Maybe he just gave up," Mavis suggested, "went back home."

"Left an empty car by the road," said Barbra K., ready for her.

Mavis had the idea that if they sat there together, they would soon be getting things to eat together. She wondered if they would go so far as to be discussing men together, but thought that if so, she would soon be taking advice from Barbra K., like going to a fortune-teller. Black women made you feel that way. All the more if they weren't all that black.

"That there was a good-looking woman," said Barbra K. "Real movie-star-type woman. She could go on the TV."

"She had her daughter in the car," said Mavis. "They must be really worried."

"It's Mr. Arnie she's after, more'n likely," said Barbra K.

8

"Dressed up," Joe Yates remarked. "Turned out like new. What's up?"

"To go back to that hospital," said Arnie, "something out of the ordinary was required . . . to see me through it."

And this was partly true.

But he had come to Yates's office to sit where he was sitting before the wall full of blown-up photographs Yates had assembled of the old pre-hurricane Coast: shrimp boats and ancient oaks, camellias in bloom, flags flying from the old white Notchaki lighthouse, moonlight on the Sound, softly blowing curtains of Spanish moss, and the one rectangle Arnie especially loved, which showed a small boy sitting on some concrete steps between two gateposts. The steps were at the end of a long front walk which led up to a coastal house with a generous high portico. The boy was sitting with his cap in his hands; he was smiling in sunlight. Arnie knew that that boy was himself. He recalled the whole visit, the whole lost day. His two old cousins had once lived in that very house— they were dead, the house was blown away, but his memory remained of that earlier paradise and himself in it. For he had been there, within! He could sense again the cotton twill, the cap beneath his fingers. Sore from some family upset at home, up in the austere hills toward Memphis, he had as an adolescent wandered here, been healed, felt healing come. He had come out front to have his picture taken. Quiet hush of a still, oven-hot summer afternoon. A wonder that objects like this could slip intact through the great sewer life is, beaching up beautifully here in Yates's office: he sat before his own lost image as before a shrine.

Yates did not believe, though often told, that the picture was of Arnie Carrington. To him, it was just the snapshot of any small boy before any dreamy old white house back in the dim lost days of the gracious Coast. But he humored Arnie that it was true.

"I had a cap like that," said Arnie, clutching to his youth.

"I gather the wife is coming," Yates said. He climbed on his high stool and dragged some designs forward, pinned them flat to his drawing board, set glasses on his nose. "Couldn't get his interest in your plans, so going to work on her."

"That poor Lex Graham up there, born for trouble as the sparks fly upward. He might just up and die."

"It's nothing to dress for," Yates remarked, noting a freshly laundered shirt, neat corduroys, the familiar sun-blotched face all shaven, with mustache clipped and combed. The new medal, the broad new belt.

Arnie went so close to the photograph he could not clearly make it out. He touched it, ran his fingers over the contour of the gateposts, the cement surface of the steps. How strongly he could smell the live oaks, the peculiar funky wetness that amounted to a fragrance, lingering. It was a smell that cut through everything present, brought back the gray muscular curvings of the great trunks, the ramblings of the wide-spreading, shallow roots, breaking ground surface in their outward reaching. He could go outside and look at some still standing, or growing back. But where to find this unity of

house, shade, and sun, the smiling boy, the brick walk, the
moss barely stirring to its familiar breeze of this hour, this
peace and precious past. He remembered a watch, a boyhood
gift, new that day, and felt again the cut of the crisp leather
band. Young blood ran through him, and like a dancer in one
movement with his day re-found—the day of the photograph—
he walked through the door in a trance.

9

In the hospital waiting room, he was certain that the same
rubbery magazines were sitting in the same old blond-wood
rack or piled under the table with the green-shaded lamp, as
when Evelyn was sick here. He knew them by heart, their size
in his lap, their texture beneath his thumb. It had been in this
room that he and Evelyn had first conspired. She had been sitting by the window in the wheelchair and no one else was
with them. They were as alone as Adam and Eve, or as some
little boy with the neighbor's little girl while the parents were
gone fishing or at work or up to things on their own. "Let's
think of something new," she'd whispered, bright and gamy as
hell. He'd started to smile, thinking: Why, she's getting better,
she's going to be all right, because there was only one something new by then to be imagined, and death was nothing
new at all. But the smile was still hanging around dead on his
mouth when the new she was mentioning (smiling herself)
grew real to him, chill as an Arctic dawn. Still smiling, even
looking casual, in an everyday manner, she yet was stating to
him that the time of migration was a presence full of com-

mand. They would only, she would have gone on to say, be obeying. Her ritual.

Even to this sacred ground, the damned Grahams were making him return. He wished to disturb nothing of it, and gratefully discovered he was tired enough to doze.

With a snort, he jumped straight up and awake.

Two women were standing before him, looking down on him. As though he had been discovered naked on a beach, he made a reflex motion at concealment, but then recovering place and time, still held for a prolonged moment to his dream sense, sense of vision. Or rather, of visions—there were two of them.

One was young, pink, and tender, a Mississippi rosebud in a lavender sweater. The other, with her chic streaked hair, her ensemble of beige with an orange scarf, could have just turned toward him with the swing of a model's step. Oh, stay beautiful and unidentified! he wanted to beg. But they weren't going to do that. Not yet the memory-switch—off and on at will. He struggled to his feet.

"Dorothy? Dorothy Graham. How are you? This must be, all grown up, Corinda, Belinda. . . ."

"Lucinda," Dorothy supplied.

"Who else?" He kissed her brow.

Myths, he thought, and stepped back, like somebody about to take a deeper, more speculative look at a life-sized painting. A pair of goddamn nymphs. Hat in hand, he stood gawking at the girl in lavender, all blush of cheek and blue of eye, blooming steadily with what was still virgin, latent. But it was from Dorothy herself that the absolute soap bubble arose, genie from the sudsy bottles of dream and memory, multi-hued, gigantic, iridescent. And he remembered, like that, their first amorous touch that afternoon of the football game when, alone in the house, they had both known that the time was now, and that knowing, too, had been like watching a bubble of desire—accessible, requitable, fulfillable—materialize. Still, he could almost see its softly shimmering presence, damply webbed with rainbow lights ready to burst in tatters of swift storm. Dear saints, to lose what couldn't be kept, what had to be lost to be at all! Now he saw her lips moving but could not hear her words. How different this day from that, the windows different. Here so high and businesslike. Outside, the warm, radiant winter sunlight of this far South blessed everything in a persistent, steady, invisible fallout of blessing, so palpable it must be something you could measure. Could he ask them, like a god, where they'd entered his atmosphere, at what point on the drive down they could smell the Gulf? He remembered what he was there to talk about. Lex. He led Dorothy aside. "You'll see the doctor, of course. He'll have all the names for things. But what you must realize is, something is temporarily on the wrong track in poor old Lex's brain. It's all to do with the fever. I guess when they get rid of it, the craziness will go too. He's worked out a long fantasy. I'm supposed to be out to destroy him. I arranged a poison bite. I'm after his money. I'm plotting and dangerous. So are you. We can all laugh at it someday. But at the moment . . . well, when you go in that room, be prepared to dodge. Sometimes he throws things.

"They've narrowed it down to three possible types of venom, but I'm no doctor. Last night, they thought of sending him by ambulance to New Orleans. The day before, it was Mobile. Changed their minds again—a good sign maybe."

In the doorway now stood the grave lean doctor. "Mrs. Graham?" She turned. "You are Mrs. Graham, I assume?"

She went to him. Lucinda then was alone there with this man who knew her father, someone she remembered from four or five years back but just as a fact, a friend they had. She was scared. "He's going to be all right, isn't he?"

"Oh, sure. No question of that, I wouldn't say. It's just an odd. . . ." He looked up because Dorothy was back already, standing in the door, her face white. "He doesn't want to see me; he thinks that you and I. . . . Oh, it's all too crazy. He wants to see Lucy. Do you think that she—?"

"What did the doctor say?"

"He said to be cautious; that's about all. Lucy . . . ?"

"Go with the nurse," Arnie said. "Ask her to go with you."

Dorothy trailed Lucinda to the nurses' desk, and Arnie followed, and with the nurse as honor guard they cautiously filed down the corridor to the closed door, Lucinda with her little unicorn's horn of blessing (so Arnie believed) to keep her safe when the door opened. But not even that might work, thought Arnie, on perilous tiptoe.

"Murderer, schemer, plotter . . . !" So Lex had yelled at Arnie. One leg was swelled to the size of a log, layered in bandages; the sheet tented above it; it lay attached and useless. His pale face was streaked with red that showed above the whiteness of the sheets like some sort of wild sunset reflection in a convex mirror. For a moment, Arnie had lingered in bright-faced wonder; though alarmed, he was feeling, too, something like relief. Finally to break free—proper old Lex—thunder from an overdue storm. "Sic 'em, boy," had been his murmured advice, just before he closed the door on abuse growing obscene.

Now back to the captive wild man's cage. The three of them stood at the door and waited while the nurse opened it a crack. She motioned to them, but Dorothy gave a pale nod only to Lucinda, then waited in pinched expectation as she entered, as though she had sent her only daughter on an errand into a Patagonian swamp. But no sound came to them.

Dorothy Graham whispered, turning her smooth, complex face fully to Arnie for the first time, "You see. He loves her." She peered inside.

Lucy was between the bed and the window, facing them but looking at her father, smiling her little cross-toothed chipmunk smile, inherited from him, down into his face. "What'd you do to yourself, Daddy? How'd you manage it?" And he was smiling up at her, foolish as a clown. Dorothy saw all that; she stepped inside the room. Lex's face, turning to her, smoothed into its usual sophistication—he was at once cool, free of fever, and aware of Arnie, behind her. "Driving all this way; it must be serious." "Serious or not, we have to get you home." She stopped, only halfway to him. And glanced back at Arnie, as though she were floating out from shore. But he had vanished, had not followed her in. And she did not know for a moment whether to go forward or back. She needed a presence but had only her own.

As Dorothy had driven south that day in the family "second car," the salt smell had struck the air at a certain point, near a small town named Pegues, as though a line had been drawn across the map, right there. At the scent of it, her blood had turned as though the moon had swayed it, and her body, waltzing like underwater seaweed, had begun to know she would see him, was going to see him again. But once she did see him, there in the hospital waiting room, dozing like an old church elder in his pew, the shock had come hard, a series of small warning tremors, then a jarring grind, and silence. She knew she'd been shifted emotionally, even before he woke up and saw them.

Of course, she'd expected he'd be older. She'd even thought to wonder, her Graham attitudes at work, whether he

still kept up his appearance in the same straight, handy, mas-
culine manner as before. He hadn't—the first glance said it all.
"Gone to seed," was the phrase that occurred. But she noticed
that something new had come to him, and recognized, worst
of all, that it was good. It spoke to her out of the quality of his
patience. It smoked up out of the precarious set of the yachtsman's hat guarded with one rough hand from falling off his
lap while he slept, dog before a door, ready to waken to duty.
All of it led her nowhere but to goodness of the humane sort,
asking more about need itself than whose need, about what,
more than who. Her name was not especially on his mind; he
did not sleep upright for Dorothy. Pious, was he? Tending to
his duty, his duty was Lex. Well, that could be bitter tea,
dreary as dried-up cake. Evelyn was winning still.

Then he'd vanished altogether; she was in the room with
the family. Yes, she said to Lex, the mail about the house was
being answered. Drapery samples had come that morning
from New Orleans, she'd forgotten to bring them. The Atlanta
furniture maker had yet to answer, but another complete catalog of select decor had come from Memphis. She thought that
about the draperies, they'd do better to go to New Orleans
and look. But the main thing was to get him well, wasn't it?
Then on to the dream, she thought, on to the perfect life.

"I can't think I'm very bad off. These accidents with bites
and all that, they either get you right away or you get by with
just a fever. The worst must have gone by yesterday. I remember feeling like hell."

Lucinda was declaring she had decided not to give up
modern dance just because she was president of the young
people's group at the church. Attitudes like that were so narrow. "I told you so," Lex said, and delighted in her puzzling,
as though he contemplated an intricate ruffle on one of his
ladies of the court, the crossing of a velvet ribbon in a portrait

by Reynolds or Vigée-Lebrun. Only find the right way. Her
answer was too choice to be real. "I had to think it through."
"Of course you did." She saw he was teasing, and made a face
at him.

Dorothy stood looking out the window, toward the green
lawn, the highway, the water beyond. Danger past, sickness is
a bore. Of course she could decorate a house—she was good at
that. Despairing, she remembered the sense of labyrinth and
discovery that Arnie Carrington had given her. Why had he
taken it back? In so many words, he never had; it just wasn't
there anymore. The last time they'd met, they had stopped to
indulge a muted, nervous quarrel on a country dirt road. It
was after a rain, the woods still dripped, and a squirrel had
talked noisily, high in a leafless oak, chattered and leaped,
seemed about to shake the woods apart. Anger in a squirrel?
What for? "Once you cried over Lex," Arnie had reminded
her. "You said he was a boy wandering in the dark." "Once I
loved everybody," she said. "And now?" "I hate them." He
was silent. What had he done? What was he doing? He was
letting her go slide down a river and over a waterfall, letting
her vanish, in a sense, for good, was not putting out so much
as his hand. His wife Evelyn's hair was squirrel-colored,
Dorothy suddenly recalled—sprinkled with gray. It was thick,
looked to have been trimmed by setting a mixing bowl on her
head and cutting around it; it hung straight down like a pelt,
almost into her live gray eyes. Real, though absent, then—real,
though absent, now. That day in the car, Dorothy turned to
look at Arnie's hand, half-curled, propped against the seat-
back, nothing in it of a caress, but her lust stirred and resist-
less, she shot over the waterfall and wound up in the whirl-
pool below, for hate to swirl and drub her like a washing
machine: she never remembered leaving the car that day,

though she had done so happily, many times before, her light step touching nothing but air. But at the last like lead.

A week a month a year later, she stopped spinning; metaphorically pitched up on a harsh bank, she began to breathe again. She could be, come to be something—what? It came to her—a great hostess. Party after party materialized: to be enjoyed, drunk, eaten, and to disappear. The wives of both dean and president praised her. Her fame spread to Jackson, where one buffet made the *Daily News:* "attractive Hartsville hostess," etc.

One day, searching for a particular silk shawl in the back of an antique wardrobe, she got all the way inside, only to have it fall down. Coffined within, she made faint cries and scared her little daughter, who came into the room. "Call Daddy," she kept saying, "five five five, four eight three two." She lay bruised and shaken, afraid to try to breathe. Rescue me, Arnie! was what she longed to cry. "Mama's in the furniture," said Lucinda on the telephone.

Lex rushed home, thinking she had tried suicide. He believed that twice she had come near it. He was curiously cool. "Sexual despair is not my affair"; he wrote it on a memo pad. It made no sense to anyone but him that his wife's sexual despair was not his problem. Still, he felt he was right. Nobody made her stay with him; he hired no one to trail her; she had gone to Arnie and returned from him as she pleased. If she'd made a mess of it, who was to blame? He did not think of it. If he thought of it, it would hurt; if it hurt, it would hurt too much.

Out in the waiting room, waiting again, Arnie too remembered the day of the leaping squirrel. The day he leaves a woman—how does any man ever know it when he sees it? "I'll call you," he had said. He kept on meaning to. Or to answer when she called—a different thing.

Scandal about Carrington came up in the spring term: a weedlike growth, though at first small and single. Then summer scattered everyone. By fall, the growth, with root system now far extended, was showing up in clumps of coarse-headed bloom. There was the librarian's story of Carrington's assignations with some graduate student in the stacks behind the periodicals room. "A good place to choose," Carrington remarked. "Large books hide more than small ones; they even hid the guy's identity. 'Call me Arnie, sugar,' he probably hissed in her ear when he heard Miss Garner's little laced-up shoes going pitty-pat." Quoting him, somebody put words in his mouth, adding that: if anyone was laying that particular student, it was a good thing; she needed it. But I didn't say that, he still silently contended, looking at a framed photograph in the waiting room: Notchaki Hospital after Hurricane Camille. It had stood firm, a concrete reinforced structure, long and low, but then with windows broken, branches hurled across the grounds, a whole uprooted tree barring the entrance. His mind streamed past it, back to the final episode at Southern Pines which had had nothing to do with sex at all.

It was just those students who wouldn't stop going. Feckless and intense, they kept on racing when there was nowhere to go. They didn't know how to be anything else but what had been so exciting for months on end, and they wouldn't drop the name they'd chosen from the first: "Carrington's Boys." So they kept up their crazy ways, only now without any leaders to give them dignity. In vain, Arnie teased and bullied them: their clothes were a mess, their grades lagging, their music was bedlam, their methods were dated and corny. But they carried on just the same, and tales got around (because he had chipped in to get them to Washington for a Vietnam protest march) that he was a behind-the-scenes director of their various tricks, and that furthermore these stunts weren't as empty-headed as they seemed—some sinister purpose was operating. If Carrington met with them at all, it was to inveigh against pot smoking. "Carrington! Carrington! Carrington!" they chanted, as in days gone by. His name had become as automatic with them as the rebel yell. By some bizarre transfer, he had managed to tap the same emotions as the old Lost Cause. He escaped the meeting early, but a general impression emerged from it: now that the great days were gone, he was trying to keep things in ferment any way he could. "He just can't give up being wild and woolly." Whoever said that, it stuck. Now it was the students who, for the most part, were fed up with Carrington's Boys. Far from wanting to be glorious, they had begun to ask about business opportunities after graduation and some had gotten converted in a Billy Graham-type revival. Only a few outlaws, wrote a solemn young conservative in the campus paper, had ever been in on the demonstrations. At that, in the name of honesty, Carrington had to write a protest. The very day his letter appeared, by coincidence, Carrington's Boys let loose a pack of coon hounds in the midst of a "Sweetheart of Sigma Chi" beauty queen contest.

The dean and the president called Carrington in for a talk. He forgot the appointment, being worried over something he had heard about Dorothy Graham, that she had exploded with hysteria in a grocery store over an order of fresh oysters for a party, which had spoiled. He had not seen her in months. She was said to be on tranquilizers. Evelyn tried to stir the friendship to life once more. Her calls went unanswered—and unreturned. He called the president's office to apologize for missing the appointment. "I'm deep into my

book, what time I'm not teaching. Every day I stroll around
Venice with Byron."

The next official communication dropped down upon him
soon after. It was delivered by a student council member with
a look of dedication to something he probably thought of as
Jesus Christ. Arnie was asked to sign for it.

The letter requested him to appear before a committee of
faculty and selected students to answer questions in regard to
certain activities now causing embarrassment to the university
in circles both within and without the university. The letter
was signed by the president and "concerned members of the
college community, as follows," etc. There on the list was Lexington Graham, among the first.

When he saw Lex's name, he started. His vital regions
registered deep shock. A six months' passion for Dorothy—
could he think that would go unheeded? And before that, the
water tower. Well, the gun had gone off at last. I was trying
to give her something! I saw her need! So he could begin to
cry out within his own mind, but who to cry it to? The committee in question? He would never bring up the Graham
marriage in public. But clearly here were two people
enmeshed with one another, neither getting nor giving life.
Sisyphus and his rock couldn't have been much worse than
that, for a daily diet. Why withhold what he could always
give? Why not transmit it, not thinking much about it later?
Could he make life contagious, like measles, for instance? He
was reminded of stories of magic, how the sacred root was
passed along, ancient wisdom. But nothing had worked that
way. He knew when he heard about the hysterics, the Lib-
rium, and the dinner parties, when he got the cold shoulder
socially, and now, the underscoring: Lex's name on the jury of
his peers. Dorothy! Whether seeing her or not, the pang was
there. Was she, on his account, sealed up in a room of memo-

ries no more living than stuffed game? The blow from Lex
was man to man, a kick in the groin, sheer pain. It sickened
him for a moment, but when the moment cleared he sat down
at his desk, scrawled out a note of resignation on the back of a
memo which said the pool at the gym was closed for cleaning,
dropped it in the nearest box for inter-campus mail, and went
home.

Over the weekend, he took Evelyn down to the Gulf
Coast with an eye to moving there. He could finish his book
on Byron, long overdue, in a matter of months. He knew it.
With that milestone past and safely on his record, he could
then start applications rolling toward a new appointment.

"Carrington! Carrington! Carrington!"

"There's a place along the road where you can smell the
Gulf," said Evelyn, seated beside him in the car. "You could
draw the line of that salt smell on the map, I bet. Have you
ever noticed it?"

"Speaking of salt," he said, "don't look back or you'll turn
to it."

She didn't. For a hefty woman she sat lightly, looking forward with interest but no anxiety. Turning back was never
her way.

What do you do when something's over? he had wondered, and knew that one path would lead him toward his
wife's fine old Virginia family, not only to find mutual respect
and love, but also a new setting, fresh scope and range. But
he wouldn't; they never discussed it. Evelyn! He knew her
best at unexpected moments, like the time he had come home
and found her in a helmet of soapsuds, interrupted by the
phone while shampooing her hair, yakking with some nosy
faculty wife, not hearing him enter: "Well, if that's the gossip
on him, maybe it's true; but if it's true, then he's doing what

he wants to, isn't he? He can stop it when he wants to, can't he? He'll know that better than I or you, or anybody else, won't he? My head is wet. I've got to go." Receiver replaced, and turning, seeing him: "Oh." A flat sound. Nothing more. He had walked past her, into the living room, on to the study, thence to the kitchen, out to the backyard where he flopped down in a chair in the sun by some orange nasturtiums. And they had never discussed that either, but they knew completely what it was all about, she with her crown of silver soapsuds, a Valkyrie of shining courage and strong good sense. "Some people would call you a fat lady," he liked to mock her. "Oh, let them," she would say, and swear when she burned her arm on a hot pan.

What do you do when something's over? Driving his hardy four-year-old Chevy south, he knew that the question Dorothy Graham had confronted was now his own.

"What do you do when something's over?" he asked aloud.

"You finish your book," said Evelyn, at once. "Everyone should be so lucky. You have a book to finish."

But even then, she was riding toward her doom. The something over, for her, would be the everything over, for Evelyn Carrington.

Maybe right then, in some tiny seeding corner of the Caribbean, a skinny black boy, knife in his teeth, shinnied his way up the long bow-bend of a coconut palm that leaned out over water. A skirl in the tide far out, riding up against a long commalike sand spit, a heat dance of glazed light, and an odd reversal in the wind so that the tree slanted sideways on its lower trunk and a clutch of coconuts, gripped together, drew back from the machete and had to be struck twice over. Only hints of a force that a year later would gather with purpose, like an army for the march.

Maybe right then, or at some other unprovable secret moment like it, deep within Evelyn, one cell was saying an awesome, forbidden word, and another had dreadfully thrilled to hear it, called it to yet another, which had taken it up in turn, until the spread set in like fire, turning life to death, hope to despair, testing a fine courage, and finally creating a myth of a lost presence, with which he daily lived.

All was past now, swept away.

The terrible tides had won.

Seated in the hospital waiting room, wreckage exhibited like a trophy in the blowup before him, hat on patient lap, he fell asleep once more.

He jumped when he woke. Asleep for how long? Who ever knows that? And who were these, but the same as before, this time sitting, not standing, side by side, with shocked faces.

"He didn't mean it," the daughter said.

"I think he's gone mad," said the wife.

Arnie rose. "Oh, come on, now. I warned you about that fever, and the doctor said— Go talk to him again. He'll have changed already."

"The doctor's gone for the day, but the nurse said—"

"Said what?"

"That it was the fever, but ohhh . . . !" She was close to wailing and Arnie dared not inquire again what Lex had said.

"He didn't mean it," said Lucinda and shed two lovely matching tears.

Arnie looked from one to the other. To ask them outright what might be the best thing, get it over with? But did he want to know? Dorothy went to look for the bathroom: her makeup, he recalled, was always at stake. Sinking in quicksand, she would ask if her lipstick were straight. Lucinda, gripping the arms of her chair, leaned forward. "He was all right one minute," she whispered, "gone funny the next. He said to Mother, 'I wish you were dead.' Then he laughed." Silent, she waited for the words to absorb, a spill on the day's dry weave. "Do you think he'll stay this way? Die?"

"It's just a fever," he reassured her. "Try to forget it."

But Dorothy's return made him see more helplessness yet, and how they were looking to him. The Graham helplessness. Things are caving in. Save us. Unable to think of anything else, he suggested lunch. Far down the hall, something howled like a beast; a nurse was running. Dorothy put her hands to her face. "I can't go," she said.

But then they had reached the entrance; she was clinging to his arm, nails sinking in. The bright Mexican medal slid forward; it swung in the air between them like a talisman. They had been followed by a crackling white nurse, the floor matron. "We've given him a shot. Go on to lunch. He'll sleep. Call in the afternoon."

Stay? Go? The three exchanged glances. Lex. The mystery.

The silver medal swung glinting before them. Dorothy touched it, just to stop it: her fingers made a delicate moment of contact. Then they joined ranks in silent decision, and went out into the open air.

10

"So where have they got to now?" was Frank Matteo's question to Mavis Henley, when he got her, finally, by telephone. "I know you'd be the one to know, if anybody would."

"Ask Joe Yates. That's his architect. He knows more than I do."

"Yes, but what has Yates got going for me?"

"You think I've got something going for you?" Mavis asked. He called on her when he needed something, wanted something. He was using her. But why then was her heart hammering and her longing gone out of her, running toward him, wherever he was. "Just what do you think I've got for you?"

"If you're still here at all," said Frank Matteo, "it's got something to do with me."

Arnie's house was where she was hearing him, with the shadows from the foliage-thick windows, and the murmur of the vacuum overhead, stopping now, and the whisper of Barbra K.'s bare feet on the floorboards and then her humming soft and low, some piece of New Orleans jazz.

"I'm working here."

"I know that. You may think I don't keep up—"

"Then what need to ask about Arnie?"

"Carrington's showing that island to somebody. Mavis? Can I see you?"

It went banging around in her head so long she couldn't answer. Can I see you? Can I see you? "He's taking her to lunch, her and the daughter. That's to say the man's wife and their daughter. The guy's got into some bad accident, God knows what. Something out there bit him."

"Maybe they bit each other, for all we know." That was some of his being funny.

"You're sounding crazy. Arnie's got problems, but he's no gay."

"Come by today. Come by at four. Can you do that?"

"I don't know . . . I'll—Frank?"

"Mavis?"

"Nothing."

11

When up is down and down might as well be up or some other direction; when black and white are the same. When morning and afternoon can't be told apart and the face you love whirls with circles like a target for your hate and Lucy has gone away, then nothing's to be said about a man standing outside your window, except (since you don't know him), "Who is it?" But as no one is there to hear—tree falling in the woods makes no sound—there is no answer. The person is a man, dark, speculative, with the look of an old-time movie star looking out from a screen. It was a warm enough day to open a window, but people don't do that anymore, they press the fan button on the air-conditioner. We are all insulated, in quarantine. The man was wearing a pink shirt, open to the waist. He was foreign-looking. He saw that Lex was awake and looking at him. "Who's that out there?" Lex asked the nurse who entered. She put a thermometer in his mouth and smiled, holding his wrist. He gave her a mental curse and turned his head, but the man outside had vanished.

Why feel loss? Because some purpose had been suggested by the figure there. Up and down have no purpose; black and white by themselves mean nothing. Morning and evening are the same unless you've got something to do, and love unanswered is a tree falling in a lost wood, but the figure out there on the lawn had had a purpose. Why get well at all? he wondered as the nurse removed the thermometer. For drapery samples, upholstery choices, private launches, and the future leisure of the yacht club? For Lucy's happiness . . . a long shot, too far away. Come back, he wanted to cry to the face in the window: Whoever you are, return!

"Lie still," the nurse said. "Take this."

12

I've got to do something constructive, Arnie Carrington thought, aware across the lunch table of Dorothy's crossed-up emotions, her inability to eat shrimp salad or stir iced tea. He was getting caught in it now, catching it all from her, like a bad cold or dyphtheria, the tension of her many contending cries. "I went by your house," she said at one point. "I thought you might be there." He pursued nothing, asked for the check, told Lucinda the way to the ladies' room. "You can drive up to some property I own. Come along with me. Look it over."

"The island?"

"No, I said 'drive.' The island's a boat ride. Come up the road with me. This is another one I've got, an old hotel."

Tense and pale, the smooth mask of her face heard without taking in what he was saying. He had a feeling the various planes and angles of cheeks, chin, temples, and brow were going to pull apart, go shooting abstractly off, like features in a modern canvas. Who knew what was both luring and wracking her? What besides himself, or some idea she had of him, or some memory? And into the old wound, rubbed raw again, Lex had just now poured the salt of malediction. She twice dropped her bag, once in the restaurant, again on the gravel of the parking area. Lucinda, being nearer, picked it up for her twice.

Arnie began to notice this girl for the first time in any
great detail. Lovely, rounded, peachlike, she was nonetheless
carrying herself with awareness, like a guardian of something.
A little distance was set between her mother and her. Whatever Arnie said to her was answered with the same smile,
polite as cream. What was on her mind? The answer ought to
have been easy, but it wasn't. Virgin flesh might be straining
at the seams, but, afraid for her father, she wasn't aware of it.
Arnie trudged along between the ladies, one apparently lost in
another world, the other at the screaming point in this one.
He got them in the car—Lucinda in the back, Dorothy on the
front seat—and by the time he had re-entered the four-lane, a
small calm had commenced. They seemed more relaxed. Arnie
was onto his spiel about Gulf Coast property, what his heart
was in these days.

"I bought up all I could manage . . . the island, some old
broken-in row housing, and this onetime resort hotel we're
going to, the Miramar. All of it will take shape for me someday. I had my dream about it, my vision of what was to be.
Any hurricane can tear things down, but who's to build them
back? You need a few people to hold out against—" And he
waved his arm in a general way toward a hideous new concrete complex: restaurants, a branch department store, bowl-
ing alley, record shop, movie house, drugstore, a parking area
as big as a lake, zebra-striped in yellow lines. "—all that. The
world," he went on with another grandiose wave, this one
sweeping skyward, "will turn into 'all that,' if we sit by and let
it."

"You were always so involved," Dorothy murmured. The
perfect hostess was answering him.

"It's been hard to take a new start," he told her. "After
Evelyn left me in such an untimely way, I couldn't travel by

the old maps anymore. There was no incentive. A new route was indicated—"

"About Evelyn: I wrote you. You must remember."

He nodded, but he didn't remember. Letters had arrived; he'd never answered them; though some he had opened, most he had not. What could they say?

"A long time ago," Lucinda was saying, "Daddy used to yell in his sleep from nightmares, even without anything biting him."

"When was that?" Arnie asked.

"Oh, after the campus riots," said Dorothy. "I think all that upset him, preyed on his mind. He likes order, everything straight."

The road tilted into a long, sweeping curve, and just off that, a drive looped up from the main road like an uncoiling whip; they took it and entered the wide grounds of the Miramar, a shattered structure, though it still preserved its long, rambling outline; it was still to be called red-roofed and white. It was set back from the highway, approached by the drive which was now an even semicircle, flanked on either side by wide-spread lawns, dots of shubbery were growing back from old roots, careful planting from days gone by. The long white building itself had been most heavily struck on the western wing, as the eye of the hurricane had come into land only five miles to the west. The east wing was better preserved; its outline was intact, two stories high, with the tall windows of the lower floor quietly undisturbed, some even with unbroken panes. A lounge or a dining room must have been inside them. "I wish we'd stayed there sometime," said Lucinda. "I did stay there," said Arnie. "Often."

Trumpet vines had clambered up the wooden frame sides of the wing and some fronds were waving above the ridgepole, savagely untended. The shell-paved drive crackled beneath Arnie's tires. The sight of this property, so long admired, so recently possessed after its ruin, broke the circuits of his uncertain feelings for the Graham women; he might have been traveling with dummies; he thought of them no longer. For, in the floor above the tall windows of the wing, a corner room, he and Evelyn had awakened to many a sparkling morning, eaten breakfast looking out on a Gulf tranquil as blue silk. Outcasts from Southern Pines, they were two birds seeking a nesting place. Once she had opened the windows that reached to the floor, and stepped outside on a narrow ledge, too small for a balcony, protected by bars. In a loose blue and white robe with wide sleeves, she threw out her arms and leaned, till he said, "It's a long way down, you know. Watch out." She leaned back to him, then stepped inside. "I always imagined that flying was just some sort of trick I couldn't quite catch on to." "Well, lose twenty pounds and try again." He was relieved to tease her: for a moment, she had scared him. Birds. You can't see them think about flying—they just fly. Here. Gone. Well, twenty pounds lost, she'd tried again, and made it. How awful to prophesy when you don't know it.

Once since, alone, the whole shell of a hurricane-stricken ruin left weirdly angled, he had entered and climbed up to that room by an uncertainly balanced stepladder and looked around it. Even the wallpaper was mostly in place, the bed still in the same corner, the view superb. Would it shudder, crumble, and take him down with it, as he had wanted the sea turtle to do out on the island, alone then, too? But it stood, another shrine for him still, like the St. Francis one she had marveled over, the one the nuns had left. Where her ghost took strongest life, there, like the barnacle and the dirt dauber's nest and the old locust shell on the tree trunk, there he clung. But he would not climb up there today.

Alighting from the car, he watched Dorothy Graham's

trim legs precede him up the broad curving steps to the veranda, only half broken in. "Are you restoring this place?" she
asked him.

"Would to God I had the money. It was one of the old
ones, a fine spirit, nothing splendid, but real. It's got to go,
though. I'm selling off the grounds as residential lots. Want to
buy one?"

"We've got a house already!" Lucinda cried, eager to in-
form.

"Make you a good price," growled Arnie, addressing
Dorothy's legs, now bending, now tiptoeing.

"What did they call it—I've forgotten." She peered gingerly through a sidelight, cupping hands to her eyes. A white-
painted fireplace faced the entrance; a reception desk, covered with chunks and dust of fallen plaster, stood empty to
the left. A mirror above the fireplace hung crooked. She saw a
glimmering of their faces as, distant, it still did its mirroring.
"The Miramar," she heard him say. Mirror, mirror. Her face
glimmered out at her, perfect as usual, though with fingertips,
she straightened anew one lock of hair. Dangerous to go in,
no matter what he said. She turned back. Lucinda had walked
a little way down the gallery.

From the steps, Arnie could see the two of them, or small
slices and abstracts of them, parcels and fragments, reflected
in the cracked sidelights. When they moved away, vines
framed them and white-painted wood in the carved designs of
another day made their background. In a moment, they would
have long white skirts and little parasols and one would be
the mother of the little boy in Joe Yates's blown-up photograph, smiling from the steps of an old Coast house, and the
howling winds need never strike at all. They would all sit out
on piers in the twilight and laugh in rippling sounds like the

soft tide along the Sound, while waiting for Evelyn to come back from a trip to New Orleans.

"It looks haunted to me," said Lucinda and she too cupped hands to her eyes to see through the cracks of a boarded-up window. "I'd hate to be here at night."

Dorothy had moved to Arnie's side—did she feel that he was distancing her, making abstract patterns of her body, setting her back in time and costume? The more he did it, the closer she came, and now it was no longer one watching two, but two watching one. "I'll just go check on the back," he said, a property owner, after all. "Stay here." But she didn't. She was following, mythical parasol and all.

All his signs out front: KEEP OUT, DANGER, NO TRESPASSING, BUILDING CONDEMNED, FINES WILL BE LEVIED BY POLICE ORDER—THE OWNER: they had apparently worked. The old place was keeping its goodness. He remembered the croquet court, right about where they were walking. No traces, anyway, of anyone having come there to picnic, smoke pot, get drunk, find shelter, make love.

King of a ruined country, he had called himself, but a country still, if only in his mind. He looked back. On this winter day, too early for sailing, a small catboat was righting itself about, making it, the wind angling into its one big sail, then pushing off for a smooth, sunny run. That, too, could have been in the before-world, where he thought he now safely had this woman, this perfect product, held in its amber. Just the same, he had to notice they were alone for the first time. They rounded the hotel corner, and he knew that humanity was required. He put an arm around her, and spoke her name. "Dorothy? Is everything okay?"

"I'm trying to think so."

"Not succeeding?" He looked down: there was a shine of

tears, though she checked them, the memory, doubtless, of Lex's raging at her, back at the hospital.

"Oh, I'm happier since he came into that inheritance, if that's what you mean. When I think of an academic future— retired professor, little modern house in Florida, comforts of home, new friends and old, all the old books in the library, Christmas card list, updated every year: some dead, some quarrelsome, some gone crazy. Well, I'd get bored enough to scream. Money is upbeat compared to that. Things like shopping, deciding, choosing things that matter. You're living for that, too, I think. Why do real estate, otherwise, rather than pecking out your manuscript on—who was it? Byron?"

"Living for money, not Byron. Well, I'm living for the day when I don't have to think about it. Living for restoring at least the shadow of what was once here. But don't think I've given up on the Byron book. Not by a long shot." He thought of the yellowing pages, stashed away in boxes. He had dropped right back into the same tone he always had with her—arguing slightly, defending slightly, slightly superior, partially aloof. "Once I get this property in hand, I'll get back to the vital part of the scholarship. There's been some interest, though I've not been talking about it, from Texas and Duke."

"So not hooked on property, then."

"Oh, it's my present mission. My dream, you might call it." He made it sound light, but serious, too. "I'm busy day and night, restoring, reviving, resurrecting this—don't laugh— this priceless image . . . right here. You and Lex could join in with me. How can I make you see it?"

"You want to hook us, too?"

"Temporarily."

"Meaning what?"

"Till the idea catches on."

"Temporarily hooked? I guess there is such a thing." She turned silent, letting the bitter undertone sink in on him. He thought probably she was holding out for something; but how, in any case, could she plead his cause with Lex? Possibilities careened around in his head, moths around a light. If Lex died, would she expect . . . ? If she got interested, "hooked," would Lex dissuade, refuse . . . ? Of course he would, in his present mood. It never before occurred to Arnie that hostility can be neverending. A sigh.

Dorothy glanced around her. One side of a summer house, in white-painted wood fragile with lattice work, had lived through the hurricane. Why? White cement walks crossed one another, leading here and there to spots of interest the storm had taken away with it. She had read that so many bodies had not been recovered after the storm that people had stopped eating seafood for months.

She sat down on a concrete slab, the foundation of something gone. He sat also, back half-turned to her.

"Have we got so beyond everything we used to know, used to be?"

Somebody had to say something, so she had done it, out of torment.

He picked up the hand that rested on the concrete, held it like a curiosity, looked at it, turned it over, set it back in place. "Since Evelyn, there's just nothing doing for me. One thing I never knew about death: it's like wandering off into the woods. You go off strolling, you disappear, you just don't come out again."

"But it was Evelyn who did that, not you!"

"You'd be surprised, how close that comes to being me."

Restive, she picked up a broken fragment of cement and held it in her palm. She was conscious that discussing turned to arguing, arguing could just as quickly sound like begging.

"I'm sure that for a long time after—after—" she began, forcing herself into expected phrases.

"'After a loved one dies,'" he finished with pious mockery, and then cut even her anger short, the way he could do: "It's not memory I'm talking about, Dorothy. Christ, I remember *you!* It's a livingness. A going on with it, with her. A power to take me with her. I'm distanced from you, from everybody. That's the mystery you feel, but I can't break it."

If he was waiting for an answer, he wasn't going to get it, Dorothy determined. She wasn't fit to deal with "mysteries." "Metaphysical," a word she'd always hated, was one of those literary terms they all liked to use, these faculty men.

But Arnie talked on anyway. "A practical-minded woman like you must have found it possible, or even easy, to move on from a broken-down old billy goat like me."

She glanced sideways, flashing the whites of her eyes. There had been one or two—she wouldn't say she cared enough to deny it. The nice garage mechanic, the brilliant young grad student.

"Oh, but you were different, Arnie."

There it was, the true murmur, rising from the depths, so pure and sweet it was like the voice of some eternal spirit, a low sough of pine treetops in a night wind. Arnie would have been deaf not to hear. Long ago he had noted that, deep within the superchic American product, a precious nonmarketable essence lived, real and rife with feeling, and he had reached it in the past and it was the why of his even wanting to touch her. How not to be lured to it again? She was shaking, clinging to his hand, and he pressing back. The chunk of Mexican silver, so oddly wrought, slid from his shirt. "Beautiful." "I bought it today," he said. "Why today?" Again her free hand, sensuous fingers, reached for it. She closed her hand about it so tight it must have cut into the flesh, and he saw her knuckles burn white. "For you, I guess."

They were whispering without need to. And so suddenly that he almost bent double, almost grabbed himself, he felt his very life, his manhood, return to where it mattered most, so natural, strange, urgent, that he almost cried aloud. Son of a bitch! Jack-in-the-box! Up for the first time in two years. I *can't*, he thought, or told it. I just *can't*. It had to understand that. But he was perishing, because it didn't.

Rising, he half staggered toward a clump of wood—trees with overgrown shrubbery, a concealing thicket. Lazarus from the tomb could hardly be told to get the hell back in there. But what to do with this unlikely resurrection? He wouldn't go back to Dorothy, he wouldn't, no. He went striding off from her. Arms of shrubs and vines clung round him, briars beaded out a scimitar of blood along his arm from wrist to elbow. Now hidden, he stopped short, about to calm and soothe and coax his member down again, promising it any-thing—Mavis Henley, Barbra K., or any female flesh it had in mind from Rigolets to Pascagoula—when there before him lay the remains he was always half expecting to find on his prop-erty: the charred picnic fire, the used safes, and on the trunk of a strong pine, the message. The bark had been peeled back to paint it on with something like whitewash: BEN AND EDNA FUCKED HERE, then, I FUCKED EDNA TOO. HA HA! It was the tree his heart went out to, surviving a hurricane for such as this. He turned back and confronted Dorothy, her face framed in fronds of winter-empty boughs, spirea and wild rose, budding forsythia. She had followed him, as beautiful as fate.

"Lex said it right out to me, an awful thing."

"I know, oh yes, I know!"

Then with arms out they were rushing toward each other, but the instant before they touched, raging with kisses, locking arms and thighs together, a scream thin as a blade came between them:

"Moth-er! Help, Moth-er!"

Both of them were frozen still. He saw two faces struggle to possess her: one appealed in helpless lust to him, and the other, as had been shouted for, was Mother. She whirled around and ran.

Arnie fell face-first on the breast of the only mother he could find, wondering among his own blurred senses what the hell had gotten to that child—had she managed to get herself raped, buried in falling woodwork, snakebit, attacked by bats out of the chimney, abducted by ghosts?

Damn those Grahams, he thought, heaving against the earth's dumb patience, waiting spent for a time, the bright medal fallen forward and caught in a tangle of vine, earth stained on his shirt-sleeves, at the elbows, along the cuffs. The drought was broken. He sat up. He got himself calmly together, rose to go wherever needed. Nothing but silence now. Had the last dinosaur grazed her up and swallowed her whole? Was somebody wandering around crazy in the old broken building? He rounded the corner.

Dorothy stood on the veranda, at the sidelights of the front door, peering in. The door stood ajar. Arnie caught up to her, came to her side, looked in.

The girl was there before them, alone in the area the mirror overruled, standing deep within—she had ventured to wander around. Some laths and plaster had fallen down around her, encircling her as neatly as a heifer put in a pen, but except for a light flaking of plaster dust settling on her or still dancing around her like so many gnats, and a loosely joined fragment of plaster which had landed on her dark head like a beanie, she was untouched by any of it, and when they stared in on her began to giggle.

"I shouldn't have done it, I was crazy. Now I can't get out, can I?" She was really laughing now, at their flushed, alarmed faces, a healthy nymph frolicking in a ruin. "Just go off and leave me. I'll make noises like a watchdog. I'll be a wonderful ghost." She moaned comically, and waved hypnotic arms.

"Don't you move an inch, Lucinda," Dorothy said. "Something else will come down on you. It's bound to."

"It's not serious. Nothing's really happened. It's not like Daddy. I was just scared is all."

"Nothing's happened to you, child, nothing at all," said Arnie with a cautious glance at the ceiling. He stepped through the door, dragged an interlocked swatch of plastered wall boarding to one side, clearing a path to reach her. He had put out his hand to her, a mild and trusting little heifer stepping forward out of her stall. She had stopped laughing. He liked her. Her mother brushed bride-white plaster trash out of her hair and off her sweater. Glancing up, Arnie saw that above the ruined mezzanine landing, the door to the room he had once so happily shared with Evelyn had swung wide. Vibrations had caused it. He glimpsed the blue and white wallpaper, the arm and back of a chair. His eyes fell, encountering Dorothy's, who, now that all was righted, had fixed a look of resumption upon him. He turned in a leaving way, heading toward the car.

Dorothy, the interruption over, stepped right back to where she'd left off, into the land of desire. Longing for him, she swayed a dizzy path across the gravel. Children were created to interrupt, weren't they? It was proverbial. Thrown apart, nothing stopped you from coming back. Where was that medal, that silver thing, swinging, glinting, twirling? That had done it. He was starting the car with her beside him.

"You didn't answer what I asked you . . . back there."

"I forgot. What was it?"

Aware of Lucinda on the back seat, she kept her profile to him; her lips scarcely moved. "I was asking what's happened to you. You said it was something about Evelyn, going away when she did."

"Condemned . . . like property." He passed the sign that said that. "I felt condemned in that sense. But maybe I'll get over it, change back to one of my old selves. I can't tell."

Now more than ever it was seeming possible to her, to be here in reference to him, to be at last a part of him once more. She bit her tongue to keep the hint of it away, erase herself as schemer, predator, perfecter of dinner parties, houses, men. Speaking of houses, there went the one the Grahams had chosen, the FOR SALE sign was down. Arnie slowed to look it over —white, elegant, cleaned up, snobbish already.

Lucinda was chanting away from the back seat; she really wanted to live down here now, she couldn't wait, she just loved it.

"Especially now that you almost got killed," said Dorothy.

"Saved by a miracle!" Lucinda gloated. "It's a special sign, a good one."

"She's giving herself airs," said Dorothy, who thought that being religious was something she had to discourage. "That was no miracle, Lucy."

"Oh, maybe it was," said Arnie. "Get you in that house, you're all going to be privileged, miraculous. You're going to lord it over us down here. We're going to be dirt under your feet."

"Don't be silly, Arnie." She turned her head. His wide-open eyes, haunted (oh yes, she had noticed it before), caught with her own, then turned away. Past Gulfport, going east, there went his own house, a clump of green, skimming by. I stopped there, she wanted to tell him once again, looking for you, stopped to ask the way. But what of those two women, especially the white one. Yours? Her heart sank. He didn't have to explain. She was a long way from any safe footing with him. "Condemned like property" . . . she, too? Lex's property was what she was, and in that sense she was certainly condemned. How to cry "Please!" before it was too late. How ever to cry out and have it work? Sweat had gathered, hot in the sockets of her eyes. His car was old and rickety, the air conditioning rattled to itself but scarcely cooled anything. He let the windows down; it was still February, he noted, no right to heat.

"Being equal is the only way," she burst out. "That way we could help each other."

"Help is what I'm needing most," said Arnie, connecting with her thought in some way she didn't have in mind. "But so far Lex is negative, won't even listen to any possibilities." He, too, had felt his own house go by. No offer to stop by and show it to her. She would have liked that. Women! Female flesh, so long nothing but memory, was getting its message through again, alive and pressing in on him, back seat, front seat, the nerve messages flickering out, like licking tongues, like the withers of a brushed-down thoroughbred filly. Earthquake might any moment start wavering under the surface.

"The thing to ask Lex—" he started out, then lagged.

They were moving toward arrangements, naturally; Dorothy knew it, so did he. Two cars of the Grahams—Arnie had driven Lex in the Mercedes from the pier—were now at the Notchaki hospital and Lex was waiting there: smitten, stung, incapacitated, a medical mystery. He stopped in the parking lot, and for a moment put his head down on the wheel. Desire had grown around him, thick as a cloud. He spoke through it, in spite of it.

"I should have told you more about my business here. Something I badly need Lex to understand. Ask him—well, as a favor, then—to think about it. Stay open-minded."

Turning, he saw the sudden hardness in her face, sharp as shock. The last thing she wanted, to be a business go-between. "So that's what you want from me, to tell Lex. 'Stay open-minded, Lex'? Is that right?" She had half let herself out the door, not waiting for him to come and open it, and as he noticed that, she gave a flick of her head, running the tips of her fingers through the turned-up ends of her hair, a bitchy gesture, getting back at him. He'd had the nerve to think her own power was nothing at all, declaring himself finished, dead, condemned, gone with Evelyn. He was knowing better now. She leaned in the car window. "And if I stop by your house and tell you what he says?"

"That's fine." He heard his own voice, felt his mouth form words he'd never meant to say. The door shut behind her. As for the girl, she was already going toward the hospital. "Thank you . . . for pulling me out alive." He was left to hear that for some time. Now she had encountered a half-grown cat in the entrance walk and had stopped to pet it. It was rubbing against legs which curved out from the narrow point of her ankles in a way that so resembled her mother's he jerked his eyes forceably aside. His heart plunged wildly. "Sick with desire, and fastened to a dying animal. . . ." To think of poetry was ludicrous, but no more so, he guessed, than the general picture of his situation, his starved senses up and yowling.

Tranced, he sat in the car, stroking his sweating palms around the wheel. He saw Dorothy and Lucinda come out again, pass the cat without a glance, pass him without a glance, their legs going clip and clip, heels, rise of ankle tendon, and oh, above those knees, the soft-haired paradise. He groaned. He must have sat there glued to the seat for longer than he realized. He had to see Lex. He had to tame this beast between his legs, get it docile enough to carry it in there and listen while he begged for money. But not today, he's sick? But just to see how he is, just to reassure him there's nothing Dorothy and I could possibly be up to. (Oh no! The very idea.) Anyway, the college try. On the way up the walk, he stepped on the cat's tail.

He did not stop at reception, or even nod to the nurse at the desk when he passed on the way to Lex's room. He would plunge through the door, humbled as a suppliant should be. What price scruples and pride? Just get back to Lex, get it over with. Say: Lex, till you're feeling better, just keep decision in abeyance. It's all I ask but, after all, remember who rescued you and do this one small favor in return until we can talk it out, just you and me. It can all come right; it can all be just fine again.

His heels hastened down the corridor. But a hand was pulling at his arm, and he spun around, straight into Frank Matteo. Back two paces, and a shocked silence. The smooth Italian, taller than he, a tower looking down.

Through the vast whirl of his churning sexual agitation, the graceful Matteo shadow cut; he was diminished, then frozen. The giant between his legs became a silent little relative, a visiting cousin. Matteo, whose problems, he supposed, had never once been sexual, was smiling at him. Why was Matteo here?

"I said, 'You're in the wrong ward.' This is women's troubles here. Probably where your wife was and just force of habit. You took the wrong turn. Your friend's the other way." He jerked his head. "He ain't doing so well. No visitors. Has to take stuff to sleep it off."

He was leaning back against the corridor wall, the white

half-smile tentative in the tanned face, the softly tinted shirt with open collar talking luxury, power.

"Must have been some bug out there, wouldn't you say? The wife's a looker, wouldn't you agree?"

"Yes, sure," said Arnie, and plodding again, he turned humbly back, correcting his direction. Matteo, too, then, was after Lex? But why?

"Your wife was down this end, I guess." He did not answer, though it was true.

Yes, it was where she'd been, and the central waiting room for both wings was the same one that he'd sat in, hour by patient hour, waiting out her rhythms of day and night and day again, in counterpoint with the rhythms of the illness itself. Tests and diagnosis, surgery and rest, chemotherapy and remission, relapse and. . . . "Cobalt?" she repeated. "No, I won't." Dr. Swiggart, the trusted blond, with the vigorous blue eyes that flashed a semaphore to Arnie, over her head, then back to her, who looked at neither. "What then?" "Why, I just mean I've had enough. That's all. I have that right, don't I?" The silence struck them all, held them together into a feeling, which was hers, then theirs, a threesome: one. Over now, and done.

The receptionist said he could not see Mr. Graham for an hour or more, doctor's orders, so he sat down in a chair in the waiting room again, and to cover the glint of the silver, he buttoned up his shirt. Medals? he thought, with general disgust. What a blind trail he had been following, vain as hell. Matteo would have something of the sort under that shirt of his, dangling on gold thread, themselves golden, something religious maybe, and one of those horn things maybe, for sexual luck. Well, he had it, all right.

He put his hat on his lap and closed his eyes. The life of an older man, what was it but interrupted dozing?

13

Down Lex sank in the fogged drowsiness of pain, into the waters of sickness, where he turned to shreds like seaweed and then, lower still, clung to the watery roots, mingling with debris. Instead of firm bottom, there was only a suspension of silt, in consistency rather like dust. The last person he had seen was a face at the window, which had, reversing, become a face at the door, then a presence over him, smiling down.

"Just call me an interested party. Think of me as a friend."

"Okay," said Lex, whose ache had quieted to somewhere in the area of stepped-up arthritis, "but whom are you a friend of, and in what are you interested?"

Matteo did not smile. "Carrington. The life he has, the assets he hasn't. Keeping nice guys out of trouble. I got no reason to think that you're no nice guy. But that buddy of yours, ever since his wife died, I wouldn't want to talk all around it—the guy's a kook. A fistful of stories I could tell you about that. Once you get out of here, Mr. Graham, your first move is indicated: look me up. What I'm seeing for you down here is pure and simple; the good life. I'm guessing, of course."

"It's safe."

"A safe guess, you mean. Bingo, you mean."

"I mean," said Lex, wearily, "that yes I'd like the good life, or a good life, whatever." But as soon as I reach out my hand for it, he reflected, all hell cuts loose.

"There are things to know about Carrington," said the handsome visitor, and sat down in a chair near the bed. "He didn't seem to me for the longest time to make all that reasonable a picture. If he'd got all this property, plans, et cetera, why no backing, why no capital? He's dying for both at this point, but anybody could have foretold that he would be. I looked around a little, just here and there. His wife had been sick with cancer. She could have lived longer, or so it would seem. What happened? There was a doctor here for a good many years. Made a name for himself saving half-dead people, here during the hurricane. The damn fool was out all night, going around in all that wind, a car and a truck both washed away from him. A power line fell and knocked him out for two hours. Got right up and continued like a lunatic: saving, saving, saving. He and Carrington—Carrington had taken his wife up to safety north of here, but when he came back, heard the stories, they got thick, him and the doc. Heroes together. Heroes on parade. But the woman had cancer, like I said, and suddenly she's dead or something, vanished . . . where? And the doc? He's in Tallahassee, Florida, now. Oh yes. Left here suddenly, set up a new practice, even got a new name to go with it. Oh yes. Swiggart to Swayze, something like that. I've sat here and worked here and, to tell the truth, I've got a number of interests here myself, so I naturally ponder on things a little. I like to think people over."

"Ammunition," Lex murmured, feeling his brow, the flesh over his spine, growing hot again. He twisted; the ache was rousing up out of its torpor. "Save it for the future."

"I'd just like to ask one question: what did happen to you out there?"

"Nothing but bad luck. Some snake or viper . . . venomous something or other out there." Well, at least, he meant that. Had he himself actually been accusing Carrington for what had happened? There was guilt all right, it seemed, but it had to do with Evelyn. "I feel like hell," he said, "like somebody shipwrecked. You're not supposed to be here. Can you . . . ?"

"Sure, I get it. I'm just leaving."

Then his consciousness was trailing away to the half-heard protest of the nurse at the door, "It says NO VISITORS, sir, you must have seen the sign, so . . ." and he was sinking into the gentle silt again, he in the lonely tide of life, out lonely in the tide of life, turning, only turning, losing whatever had been wild, strange, vivid, perilous, dramatic. I will gently live or gently die. But my rage was not entirely wrong. There was something to suspect; there was truth in what I thought. I got a thread of it, and now I have another. Even a thread of truth is what you have to hold to. Even a thread will hold you swinging in the restless sea, something to climb out of it on, to wind up with, something to have. Oh, Dorothy and Lucy! I'm out here in the Gulf, sunk down deep, but I can rise from all that, come ashore, find life again, or maybe not again, life for the first time . . . only to be. . . .

So rose the voice of his thoughts, in sickness rising like a bell or a calling of some distant sort, far out on foggy waters. Swiggart to Swayze, in Tallahassee, Florida.

Lockstep they arrived, two in number, the specialists. They prodded their way through his fever with their muffled monosyllables. Samples, once again, were being asked for. His arm was peppered with needle marks.

Someone rose in white to make a speech. His glasses were horn-rimmed, he had a paper before him, he looked like Lex Graham. "The only known source of such inflammation and fever, developing within minutes after contact, as we know that it did, is a particular species of asp known to exist only on the semitropical slopes of the mountains in Laos. How to account for its presence here? In one of the few instances of its appearance on this continent, a customer in a department store in Toronto fell down while trying on a cheap quilted jacket of Oriental cut, made in that distant area. The asp had been sewn into the shoulder and had come out with the shipment. Perhaps it had been dormant until roused by being tried on. However, many species of poisonous toads, reptiles, spiders, and even insects exist in the West Indies and also in the Gulf islands which have not been specifically cata- logued as to types of venom or as to symptomatic reactions in humans resulting from their bites or stings, as the case may be." The scene vanished, but the language lingered. Venom was what he'd hurled at Dorothy . . . ejaculated. But she had venom, too. The green and white cat glance, sidelong; the sexy turn-on of her amours (there had been others since Arnie), her comings and goings, passings in corridors, dress- ings and paintings, sleekly secretive. Buy a white wig, tie a black ribbon at your throat, dot a beauty spot on your cheek, he wanted to cry. But no, she was definite, controlled, almost tailored. Blouses with sharply cut collars became her, slacks and straight skirts neatly cupping her neat behind, receding with a snap of heels. Could he imagine that he sometimes caught a whiff of sex-damp sheets she'd just left to come home? Ask her right out. Go on and ask her. What would he get? The white-green flash, upturn of eyes. Don't be crazy. I don't know what you mean. At long last, he'd said something. Only by then it was excessive, mad. "I wish you were dead." Did he, actually, wish that Dorothy was dead? She, the party- giver, the conscientious mother, the chooser of fine decor?

If he didn't wish she was dead, did he desire her for him- self? No, by now he could swear that he didn't feel much desire for her. There was Lucy to soothe him . . . only her. He felt more for a Boucher nude than for his wife.

The grand ache in his limbs was running toward a softly swollen stream, a warm spring, flowing. He roused with a jerk, found that it was Carrington now, sitting on the metal chair, and he smiled.

"I thought I was somewhere else."

"Where?"

"Oh, back home."

Make me a boy again, thought Arnie, only for one warm spring afternoon, in one of those sweet North Mississippi towns he, like Lex, had come from. Only to be reading in the back sun porch on a green glider, drowsy from lunch, sounds of the kitchen being cleaned for the day, sound of a dog trotting past the corner of the white house, faint smell of yellow jonquils in the room, then some shy little girl with a knock at the front door, leaving a notebook he'd dropped on the sidewalk, stuck it in his mother's hand and fled. Outside, green of shrubs, white of blooming spirea, blue skim of a jay's wing, news of spring bursting around this safe womb, pocket of tranquillity. These memories brushed him, went past. Flutter of irises—what they called "flags."

"I remember the Coast from when I was a boy," said Arnie. "I ran away from home once, came down here with just two dollars in my pocket, didn't know a soul. I found a room for fifty cents in an old wood-frame hotel, ate a big plate of gumbo for a quarter, woke in the morning and didn't know where I was. I saw a palm tree out the window, a bougainvillea vine, then I smelled the salt air. I thought I'd died and gone to here, and that would do for any heaven. Afternoon and I went to find some cousins I'd heard about but never met, who had a big house along the waterfront. They telephoned up to my family. Somebody came for me. But till they got to me . . . well, I loved it. I rambled the yard. Strange plants, a pool choked in lilies. One cousin took my picture on the steps. That was paradise . . . here."

"Back home," said Lex finally, looking out the window.

"I don't guess I ever ran away. Afternoons in the spring . . . I'd had fever. It was a feeling around the eyes, an ache, like this ache I've got now. There was green outside, and down in the hollow. . . ."

"What was in the hollow, Lex?" Arnie gently inquired.

Silence, then: "I can't remember. Some old outhouse, a privy, fallen in among the snakes and honeysuckle. What difference?" For his study in the new house, he had ordered framed hunting prints from England. He wished to see them now. He had a clean feeling about them. Memories were no use. Some were deceptive, luring, but most were full of meanness. Chickens' necks wrung in the yard, their heads lying later by the kitchen sink, the cook's black fingers pulling out the entrails, blood washing in the water, and he one afternoon rushing in with a cry to where his mother sat in her upright chair talking to another lady in the parlor, "Come quick, sister's bleeding. It's in the bathroom!" Her face went from white to blazing red as she forced him from the room, marched him to his own room, locked him shivering and namelessly afraid, there in the cold. What had he done? Oh why, oh what? Let memories come up over a hill where they'd been playing behind it like children, and one by one he would gun them down, order French draperies, California china, English hunting prints, a sideboard from Japan, a Spanish table, a French desk. He would do anything but return to the impure messes of the past. Even Carrington had run away from home—why?

"The past should continue naturally, live on," said Carrington, half to himself. "Flow in one stream."

"The past is quicksand," said Lex, perverse as an adolescent, closing his hot eyes on the gloss of pale gray enameled wall, devoid of soothing green. "I wonder," he said peevishly, "when the damn thing starts itching."

"It's odd I can't connect with you anymore, Lex, my friend," said Arnie Carrington. He turned the shabby yachtsman's cap, round and round. The strap across the bill was loose. "Suppose land down here were an old estate in England, where Charles the First might have hunted, or old John Dryden nosed around in the library, wouldn't you see everything in its place had a certain life to give?"

"I'm doing my own house down here, the best I can."

"Sure, I know. It's a bad time to talk to you."

Lex lay profiled as a corpse. The beseeching enemy beside him was his accomplished revenge. His soul, though all alone, was dining grandly in a splendid room. Extend the minutes, savor every bite. Still, he missed something and knew what it was: the feeling of the island, something it had given, then snatched away. How could you sulk at an island?

Arnie thought that Lex had gone to sleep. Empty, at road's end, he was about to leave a onetime friend, possibly forever, when Lex suddenly turned his head:

"What's so wrong with your friends down here, Arnie? Why won't they help you?"

"Nothing's wrong with them. I don't know if I look for being helped. I never thought in terms like that."

"But now you do."

A thin band of pain—fine-honed and flexible—had thrust itself into the sole of Lex's foot and now was threading itself up his leg, radiating like fragments internally exploding, then stubbornly continuing its upward exploration, sinew by sinew, nerve by nerve, scraping bone and needling flesh, his face blanching at the outrageous attack, this time when he closed his eyes it was to fight down unmanly tears, and in the womanliness of pain he wanted to cling to the hand that turned the hat, as though it belonged to a grandmother or a colored nurse. Let go, he'd thought before the steady thrust had so determinedly begun. Let go forever of Arnie Carrington. Call the books closed, accounts settled.

"Not now," he said. "I can't think of it now. I can't think at all. We'll discuss things later. Yes, later, Arnie."

The rough hand did take his own and press it, the feel of brotherhood amid pain was giftlike, surprisingly offered. The door closed behind him and, alone at last, Lex dared to let his tears flow. They were soft, warm, salty, large, but not bitter. They were natural, that was all. He dabbed them off on the corner of the sheet. Arnie returned from the men's room across the hall. "I thought you'd gone," said Lex. His restive head turned; the pain was less. The eyes had no horn-rimmed glasses to clothe them in. They were smaller than Arnie remembered them, small amber lozenges, Smith Brothers eyes.

"Did you get your glasses from the island?" Arnie asked.

"I never lost them. It was just that my head hurt." He gestured toward the night table, then put his hand to his forehead. "No, they never even came off, those glasses. Must be well-fitted. If you've overextended yourself, what the hell business is it of mine?"

Arnie felt disinclined to answer, except to say: Let's forget about it; get well. But like a priest asked a theological question at an inopportune time, he nevertheless felt compelled to answer. "It's everybody's business to restore what's gone, to resurrect. . . . Either you don't follow me, haven't ever, what I've been saying . . . or you just don't trust. . . ."

"'Trust'!" The word went around the room several times, echoing, somersaulting, flirting, shouting, whispering. Finally, since no one took it up, it fell on the floor like a large flying insect hit by Raid, kicked wildly, then piteously, and died.

Lex drank some orangeade through a glass straw. "One thing I'd like to know. Out there—what were you doing when I saw you?"

"Clearing up some brush, I think. It's an old religious shrine out there. I promised the nuns I'd. . . ."

"It looked more like a grave." There was a long silence during which a nurse entered, asked if he wanted anything, took his temperature, and left. NO VISITORS certainly meant Arnie, but she might have been absentminded or thinking of something else: she didn't notice. "I think it was a grave."

"If it was a grave," said Arnie, feeling like a puppet set upon the knee of a ventriloquist, giant and invisible, who worked the motions of his hinged jaw, "then whose grave was it?"

"The only one you'd be tending," Lex said. "Only one in the world. You were always a little bit crazy, Arnie."

Arnie sat, feeling old, feeling the want of sleep, looking down at his hat. Lex with the little lozenge eyes, Lex of the unfeeling silences. Are we fighting each other, then? In spite of all, and after everything, dueling with poisoned blades?

"You still haven't told me who."

"I wouldn't if just guessing. I wouldn't say."

"It was a shrine to St. Francis. The statue went shooting off in the great blast."

"You're not the type to tend a shrine."

"I've just brought you back from out there, Graham. You might think about that."

Lex looked at the ceiling. "I wanted to go back to find the butterflies; they were floating out over the marsh."

"Butterflies!" Who's crazy now? he almost said, then he remembered, and said, "Oh yes, the butterflies."

"I would like," Lex said, "to invest money only with sound people . . . to know, in other words, what I'm doing, that it is, as I said, sound."

Soundness was a big Mississippi word, as Carrington well

knew. He himself, up in that state, was "unsound." First a wild sun-blazing glory, then a total eclipse.

"It's 'sound' to sit on money," he halfheartedly pointed out, "but all it does is shrink."

"The Graham alternative," said Lex, "is always you."

Arnie turned his hat in his hands. He was beginning to feel like what he undoubtedly looked like, an old country man, corn likker in a paper sack, bottle stopped up with a rag. Come to beg the local moneyman, on the grounds of long-ago friendship, for the cash to see him through.

"Who's in the grave?" Lex asked again. I'm not having this conversation, Arnie thought. He'd never, in the past, have had the nerve to ask me that. To point a gun at me, yes, provided it was on the sly, nobody looking, he thought. Does money give you courage, too? He guessed it did. Power, a power sense, yes; but real courage?

"In the grave? Me, I guess. I'm in it. Six feet down."

He got up. A passing cloud, a threatened shower, had made the room dim. But the appearance, in the doorway, of Lex's young daughter, in her lavender and pink, created brightness by itself. She smiled, and he thought of rainbows. He had turned his head automatically, and there she stood.

"Is Daddy awake?" Arnie said yes he was, and left, but heard her voice persisting still behind him, echoing off the bare large door and into the early afternoon stillness of the corridor: "Mother's upset about something; she's crying and now she's got a headache. She said the ignition of the Mercedes wasn't working right and she's afraid she hurt it some way, but I don't think that's it. Can we leave tomorrow?"

"I'm not well yet, just mending maybe." That was Lex.

Arnie loitered, letting the sweet Mississippi notes of the girl's voice pass him like a thrush's song, then turn and circle, like wavering bands of colored smoke. He permitted enchantment.

He pretended an inability to move, which may even have been so. Oh, soothing voice! He felt dipped in nectar, laved in balm. He dawdled in the corridor, nodded to the nurse while passing the desk, lingered at the hospital door. Finally, she came out again. "Lucinda?"

"Oh." She smiled again, and that alone was worth the wait. They stood half confronting, half side by side. He said quite naturally, as if he were a high school boy again, or at the most a sophomore in college, just in from tennis or the swimming pool up in Corinth, that pleasantest of towns, town of his birth, catching her hand in his casual grasp: "Let's look at the lighthouse before you go. I'd love to walk with a pretty girl again."

14

And so, as if he were at home in the summer from the university, making a date with somebody he'd met on the tennis court or at the pool, they began to walk together.

The cloud having passed, the Gulf was sparkling, brisk, and bright, whitecaps playing beneath the sun, and before them stood the old Notchaki lighthouse, earliest of all structures there, save one falling-down showpiece of a Spanish place the hurricane had unaccountably disdained to blast to splinters. Brave around its whiteness floated many flags: Spanish, French, British, Confederate, American. A few old palms and many new small ones, low as midgets on the grass, blew fronds of dark green and Lucinda's own hair was shaking out of its pins and blowing free, and her laugh was there, and (marvelous) she was able to catch a mood, even to seek to match it. The lust that had dampened down from Dorothy into something like a narcotic sleep, enforced and aching, lasting till now, was waking to Lucinda in cublike frolic. They crossed the boulevard. The wind was beautiful. From far out two shrimp boats were returning, late ones in the midafternoon, making stiff progress against the shore wind, in rhythm each with the other, and as he looked a third rose up like something come from a world away. He expected any moment to glimpse the bold flag of Spain. But no, it was just an old shrimp boat, like his own—like himself. But would she not accept him anyway?

The girl—lovely, rounded, young, now laughing, now not, now talking, now not, now near enough to sniff and nuzzle, now drifted out to a dancer's length away—was doing the real thing to him, was giving him the good awakening, not the sudden hypodermiclike jolt into lust, but the slow natural freshness, the life of clear water, warm sun, fresh bread. He knew it now: he was going to be all right again. He *knew!* Oh, Barbra K., he wanted to shout, loudly enough to be heard five miles down the Coast, I'll be coming to you, while the angels clear the way. Oh, Buddha! Oh, Mavis! Oh, ducks! He was carrying on within himself like a nut. But even an old turtle, stranded in a dry gulch, struggling up one side, then the other, always falling back, might shout (in turtle language) to feel the rush of rain, see walls dissolve to mud, float to freedom in a freshet. How pure was rain to seem so pure? it would cry. Well, at any rate, Lucinda seemed that way, had no particular knowledge of hanging rich, ripe, and ready as a peach on the bough, with skin unbroken certainly. She ran charmingly off to look in a gift shop window. Now she was coming back. He all but groaned.

As for Lucinda, fleets of impressions were sailing through her head; she connected with none, being troubled, still, about her parents. She was a good little churchgoing girl, having been converted at school during the reaction period, "born again," she called it, braving the embarrassment she caused at home. She also thought about boys and dates and got her lessons up. Her papers were neat; she worried over a C. Her nicest habit was listening to others when they talked. Arnie Carrington said funny things. "You laugh when you laugh," he told her. He meant she wasn't a giggler.

In a patio planted with palmettos, small potted palms, stiff wax-leafed camellias, he suggested ice cream, but she, in a grown-up mood, ordered coffee the same as he. Spooning sugar into her cup, she sat straight up, the way she'd heard about, felt the top of her head angle into the fall of sun, shook herself into place as if grown by an inch: she felt, for the first time, mature.

He saw her Renoiresque against a drapery of purple bougainvillea and asked if she had studied Byron. She had. She leaned a cheek on her palm and soon was talking. Yes, she had read a lot about him: Byron was not the way people thought of him. "You mean he was misunderstood?" Arnie inquired. She nodded. People had blamed him for what they caused him to do, women, especially. They chased him, they worried him, it was a wonder he hadn't hated them. "He may have hated them, some of them," said Arnie. "I think he saw them individually," she insisted. The old Byron magic, Carrington saw, was still at work. What would he have made of this Maid of Hartsville, Mississippi? A poem to Lucinda, Carrington supposed, which she would have deserved, wouldn't she? Damn right, a good one. "And when he went off to

Greece like that," Lucinda pursued, "it wasn't all just some dream he had. He really helped them out. They knew it, and loved him for it. It was my book report, a biography I had to read." She stopped, blushing.

Went off to Greece to die at Missalonghi, thought Carrington, taking up where she had left off, and the blood-letting, blood jetting from the handsome vein. To make him well, the doctors said. It killed him. End of the line. He knew that. Dead end. Uncomfortably, as if having to act in Byron's place, he wanted to praise her, praise Lucinda, not in poetry but aloud, in the here and now. He sat remembering how great it had been, at times, to teach, feeling he could start that certain light in young eyes—oh, beautiful! Out of nowhere, it occurred to him to wonder why Lex Graham taught, and there was the answer: to be precise, of course, to define, to package neatly. But for him, Carrington, there had never been anything more precious in the whole of academe than this calling forth of the intelligence, shining, eyes flashing, wading up from the surf, hair falling to the shoulders or (the boys) capped about the brow, the knees sluicing bright water, the Grecian thing. How like Byron to die in Greece. Now she was bringing that back, too, his feeling for that yellowing manuscript. From Italy to Greece: *The Last Adventure, A Study of Byron's Final Years*. The poet-hero taking his last fatal step, in full self-knowledge, by midday's blaze. "I was writing a book about him," he told her. "Who? Byron?" She took it as news, new and marvelous. "Were you *really?*" He knew then, as her words fell, that he would have to find—impossible though it might seem to plan for—some gesture, some action: he was obliged to it.

They left the patio to walk to the lighthouse, lamb and lion, and it was only as he went, believing himself stifled in impasse, pacing behind bars, consigned to dreaming about it, that he suddenly saw the lighthouse as hope's beacon, its white door set in a slanting wall as the secret code that could suddenly be found lying carelessly among all the ordinary world's reasoned visibilities. If it would only by added miracle be unlocked. He walked, his fingers already curving for the brass handle and the bolt above. He walked with purpose among waving flags, moving free.

From his hospital window, Lex Graham saw them pass. They crossed the rectangle of the window frame from one side of it to the other and passed from the field of vision, conscious of each other but not of the hospital nor of him, back and shoulders sliding from nearer to farther, then cut off by the frame. He went from cold to hot and back again, paralyzed, contained in each, freeze to flame. Then he laughed, aloud, alone. It just wasn't true. He'd been seeing things again: the fever. Those two happy together, when, really, she'd left long after Arnie—no, it was only his fear visions; that one, way down deep, might well be the last, the hardest, the most taunting of all. He rang for the nurse. "Look out the window, Miss Bishop. What do you see out there?" "Just the lighthouse, Mr. Graham." "I mean, who's out there? Anybody?" "Not a soul, Mr. Graham. Out in front of the hospital, you mean? Nobody. Just the lighthouse."

So he could breathe again. . . .

The lighthouse door, which had rasped open on hinges plagued by sea rust, swung closed behind them into its frame with a loud touch still being echoed, re-sounded, far up at the narrowing trapezoidal peak; some nook or ah pocket there was apt to pick up what it liked to hold.

"Tell me about your house," Lucinda was saying, but finding herself in the small space, a square officelike room with a desk, a set of steep iron steps backless as a ladder, rising up to a landing and a second flight, broke off to look around her, and then repeat, lowering her voice which carried straight up from her as it might in an empty church, "Tell me about your house."

"Well, for starters, I think you'd like it, find it interesting. I built it mainly out of what I could scavenge." He was half whispering, murmurous, at her shoulder, at her ear. "Some of it I had to throw out, couldn't use it. Oriental rugs, half-rotted, stinking with bayou water—I had to throw them out. Dutch spoons mounted with little galleons in full sail, some acid had corroded, no good. But most of it was sound, usable. What really decided me to stay after the ruins was the Buddha."

"Buddha?" She jumped, spoke louder. ("Oo-dah," the tower said.)

"I'd call him a god any day. If he's after me, he can have me. A rich lady's property. Got blown into my backyard. As soon as I saw him, all debased in the mud, former glory fled, proud serenity and wisdom kicked to hell, I knew I'd have to see him through."

"How did you?"

"Oh, cleaned him. Put him up straight, even gave him something to preside over. If not an Oriental garden such as he was used to, he's got white ducks, Oriental."

"Ducks!" ("Ucks," said the tower.)

"Well, yes, I know it's a string of odd things. But it was on account of pollution control, testing duck livers. I earned a modest fee. Don't worry your pretty head. They're there with me. Good ducks. I'm fond of them. It's the mosquito spray that was a bit of a problem. How to keep them under control and still not damage the ducks. If I keep this up, you'll think I'm crazy. What I'm talking about isn't gods, or ducks either. Only happiness . . . Will that house make you happy, the new one? It sits up too high, it looks too much on show. Maybe your folks want that." Leaning back on an oaken desk, there near where the steps began, he folded one brawny forearm with broad wrist glossed with bright hair over the other, then, a hand forward to her, took her fingers to his wrist, setting them equally there, watching them close round his rough flesh. "Come visit me. I'll show it all to you. Will you?"

"Oh, Mr. Carrington! Why, that would be. . . ."

"Can't you say Arnie?" He lifted her hand off his arm, turned her a little as though in a dance, and leaned his face to brush a kiss against her hair. "Go up the steps a little now, will you? That's right. Just a little more now, a moment more and we'll go." Obedient as a dancer, or a little skiff with its spread sail, she climbed the first few steps. He hardly breathed. There was so little here that had to mean (slender bridge of perilous matchsticks over the bottomless pit) so much.

Her back was turned then, as in a game, but really for him to appraise her, a good judge of flesh giving the once over. But tenderly . . . he felt the spirit he savored most, soft and sweet. She was, he agreed with himself, extraordinary; his eye roved from ankle to nape, rounding curves, aware of grades and declivities, sudden drops, dizzy rises. But along the journey came the feeling that she was both amiable and bright, the lineaments said so, and forgetting his selfish need for dead currents to come alive again, he found himself demanding silently the answer to one question: How could they have done it? Dorothy and Lex produced this wonder! Impossible. It was not the physical act he meant (he guessed they'd managed it somehow), but how produced in the sense of raising, the old Southern sense of upbringing: she must have gotten it somewhere, but not, he still refused to think, from those two. She wasn't even conscious of it! His heart constricted, almost with pain, before it burst forth, blooming with utter wonderment. And straight on the heels of that came power, like a flash of fire. The old lighthouse on its green lawn must have teetered from the force of magic within. He called her name, softly, and she turned at once, face flushing with sudden bright expectancy, and in a word, which burst out (though just what it was he could never quite remember), she was his, all else thrown aside, claimed forever. Light struck through a little window, high in the tower, marking a certain hour of that afternoon. "Understand me," he was wildly pleading, rough hand to soft cheek. "Please do! I was never any age but yours!"

15

"So where have they all got to now?" asked Joe Yates, the architect.

"I called to ask you," said Mavis Henley.

"At Matteo's request." She got angry at that and hung up. Then, afraid she'd made a mess of it, she went around to see Yates in his office. She had never been particularly friendly with him because she felt he didn't like her. They were into some sort of contest over Arnie, but wordlessly, the way two pets in the same house will contend.

"It's nothing to me," said Mavis, "except that, as you guessed, Frank got curious enough to call me up about it." She sat down and knew the charm bracelet which clinked on her wrist when she moved was irritating to him, and recalled his wife, a plain, pretty woman, so devoid of ornament she was like a beautiful piece of unfinished furniture. "I don't see Frank these days—hardly at all." It hurt to say this.

Yates at least got himself to glance at her. "Then what worked him up to the extent of calling you?"

"Well, he knew Arnie went out to that island with a stranger, a well-heeled guy from up in the state. He heard that from somebody down at the small craft harbor. Frank doesn't know anything about Mississippi or anyplace like it. I don't know much, but I can imagine it better than he can. He thinks everybody up there, for instance, is a cotton planter or an oil millionaire, or some big bank operator, that they're all rolling in cash."

"Matteo's doing all right with his restaurant—that and whatever kind of little playroom he's got upstairs. What's he need with an island?"

"He's got the cash for it and Arnie keeps stalling."

"I personally think he's got his orders from somebody, somewhere else. I think they're putting up the money. Now do I wind up in my own garage with my head bashed in for saying so?"

"Everybody wants to give Frank a bad name, and terrible connections. Just because he's Italian and runs a restaurant."

"Would you know it, if that wasn't all?"

Provokingly, hardly looking at her at all, he was back on his high stool, twirling his Lucite triangles, or he was going to answer the phone. He was gray with his own convictions: gray shirt, gray hair, gray eyes. She was neater than usual in a blouse and skirt, and so had dared to appear. But nothing worked with him. Arnie, she knew, esteemed him and his wife but hardly ever went there.

"I know you don't like me," she faltered, for like any animal, she had gotten scared of abandonment, since the real rival had invaded from the north. "I just want you to see that

what you think about Frank might not be so. It doesn't have
to be, does it?"

"It's nothing to me," said Joe Yates, "if he is or isn't."

"Well, at least, then, you could stop believing it."

"How did you get here?" Yates asked. He had an appointment in Ocean Springs.

"My car's in the shop. I walked."

"I'll drop you."

He was taking her by the garage where she'd left her car,
when, on the highway that ran by the water, a car passed
them and they both saw with astonishment it was Arnie himself, humped over his steering wheel like a troll and going
fast.

Mavis gave a little sigh. "I want the best for him," she
said, with simple feeling, and Yates, for the first time, looked
at her with understanding. He even smiled.

16

For some weeks now, Joe Yates had busied himself in a last-
ditch effort to help out Arnie Carrington. That he stood to
gain if Arnie kept afloat was clear; yet he had enough work
without Arnie. So his activities fell under the heading, he
ruefully thought, of quixotic, if you had to get literary about
it. (His wife had thrilled to lectures Arnie had given on
Byron.)

Yates had business connections from Miami to Memphis,
from Houston, Baton Rouge, New Orleans, Atlanta, and Bir-
mingham. Some were tenuous, worth a letter; others he could

telephone. "If you buy a lot or two and build, then the resale value. . . ." "If you put capital behind the whole little street of shops, your rental alone would be. . . ." "The plans seem old-fashioned but, according to the cyclic theory of architecture, in less than ten years, demand is bound to show a trend. . . ." He even took a couple of trips to meet with possible interested parties. Some, appearing in the coastal region on other errands, he had actually presented to the owner himself. That was when everything would get more shaky than not, for Arnie was scarcely the greatest at inspiring confidence. In fact, in a certain well-brushed business type, what he inspired most was unease and, in a certain uneasy business type, what he suggested was absolute terror. There was yet another type—the understated, quiet type—noting everything, mentioning nothing, hardly breathing life enough to keep a conversation up, but saying, out of the side of his mouth at the end of a lunch, "Another planet, first turn to the right." Yates was angry more than once. Arnie was not that bad.

Arnie was not that bad, but he lacked the sense of someone at central points in a society. The old order on the Coast had scarcely trembled after the storm. Its houses might be gone, but it never missed a single executive committee meeting on blown-away yacht clubs. The dead were buried, and the ranks closed. Arnie was okay in the little interested group circles—academic, artistic, conservation-minded. Arnie would have been all right in business circles, but only by the hardest, providing the biggest *if* of all were not there: *if* he had capital.

"I may be flying out to Houston to see a client," said Yates, driving along with Mavis.

"Houston? Does Arnie know that?"

"I haven't mentioned it. Why?"

"Just that he's got a son out there . . . Kelly, I think his name is."

Late afternoon and back in the office alone, Yates, at the lower right-hand corner of his drafting paper, inscribed his name, address, and the date. He let the paper scroll up and put it aside with others, one of a number, ready for photocopying. Maneuvering down from the stool when the phone rang, Yates smiled to think how quickly he had gotten that piece of information out of Mavis. Meddling was what he was doing now. It went beyond helping, certainly. He cast an eye toward the blown-up photographs, the child on those friendly steps of a lost day. He, too, had caught the purpose, and felt he had a stake in things.

17

Having recovered her car and paid for its cure, Mavis went to telephone Frank. She was going to tell him she hadn't found out anything, nothing at all, not about any business dealings, but he asked her by to see him, wanted to talk to her and before she could stop herself, she'd said okay. Stunned at herself, she stood staring at the silent telephone after she replaced the receiver. Back of the garage, nobody there; smell of greased metal, rubber tires, dusty cardboard, oily rags. It wasn't believable that the world could even consider turning golden again. Yet the minutes were doing that and she was moving through them, along with them, leaving. She was combing hair and freshening makeup in the ladies' room, where heavy liquid soap was rank in the glass globe. The min-

utes, like a line of golden bees, curved along her path. Now
she drove along a Gulf crowned by clouds in silky bales of
high spun light. She stopped the car and mounted the long run
of steps along the side of the seafood restaurant, up to the second floor apartment where he lived alone, thinking: At least
he wants to see me, and I can see him if I know that least is
all, is everything, only remember that. . . .

The door gave an answering buzz to her ring and flew
open at her touch. And there he was. He was holding open
the second door beyond a screened platform area, which led
right into his big living room overlooking the Gulf. Caramel
slacks, fine leather sandals on brown feet, soft beige cambric
shirt open to the brown navel and the gold religious disk
dangling flat, half-hidden among the dark chest hair. Once
she might have fainted dead away from desire. Now she just
walked crisply in, scanned the remembered luxuries, dropped
her bag beside a chair, sat down, crossed her legs, and said:

"My job at the school is important to me."

She had run up a matter-of-fact flag of independence
among chrome and glass, rich carpets and towering house-
plants, among scenes of her former passion. There was the off-
white pouf he had made her lie against in slit skirt and bra
printed in tiger lilies, bracelets to the elbow, dangling earrings, flower in her hair, while he snapped her time and
again with his Instamatic, kneeling, while by request she took
off one thing after another, down to the earrings and the
bracelets which soon went also, then the camera went too,
and it was heaven right here and now. But that scene had
sunk below water and come up empty, long since.

Now, quietly polite, he brought her a drink in a huge
chunk of modern glassware one-inch thick, amber-colored at
the base; she could hardly lift it. She sat sipping in her cotton
skirt and striped blouse and waited to know why he'd asked

her there. Through the window, those gigantic clouds she saw piled up over the Gulf once had seemed the very shape of happiness.

He sat down in a chartreuse chair of ribbed velvet, whose arms branched out like duck wings, whose back rose in an arch just to the crown of his head. One hand held his drink, the other dangled off the chair arm. Princely. In Italy, he should have been a prince.

"Jobs aren't everything." She said nothing. "What's up with you these days, Mavis? You're making out with Carrington? A little on the old side, but it looks okay."

"Not what you think. We're not like that."

"Your business. Just tell me what he thinks about?"

Frank Matteo spoke in short sentences. He had studied his English, she always felt. He put capitals at the first and periods at the end. He used stock phrases.

"Think about personally, or what?" Was he asking her to blab on Arnie? She felt a sediment-stir of feeling whirl up, mixed. "He thinks about his wife and she's dead."

He looked away. "You should think of yourself, then."

Seeming to mean it. She thought of eager faces in the classroom, following her every move as she taught the mounting of a collage, the sketches for a graphic. She thought of the sour-sweet smell of children working.

"That's my business, too."

You've ruled yourself out of it! she wanted to shout at him, but only for a moment. Half of her watched the other half.

"Why won't he have dealings with me? Can't he give me an even break?"

"For the same reason nobody will deal with you, Frank. They think you're underworld, Mafia. That scares people.

They keep asking me: Is he? Isn't he? What's my answer? What do I say?"

He had crossed one ankle over his knee and now looked carefully just past her head.

"What's so unreasonable about me? Do they know any facts? Then why make a judgment? Try me. It's all I ask."

He wasn't going to tell her anything, not ever. It was the only room she had ever been in where no sound whatsoever came from the air-conditioner. It was silent as the day before creation, except for the faint velvety melody of FM from the bedroom.

"I'm honest and fair in my dealings," he persisted. "I say, 'That's it. No more, no less.' I deliver."

"Well, then, I think that people look for something human in you." Her voice struggled to get out the words. "I think they keep looking for that."

"Human?" He always had a way of not precisely referring to what had just been said to him. But now he did. Significant, she thought. He had got up and was coming toward her. She stood up to go. He caught her wrist and gently took away her glass. "Sometimes I miss you. That's human."

She must have gained fifteen pounds since she had lain, slim as a tropical serpent, against that off-white velveteen. Leaves fallen from the golden tree. She pulled her wrist away and picked up her bag.

"Those people from up in the state, the ones you asked about. I didn't meet them. I don't know what happened. I only saw the man once, when they were going to the island. He was a professor type, but he's got a lot of money, I think. He came to see Arnie because they used to teach together."

"What's he here for now?"

"Some people are just friends, I guess," she ventured. Still, he was against her, standing close, then bending to raise her face for kissing—and, failing that, asked her to stay with him. He asked her the way he had asked Arnie to sell his island. He would ask for anything he wanted, right out, just like that. It puzzled him to be refused. He recoiled from her, went and stood at the window with his back to her. Leaving, she turned from the door.

"Staying would take a stronger person than me," she said to his back. "I'm only just so strong."

"You were strong enough one way."

"Meaning what, please? Oh, back to that. Getting rid of it, you mean. I did it because you said to. I would have done anything you said, Frank."

He wheeled around. "Don't tell me that again!" Angry, shouting.

"But surely you don't mean that if I'd held on, you would have done right by it."

"Don't speak about it!"

Oh, she thought wearily, but I'd be the one taking a chance that great, just like it was me actually hurt, my risk, my loss. But on the last count, evidently, there was something he felt, too. Why should he care so much? He did, then, more than she'd realized? She remembered a funny thing, how one day she had come to the restaurant, back when things were good, and he'd been out in a boat of his with nothing but children in there with him. She'd heard the laughter of children, the cry of what seemed like fifty happy little voices babbling, and she hadn't been able to believe her eyes when he docked and took them up out of there one by one, reaching down his arms, tossing, landing them, laughing too. His back now turned to her once more expressed feelings in many-layered confusion, but that day, she wanted to think, was among them, mixed in, as it was in hers. Neither of them, parents of a lost darkness, could have reached into that dark for any certainty.

At some moment she could not have told, she forgot about herself completely. She did not ever remember crossing the room to him nor did he seem to know she was there till she hooked her fingers softly through his belt. He turned then, and drew her in.

When she left it was late afternoon, though still light. She left wordlessly, no mention of another time, no promises extracted. It was the child they'd done it for, the lost child.

Not wanting to go home, she went to a motel she knew with a big pool always half-empty, lay on a beach chair under a far-off umbrella, hoped nobody would chase her out, went sound asleep. Waking again, now in the dark, she thought of Arnie Carrington because she was getting her senses back and because the weather was shifting. It had started to rain; first a sprinkle, then a shower.

It was a true, gentle, steady rain slanting in the air without thunder or wind, and as she went about in it, by car and on foot, her cheek and hair and clothes got wet, a wetness that persisted in a total sense after the rain had stopped, so that, soaked through, she was walking in the memory of Frank, a salt taste to the still-welling wetness on her cheeks, seeking Arnie. He was to be found—oh, he had to be—but where?

At last located, he was not far from his house, but on the other side of the highway, out on the beach, a troll-huddle in the dark.

He was far out on one of those spits of land which, despite the white sand beach laid down along the Sound, jutted out into the water same as ever, furnishing marsh grass as havens for small birds, shore terns and the like, and the kind

of rugged beach favored by white boys and Negroes who pole-
fish the inlets the high water leaves. He was sitting out on a
mounding up of concrete slabs, part of the old seawall the
hurricane had smashed. Buoy lights gleamed beyond him,
marking the channel outward, and along the horizon a lighted
freighter passed slowly as the drawing of a meditative line.

"Oh, Mavis," said Arnie without turning his head, "what
a day lies just behind me." He seized her hand, her arm as
well, brought her down beside him with a sure grip. "Oh,
Mavis!" He was holding to her and a warm friendly flow was
running between them. How could she feel anything after—so
recently—Frank? She didn't know; she did. (How could he, he
wondered, feel anything after Barbra K.? He didn't know; he
did.)

"What's happened?"

"Nothing. Everything."

"About the money? He's going to lend it to you, go partners or something?"

"Lex is no lender. I should have known better. But they'll
be going now, and I— They've given back what I lacked more
than money. The Miramar, and then the lighthouse. Oh,
you've got to know the truth: I've returned to myself, Mavis."

(He had gone from Lucinda and the lighthouse straight
to Barbra K. who, though she had just come through her front
gate dripping with packages from a New Orleans shopping
trip, was better than glad to see him, and had news from her
husband, who had spent some months on an oil rig down
below Grand Gulf and might be showing up any minute; it
wouldn't do for Arnie to hang around too long, Reuben was
apt to be one mean bastard.)

He screwed somebody in the lighthouse? thought Mavis.
The guy's wife? His daughter? This could get ridiculous. Also,

it was a big coincidence to think that, while she was busy with Frank, Arnie had gotten himself going again.

"Who'd you make out with?" She laughed. "Seems like you could take your pick." He might have been some old chum.

"The fire that's really lighted will burn forever," said Arnie. He caught an arm around her bent thigh beside him, and anyone from the highway would have seen them as one shape with two heads against the faded sky.

18

"Let's go back to the ducks," said Arnie after drinking to the last of it his long silence. (In truth, his heart still beat to the lazy African tom-toms of Barbra K.; his veins still drummed and throbbed. She had sat on her little sofa in a brown robe starred with milk-white daisies and read her husband's letter, first to herself, then aloud to him. "Sounding his horn from down the road," she remarked. "That's the substance of it." She folded the letter, and got up to light some incense out of a bright packet she'd bought, maybe down in the Quarter or out on Bayou St. John. She helped him dress. "You ain't going to tarry none with me, I doan wager." "You ain't to know that for sure," he told her, and moved away like a whole cargo from the Indian Ocean, gunwales deep in sensuality, arms come to wind easily around Mavis.) "Let's go back to the ducks," he said to Mavis. Everything easy now.

He drew her up and moved with her down the break-water to the sand and all across the sand he took her with him, back to the house, scarcely wanting to part with her to let her get the car she'd left in one of the parking bays. But get it she did, and entered the house after him, finding him in the living room with her hemp bucket over one arm, about to go for duck food. She was intent on telling him what she thought he had to know. "My lover's Frank. Did you forget? It's him I love."

He turned with radiance, his eyes, in the half-light, had a cat quality and shone like gold or bright liquid. "I could tell you'd seen him. So, good. But 'love,' you say? It won't last."

She opened her mouth, with an angry cry about to come out of it. Was he trying, then, to snatch her love away? How could she know but what a second child from this afternoon might not be theirs?

"Living, that's all," Arnie kept right on. Castles in air, bulldozed to rubble—was he trying that? "To come back to life. That's all. The ducks are hungry, waiting. Come with me."

"Out of friendship," she insisted.

He looked at her and laughed, eyes a blare of brightness. "Okay, okay. Just come on, will you?"

They went out together. By then the moon was white, full and round, beaten silver overhead. The Buddha was in such thick shadow you could imagine you didn't see it at all. Only the head floated free of shadow, and it had turned a luminous gray in the moon, as though varnished. Back of the palings, the ducks were silent. They had tucked heads under wing and gone to sleep, mostly, though one or two, faithful and hopeful, waited by the fence in the dark.

Mavis and Arnie spread food in the troughs and the shapes rose, gravid, sounding a hungry quack or two. A distant trough far down the walkway at the low pool's edge was empty, but no ducks were near there. Mavis took the bag and went down there and, on returning, passed among the ducks,

now standing, white awakened forms. Arnie caught his breath
at the sight. It was joy—beautiful, and it hurt. Oh, if he could
have held that girl today! But she was elusive—girls were
nymphs, elusive, so they should be. Given choice, he wouldn't
anyway. Youth . . . innocence, etc. Fading, she would never
know her own awesome gravity. Mavis then could be her
image. And after her, others would come, trooping through
shadow and sunlight, lighthouse and duck pond, pool and
pathway, on forever, in ranks of gracious seductiveness. Was
there any final, finalizing *she* ahead in the minutes, days, and
years to come, just for him? He did not know. But it had better not be long.

Meantime, he watched this girl of Frank Matteo's among
the ducks, waist-deep and graceful, the smell of love and rain
upon her still. She stood, immortal, Grecian among their
moving forms. Returned, he put an arm of kinship about
her.

"Of course, you're Frank's girl. Just let me know when
you're not."

"How could you know about it—that I'd seen him?"

"A UFO took me for a spin. One of those little green air
hostesses aboard, she told me."

They both started laughing. A duck ran at them out of
the flock, head stretched out and angry beak open, it bit Arnie
on the leg, and still they clung together, happy and laughing,
with the face of the Buddha floating over the palings and the
moon sailing high. That day, he thought, with a high heart, in
different ways, was theirs—their own.

But I'm still ruined, thought Arnie, after she'd gone home
in her little car, leaving him alone to sort things out. Nothing's
really changed for me in the money world. Financially, I'm
two jumps from the world's edge; I'm floating toward Niagara

Falls in a washpot; the levee is breaking in a dozen places; I'm going to hell in a handbasket.

But emotionally the ferris wheel which had borne him high was still stalled at the zenith and, head among the stars, he gazed outward over magic seas toward islands of the blest. Poor old Lex and the butterflies. Even benighted souls grew light with marvels, bloomed in warm winter air. Right? he turned to ask the Buddha, but the face was gone into shadow, the moon having shifted lower, getting ready to set.

19

Circling the yard, feeling the sponginess of earth the spring-time worms had worked, out near the camellia bushes, hearing the rattle of a snake's passage through fallen magnolia leaves, stopping to pat the Great Danes' stony heads and view the lonely swift scudding of starlit clouds, he remembered something, as though the brain too like the planets and their satellites had a dark hemisphere and a light, and his sunset came abruptly. His mind on that dark side had all along been calling out what Lex had said: ". . . a grave." A grave.

Should he run immediately to the hospital and wake Lex Graham up? "There isn't any grave out there; she's buried in the cemetery." Would that hush him up? Lex spying and wondering was one thing, Lex really getting hold of something was another. It occurred to him now to know what he had dreaded from that first moment in the drugstore; it was not the dread of discovery—no, not that, of the discoverer. For none should discover us, he thought, who cannot also love. Self-righteous Lex: "Those organizers, those do-gooders, coming down here on us, they don't care what we're really doing here." Old-fashioned Lex: "A campus is no place for active politics." Wrathful Lex: "I certainly cannot attend any late-night debating sessions. I have to get up and teach!" Trusting, gentle Lex, even his mouth shying away from the formation of the words he sought, choking them out some way: "I never had a brother, Arnie. Can we be brothers?" How awesome a release to fall at last, wild and wordless, on the wife. Dorothy and he, sweating at their toil, were accomplishing not so much ecstasy, but extinguishing Lex. But that was done. An even better service rendered by Lucinda, blooming innocent and voluptuous, there in the lighthouse.

He would go up home now, he thought, and find a bride. Some family in the old town or one near it, known to his family for the last hundred years, someone not so young as Lucinda, wrong the first time around and now divorced, working in a quiet job: legal secretary, town librarian, small city reporter for social and civic news, russet hair, neat skirts, loyal eyes. He could see her. She was waiting for him without knowing it.

"There wasn't any grave." He remembered now, going in the house, that he'd told Lex that, remembering that the eyes were following, no glasses, the flesh around the lids looking stripped, naked, the pupil half-squinted, narrow, as though watching life out of ambush. Grave! What wouldn't Lex do? Go so far as to look into death records, find out the attending physician? He was sure to be checked, wasn't he, by conscience, by decency, by just knowing himself saved and rescued? But word, somehow, would get around: the state, up there, was a web of news: touch Amite County and Itawamba trembled. Okay, so he wouldn't take a Mississippi bride. A Yankee girl. They were understanding, they fit in well with husbands, they didn't think so much about family networks. He'd take a business trip up North a few weeks from now.

Talking with Evelyn was, at this point, essential, but before he could start, she was already talking to him, right out of the air.

"Arnie! You're not sounding like yourself. You know you always had to be in love, at least for marrying purposes." (She was right.) "But," he pointed out, "you know who that would be, don't you? Barbra K. Work out of that one." She was silent for too long, thinking it over, he knew, but did she seriously think he could get away with it? Why not? he sat wondering, the very question that had gotten them both—him and Evelyn —into most of their jams. He could take her far far away, couldn't he, where her skin color would just be called pretty. But the why not was clear: she didn't want to, had Reuben, a good man when he wasn't drinking, loved him. 'Nough said.

Half falling asleep, he dreamed, twisted in the sheet, fell out of bed in dreams with his ankle hurt, suspended in a white length of sheet. Lex, refusing him—the question was not of money but revenge. First spy, then bloodhound. Who maps our position in another person's life? His with Lex may have been taken the moment they met. Arnie was on the spot reserved for one who is struck at. He rose and told the Buddha so, for he could see his bachelor companion now; the clouds had broken up and sailed off in a grand fleet; the sky, cleared, was bright with starlight; the dusky face floated smiling in secret knowledge, but listening too. He too had smiled, he remembered.

Yes, had smiled with tenderness no Buddha would ever know (for, being complete, what need did the god have to reach and touch, meet flesh with flesh? Himself his own source, denying others). But Arnie had held Evelyn's hand, both of them had smiled when his hand had set the needle in the vein, his thumb had pressed the plunger . . . and she had smiled at him, dying. "I, Evelyn, take thee Arnold. . . ." That was it: done. He had killed her while she watched. They had dared to do it together. "You know you have to," she had told him. "Anything else would be a cop-out." "I know."

Whispering through the raised window, he told the Buddha about it. (Do I kneel for this? he wondered.) He reasoned that if a god was there, he might as well be confessed to, or at least talked to. Finished, he fell down to sleep again, washing into sleep with the soothing memory of Barbra K. ruffling, furling wavelike over and about him, prevailed over by her Negroid scent, her softness sooty and buttery, the memory of her depths and valleys, knolls and shades, her nooks, caves, and sinkholes, her whisperings for Jesus and her Lordy-lords of glad despair. He heard them soft in his first waking, just before the current of them, threading ribbonlike through his senses was as with the flash of large bright scissors cut through, not diverted or pressed back or allowed to be temporarily suspended, but cut off, canceled.

He was not alone. In the moment before waking, he knew now, a head had mounted over the top of the stairwell; in the moments before that, someone had entered the back door which he must have forgotten to lock; and this someone was now in the room, standing silently with a silent downward look, watching him awaken.

His hand moved toward a little bedside light and, when he turned it on, she showed no effect of it, but was the same presence as when it was still dark, and just as silent. He watched her as she pulled her sweater slowly upward, then stripped it off in one movement. Nothing under it: never was. She bent to the latch of her sandals, as her hair fell forward, touching the floor. And straightened. There had been no sound since the faint click of the light by the bed, no light but that either, a dimness that scarcely pricked the skin of the dark. She stepped free, bare feet on the floor, and said:

"Our only chance. Maybe forever."

The words fell with a sexy sad liquidity—like tears maybe, blood maybe, not rain—and he knew with regret that, as certainly as the air had turned to the Parisian scent she wore, his grain was to be sowed in this dark dawn to assuage an old passion. I don't want this! he longed to cry, but she had dropped her skirt already and was moving toward him, the soft thud of heels in measure to her words:

"Lucinda told me, made me know by telling me—oh, she didn't have a clue—that this was the way, the only way."

"*Told* you? Told *what?*" The lighthouse.

"The lighthouse. Oh, I know you said, 'Don't listen to me, an old man with silly ideas. Shut up your pretty ears.' But don't you know what girls are like? From Eve on. Try saying 'don't' about an apple . . . or anything . . . you name it."

"But I never harmed . . . I never. . . ."

"You spoke to her that way, my daughter. Don't you see that I . . . ?"

But, oh, he had trusted purity, felt drawn by unicorns across the green grass. The lighthouse. And his rough hand in the untried palm. Freedom. Flawed now (Dorothy), but too alive to die. The bed gave to her weight. Only chance . . . "forever," she had said.

She meant, then, not to conquer but to end it, finish in a flash of glory, where surrender has the air of victory. That was the spirit of her touch. They fit together instantly, the way they always, fatally, had.

part III

1

"Oh, sure," the young Houston executive said. "Sure, you're welcome to the whole morning. People that knew Papa used to show up and call me on the average of one-and-a-half times a month. Now it's dwindling to two-point-something times a year, and now it's been six months, just a little bit over, that I've gone without a call. Tell me, what's the latest? Still trying to resurrect the whole Gulf Coast?"

Joe Yater said that something like that was occupying Arnie Carrington's mind. He had telephoned the afternoon before. His dinner suggestion had been politely refused on the excuse of Kelly's long-standing engagement with old friends. Kelly Carrington. His office was ten floors up in a new high-rise building, just off a new shopping mall. There was a bright abstract on one wall, and a color photograph of Kelly himself on a ranch, perched on a tall horse, half-engulfed by a Texas saddle. For he was small, a neat, nimble young man. Worked with his loafers off, in sock feet, did not replace his shoes for coming from behind the desk, shaking hands, then, as if acknowledging the nonbusiness nature of the visit, curling up in an overstuffed chair covered with brown corduroy. Couldn't be much over thirty. A wartime product. Yates had heard you never knew about them . . . what they'd turn out to be. But did you ever know? Childless, he stared in on such things, like a window-shopper.

"Your father's been having it uphill lately," said Yates. "Tough going. Don't know if he's let on to you."

"We talk on the phone now and then. I'm not much on letters." He went to his desk, pressed a button, said he did not wish to be disturbed, resettled. "What's Papa's problem?" he asked.

"He's trying to hold on till his property sells, or rents. You know his ideas aren't just run-of-the-mill. So you need buyers with some taste, and they don't come that fast. The Coast is shaping up again. Well, you know that if you've visited."

"I was just there once since Mother died. Evelyn, I mean. She wasn't really my mother. Just like one."

"I guess you stay pretty busy, too."

"After I got off probation. That was my slowdown period. But then I got in this firm, taken on by this guy I met in the same clinic. He was on acid—took him longer to click. By-products paper is what we're into. He learned a way of making paper out of every sort of waste product. Especially from the oil refineries. There's next to nothing about the oil process you can't find a use for. We're into big bucks already. Next year we're aiming for the same, only in net."

"You don't say."

"Well, I did say . . . but that's enough. You've come about Papa."

"Oh, he didn't send me. Doesn't know I'm here. I came on other business."

"Yeah, yeah. I understand. The thing to understand, Mr. Yates, is this: Papa's up the creek. He gets hold of these ideas.

I really loved my stepmother. She might have got all right. I'd talked to the doctor, two specialists. Well, no sooner was I headed West and over the horizon, than what did he do? He killed her."

Yates went from shock to blank-eyed wonder. He looked about him, from the brown, alert, intelligent eyes before him, to the window which showed a few gray-white tall buildings and a cloudy sky. He looked back at the abstract painting. He knew of nothing to say. He had heard rumors of what the young executive had mentioned, had suspected himself it might have been the case, but had never dreamed of receiving any such confidence from Arnie, had never imagined anyone's saying it aloud, much less a son. He looked back at the eyes, as though risking a glimpse at something grotesque. And the eyes in the normal, frank, American face were brown, alert, and intelligent still.

"You knew that. Nobody wants to talk about it. Papa had enough capital, then, to carry on. My guess is that somebody involved in the transaction got it out of him. Blackmail."

"Transaction!"

"What do you want me to call it? Murder? He may have gone a little crazy afterward. He called me with some nutty message. She was gone away, a burial service. I could come, but really she was on the island, not in any coffin. Sucker: I went. Then there wasn't any funeral. Do you remember any?"

"No, but I didn't know them so well then. I assumed—"

"Cremation. He said he'd had it done over in Pascagoula. He had some papers from a funeral home. And the ashes? He was in some wild state, drunk half the time. I didn't want to ask."

"I don't see anything so suspicious," Yates said. "Anybody might—"

"But Papa's not just anybody. He'd have to have a funeral of some exalted, private kind. Once, at Southern Pines, he built a bonfire twenty feet high. It was during the protest period. When his feelings came out, they were bigger than life. Cinemascope. What would suit him for a funeral? He might have hired a torchlight procession of jazz musicians from the French Quarter; he might have dug a hole at midnight in that big fantastic Indian mound up near Natchez, or found an ancient Spanish crypt under some old church. My guess is he painted his boat black and floated her out beyond the Sound, maybe to the island. Maybe she had some dying wish or other. Between them, they could cook up some humdingers.

"Whatever he did, somebody knew it. It's why he hasn't come to me about his troubles. I know that. I think he's counting on the fates, or something like that. I think about it, about his doing that. He might even have talked her into it. Maybe she helped him. She was helpful—brave." His voice faded, then he suddenly laughed.

"You've got all these things in your mind about him," Yates said, "but you don't actually know them. You do know he's up against it now, for money. He saved your life once, I think. Some crazy bunch you were running with. . . ." Why spare him anything? "He went and found you, so freaked out you couldn't tell day from night. Went all the way to Colorado, wandered in the mountains. Didn't he?"

"Sure, he did all that. It takes a type like him to do all that."

Kelly was wearing brown-ribbed socks. He leaned forward, straightened the seam of one to its place beside his big toe, smoothed it, leaned back again. "You might think I sound ungrateful, but frankly I think in the long run it would be better for Papa to give up this property idea. It's just like everything else he's done. He's trying to fill out some idea of himself. My real mother, she was from this grand family up in Little Rock, Arkansas. Very wealthy people. She couldn't take it because he wanted her to put money into some project he had out in Hawaii."

"Where?" Yates had never heard Arnie even mention Hawaii.

"He was stationed out there for a while, the last year of the war. Second World War—not Korea. You know, he joined up for Korea. Idealism: what a nut! No, this was an education program for some bunch of natives he got interested in elevating. He wanted her to stay there the year-round, and he would join her from time to time. He had got mixed up in the early movement for statehood. He wanted to get on with his book. That's the one he published. He said it would have been better, but my mother was suing for divorce and he couldn't put his mind on it."

"It was still a good book," said Yates. "Distinguished." He was quoting what his wife had in turn quoted, from somewhere. *"Byron's Friendships."*

"I know. I read it once. Hell, I never saw him for nearly ten years. Then I took it on myself. When they thought I was off at camp the whole time, I sneaked in a visit with him. He came up to the Smokies. We stayed in an inn with a big fireplace. He said Scott Fitzgerald had stayed there. Described the whole thing about that man, the writer, and his wife, that crazy one. I didn't want to leave, we had such a fine time. We made a pact. We'd always see each other, no matter what."

"Did you promise to help each other, too?"

"Mr. Yates, I'm telling you. To raise money for Papa wouldn't be helping him!" He leaned forward to say this, then leaned back smiling and, for the first time, hands behind his head, chewing gum. "Even if I could. I can't, you know. Too many commitments. You get a new business going, you get just enough money out of it to eat, sleep, and pay the rent. The rest you plow right under. You're in business yourself. So you know. I wish I could ask you to lunch."

He was back at the intercom before Yates got out the door. Yates trod stiffly through the plush office, out to the noiseless elevators of satiny steel. A boy entered the corridor from an office door whose lettering was too distant to decipher. He was carrying a birdcage with a canary inside. He waited at the elevator beside Yates while the canary, evidently used to the journey, swung slightly on its perch. It did not sing. The boy went down in the elevator with Yates. At the door to the building, they went separate ways. Of his own way at the moment, Yates was not sure. He stopped at a street corner through two changes of the light, wondering how to get to wherever he was going.

Killed her.

It kept running on and on through his thoughts. Would Arnie do that? If he'd gone to that extreme, shouldn't he have killed himself, too? Wasn't that the next step? He must have debated it, then decided not to. In a way, maybe he thought he had actually done it.

Why don't you explain? He thought "you" instead of "he," as though Arnie in all his oddness was walking beside him in Texas, not brooding in a tangle of mystery over on the Coast.

2

But Yates when he returned found Arnie optimistic, bounding with pristine life, spruce, fit, and sharp, looking ten years younger, though finances had trickled even lower and the electric company had threatened to cut services off. "I'm back to myself," he said to Yates. March winds might froth the Gulf to the color of a snowbank, and shriek through the pine tops; rains might slash through the nights, with bursts and grumbles of thunder, and lightning snipe through every chance errand, but Arnie strolled about in perpetual sunlight. "What's wrong got right," he might remark, or, with a deep sigh of content, "Women are wonderful." Looking for matches in Arnie's living room one night, Yates saw the silver medal and leather belt Arnie had been sporting recently, stuffed in a drawer, apparently forgotten. Yates regarded them with a tenuous feeling, somewhere between contempt and envy. He remembered boys his own age, mounting motorcycles, bands of leather buckled to their wrists, black leather jackets, himself in a modest, studious suede. He found the matches and closed the drawer.

Arnie had taken up church, of all things, become a sidesman, wore charcoal trousers, a butternut linen blazer, could now be found a guest at Sunday dinner in one of the old residences that had escaped the blast, or a new one of those now going up, slowly, here and there.

"I went over to Florida," said Arnie, "while you were away in Texas. Looked up a boy I used to know, out in Korea. Bad hassle, but I got him out. Arm shattered, sense of direction gone. I took him for the princely sort. For years, we wrote. I thought of golden youth, turned gray in patches, but shaped up for good. The worth of citizens. Instead, bald with a beer belly, beet red where the hair's gone, running a kiddie amusement park. His family hadn't liked the girl he married; there'd been a quarrel and somebody shot. Jail. I never knew that. Now an amusement park near Miami Beach. A going thing. Said I could come in with him, buy into the business, maybe set a branch up here. Just what I'm trying to escape. Can't you see me—handing out tickets for rubber-bumper kiddie cars, raking sand over the miniature golf course, breathing beer by ten A.M.? He loves it. For this, you save the world. Kelly, now—my son, now—paper products. Desk memos, office stationery, notebooks. But this Florida boy—once golden—now gone bald and flat-chested, wears shirts with palm trees and MARILYN MONROE printed all over them. I'd sooner go decently down the drain. At least I won't have on that sort of clothes. He puts his money all back into business, is in debt to the bank."

"So problems remain," said Yates. "Well, what about a lecture circuit? My wife says you're rhetorical as hell. You can start out: 'All around us now, a new Gulf Coast is arising. . . .'"

"Oh, stop it."

"What happened to that family that was here, those friends?"

"The Grahams? One reason I left for Florida. Complications of a former life. The guy got well enough to travel. They went home."

Yates thought there was more to it than that.

"The girl," Arnie burst out suddenly, musing, and stopped. "She—oh my God, but she was lovely. To have a daughter like that."

Yates remarked that the house they had bought was still standing there empty. He wondered when they would move in.

"I'm too much for them," Arnie murmured, half to himself. He thought of them now as passed into another realm, like those known in wartime change to other spirits when peace comes.

He had called Yates because he was busy getting a

scheme together to obtain free city demolition and removal
for the old hotel. At first, after the storm, the authorities had
been obliging. Now, their appropriation exhausted, you had to
prove a health hazard to get them to act. Rats were indicated;
if only it were infested. But the hotel was remarkably free of
them, pure in its bashed-in state, held tenderly in the arms of
vines. It was Arnie's scheme, carried out on the next clear
night, to drive up with Yates to Stony Hill, a town about ten
miles inland, and at the town dump trap enough rats to put
into the Miramar, then call the city to witness the hazard. As
it turned out, once did not accomplish what was needed, for
the rats left the hotel as soon as they were released in it. On
the second trip, they fed them food with arsenic and put them
down, some already convulsing, in the downstairs rooms. The
next day Arnie met with the health inspectors.

In the little morning room where he and Evelyn had so
often sat before lunch for sherry or for visiting with friends
from New Orleans who had driven over to see them, dead rats
littered the floor. Two had died on the white-painted, cre-
tonne-covered sofa, the teeth bared in agony but limbs
touching still; a couple had existed, even among this kind.
One of the inspectors threw up. Arnie's exhibit was successful
and he saw the order for demolition processed that afternoon,
but he was sick himself by now—heartsick. The golden robes
of his manhood for the first time faded to an ordinary cloth,
and he longed for the island, its distance and winds, its warming sands.

3

With Arnie gone out to the island, Yates, in passing by his friend's house, saw a truck the size of a moving van, though with no painting on the side, ease out from the driveway and rejoin the road, thence to the highway, so he turned up to see what it had been about, and found that the Buddha was gone, only a bare patch of ground where it had stood. He was stricken and stood disbelieving, grieving even, extravagantly shocked. Why, he thought numbly, do I take it this way? He tried to get in the kitchen for a drink of water, and found the door locked, and felt this too personally, as a rebuff.

Arnie spoke of his Coast, its nurture and return from disaster, but Yates had felt a township and community in that very effort, pieces of wreckage, the derelict statue, piers of smashed seawall, upended trees, the eccentricity of white ducks. He had wanted, in this curious sense, everything in place. The heart makes houses for itself. They get broken into.

But about the Buddha it was even more than that, for him, Mavis, Arnie . . . who else he didn't know. They had been presided over. Not precious, or even noticeable, once you got used to it: till it was lost.

He shouldn't have been so surprised. He had heard Arnie say that the owners were about to reclaim it to sell it to a museum, had found a place for it, curators and appraisers had come to visit at various times. But none of this had registered and, walking back to his car, a frowning, gray, thin man, he was missing the image they had carted away. "Not 'it,' 'him,'" Arnie would insist. "A god has a right to his pronouns."

Maybe he was a god, thought Joe Yates.

One evening, sipping beer with Mavis and Arnie—his wife there, too, that night—he had first heard Arnie acknowledge that he actually needed the Buddha. "We all need him," said Arnie. "Why? Because we feel something come from him to us. Because he seems to float above us, smiling, beneficent, the way he still might if he weighed ten tons instead of one. The smile. I thought at first of the Cheshire cat, because his smile might be like that: it had a way of coming out of trees at me, out of the foliage. But then I saw the difference. There are smiles and smiles. The cat's is the Mona Lisa's. Only the cat has found a trick the woman—poor, tired, smiling thing —hasn't found yet. The cat can disappear from the smile. But Buddha's smile is part and parcel of what he knows; he attained it, with his ever-loving spirit. There's nothing he can't take and smile about it. He's got fat from swallowing the world. Good and Evil, man and woman, thief and saint . . . he's worn them all down, digested them through the long secret process of twenty stomachs, dumped them, exalted them, killed and resurrected them, not one or two or three but hundreds of times. We think power has to be fast, a stroke of lightning. His is slow as Christmas. Sometimes he thinks that's perfection he's attained—most of the time. Still, he lacks something. His time span's nil, infinite. He never got to be any age at all. So he needs us, here. The millions of Eastern souls playing around his knees don't worry him—they're all part of his daisy chain of being. But here he can't quite make do. We challenge him, maybe just by not really understanding. So he's got no threshold to us? So he's lonely? A boy away from home. I can see only so far into it."

He had done all that speech for Ellen, Yates's wife; this much Yates knew. A pale, quiet, sweet woman, he had almost lost her to a drug addiction he had learned about almost too late. Then, after the cure she'd taken, nothing seemed to stir her until the day she went to a club she sometimes attended and heard Carrington speak on Byron. She came home thrilled. It was then for Yates to seek Arnie out, thank him, make friends.

He had wanted to thank him again that night when the voice fell silent. To make fantasies like that, circle something with thoughts, feelings . . . so few people could do that. (If he himself were more interesting like that, would his wife have gotten so hooked, in secret?) The Buddha's removal was a real loss. Things encircled, sacred, set in place, how could they be moved? He wanted to kick a rock, to strike a tree with his fist, to butt a wall. If one thing could go, so could everything.

4

Arnie's only hitch in getting to the island was that his boat, dry-docked for caulking in February, was not yet seaworthy. He suspected that the boatwright's spells of boozing had gotten worse; still, what he was told had to do with new planking and that took time to shrink in place. He went by the Broadwater marina and bummed a ride on a six-berth cabin cruiser whose owner was taking a full contingent out for deep-sea fishing; it set out in late afternoon. He had his sleeping bag, Thermos, a hamper of food, and a spirit still sick about the rats, but needing to contemplate, to experience wonder.

Only when the land dropped behind the boat, a silky gray veil of light mist thickening with distance between the boat and the shoreline, did he feel shaken with a wrench of breath which freed him from the recent ill within his kingdom, and left him light and fit to redream the world so gardenlike and fair, all for him to wander in, resurrected. Rats in Eden were worse than snakes, but he was moving with the boat, graceful and deliberate and strong, feeling the deepened strength of water beneath her, strong in movement. He sat on deck next to his pile of belongings; he was near the prow, facing seaward. Free, at last, to contemplate. Yet thinking nothing, holding it off.

Ashore, he watched the boat dwindle into the dwindling sky, the brightness, pursuing the west. He had waved goodbye, and saw himself as he might have been seen from the boat, an older figure, man on island. Sturdy yet, with heavy, bent shoulders. Then he made his camp, on the stretch of beach to the sheltered north, just past the dune, near the shrine. He drank whiskey raw with a little water, heated soup on Sterno, pork and beans, too, and a packet of boiled shrimp, then coffee hot from the Thermos, but still no thought came. And he knew why, for with the sweeter, fonder memories, the betrayal would come, too, and he dreaded it.

He went directly to the tomb and lay there and then he knew that the women were coming, whispering, a laugh at times, feet bare and whispering on the sand, pressing down some island grass, or skirts rustling in dry brush. That was Lucinda, her laughter.

The moon had risen, silvery, full and bold, and Dorothy was out in it with her streaked hair and careful makeup, a sullen mouth. The shadows, dusky, multiple, attached to earth, the ground—these were all Barbra K.: he could hear her breathing, breath among the shadows. Mavis was out on the beach, back turned, knee-deep in her white flock, feeding them. The four he knew best now.

Dance! he commanded in thought, wanting them wakened into sweet orgasmic madness, to leap in moonlight, to tell him by accident how to live with the dark side of memory, with (it was coming back now, in spite of all he could do) the trusted young doctor who had so "understood" them both, had helped when they wanted to hurry death. (If he's out there anyway, ask him in.) And more: had been one with Arnie's private motives for bringing her here. (You lose your madness by living it.) Had faked records, stolen lethal drugs, sneaked in dark of night over dark waters with Arnie to bring her here. Side by side, had swung the shovel with him, digging deep. All leading to the day (one fine morning), when that good young face had said, "It's got out. I don't know how. All on your account, because of you. I'll be ruined in medicine, not only here . . . everywhere. If you don't turn loose enough capital to help me settle elsewhere, I might as well leave for Ecuador, just to choose a name of someplace."

He'd let the money go, gave it. No strings. Learned a month later the real reason for leaving, changing his name, starting up elsewhere. Some trouble with a woman: banal as that.

Why is it harder when the villain has blue eyes, blond hair? There are rats to be found everywhere, he guessed. The face you are looking into with frank eyes, sharing a common history, mutes only a little. The long gray whiskers catch the light. They were there all the time. You didn't notice.

Come, ladies! his thoughts cried out, and he seized a broken limb and flung it out into the moonlight. Come clean this place up for me! Do some blessed housekeeping. Down the drain with Dr. Swiggart . . . I might have known him from the name alone. Tie him to a turtle's back; ride him out to sea.

So they came. He watched them laugh, talk, dance and walk and breathe by mad moonlight, till finally he said,

"What's to become of Mavis?", addressing as he well knew the grave he was lying by. No answer, but sleep came as mysterious and sudden as a cloud across the moon.

He awoke with the moon slanting its light across his face, through a rift in the small trees, ragged and large, like something torn out. The moon was low to the water and platinum-white. He raised a hand to shield his face from the light, remembering some superstition about sleeping in full moonlight.

Then, between one breath and another, he knew something as positive as seeing it: he was not alone on the island any longer. Fantasy flown . . . time for business. But what?

5

Two A.M. and a man solitary on the pier, sitting in shadow on the pier's edge, on the south side of the island. When the wind stirred, he shivered, debated going back to his boat for another sweater. It took the climate too long to get warm. Wouldn't change for him.

In summer, and as late as November, he had been able to lie on warm sand face up when waiting, watching stars, while the sand, responsive, had crooked around him with a coarse blanket's thin, dry feeling. But tonight even the moon looked cold. It was too white. He was an hour early. The Coast Guard had passed by before he came. Lagging in the island's lee, he had seen the patrol boat plowing on toward Ship Island, from there to Cat, then the Rigolets. Doing its job would leave it no time to return. In the new season, warming toward summer, the sea traffic would thicken. He would have to have real fishing going on, maybe a passenger or two. It could be trickier than hell. He rose to take a walk around the central dune, made restless by the chill and the pale solidity of trees and driftwood, weeds even, by a hopping toad, which cast a shadow, as it would in the sunshine. Be careful of whatever kind of poison thing it was that guy, the friend of Carrington's. . . . Far off, then, he heard it, a stumbling sound, rumbling, then silent, then repeated—a muffled motor.

He moved to the pier, walked nearly to the end of it, leaned to place a small brick-red wad into the crotch of a tripod, struck a match. The short flare arched upward suddenly with a sizzle like bacon, as suddenly dived, its life gone into water with a hiss. Out ahead, a hundred yards from shore, a vessel broader than a ship's lifeboat, but no higher off the surface, righted its wide prow into land and so became visible. He quickly left the pier. His boat rode in shelter, behind a wooded spur; from time to time, he could see the high gray-blue fishing nest, perched above the center deck, nodding slightly.

The part he didn't care for was walking through the woods, small woods, more threatening than large. Large ones too big to pay attention. A twisting path, a stream to jump. Toad in the path again, what luck was that? Ahead, moonlight.

A sharp turn and there was his boat, graceful, ready to break the Gulf's strong swells, to pull the catch out: marlin, pompano, redfish, bluefish, cobia. The boarding plank he had set before leaving had slipped, fallen to one side in the tide's motion. He glanced at his watch dial, righted it, came aboard bent, an ape walk, to keep balance, not to cast a shadow. The moon went under a cloud and the approaching boat became at once less distinct and nearer. His watch was

running now in the pit of his stomach. What did it do to him
always, this mystery, this connecting point? It made him real.
Before the connection, he was merely himself: a fragment,
one man only. Once a connection approached, on time,
planned for, and he united with it, he knew the earth, he became something. Like everybody else, he needed to be something. Well, didn't he? Of course, he did. And this was it, his
job.

He drew in his boarding plank, closed the slot in the forward rail, then moved along the rubber-carpeted passage past
the cabin to the stern, and looked down, over the taff rail.

What he looked for was already there. The dark low
boat, its central cabin painted a metallic gray, like the rest,
showed itself to be a relief ship where, on deck, riveting ma-
chinery and bins for tools were bolted to the floor, canvas-
covered, while the few men on deck, until they moved, turned
faces upward, might have been another part of the equipment.
The faces were broad, the color of ashes in the thin light. The
moon still lingered back of the cloud. He hoped the gray boat
would not touch his clean little yacht. What were they? Oriental, okay, but what kind? Or maybe a Mexican or two.
They stood, broader than most men, inclined to broadness,
two of them shirtless with trousers low on the hips, cuffs drag-
ging the deck or rolled back, feet in heavy leather sandals. A
third had on a frayed undershirt. A small crane, like a toy,
was waiting. One of the shirtless men knelt to turn the winch,
and the other hooked a net containing two large brown-
wrapped packages to the hook which swung outward. At the
last minute, a fourth man, wearing a shirt and trousers,
stepped out of the shadows and caught the net. He stuffed
something in that was small and flexible: an envelope, it
looked to be.

Frank Matteo disliked the moment of contact which ap-

proached in a slow rise, then a pendulum swing. If no great
shock was in store—anything was possible—he shrank from the
idea of dirt, its stench, of sludge, of the oddly corrosive smell
that attended men who did not care about anything. Yet he
caught the net, wound his fingers among the threads, found
the opening, lifted out first the envelope, then the packages.
He put the packages on deck, but stood hesitant, holding
the envelope. "Wait . . . *momento*." What language did they
speak? Some English, maybe nothing else. They couldn't work
in Pascagoula if not, and maybe all along they'd been Florida
Indians, Seminole, not Mexican. Or West Indians of some odd
recipe in the blood. He knelt, hearing the motor cut back to
neutral, idling down below. The envelope was brown, FM
NEWS (it read), stencil-printed in large letters across the front,
and within, mixed in what might look like advertising for
some new Mobile, Alabama, station, he picked up the code,
kneeling by the dim light of the stern. "Package B not routine.
Save for transit north upriver to Cairo with Steamboat Bill
late summer." The first time they'd brought one like that, this
crew. "It's okay." He rose, stood tall for a moment, not only
above them but in every way their master, standing in the
black cotton canvas zip-closed Windbreaker, the trim black
cotton slacks, the black canvas yacht shoes, revolver snug in
the inner pocket of the Windbreaker, weighting it only by a
threadlike pull against the chrome-buckled waistband. A luxury river cruise in August, why he might . . . some distance
from Mavis might be a good thing at that particular time.

Just then a face, one of the dirtiest, broadest of the men
below (who seemed to have come not over the water but out
of it, sluicing silt and slime, hung with sodden seaweed) was
calling. "What?" "He want go island, one minute. *Agua*. One
minute." "Well. . . ." He watched then the dash and scramble, the man off like a runner at the gun, overboard, a few

splashes to the shore, then scooting into the wood like an animal, half-seen, or seen only at the point of vanishing into foliage. Back so quick with a bucket, and the bucket lifted up out of the water by one greasy arm and caught greedily by someone leaning down. The men on deck were drinking from the bucket of pure water. It splashed on their shoulders, their chests. The one who'd brought it came over the side to join them and they let him drink, too. I never thought of it, never tried it, Frank thought. So the scorpion that bit the guy had come all that way; maybe he was thirsty, too. Then he heard the motor catch and saw the gray boat back away. He waited till the outline grew distant and the one small red light either faded or was put out, then he moved to conceal the packages beneath the planking, prime and start his motor, free the mooring ropes and bring them in.

He mounted to the pilothouse and closed himself in, touching only lightly the knobs of satiny-steel fitted into mahogany paneling. The smooth enclosing chrome and glass shimmered. He went below to scrub his hands and wrists, then return.

Lower than ever, the moon lingered to light his way. He rode high, above glistening waters.

6

"So they were there all the time," said Carrington to Yates. "Have been, are, will be. Whether he owns it or not, he looks on it as available, he uses it as if it were his. Rights of passage, strange cargoes, scorpions from Oaxaca or Borneo, who knows what gets in there?"

"The whole coastline is like a sieve," said Yates, "from Miami to Key West to Galveston." He was swiveled back and thinking. It was Sunday, a cool-warm morning. Yates had come down to the office when Arnie telephoned.

"My dreams of the Coast," said Arnie, "why, they're chicken feed, gobbled up, blown away in a breeze. Nothing belongs to us here: power's loose. They take what they want to. Sure, I could go to the police, but I didn't see anything. He could say he had motor trouble, put in at a friend's dock, saw a rig boat come in for spring water, ran them off. Even if they catch him, out with him, what then? Matteo, the poacher, exploiter, smuggler, corrupter . . . out. In with somebody else, some greasy little cigar-smoking Dago. . . ."

"Cut it out," said Yates. "It's no good just spinning your wheels."

Arnie looked at Yates's array of Gulf photographs, the softly stirring Spanish moss, the smiling shrimp fleet, the sloops running white before the wind, the big somnolent white-pillared houses, and when he came, last, to the boy on the steps, his eyes filled with tears. Yet he had known this all along. Power fed on itself. Matteo was within a structure, its foundations laid out according to some plan, its walls gone up, now to be enlarged. But at whose expense? And what about the ever-growing legal enterprises, the coliseums, the Holiday Inns and Howard Johnsons, the waffle houses, and shopping malls—what were they but squeeze plays, draining off money, tormenting out of existence whatever wasn't aimed at power but at preserving, understanding, leaving intact, enriching. . . . Yates let the words flow over and around. "After the storm, a man down here, a Yugoslav—been here for generations—blasted out of house and home; saw his wife and baby drown; ran, half-blown along, to safety, in a clearing; spent the night in the lower limbs of a tree; at dawn, looking out on what he had taken for vines softly hanging around him: they were really snakes; the tree was full of snakes, refugeed, like him, and he had slept there." Arnie sighed and was silent, except for one more remark.

"I know we live among sleeping dragons, sprawled all over the place. Let them sleep. If they wake up, what can we expect? Poor old Lex, he stepped by accident on a dragon's spawn, his head in a cloud of butterflies."

Yates sat thinking of Kelly who said that his father was up the creek. If you sat repeating things you already knew, that was the meaning of "the creek," he supposed. Then the storm wore out. It would come again. "You should list your contacts," Yates said.

Arnie spun around. He had been in the back of Yates's office, extracting a beer from the refrigerator. "Contacts where? What sort of contacts?"

"You have them. Politics, both national and state. Educational . . . not so important. Media? No. Newspapers? Doubtful use, but to be considered. High finance? Know any? Yes."

"If you think for one minute. . . ."

"Oh, I know. You think they all let you down. The university started it, then your wife's death, and some sort of political swing back—I can't quite see that yet, can't make it out. But it's there."

Arnie crept closer. He was feeling a little like an interested stranger, listening to his own story. "Go on," he said.

"Then you might be ashamed, too. I don't think that's necessary, but you might think so. Success is a big old scare word once it's left you. You might be scared of being sent around to the back door, a country cousin. I doubt it would happen, but I see how you feel."

Arnie was leaning now; something was waiting to be said.

"The doctor who took care of your wife," Yates said. "What was his name? Swayze? Swenson?"

"Swiggart. Changed to Swayze."

"I doubt he could do that without some hanky-panky. He can't come back on you, you know. Not without swamping his own boat."

"You're believing some gossip, is that it?"

"Not believing, not disbelieving. Just saying it exists."

Arnie was stopped dead. Speechless. Among the sleeping dragons, evidently, there had been this architect, this mild gray man. He hung between wonder and anger.

"You're just plain trespassing is what you're doing. That and trying to take over."

"I'm your partner in the rat crime, remember? You might have had other partners, mightn't you?"

Oh hell. He bent his head. Crime was what you called it when other people did it. At any rate, he didn't care to discuss Evelyn. She had been, after all, his own crime.

"Make a list," Yates urged. "Contacts. People here. People at the university. People in Jackson and Washington. They might make that island part of the new Gulf Islands National Seashore."

"No, the surveying left it out. I even saw to that."

"Saw to it?"

"I mean I checked to see that it had been left out."

"If you could get it left out, you could get it included."

They adjourned to Yates's house for lunch. Arnie went home. Yates came to see him.

"I'm going to Washington next month," said Yates. "My wife's not a congressman's sister for nothing. I got contacts, too." Then he said, "Go on, sell to Matteo."

"Don't think I don't get the drift. Sell to him, the government shifts survey lines, he's out, I keep solvent."

"The island's sacred, I know, but you could go there still."

"If it worked. . . . But no. God, it can't work. What would they do to Frank? Eat his heart with scrambled eggs?"

"You think he's got one to eat. That's probably your big mistake."

Arnie shook his head. "And then there's Mavis. . . ."

Silence. He was sitting in a chair, looking out the back window, past the kitchen wing, out to where the Buddha had been and was no longer. On the table behind him, neatly typed, were the list of names, identities, "contacts." Yates had become more voice than anything else, pursuing, inexorable, at his elbow, stating, arguing, reasonable. If the voice stopped, it was to rest, like a runner, only to run again.

"You know how I feel about Mavis, about her and Frank both," Yates said.

"How do you feel?"

"That they're nothing. Worth nothing. Thinking they're worth anything is as wrong as believing what you see in a movie. It's worse than that. A movie can't hurt you. They can."

"I don't share the view," said Arnie, "because, so far at least, I don't have to." He couldn't sit there forever, looking at where the Buddha used to be. There went Mavis across the view, going out to the ducks. And there went the ducks, with melodious quacks, long-necked to the fence, her greeting. He couldn't sit there forever.

"I'll see Matteo," said Arnie. "You're right that I can't carry on."

7

But Frank himself had gone to Florida. Dancey, the Negro boy who seemed to know more about Matteo than anyone did, said on the restaurant telephone that the Boss was away, and Arnie, hearing the word "Boss," remembered the plantation—country—sound of it and how that had come to blend with the city sound and the present verity. "Boss" Matteo— how far did Dancey think that went?

Arnie referred himself to Barbra K. "Do people here think Frank Matteo is the boss of everything?" he asked her.

"He got this one and that one," she said.

"Got who? And what? What does that mean?"

"I ain't so well up," she said. Then she said she had worked for him. "Doing what?" "At the restaurant," she meant. "Just at the restaurant." But then she had worked for lots of people. At some other restaurants and once for a long time at the air base in Biloxi, in the kitchen. "But over there, there was always something going wrong. Too many bosses," she said. "You never knew who you worked for. But with Frank Matteo you knew." "Knew what?" "Who you worked for," she said. And that was all.

He tried a different tack. "When Matteo left town, where did he go?" "Florida," she said. "To do what?" he asked. "Tampa, Florida," she said. "Why?" he pursued. "Lord know," said Barbra K. She said he ought to ask Dancey. He asked why she couldn't ask Dancey. She said she hardly knew Dancey and wasn't too fond of what she did know. It seemed to him that Barbra K. ought to do most anything for him. He had fixed up the front of her house so she could work mornings, taking care of children whose mothers worked. She was earning money. It looked as if she felt no gratitude, though in many ways she was accommodating.

Arnie said to Yates, "Whatever you wanted with all those addresses, I wouldn't like to know about it."

He said this not to engage in contesting anything, to stay clear. Weren't Frank and Mavis as much a part of life here as Barbra K., or Yates himself, or for that matter the ducks? When he drove about the Coast from place to place, teaching at the junior college, or drinking in a bar, or having his boat mooring changed, meeting with the ecology group (once off pelicans, they had gotten hung up on shore terns), or unraveling interminably the problems of real estate (four lots had sold), he felt that distinctions were no longer possible here, that all of life, good and bad together, was simply one thing, a growth, a creature made of many creatures within the area of its original simple structure, yet complicating itself the more it let new creatures in, and he felt the generosity of its doing so. Whatever Matteo was going to the island about, was it so impossible to see him as still human in his motives, actions? Perhaps he moved from fear, maybe he was the channel, only that, for operations he had not much idea of, and maybe it was only marijuana traffic, which to Arnie's mind was not so bad; it took him back to army life, then college. A commonplace.

Besides, Matteo was united with him and Mavis against that gang of squirmy boys who fooled around with guitars and, yes, drugs, too; some sort of dumb language they talked in, and prided themselves on bringing off petty crime. Matteo was way beyond that, intelligent, could have been a good straight-up businessman. He had said something once to Arnie about not offending the community. Ergo: he knew there was such a thing as a community to offend.

If he was part of a vast network, organized crime, it might have harmless parts in its makeup, fairly innocent working; restaurants had, after all, to sell food and drink, pay waitresses and cooks and handymen like Dancey, and a restaurateur might need the love of an attractive waif like Mavis, who if she thought there were anything so brutally terrible about Frank, might have loved him but would scarcely have followed him, stayed near him.

She did love him, Carrington knew that. And so doing made the crux of the problem of Frank; the knot he shrank from cutting was, purely, her love. It was why he said (when in a state of outrage over finding Matteo on the island, he had given Yates his store of "contacts"): "Take them, but don't tell me what you do with them. I wouldn't like to know."

But secretly he thought himself so out of things, out of the world he had once known and influenced, that he could not imagine the addresses doing anyone any good at all. Who were they all? Where were they now? Some out of it, like himself, dropped and set down on the sidelines by the rush of time. And some even better known than before but no doubt, for that very reason, changed, unrecognizable, ready to say "Who?" and, with a little frown of genuine concentration, murmur, "Oh yes . . . certainly: Carrington. Oh yes, of course." An interruption, a riffle on the day's stream, for the busy photographers from *Life, Time,* and *Newsweek,* the editorial writers for the *Times* and the Chicago *Tribune,* the Los Angeles *Sun,* the Washington *Post,* the editors of *Rolling Stone,* for professors and lecturers at Berkeley who had headed a network for getting dissenters out and away to Canada and Sweden, radical congressmen and liberal senators, reporters with an "in" at the White House, and reporters of

whom the White House was wary, journalists in scattered lo-
cales, key men, shrewd judges of what really went on. "But
the sixties," as he said to Yates, "are dead now. You know that
and, even if you look up these guys, what good exchange can
you have about anything here? They've followed separate
paths, turned into other people, just as I have. But all right,
try and see, but don't turn me into some down-and-out has-
been. Stick to lofty principles. The great issues! The common
good!" He was laughing.

Sometimes—though each, as they regularly came from
women, returned to women—they seemed like two old bache-
lors, living together with a kind of vague ritual of politeness
established between them, times for talking, drinking, eating,
so well worked out between them, no one discussed it anymore. Yet they often did not see each other for a week or
more, or call, and were like classmates in a university, not
well-known to one another. But they had taken on, it seemed,
a common cause. It had to do with how life in this place
ought to be lived. It was better than working hell-for-leather
for money, or power, wasn't it? There seemed something extra
good about it, because they had so little to gain.

As if a kind of musical accompaniment to this commu-
nion was Mavis Henley. She was often with them, or nearby,
peripheral. Joe Yates was to move into one of the shops in the
row Arnie had bought. His office would be moving there, and
Mavis had plans for a handicraft shop in another, the one next
to Barbra K. That would leave three to rent. She had the
ducks, too, over at Arnie's house, and the art classes, at the junior college. And within, as their common chemistry knew
constantly, she had Frank's child.

But they didn't talk about it. They talked about business,
about food, about architectural drawings and the talent of the
art students, and whether Barbra K. could get a permit to set

up a child day-care center, and what toys would be available, wholesale, and wholesome.

They did not talk about Reuben, who had got his ear half cut off in a fight in New Orleans, or about Frank's business being crooked, or about Frank being the father of Mavis's child, or Arnie vanishing in Barbra K.'s direction from time to time, or about Barbra K. being black and the others white. They did not discuss Ellen Yates's former drug addiction, though she was still under supervision, or whether Reuben would get it in for Arnie if he found out, or what would happen when the baby came. Their lives lived in the spaces they could live in, stronger than if they could live freely in all. It was what I meant all the time, Arnie thought. He had known you couldn't order such things like a meal, or write a check for them in a store. That time he'd run away from home in grand rebellion, and the family had sent for him: "You've just come for this nice visit with us," his Biloxi cousins said. "You know where we live now. Come back again."

8

So Frank was gone to Tampa, Mavis thought.

In her head, she could see the vision of his travel, how the road lay for his passage, first along the beach, then through the flats where the road level had been raised to escape swamping in the rainy times, the trees at some distance, a lonely trailer park maybe out among a live oak grove, the ground cleared and bare, black, the beach and Gulf visible through the thick bolls of the trees. She pursued his flight, but he did not turn his head; the purple car went around a bend.

Then she half dreamed, or daydreamed, that he made a detour by the city where that doctor—Dr. Swiggart, was it? or Swayze—stayed. The one Arnie had gotten ripped off by. She'd heard the story from Frank, and while she put it down to speculation, she thought maybe it had some truth in it, or she wouldn't envision anything about it. That city would be covered with a black cloud, like a hood, a spring storm, streaks of lightning, bands of rain. Frank might stop for gas, look in the phone book. There it was: Swayze, M.D., off., res." Frank liked to know where everything was. Frank was slowly drawing Arnie in; she saw that or, rather, felt it. But she didn't see how Arnie would be harmed by it. There was money to be sunk somewhere, better on an island than somewhere else. A fishing resort. What's wrong with that? So what's wrong?

The way she saw it, certain groups had money, lots of power; what they did with it was for them to decide. Governments, according to Frank, were just the same. Using power . . . it always came to the same thing. The bottom line. If somebody got in the way too much, you had to find the means of—what was the word?—"finessing" (so Frank said) their presence.

Frank was going now to somebody named Eddie. She knew that much. At Eddie's motel and golfing resort, Frank would be given a luxury room, indirect lighting, a bar (equipped), TV the size of a drive-in theater screen, and on a sleek white telephone he would check in with Eddie. His appointment would be for the afternoon; he would go for a swim, lean and brown, in the sparkling pool with its bathhouse, its deck chairs, the flat blue plate of the Gulf just beyond the low brick wall where the oleanders bloomed in big-bellied pots; and then, oh then, he'd see the girl, the slim brown girl who'd been sent there just now and know immedi-

ately she'd been sent there for him, just as he would not acknowledge her presence, nor she his until the last moment, the
moment when he came out, fleeced in drops of water, bent to
pick up a towel, but first to lift, then strap on, his watch; now
drying his face, setting on his dark glasses, then turning to
find, connect with a glance just turning to his own. White
teeth, latent under their lips, now smiled, each to each—flash
. . . flash. Semaphores. The bar was shadowy, a cool cave
behind glass doors slid back, off from the pool. Plants. He
would slip on his robe, order daiquiris, sit with her at a small
poolside table, talking beneath a striped umbrella, straight
chairs, crossed legs. Teeth. White. Skin. Dark. Glasses. Black.
They'd leave together. Oh no! she thought. No! They would
like whatever they did. Don't. Please don't. Don't make love
to her! Don't do it!

All this time she was teaching a class, moving among students who were doing collages—"The piece of mirror there is
interesting." "Do you really want two reds?" "I think you've
left too much blank space. Can't you fill it some way?" Her
mind in layers. She began to ache. "Yes!" she cried, as a
Negro student glued a piece of cord across the neck of the
drawing of a man, as though to strangle him. Her heart quiv-
ered in its hidden violence, shuddered away from what she
wished until she didn't even wish that she wished it, then
withdrawing even from the image of it, cried silently at herself, the hateful woman within: You're awful, just terrible!
and a tear fell on a girl's hopeful blue watercolor, a Gulf sky
ran. "Those water pipes are dripping again," she said, and
took up a brush to help. "Let's make it a gull."

So many things to think about him. She was glad to get
home to think them. The things he'd told her—how she'd gotten hooked on him after the sex had gotten a little bit calmed
down. Like how he'd been a boy, an only child, in the base-

ment apartment in Philadelphia that was also a shoe repair shop, how he couldn't stand the smell of shoe polish anymore and would always wash his shoes to this day rather than shine them, though for some odd reason he loved the smell of good leather. His father and mother kept late working hours, joked with neighbors and customers but were silent with one another, bent together over account books, their heads touching. He was generally cold: the apartment had no sun; they saved on heat. The houses on the street were joined, all alike. Theirs, near the corner, had a sign out. A big laced-up black shoe hung from two chains. It said EXPERT SHOE REPAIR and, underneath in a swirling hand as though in a letter, A. MATTEO. When he got tall enough to reach, he would go out every night and take the sign down. Each morning one of them would put it up again, whoever had the time. One morning the wind blew the sign out of his hands and into his face. It knocked him down off the steps. His father thought the sign might have cracked but it hadn't. His mother kissed him, but he wasn't hurt. "How do other people tell which house they live in?" he asked. It was at the table, eating. His parents looked at him. "They don't have a sign," he explained. "By the number," his father said at last. "They have a different number." Philadelphia.

He went to school. Quiet, did what he was told. Listened. He had his own room, a cubbyhole. Books and pencils, neat piles, clean pages.

One Saturday at the shop, a cousin came. A young man with side whiskers, very black and furry. He talked a lot, all day, the voices went up and down, fast, loud, in Italian. Then softer, loud again. It was dark when he left. But when he left, everything had changed.

For one thing, there was money. For another, Frank was going to be sent off somewhere he had never heard of: Montreal. He said it over. Montreal. Out of the country! But not so far. Far or not, he was terrified. He knew then for the first time how he was holding on to America like somebody in the bottom of a ship at sea in a tempest. Maybe it had not been comfortable, but it was all there was. To leave the ship was unthinkable. But where had he gotten this idea? He didn't remember anybody saying that, not in so many words. On the bus to Montreal, he sat like somebody petrified, thinking that when he got to Canada the ground would be orange, the grass purple, the trees grow upside down, anything. Here he was, fourteen years old, thinking that. Also, he thought it would always be snowing. (He told all this to Mavis Henley, late one night in bed, making a joke of it.)

In Montreal, marvelous indeed, where some people had gotten in the habit of always speaking French, he lived in a luxury house with Uncle Luigi and Zia Gianna, had his own room, cried at night for his mother, but otherwise went about happy, in good soft wool clothes they got for him, glossy shoes. He went quiet and sturdy, answering when spoken to. Zia Gianna used to hold him in her arms and her eyes would shine with tears for the children she'd never had. Uncle Luigi about once every week took him down to a restaurant where he often ate, and cigar in mouth introduced him to a variety of friends, holding his shoulder, roughing up his hair, slapping him with pride: "Toni's boy. Remember Toni? Just for this year, we've got him here. Quite the scholar." He said this because Frank was often in the library. The library was the one room in their old made-over house which hadn't been bothered. It had a bowed-out set of windows over the street, was small, with a fireplace, rug and table, sofa and two chairs, all silently gathered. The books lined the wall, but when he reached up for one a whole painted cardboard facing toppled off on his head. From the taller, bottom shelf, large volumes did come separately out in his hand, but they were empty boxes painted with encyclopedia titles. When he put everything back, the library feeling returned, so he used to take a magazine in there and read it, sitting in one of the chairs.

Uncle Luigi sent roses to Zia Gianna, red ones with long stems, which she arranged in her beautiful blue and gold vases. Then she had a closet lined with cool, thin metal where she kept her fur coats, four or five of them, with some smaller coats and hats in all sorts of fur. One day Uncle Luigi got killed. It was in his restaurant that somebody walked in and shot him. Just before that, everyone there had walked out, as if signaled. All the papers wrote about it. They put the casket containing Uncle Luigi on a table in the library and all his friends and relations filed by and around it to look in. Then they covered the casket with red roses and took it out and Zia Gianna had to be taken out, too, to the hospital, the next day, so he was alone and frightened and forgotten, there in the house, eating out of the refrigerator. Zia Gianna came back, eventually, and cried over him.

In the dead of night they awakened him, made him pack, gave him papers with another name on them, drove him to the border. Two men. At a certain New York town, he caught a bus home to Philadelphia, in the stony, snowy hours, just before a late dawn. But before that they had taken him somewhere, impressed on him that he could never talk of Montreal, and he said he wouldn't.

"Impressed on you how?" Mavis asked, and he flicked on his lighter and showed her the thin crossing lines on his chest, above the heart. "That wasn't all. I was a green kid, scared shitless." "You're talking about it now." "It's long enough ago. And anyway, not everything."

No, she thought, it was never everything; she knew that. Still, she knew he had gone home, found his father in a regular job, working in a factory, moved into a new apartment, everything better. He finished high school, worked at different jobs, finally as a receiver and checker of materials for a construction company, so now he was making what they called "good money." But he was shy. Ever since Montreal, he had been shy. In his dreams, they came to get him again. He had let something out. It was known. He dreamed the chill of knife blades, the chill of the fur coat closet, metal-lined, the empty mockery of the false books, the blood-color of roses. It took him a week to get up courage to speak to a nice girl who ate at the same sandwich shop.

She was pale and blond and worked as a secretary at a hospital nearby. When he took her out to dinner, he sat speechless, without eating much, unable to talk. Next he took her to the movies, so talking wasn't required. When she asked him home one Sunday, her father, a chemistry teacher in a high school, wanted to know certain things about him. He must have said something that was all right, because they let him return. One thing he said was that his parents lived over in New Jersey.

Her name was Annette. Her mother was dead. She had pale silky hair and, when she finally let him stroke it, run his fingers through it, kiss it, he felt something shake loose, like a stuck lock opening, and then he could talk again. Not to tell everything, but much. He said his parents came from Italy, brought over by an uncle in New York, then moved to Jersey. He said he had visited relatives in Toronto, that his aunt in New York had several fur coats. He told this last at dinner with Annette and her father, and they seemed heartened by the news. It occurred to him that they were afraid.

One afternoon he and Annette got married. She was five years older than he, it turned out. He thought it didn't matter. He guessed he believed that. He felt innocent about her. They stayed together in his little apartment and then he took her home. They hated to tell her father, who was so alone, she said. But after a month, they told him.

To Frank, his father-in-law, whose name he could not remember, was in a small way a heroic man. He had every reason to throw a fit, but he didn't. He asked them to live with him; he offered all that he had. He even promised not to get in the way, to move to a room at the back. "Daddy, Daddy," Annette sat saying. She was looking down at her plate, smiling, shaking her head, and with tears in the corners of her eyes. She must be looking like her mother now, Frank thought. But they were funny. She went away to wipe the tears off. Didn't like them seeing her touch her face.

While still considering where to live, Frank came home one day and found a dark woman waiting for him. She was from Montreal, she said, and had looked for him everywhere. She didn't have many ties in Philadelphia. He remembered her and went out with her for a drink in a dark restaurant and bar he had never been to before, which glowed inside like a dark jewel. They sat at tables cupped around with curved sofas like young moons, drank from heavy green glasses set on tables of glossy wood, nearly black. She talked about Zia Gianna, not Uncle Luigi, and he was reassured, took a second drink, and said he was doing fine. That was all.

But that same night he took Annette to the movies and felt moved to tell her that his parents didn't live in Jersey but here in Philadelphia, that soon she must go over with him and be introduced to them. But she only said he had lied to her. "A little bit, not much," he admitted. Then she said her father had suspected something all along. "What?" "That you were in the wrong element." "Wrong element?" "Aren't you?" "It's just how everything is," he told her. "There's no element about it." "You mean you don't know the difference," she said.

He stared at her, carefully sizing up new possibilities; now she'd gotten on to him, or thought she had. "We'll go back to my place for a while," he quietly said. So that's how they got to the bad part.

It should have been the good part. All he wanted to do was love her. Not the polite, gentle, regular way, which was all he had allowed himself before, but the wild, strong way he had picked up here and there and now wanted to bring her into, nerve and muscle, wild mouth and ready thigh, loosing all that her pale hair had stirred him to want. But she couldn't, she said, then she could but then after all she couldn't really, but he scared her, he hurt, humiliated her. And over nothing much. But in the car, he kissed her gently and she said she would be okay tomorrow. It was a promise.

The next day she wasn't home, and the next she had her period and was sick, so on the weekend, worried crazy, he dodged a number of phone calls from the woman he had known in Montreal, inviting him to a party. He felt there must be all sorts of ways around things, out into a simple world where blond girls had daddies who taught chemistry and watched "I Love Lucy," but it was right there he got trapped, her father seated back of a desk to face him, and she standing beside the father, facing, too. "You must tell us, you see. We talked and decided. It's the only way. You must tell us everything." He thought about it. "It's impossible." "Why?" "I don't really know anything to tell. Some people I've known have been mixed up in things. That's for them to say." And the terror stirred in him again: the motel below the border; the burn scar near the groin (a live cigarette—he had not told even Mavis, but she'd found it, and guessed); the thin, chill touch of wandering steel, leaving the fine blood beads; and the dreams. "You mean you won't. Not that you can't." She stood there pale, her mouth as thin a line as a scar could be,

but that was worry. She worried. "I mean what I said." He
was looking down now, and they were all silent for a long
time. Then he rose and went to his wife. He kissed her brow
and touched her hair. "*Sei bella. Ti amo.*" Then he left.

Some days later, he went to one of the parties the woman
from Montreal kept asking him to, and there he met her
younger friend, a girl with dark curly hair who wore bracelets
and was strongly built-up. He drank a lot of wine and went
home with her and they did a lot together. He decided this
was the company he would need to turn to now and then.
When things got all right about seeing Annette, he would still
go to these from time to time. Nobody need know. But maybe
he wouldn't. He couldn't guarantee.

Then he got to thinking of her, of Annette. He thought of
her with tenderness, with pity, with devotion. He saw she
couldn't help her fearfulness. He wanted to see her. He read
by chance in the paper that her father had been killed in a
street accident; a truck had hit him when he stepped out from
behind a parked car. He rushed to the phone, but her line was
busy; he went to her house, but there were people there; he
waited till twilight when she walked out alone; he came to
her out of a side street with his arms wide. But she froze away
from him. "You did it," she said.

"Did it? I'd never do a thing like that. What do you
mean?" "That gang you're mixed up with, they did it." She
walked on, stiff as a stick. "But why would *they?*" "To keep
you. They had to or you'd leave." He writhed along the sidewalk like somebody shot by a sniper and not knowing yet
what had hit him because he was wondering if she might be
right or not. Could they have, and why? So he didn't call her,
or go to her again, and guilt surrounded him like a mountain
cloud.

The dark-haired strong girl, friend of the Montreal

woman's, turned out to be rich. She got him fine-colored shirts, cuff links from France, a suit cut of English material made up in Italy. He slicked his hair closer to his head and remembered those other soft wool clothes chosen by Zia Gianna and the short beige sheepskin coat with the fleece lining. And he was older. And some things he'd only thought about back then, begun to hear about, now were done. A job change, too. On his own, he'd done it. Advanced. *Ben fatto.* Still, he remembered Annette.

She had a wool cap with bright threads which zigzagged; she wore it when the wind blew cold. Then, too, she had mittens, like a small girl. "But you got a divorce," Mavis Henley said, years later, down in Florida, in the dark. "Or she did. Didn't you?"

"No, not divorced." He turned his face into the pillow.

"Why not?"

"I didn't like to disturb her." He said "disturb" with the faintest brush of an accent, like "di'turb." Mavis could hear it still, how he sounded in the dark, remember that she hadn't believed him.

His phone is ringing, she suddenly thought. It's ringing in Tampa.

His phone *was* ringing, down in the motel south of Tampa. He caught it while the brown gypsy girl turned languid on the white sheets. "Sure, Eddie, right away." He drew a hand across the bare behind beside him, a parting caress. She would have given a name but not her real one. He'd never be able to say he knew it.

Mavis thought that, anyway, one more was gone for good. She knew the way things were, the way they had to be.

When Frank got back to the Coast in the small hours, he wanted to call Mavis and tell her the truth: his life was all

like a movie; he was living in a movie. He had found life less
of a shock, less of a kick in the ass, or a pain in the neck, or a
sickness in the down area of the stomach when it had the
movie-feel to it, as if he were parroting out a script somebody
else had written, walking onto sets instead of entering real
rooms, swimming in real pools, screwing real women who had
names and might get pregnant. He had been shocked into
this; it wasn't fair. Whose father turned out to be a rip-off in a
safe factory? Whose uncle turned out not to be top banana
after all in far-off Montreal? Who, because of blood ties to
these things, got tracked down and sucked in? It wasn't fair,
but thanks to God he looked made for a better part. Straight,
lean, a cutout figure, flat at the waist, with a clear, flat, tan
face. The sets were made for him and such as him and, without him and such as him, they would be lacking something.
Yet he too could get shot full of ugly, blood-oozing holes. Or
shipped off to two hundred miles south of nowhere. He was
replaceable. The world contained others who looked as good,
who did as well. If he could acquit himself well enough here,
he would go West. There were spots in Arizona—the ranch
life—and California in the High Sierras, where life wasn't bad
at all. He could do without Vegas. But meeting somebody
now outside of who Eddie knew, that was his next move. It
was funny that he thought for a long time that Arnie Carrington had some track, that he was tacking close to some mysterious force that Frank needed to know more about. He wasn't
altogether sure yet that he hadn't been right. He was no
longer the boy in the new suit from J. C. Penney who sat
through an evening with his girl and her father before the TV
set and wondered how long it would be before he could go to
the bathroom where, in addition to relieving himself, he could
pull his sock up where it had slipped down into his shoe. All
that time lay in the world of shadows, while the movie world

of sleek suites and offices, crystalline pools and nameless willing girls, had become the real one. He wanted to tell all this to Mavis, who had once worn gold bracelets and a tiger lily skirt with a bold hibiscus in her hair. But oh damn, no more, those days were gone; she was having his child. Having it.

He had reached home, parked the car in thin dawn light, mounted his stairs, and now, locked in, stripped to his shorts, with the blinds drawn, he fell exhausted across the bed and formed in his head the image of a handsome male child, leaning out from a mother's anonymous shoulder to put his arms wide toward him, the father, tall by the window on the sea, accepting that the picture had come to life—a great wonder, but it did happen. If only life wasn't so Jesumaria complicated, trouble, the sort you didn't finesse—the fucking damn human trouble. He turned back to the image, the dream, and fell asleep in its folds.

9

When finally Arnie Carrington came to see Frank Matteo, he did not fail to note that it was a fitting journey to make by climbing. Stair by stair, and within, spaciously opening out from the mysterious entrance, an ideal. Carpeted thickly, lighted softly, with broad sea view, the murmur of music, the air tactile with power, the small sharp sound of it (struck crystal) almost to be heard. Yet nobody, they said, came here. Momentarily awkward, a sea-wind-beaten feel to his very skin texture, ankle-deep in wall-to-wall, he perceived the sense of having a place the way it was just in order to have it; no other eyes had to see it for Frank to feel it. One god (the Buddha) gone but here were strong signs of another. Matteo shook his hand and, for a moment, they stood in poised equality, strong lords before a duel. What to prove?

He was almost licked and down to nothing, which is to say that if the island went up for auction because of failure to pay back taxes, then Matteo might or might not have a chance to get it. But Arnie, in that case, would realize far less than what he needed to realize, far less than what Frank's offer had been. Yet his seeing Frank, asking for this meeting, had nothing really final in it at all. He was simply Carrington, doing what he was always doing, exploring his world.

Relations: to Mavis, to the child unborn, to land, to crime, to love. And, yes, to architecture.

"Architecture!" Matteo jumped like somebody shot. He was before a wall bar lined in blue glass, pressing the button on a machine that spit out ice, chunk at a time, and was now about to squirt a slug of bourbon into a glass crater.

"Well," said Arnie, "you haven't done too badly with your restaurant. It's got a driftwood look, fits in with the marina. My friend Joe Yates is an architect, and likes it. If you got hold of that island, now, say, and we have this trade, I wonder what you'd put there."

"There's not so many ways to build a fishing camp."

"I'd say there's every way to build one. Why do you think that?"

"Because," said Matteo, "the only thing a fishing camp can be built like is a fishing camp."

Arnie sat back with great relief. It was, he supposed, the main thing he had come to find out. But, like a shopping list, a few other items were needing to be picked up.

"I'm curious why you won't marry Mavis." Matteo, who was given to handsome pacing, came about on one heel.

"Your business, I suppose."

"In a way, it's my business. Hell, I've been looking after her off and on since last fall, picked her up when you were out of town, leaving her flat—emotionally flat, the worst flatness there is."

"She's not so flat now, but that might be thanks to you."

"No. One thing I know for sure. It ain't me. One thing she knows for sure. It's you."

Maybe it was the first time he'd been convinced of it. His dark Latin eyes grew suddenly larger, lambent. There could be more to this, thought Arnie, seeing in their light a glimmering of future hope.

"A mother needs to be a wife was my impression." Thinking it would do no good to argue with Matteo, he argued anyway. "You could be a cub scout master in a few years." He strangled back the suggestion even of thinking that was ridiculous, and saw, to his astonishment, that Frank was taking it seriously. He was thinking it over. If Mavis was here right now, moving around to get them something like peanuts and cheese, Frank might work into a new role in nothing flat. Arnie wished she was.

"This domestic plan you got for me," Frank Matteo asked. "Is that the price of the island?" He was walking again, back and forth, past the window and returning, in rhythm like a stroll, until in midstride the change occurred—he became one balanced line of animal tension, destructive. A great dancer could achieve that sometimes, and Frank could have been that, Spanish with elastic hips and clacking heels. "Why're you telling me I have to do something? You've been walking around here for months, not doing much of anything."

"It's a free country," said Arnie.

"You've been allowed to enjoy thinking that. Me, I've

personally never seen much that's free about it. There's something to be said when a poor kid like me gets to talk on a level with somebody like you."

"I imagine you'd like it more than level. Making me the poor kid, that would suit you fine."

Matteo at the window, turning. "You think you know something? Let's talk about it."

"I don't know anything," said Arnie Carrington. A gull planed past the window. Just beyond a net mast rocked, in the heavy wake of something they couldn't see, and a few moments later, scattered out and beating against an offshore wind, a small regatta entered the field of vision, and they both came to the window to watch it. "Yacht club stuff," Matteo said, "from down at the Pass." "Who's taking the most orders now? On the new stuff?" "Fraser. And Christovitch for the custom." For a moment, they were Coast men together. A little more time and they might have bet on the outcome. Matteo sank down on a hassock near the window. He had refilled his glass.

"I cannot marry Mavis," he began softly, "because of already having married somebody, a girl a long time ago. Never divorced from her. She was older; I was just a boy. But what is love to pay attention to a small thing like that? I felt so much—to my fingers, even, to the voice I spoke with. Lived with her father. Kept house for him. What was marriage? Something to make her feel okay. Then the father died, by accident. She had found out, and so had he, that some friends of mine might have a kind of influence she didn't like, that she feared. She thought they'd done it, to him . . . the father. Whatever I did, said, her mind stayed fixed; and she was changed forever. I send her money still. After that was Florida, then here. In between, Mavis. She knows all this, I never fooled her. She comes here to beg on your account." The change, swift, had come again, on face, tilt of head, lighting a cigarette, hands cupped around the flame, lips curling with scornful fun. "Now you're here begging on her account. One way or another, you've got to dump that island. It's my advice. You want some more? You go marry Mavis yourself, you want her married. You're still putting them down. There's that nigger girl. And the sexy wife come down about your friend got himself snakebit. I heard you scored."

"It wasn't a snake," said Arnie. "In fact, the speculation was it was something had no business out there."

"Like what?"

"Something might have got brought in there off a boat had no business out there either. Come from afar. Medical research revealed all. Can't beat it."

"What's it prove?"

"Enough, maybe."

They were really silent now, Arnie holding his empty drink on his knee, Frank in silhouette against the wide windows.

"As for Mavis," said Arnie, "maybe I could arrange to go so far as to marry her, provided she would consent, which I doubt. But what would that make me, the father of your son?"

"Son?" The word, like architecture, seemed to have sneaked up on Matteo, and he said it again in exactly the same tone, steady as an echo. There's a melting point in every situation, Arnie believed. He'd almost got one when the regatta passed and with it, like trailing veils, the long thoughts of first love.

What difference if Mavis had been with them, in and out of the kitchen, or reading or sewing in a corner, as was her way, a presence, not listening but not disinterested? Then Frank would not have mentioned his love. Though he might still have grown concentrated and dense, tense as a gambler before a decision to play.

"There might be other items out on that island that ought not to be there, that nobody had a license to bring there."

"For example?"

All grace now, the dancer all but whirled, the voice sibilant as whispers at a distance said, as if to someone else, "I chanced to be in the hospital when your friend was there. We had a talk. Naturally, as he was a friend of yours, I felt concern."

"Concern for Lex Graham!" Arnie couldn't keep from laughing. "He was raving, poor Lex. Didn't know what was coming out. High fever. Broke the thermometer."

"Not when I saw him. I'm telling you."

"What did he say? He doesn't know anything to say."

"There might be something he'd picked up somewhere. Along with what's thought about that doctor friend of yours— the one that left for Florida."

"You're believing gossip. You just said so." But he couldn't have the island watched. Somebody could go there, find out for sure.

"I hope you've got it straight," Frank said. "If you think I'm going soft, you and Mavis—"

"Is it soft," Arnie inquired, "just to be human?"

"I'm a soft guy, and you know it. But what I do, and what I feel about, that's two worlds far apart. You'd take good advice to know it, write it down. I'm set to work against my tendency."

"Why?"

In the long pause while he waited for his answer, Arnie saw the light on the Gulf shift and gather, beat against the wide window in a new way for that summer afternoon, so that when the dark long head came up once more the light seemed to blur the features but to outline the head. Or was it just that Frank's idea was monolithic, a world force, never in debate with its own nature. Finally, Frank spoke one word,

"Business."

His mouth had hardly moved. It was just simple, ordinary. The president of the Rotary Club, any local realtor or banker, might have said the same thing as sufficient answer to end any debate on ethics. But to Carrington that afternoon, poised above the sea, the word seemed to rumble in Mayan mystery from a gigantic head meshed in some jungle-plundered temple. A god was speaking. Smoke drifted from the great stone lips.

However, when gods spoke, did they have to be 100 percent correct? "She had an abortion before, and you hated her for it. She told me so."

The face creased now, white at the cheekbones, and rage was taking it over, an explosion. "I told you, Goddamn it. Told you the whole of it, everything. What I feel is not the thing that I act for. Get it into your head, Carrington. Take it to heart!"

With the quickness of a performer, knowing the show had ended, he suddenly left the room. Carrington heard a door close and, alone, he presently let himself out into the ordinary world, which lay below the long stairs. In the doorway, the speaking grill said his name and he jumped, then looked at it like a person. "We might be close to a deal. Don't you think so?" He had no time to answer. The mechanism clicked off immediately. He would not have known what to say anyway.

"I just hope it's a boy," he couldn't help saying to himself, and began the long descent.

10

And in the June morning, just past eight, taking a shortcut to his street of shops, where the work was now, he passed the property line of a huge motel, its name known to more of the world than any Caesar's had ever been, its importance asserted further by an upended cement slab spelling itself out, and spelling out, too (or, rather, misspelling), the day's menu in seafood and music, the whole construct dominating the beach highway for several miles, drawing to mind some shoddy period of any empire, the cement gritty and dull, the colors of doors and walls oddly mixed, the harlequin curtains, drawn or drawn back within, anything but gay.

Yet passing through the back, not a hundred feet from this monster, he caught his breath, stopping.

A live oak with a seat circling it—as in the olden days; somebody had remembered—stood central to a play area for children, with tiny swings hanging from the limbs, and nearby a little seesaw, painted yellow. A Negro boy was alone there, raking leaves. He was wearing overalls and a dark-checkered shirt. The oak leaves rattled against the wire rake, and just now, moving on to a magnolia tree in the far corner of the plot, the response of the fallen leaves was all according to their nature, some being stiff and dried and brown, and others of the same brown, thick and leathery. The air, still and fresh, was like green silk, and the boy's movement was in tune with all they both—worker and watcher—knew. And not only they but oak and magnolia (both evergreen, shedding leaves in early summer as new growth came), the seat around the oak (how it cut the bark in places), the silent swings and seesaw, and whatever there was of bird or vine or lizard, all in one breath's tremendous knowing, held.

He held on to the fence to extend the moment. Who knows any place like it knows itself? Why would I—why would anyone—be needed here?

In the continuance of the Negro's steady motion, he could himself continue, along his shortcut through two back driveways, two streets, to the street of his own shops, knowing how along the way the smoke rose from the one at the farthest end from the water, that being Barbra K.'s morning fire from that ridiculous little wood cookstove she was fond of (it had seen her through the hurricane and she bore it a personal gratitude), knowing that, in the stillness there before the traffic started, he would be able to hear the *pock* of balls from the tennis courts back of a private club, just rebuilt and raw in itself, but with trumpet vines already thickly dominant in the backstops, and the girls' knees, ruddy with sun, flashing below white shorts, and over all, the Coast breeze, high above. Spirits made their place and place their spirits; who was needed to prove that? Not me.

Yet, as he walked, the major picture in his head was a map: the island, the three small mainland areas—house, street, and hotel property—that were his own, like the holdings of some small seafaring principality, cropping out in orange here and there.

I haven't hurt you any. Say that.

It said nothing.

11

The gang that hung around the Coast that year worried
Frank Matteo more than all the law enforcement officers and
agencies in the entire county. The Punks, some people called
them, though Yates, more original, had named them the Weasels, as they all looked mean and sneaky. "With that name,
they'd make a fine rock group," he said. They worried not
only Frank but everybody else.

Arnie and Yates, coming in from a look at what yachts
were moored in the Broadwater marina, saw from the car
windows how a bunch had gathered like crows on the lovely
slope of lawn near the entrance, and how two, apart, were en-
gaging in some sort of sexual play, to be seen in the shadows
leaping like snakes. Yates snorted with disgust. "God, why
can't they take to the woods?" "They're show-offs about everything," Arnie said. "They'd be glad to sell tickets." "It's
bad enough to see girls in cars at Easter putting out for their
boyfriends in broad daylight. But stuff like that just now
ought to be reported. Talk about rats . . . we should have
saved some arsenic." "People do report it," Arnie said. "In
fact, they've been reported for just about everything."

Sometimes they worked as busboys, parking lot atten-
dants, bartenders in cheap motels. But mainly they loafed and
thought up things to do. Or so it seemed. At lonely spots on
the interstate at twilight, cars were rocked with broken pieces
of brick. Shadowy figures fled away. On the curve of the
Sound, at the farthest point west, somebody set fire to an old
lighthouse, a classic hundred-year-old wooden structure, ap-

parently just to see it burn. Someone broke into the town library at Gulfport, newly rebuilt, tore the fire extinguishers from the wall, and shot fluid all over the books—but he turned out to be a loner, high on pills and booze, just released from juvenile detention, not one of the Weasels. Nothing was ever quite proved. The rector said to Arnie Carrington at church that he would have prayers for another hurricane if he thought it would get rid of this gang.

Frank Matteo called his nephew, Antonio Stallone, into the office at the restaurant and told him all this cheap stunting around had to stop. "It serves no purpose," was what he said. The boy had a way of looking to the side of whatever was going on. He belonged to the sallow part of the family. Even so young, he had hollow cheekbones, a frown, no youthful glow. He didn't smile. He said he thought he was due to have found a job there, with Frank. "I told you before," Matteo said, "I don't go in for music; the place is not set up for that. To say it right out, I don't need you. You want to eat, they'll feed you here. I'll find some work for you, not what you asked for, but a job. Meantime, you're giving me a bad name. I can't take life easy when that happens." The boy's name was Toni, same as Frank's father. One drooping eyelid; that, too, the same.

"Where do they hang out?" Yates pondered. "If we just knew that, we could do something."

Arnie learned of one place anyway. He heard guitar music coming from his own backyard one late evening and walked through the shrubs and trees to the Indian graveyard. There they were, sprawled boldly around a fire, talking, smoking, and laughing like owners, or renters, at the least. He stood there, out from the trees, in plain view, till they raised their heads and hushed.

"Get out of here. I'll give you five minutes."

"You try making us, Pop."

It was the "Pop" that made him mad.

He went back to the house, climbed to the spare room where stuff scavenged from the hurricane still awaited use, and dug out from beneath some dried Oriental carpets, first removing the parrot cage that sat on top of them, a drover's whip, coiled, with a stout hickory handle. Then he went back.

It was the next day he told Yates about it.

They were moving into the shops now, Yates and Mavis, while the students still were working there. Students were wonders if they liked you, and Arnie had never had students who didn't; now Mavis's came—the same. Warm weather made them comrades. They spent Saturday after Saturday there, finishing the insides, even shoring up walls and installing windows in empty frames. Now that the roofing was on, anything seemed possible. Mavis had already started her business. ARTS AND CRAFTS read the sign. QUILTING, KNITTING, MACRAMÉ. WHAT YOU DON'T KNOW, WE'LL TEACH YOU. With people building back everywhere, Arnie guessed she couldn't lose. COLLAGES, PRINTS, AND GRAPHICS. She went around like Old Mother Hubbard, except she was still noticeably young. The flowing Indian dresses suited her role, he guessed, but more than anything else they kept notice away from her changing waistline. When everybody did notice, finally, he wondered if they'd think he or Yates was the father-to-be. Everybody by the time it actually got born would have forgotten that the mother had once been Frank Matteo's Florida girl friend, chic, tanned, and sexy, with her dark flip bob and dangle of gold at the wrist. Transformed and out of mind.

"Myself," said Arnie, "I think the Buddha did it. He sneaked when nobody else was at home. Poor old guy. I bet he misses us."

Yates had already fastened his collection of Coast blow-ups to the wall of his new office. The boy on the steps looked out on a wall of old brick, newly scraped down, finished with new moldings. The high desk was there, with the slanted drawing board and the Lucite rulers, the pencils in their drumlike holders, the stool he perched on, legs wrapped around the spokes. And the telephone had just been installed that morning. There were birds in the few trees left standing outside, and sun in the ruined street, a sense of life accomplishing itself. Then, noise out of quietude, there was a burst of student voices, the rattle of stepladders going up, the smell of fresh paint. Working on Saturday. Flats of bright petunias to set out in an old washpot. New window sashes for Barbra K. Everyone, it was probable, knew her place in the scheme of things, but wondrously nobody seemed to mention it. Perhaps she did not mention it to herself. Her Reuben worked away from there, but she had him at home sometimes. When he left, she would go to the telephone and call. "How is you today, Mr. Arnie?" He was always "Mr. Arnie" on the telephone. Better than "Pop." Arnie had come in from the outside, to think. The Gulf was turning deep-colored with summer, but in the early hours it shone a silky blue, clear as the eyes of good old men, who hold no bitterness, bear no grudge. Goodness of young ones—painting, planting, climbing ladders, setting in window sashes. I'll pick up three dozen hot dogs, he thought. I'll call them all by name. "Sitting over there grinning, like a mule eating briars," Joe Yates remarked, looking over the top of his steel-rimmed readers. "I don't know what you got to grin about." "Wonders," said Arnie. "Life is a wonder." For a moment more, his attention held on no visible thing, eyes fixed on nothing but the invisible thought of this wonder. He felt if he could hold it still a moment longer, none could take it from him—none. And no body, no thing could take it. So did he hold and possess.

At the moment's end, the phone rang.

"Get it, will you?" Joe Yates said, and he did.

The next minute he was bolt upright, phone gripped tightly enough to break it. "What is it! Wait! Hey, calm down!" But she was screaming. Mavis. Yates himself could hear her voice coming wild and inarticulate out of the telephone. Then Arnie was up and moving. "I've got to get on over there. Some kind of mess." He was gone, walking, half running, not bothering with the car. If he cut across backyards and through an alley, he wasn't far. And through a wood, his own, a path through it. He broke from it, and there she was.

At first, stopped stock-still, he could not credit what he saw. She was kneeling, the layers of thin cotton stamped in the exotic, strange prints of India or Pakistan, Taiwan or Burma, fallen around her in an ordered way, as though responsible in shock and grief. The Mexican hemp bucket she fed with, heaved over at her side, spilled out its contents. She was down on one knee, the other crouched but bent, and her hair was fallen forward like a curtain, shielding her face, while the hands to the wrist were buried beneath her hair, holding her face while her shoulders heaved, there in the duck yard between the hutches and the pond.

All around her the ducks were lying, their white astonished necks distended in death. Blood had run into the pond waters. A slaughter. To Arnie, the belief in what he was seeing came slowly. Not till he had run to the enclosure, gotten through the gate, kneeled beside her, cradled her sobwracked body, did he begin to know he had to begin to believe it. That somebody had gotten in there, had caught them in their niceness and innocence, had taken out knives, sharpened for this, had cut their throats. And one or two were left, quacking out their distraught feelings in a far corner, but could not tell what they'd seen.

"Come in the house. You've got to get away from all this."

She'd loved those ducks. Had cared for them from the first. They had been the link in their getting together. ("I've got to go feed the ducks." "Why do you look after them?" "I want to—I've named them all. There's Patsy and Frieda, Gretchen and Margy." "What about Eula? Eula sounds like a duck." He'd said it for a joke, but she'd given one that name.)

I've caused this, he thought, or said. "It's my fault, taking a whip to those damned boys. What's to keep them from killing us all? They've just been practicing on ducks."

But she was crying still. He thought he'd never stop her. Wherever he led her, put her down, chairs or bed or couch, upstairs or down, she went on crying, hair fallen forward, hands to her face, the garments of the East falling with a secret knowledge, like those of a priestess or one of the great Oriental majesties: Shiva, Quan-Yin, one of those. And since she kept on still—sobbing with the monotonous fervor of a devout ritualist, somebody whose devotion, known only to herself, is powerful just in and by itself, never to waver—he thought: By that reasoning, she'll cry forever, till she turns to the salt of her tears. But then he knew.

He knew that though ducks certainly (as an end in themselves) were enough for tears—Patsy, Frieda, Gretchen, Margy, Eula, and all the rest: for love was love, for ducks, for men, for friends, lovers, children, mothers—that when all for love that could be thought of in this case had been said, that still was not it, nor why she was crying so. No, she was crying for all she knew, for everything that had ever walked rough-

shod and without so much as knocking through the private
soul of Mavis Henley. She was crying for herself.

He in no way begrudged her. He had dampened his mustache with a few droplets himself and thought such things as
wishing for the Buddha back. But his caution was going to the
baby—hers and Frank's there inside was in some odd way his
own rabbit's foot, his something to charm the future with.

"We're getting out of here, just for now," he told her several times, pulling gently, finally succeeding in leading her
out, weeping like a fountain. So he brought her to the car. She
let herself be tucked inside, though her Indian robes were getting tear-wet past the waistline, and turning royal purple. He
drove her to the small craft harbor, then telephoned Yates.

"There's been a duck slaughter. Yes, that's what I said.
Pure spite. It's that gang came back and did it. Go ask the
neighbors; maybe somebody saw it. If so, I'll go right to the
police when I'm back. Broad daylight. Make a bundle of
corpses or get somebody to. Leave them in a sack. We'll hold
the funeral when I get back. I've got to be with Mavis."

12

On the boat ride Arnie and Mavis took that day, they both
figured later that she had cried enough to raise the Gulf water
level by two inches, though in that case she would have
swamped the boat.

Someone who saw them go—decorous and almost ceremo-
nial, he with his arm around her, leading her aboard his old
shrimper—thought she must be a person of some advanced

age or uncertain vision or both, and in her long Indian dress, too, and he in his jacket and old yachting cap, perhaps a faithful retainer or secretary or relative. Not even on board did he let her go, but continued to hold his hand on her shoulder, keeping her near him in the pilothouse while he took the boat out and moved at low speed along the shoreline, scarcely half a mile out, decorous as a gondola. He should have raised a black standard: MOURNING.

She was doing just that, she realized, but couldn't stop it, kept telling him, between spasms of sobbing, things she'd already been over with him in the past, like, for instance, why didn't the charming French boy she'd first gotten married to at such an early age (Gerald: pronounced "Jer-al") tell her before he went back to France with his family, they having first taken him out West on a trip, and she still waiting down south of Daytona which he didn't even come to when the family got back to West Palm Beach but only wrote a letter from there (which he mailed later from Paris) describing their marriage only as their "intimacy" (which to him had meant such a lot). Whatever you called it, the family had it annulled. He was underage and had lied about his birth date and the place, too, for that matter, having put Boston instead of Dijon. "Oh, that was a bad thing," Carrington agreed, and noted that they had come a mile up the Coast. He reckoned another mile or so for the second marriage, then back for a long slow turn around the tip of Deer Point for a rundown on Frank Matteo, but all the time he was thinking it would be good for her to get it all cried out and was wondering how it was that animal sacrifice could do so much; at the same time, he too was feeling rather more than a little god-awful about the ducks and would have at the moment cheerfully shot the murderers; that is, if he'd caught them in the act, or even now.

Clifford Henley, she was going on, her first real husband, for she couldn't count the marriage to Gerald as ever having been serious—oh, Clifford had had two children, the first wife had died, he said, but it turned out (he told her the truth before they married) that she had run off with somebody else. Now Mavis had the children to see to, and Clifford, a caterer in Palm Beach, was good at earning money and the nice house was hers to stay in with the children, except she had to stay in it practically all the time, curtains drawn against the glare, all in the Sunshine State, she loved the children but she got bored. Then there was the day of the big blowup with those kids when she burnt her arm in hot fat, a big long painful splash, and when she cried out with pain, the children jumped up and down with yelps of joy and danced around her when she fell down on her way to the telephone. One of them, the boy, tried literally to keep her from the telephone; he had his arms around her waist, pushing her away, and she finally struck him; so when he got deaf in one ear after that, her husband blamed her because the boy said that was why. She tried to get the girl to back her up, but she didn't say anything; she kept saying some silly rhyme and jumping up and down. After that, she sometimes got a girl to baby-sit while she said she'd be at the movies, but instead she went off to find a marriage counselor, anybody to get help from, but a girl friend of hers said, "Go to the fortune-teller first," so she did. The children, who were being good again, promised not to tell Clifford about the baby-sitter, but they did anyway and he turned mean ("relentless mean," she called it); and meantime, the fortune-teller had predicted she'd meet somebody in a restaurant who would ask her to dance and the thing to do was say yes she would, and Clifford Henley took her out to cheer her up he said but only partly that and partly because he was catering a party in a special dining room upstairs in this res-

taurant and had to keep leaving to see about it, and in walked
Frank Matteo—

Arnie had reached the tip of Deer Point, where he cut the
motor and let the old boat nose around at will, drifting; he
knew the depths here. He took her out on deck. "I should
have taken you out to my island," he said. She had stopped
talking, stopped crying, too. She just clung to one of his hands
with one of hers and gripped the rail with the other and
stared at the long, low tongue of land, peninsula rather than
island, at the remains of a picnic fire, the line of low pine trees
marching up out of the sand. Someone fishing saw them
standing there, thoughtful and composed, and judged them
not of this place, strangers.

She stood there looking outward and grew calm. He felt it
when she let his hand go. Calmly, he asked her, "What decided you to come over here after Frank? Did he send for
you?"

"He asked me when he first left, said for me to come, but
I didn't decide till later. It was the hurricane over here got
him out of Florida. He had some business ideas, he said.
Clifford had found out about me seeing him and was mad at
me all the time, cold as ice. Clifford had a book he added me
up in, like one of his catering accounts. It had my name on
the cover. It showed what I'd cost him in dollars and cents, a
bad investment. The day I found it, I packed and kissed the
children goodbye. He asked for a divorce by mail, but by that
time I had a lawyer, and evidence from the baby-sitter, and
the scar from the burn, plus one or two slaps on the jaw he
couldn't deny. I'm waiting for the decree to go through and
maybe some alimony. He'll write it in the book." She gave a
small smile. "Everybody has hard times, I guess."

"There ought to be a limit," he remarked and left to start
the motor, for the boat had scraped on sand. He was just in

time to pull off. She followed him up to the pilothouse and sat down.

"Honey," said Arnie, "you don't have to look for bad luck. It just comes and sits on your lap and purrs."

"About Frank, I knew it wouldn't be any marriage. He always said that. He told me he was already married, but I could come along with him and work wherever he was. I worked. A kindergarten in Mobile, a receptionist in Pascagoula, the school here. It's just that I thought it would have to always be constant with Frank because of how I felt. I thought he'd be bound to see things my way, as being the only way he could see them."

"You found out there were other ways."

"I did," she said, "but I still don't understand what they are. Or even why they are."

"Just that they are."

"That's right."

She was laughing now and combing her hair, sweeping it back, twisting it with expert fingers, shaking herself together, phoenixing up out of her ashes there in the pilothouse with the old motor chugging away to keep them just clear of shoals until they hit the channel, with sunset lighting up a sky made lurid by a dark cloud to the southeast, out toward Florida. "A good girl." He reached to stroke her hair. "A little on the dumb side, let's admit." He pulled her hair down with his fingers so that she dodged away to put it up again, smiling and scratching around for powder and lipstick in her bag.

"Life is better for me than it was."

"An unwed mother," he cautioned.

"Even so."

"How can you say that, honey?"

"Because of you. You care. That's what it is about you. Caring."

Saying that, she threw her arms around him, a girlish moment, daughterly, and he asked himself if somewhere along in a myriad career—that long road stretching backward over hill and river to his misty origin—he had ever had a daughter, but no, he didn't believe he ever had. "You know, doll," he said, laughing, disengaging her gently, "I'm just an old sinner. No great guy. Maybe caring is all I can really do."

They docked at last after dark, and he helped her ashore in her bedraggled robes, a princess long at sea. A couple passing through, seeing them, thought she might have been saved from a shipwreck, boat from some exotic port, for the cloud had taken half the sky, and was purple as her dress in the sun's last ray.

Back at the house, the good Yates had cleared away the carnage and, with neither Buddha nor Oriental ducks to companion them, they felt rawly exposed when wind struck the shore and a wild peppering of hail belted against the windows. They found themselves locking the doors, turning on small lamps only, building a fire, the temperature having suddenly dropped. "Hail after sundown," Arnie grumbled. "There's no such thing."

Mavis went out to seek the two remaining ducks. She found them huddled in a distant corner, on wet ground starred with hail pellets; their wide feet were cold against her flesh. She appeared at the door with one under each arm. Arnie laughed because they looked so puzzled, though survival was hardly funny.

"It's Lena and Olga," Mavis said.

He had found smudges of blood all along the wall when he went in the kitchen for drinks. He stopped getting out ice, put the tray down, and went upstairs. Door by door, he checked the rooms, but no one lurked there. Had they come inside, then, and left? If so, why? Had Barbra K. come in

looking for him and cut her hand some way? Mavis herself
. . . but he did not ask her. In the kitchen drawer, the knives
lay quietly in their case, looking somewhat cleaner (or so he
imagined).

When he finally came back with their drinks and sat with
her before the fire, his feeling was more than ever that of wil-
derness and distance, of being on this shore not now but two
hundred years ago, and of some strange girl like this, half-
wild with injury, he might have met there. "That stupid
gang," Matteo called them; "The Weasels," Yates's name. His
mind turned to them now, and also, surprising him, his heart,
in all its sudden generosity. He had seen their faces when the
whip fell. What fire did they sit by, defiant maybe, but also
lonely, and afraid?

13

The next morning, as if to reward him a little, blessings
stuffed in a bottle, pearl-laden shells pitched up on the shore,
two letters arrived, both with money in them. One was from
Kelly, containing a check for five thousand dollars. "Heard
you were having it tough. Hang in there. Hopefully, this will
un-bottleneck you." That sentence on an English theme would
fail him, thought Arnie, and clasped the check like a lifeline.
The Florida army buddy wrote, offering to sell him stock in a
citrus fruit plantation, bound to double in four months, maybe
less. In another sheet, a check was folded. "Maybe a little
hype like this is all you need for now." Five thousand. A good
round sum, easy to pick out of a hat if you were just wondering what to send.

He felt suddenly exhausted. He called to Mavis, but she had gone home. He thought of calling Yates, but instead he did nothing. He walked to the empty places of his property, the spot where the Buddha had stood now greening over with grass, the quiet empty hutches, like Pompeiian ruins, and the silent pond in shape of a comma, where a feather or two still floated, the bare earth still marked with the blood that had soaked it, and he walked past, toward the Indian graveyard.

There at the edge of the farther line of woods, property line of a large house on another street, an Indian was standing. This was often the case. Their contract gave them the right to come there and look upon the burying ground of their Notchaki ancestors, so they would just come and stand there, look for a while, and go away. Once they came in numbers— about thirty—and did a ceremony of some sort, by moonlight. Arnie almost went to the Indian to explain what the remains of a fire were doing there at the center, but he didn't for an odd reason: hands close on the two letters with their sustenance inside, and pulses of the fingers beating against the paper which had witnessed to him that cries are answered from out the human rush, he felt overwhelmed with a great drowsiness, a singular heaviness like a spell, as though he had wandered into thick mist or the smoke of sacred fires. But I just slept; I just woke up. He started back toward the house. Maybe the tiredness he felt extended backward through the many strains and tensions his generation had endured, all the way back to Pearl Harbor and the monotony of radios, reiterated shock news on a Sunday morning in December—opening gun of the American Age. Upstairs, he reached his bed and fell across it, closed his eyes with the leathery lids of a hibernating bear. Never to wake again . . . so ran his dazed unregretful thought, hands still clutching the letters.

14

It was when Mavis got back home and was alone that she got frightened. Before, she had had company for her anguish. The one thing she had loved with any success—the flock of ducks. Who had wanted to take it away? The gods—she had heard Arnie refer to them from time to time. "They kill us for their sport," he had once exclaimed when he hit his thumb with a hammer. He would say that, rather than "Goddamn." But if not gods, demons? Entered into those boys, that gang? Wifely in her feelings, she wanted to run to Frank. Motherly, she had worried that the shock might hurt the child. And that had been in Arnie's mind, too, when he took her in the boat to let her wail and cry. The thought of demons brought back the dancing stepchildren: some demons must have gotten into them. True, the ducks had been originally raised for slaughter by an oil company to test their livers or something, but Arnie had let her keep the flock on when the contract expired. She had liked so much the musty smell of their stiff feathers, the more meditative tone of their quacks. The ways they asserted the pressure of their orange feet in walking thrilled her, those same feet which had lain to one side, limp as large leaves struck down by rain. The wanting to cry about it all to Frank grew too terrible to bear.

She wasn't nearly so dumb as people might say. She knew well enough that Frank might be into things involving slaughters worse than those of ducks, but she had never seen it proved before her eyes. She wanted to measure Frank by the same rule as Arnie or Joe Yates, doing organized, practical things to get to certain goals. There was danger in what he dealt with—that's all she knew. But Arnie had never been in any danger, though by not selling the island he proved he wouldn't play ball. Frank ought to know what had happened; who else could order those boys around? She spent a sleepless night, resolving not to call him, for she had sworn herself to nothing less than that.

In the morning, she picked up the phone.

It had honestly gotten to where getting to see Frank Matteo was like getting an appointment with the governor or the President or, if this was Italy, the Pope. An audience. You could call it that. It had started with that purple car he drove, then when the secret apartment went up over the restaurant, with its lookout like a crow's nest on a boat, and its fancy electric-eye way of getting in—from then on, it had seemed like he was everybody's ruler. As long as the Buddha was at Arnie's house, she didn't hesitate to think that Arnie was the top cat of the whole area, but now that it was gone she wasn't sure, and when the duck slaughter occurred, she knew within herself that Arnie wouldn't really do anything about it. Since he'd whipped those boys with a cattle whip, now he'd have to do worse than that. But nobody had actually seen them, he told her. Somebody had once long ago poisoned an Alsatian he had; could he do anything about it? "But you always have a pretty good idea who's done something like that," she pointed out. "Yes, but even if you do, what's there to do? Are you going to stage a fistfight, challenge them to a duel, complain to the police, sue? Anything you do, the guy just thinks of something else, like setting the house on fire, or slashing your tires." So that, she knew, would be all.

All. And she came near to rage. It was mixed in with her feelings about the child, she knew that—the lost child, and this child she carried, who, fatherless to date, was going to be lost, too, in a sense. But knowing all this did not keep her rage away from those boys. She could have killed those boys herself.

"You have a pretty good idea who's done it, don't you?" she asked Frank. "In fact, you know, don't you?" Obsessed, she had simply gone there and climbed up the sacred stairs, when he wouldn't be gotten to the phone. Dancey had told her: "Mr. Frank ain't taking no calls today." To hell with Dancey. She'd probably find him with that girl who served drinks down in the game room, but there was nothing in the apartment to say she'd even been there, not even a whiff of perfume. Frank was alone, and let her in.

"Of course I know who did it," his anger becoming, just for the moment, like hers, tight and irrational, till he cooled it. But not before she'd seen. What she saw was that they were, all at once, together: she, as though she'd never been away in other places with anyone else, teaching, opening a handicraft and sewing shop. And he, as though the wide swing of his life could be summed up in a traveling man's answer: Away on business. Just for an instant, she had seen that now he was home.

"Things like that will keep on happening," she said, and buried her face in her hands until he pulled them away.

"You've got to cut all that out. There's nothing I can do about ducks. It's just that gang doing anything they get damn good and ready to, that's what I can't accept. They know who's running things, but they fly in the face."

"Running things?" she echoed. She'd never heard him admit it.

"Whoever runs things, it's not them," he amended, absentmindedly. "They know it's not." He was pacing now, one side of the room to the next. What could he afford? To act might be too much. Not to act might be to let too much get by

him. And he was circling, too, as though she, sitting on a hassock with Indian robes spread out around her, might be a
mooring point. "What do you do in school," he asked her,
"when kids start acting up?"

"Those kids *were* in school, some of them! They were
stealing supplies before anybody knew it. Things just
vanished. They raided the school cafeteria once too often and
the principal ran them out. First, he had a talk with them."

He stopped moving, looked afraid of what he couldn't do
well, but had to try. "The same ones?" He disliked having to
ask.

"Well, that nephew of yours. . . ." She didn't go on because of the waves of anger that were coming on, out of his
direct gaze. "You, why should you bother with it? Ducks,
school supplies, worry in the community. All that's nothing to
you." And a woman having your child, she wanted to rush on
and say: Why let that worry you, you're above everything;
but she didn't want to say that, she'd grit her teeth and die
before she came out with it; besides, she saw that she was
worrying him anyway. A shadow alignment appeared across
his face, shaping it for a future she didn't want him ever to
get to. Mavis saw what ought to be changed about life; she
just didn't know, ever, how to work it.

"Carrington," said Frank. "What's he doing? Ass-sitting,
like that statue he used to have? Look, I'll show you something." He unwrapped the box carefully. It was a wooden box,
either from India or the East Indies, carved with a serpent
pattern across the lid, such as one might buy in a bazaar and
use to put trinkets or scarves in. With a penknife and cautious
fingers, he lifted out the false bottom. The jewels lay below it:
three emeralds, six rubies, the rest sapphires; and in the center
the settings, a necklace still sparkling with a crust of diamonds, and two pendant diamond-covered earrings, but the

central stones were pulled out, like drawn teeth. She wondered why they'd done that.

He knelt to let her see; wondering that trusting each other
was what they both were doing, yet knowing (at least, she
consciously knew) that trust was there. How could anything
good come out of what she knew was stolen goods? In other
words, if I got married with one of those diamonds, would I
be less married? "I wasn't supposed to open it," he said.
"They're staying here, in my safe, till late summer. I couldn't
let anything cool that long on the premises without knowing
what it was. Then to New Orleans and up the river. Nobody
has told me enough. The worst of it's thinking: Who's after
them? Why send them through an off-route like this?"

He began to fit the box back together and, just before he
put the slotted pieces of wood in place over them, they all
flashed together, like the tomb of some fabulous ruler being
closed up again. They burned against her eyes for a moment.
He snapped the box shut and kissed her gently. She never
knew him to be in quite such a mood and wondered what it
was—it wasn't cheap, she decided, but had quality to it; this
kind of word she'd learned from Carrington.

15

For three days after the checks came, Arnie did nothing but
sleep. He descended into mysterious depths, drifted through
the feathery silt on the sea floor of all things, dim lights far
above, soundless, timeless. He woke on the third day, full of
sharp certainties, decisive. Where have I been? he wondered
while shaving.

Unable quite to recall, he turned on the Ansafone and asked the question into the recorder, "Where have I been?" "Well, not to the island," he knew Evelyn was telling him—he had made contact with her right away. Why not to the island? he wondered. Did Matteo spoil it?

While putting up the straight razor he always used, clearing the basin, it slowly came to him: an island here was where he'd spent his time, and he saw the vine once more spread live and green as a great benign lizard against the screen of Barbra K.'s room where the dark smell of her flesh was spread as evenly as butter. New Orleans music murmured from the record player. Another one, a white singer, crooned that "Love Is Blue." But it wasn't, he was here to testify: its color was milky brown. He should have gone through a chameleon change. He wondered at the whiteness of his arm.

He puzzled about Evelyn—she was making him think all this: think of Barbra K. Color was a trick, *trompe-l'oeil*. Black and white together, they had brought his island to the mainland, led by a scarlet cord. They got along together. Oh, joyous thought, when women got along.

As for his long suspended sleep, there was life in the deepest sea tomb, after all. He went through humble, beautiful morning rites, bath finished and breakfast next, but before that, without debate, he was telephoning, finding wires and switches usually so devious letting him right in to Frank Matteo, who answered at once.

"I'm selling you the island," he told him. "I'll come up this afternoon."

Frank said that the afternoon was gone; it was six o'clock already.

"Then I'll come up in the morning," said Arnie, and went to get some breakfast for a new beginning.

part IV

1

Lex Graham had become what he had never envisioned when he bought the Mercedes—a driver merely, always behind the wheel. If it wasn't driving Dorothy to New Orleans, first to shop, then just for a good meal, a good time, to break her depressions, then, when these turned into flat failures, to appointments with psychiatrists; if it wasn't any of that, it was taking Lucinda up to the select Virginia college he had enrolled her in to get her out of the way of her mother. More, unthinkably. If there was a day world, there was a night world, too. He had to be ready for its events and eruptions at any dark hour, instant in starting up at the ring of the telephone to hear a strange voice saying, " 'Fessor Graham? Better come get your wife. We don't want no trouble in this place." A roadhouse or some motel bar, a disco joint in another town—the places would be something like that. Once he drove all the way to the outskirts of Jackson to a barnlike club where a strip show nightly held a clapping crowd—she had been recognized by a colleague who telephoned him—and he reached her, took her out, just before a raid. By rights and common sense, he should have taken away her car, since she

was always keeping him in his, to find her. But he didn't, and
he didn't watch her closely either, and he sat and wondered at
himself, in the wee hours while she slept things off, who
would soon awaken and give him a long explanation he would
pretend to believe, or at least never challenge, about how a
couple they had met at the last Sugar Bowl game had rung up
to ask her to meet them at this unlikely spot and then they
weren't there or had had to leave soon after she arrived and
she had stayed on for one extra drink was all, and what was
wrong with that and why was he so worried? He was developing a rare thing: the philosophic mind. He could wonder at
himself. She was trying to provoke him, surely, but to what?
To leaving her, beating her, to discovering some torrential
hurricane of passion for her pleasure and satisfaction: she
should know by now they would never find what wasn't there,
she was fishing in an empty pond. Still he would reach out to
her, thinking that trying might make the difference, only to
see her recoil, so violently once he could almost see her re-
treating through a wall, leaving a hole in it, the shocked
fleeing outline of herself. They had a negative of a marriage:
black, white, and smoky gray. But was that something? It
wasn't nothing: all the answer he could give, because he
didn't know anything. She kept changing. Like a moon hur-
tling around some distant planet, she seemed to go through
forty phases in a single orbit. Finally, he would get in the car
and drive to find Rosie, a waitress he knew in another town.
She was like a dozen others in his life, stemming directly from
the librarian in the Yankee university, only sweeter-tempered
—he was careful about that. He rather liked her; she had a
plain mind, said what she thought. He also usually liked the
people who called to say he should come and get Dorothy;
they knew not to talk, had a feeling for being decent about
things.

Also, he now and then talked to Lucinda, who knew a good bit more, it turned out, than he did. She had known about the graduate student—who kept a fishing shack down on a bayou where he did what he wanted to: smoking pot (yes), women (yes), even fishing (that, too). He had been one of Carrington's Boys, a dark Indian-looking guy, with curious light eyes, and an odd name, Cottrell—not a bit friendly. Dorothy had driven him home once as a favor, that much was known—what happened later could be guessed. She still drove out there, from time to time, and once when he could find her nowhere for all of a long night and no call came to summon him, Lucinda told him out and out and he went down to that camp, over twisting little roads, some soggy and many only two matching tracks with weeds grown up between, but not finding any sign of her at the camp, he wandered more and by moonlight along a wet green road, saw her little car, pale and silvery blue as a fish, parked by a young tree, and she farther on, wandering around the fallen-down ruin of a paintless old house, in the garden, which was blooming for spring in wild weeds and also shrubs like canna lilies, climbing roses, wisteria, and bridal wreath. Fragrance in the spring night, and she like a ghostly bride, or chatelaine lost without her household, returned to check the linens, count the silver. He called to her. When she saw him, she began to cry. "Lex!" Unbelievably, she came through the fallen gate. They put arms tenderly around each other, kissed. Her hair was dew-wet. The kisses were for that boy, he thought, but how amazingly they returned to those of their first dates together, the great before. But he took her kisses anyway, along with the stale bourbon breath, because she did know him, and had been (literally) lost without him.

Back at home, it never happened.

They would never move to the house on the Coast; he

had known that for some time—precisely, from the day they drove him home from the hospital, his leg distended on the silken-soft leather of the back seat of the Mercedes (Lucinda driving), and Dorothy following in the little car. And how when they stopped for gas on the highway just outside a town called Pegues (one dusty stoplight swaying equidistant from four identical corners, Lex recalled, accurately: he had once known a beauty parlor operator there), Lucinda had gone twice to look at the highway, once when the gas tank was being filled, and again after they had paid. Returning, she had said: "Daddy, Mother's not back there," flat, a statement like reading him something out of the paper, and right then, the way it streaked through him, meeting no resistance, he knew he had expected this word all along, that he had, in fact, known it already. The house was over, he plainly thought—a whisper, quickly rejected, easy to unhear. But can you unthink Eden?

She came home finally, though delayed some hours, and saying nothing about why. They talked about the Coast house as though it waited for them—white, beautiful, remote, with magical survival powers, even its waiting was courteous. Searching something, he went into the guest bedroom which Dorothy used at times as a household office, keeping accounts there and paying checks. He opened a closet door. Ten empty gin bottles were there, in grocery carry-sacks. She threw them away at the town dump, he supposed, or in some innocent neighbor's garbage. So the house would never be, he thought again.

He went down and looked over all his eighteenth-century belles; they were buxom, cheerful, and younger than ever. Forever wilt thou love and they be fair. Whether he moved them or not, they would look just the same, the blue ribbons would still be blue, the King Charles spaniels' ears just as silky, the hands, the alabaster brows, all just the same. "The house is over," he said to them. They continued to smile.

Lucinda spoke of the Coast as something they were still going to do. Once, when Dorothy did not return for dinner, she said to him at the lonely table, "I think she might be better on the Coast. It's the air; it's always smelling new. That day in the lighthouse—" She stopped.

Lex's heart stopped.

And now to know that, too.

For he had thought it over, not thought—but seen it pass many times like a clip from a movie, just that, not starting anywhere but simply existing in motion from the edge of his hospital window and forward across the wide lens of its rectangle, past the middle of which he had seen them both vanish into the lighthouse and, doubting his own vision, had never thought anything but that he really hadn't seen them; if anybody had a right and reason to hallucinate, he did. So when he asked the nurse, "Who was that out there? Out on that lawn?" and she had said, "Nobody that I see," he had believed her. But then, by then, they were gone.

"So what happened in the lighthouse?" he lightly asked his daughter, now that she mentioned it, speaking as though it were nothing important. Because he knew that, if he asked as though it were serious, earthshaking, and hitting close to home, he would never get a straight answer. So he kept his head, though his heart was jumping around, once it started beating again, like a limb in a crazy storm, torn every which way at once, and saw her blush scarlet without seeming to see him, and now remembered what he had heretofore put aside, that she didn't mention being "born again," or do so much Jesus talk as before. He must talk to Dorothy about this last, if she was sober at all, when she got home. They had worried about Lucinda's getting too religious, as if she had a nervous habit, a physical defect—too much body hair, or a need for braces.

Lucinda got up, went to the kitchen counter for more coffee (not like her), came back hesitantly: "Oh, nothing. It was just a walk with Dr. Carrington when you were in the hospital." Pause. Then outburst. "We talked! All kinds of things. It was such a lot of fun, like we'd been friends forever. Then we were walking, talking, laughing, all at once together. I don't exactly know what happened. It felt like floating. And all of a sudden, he—"

"He what?" Lex casually prompted and stared out the window.

"He opened the lighthouse door, and there we were . . . inside."

She stopped, just stopped. And now his heart had started its descent, down the elevator that had no stopping place—there wasn't any ground floor, the basement was forever.

"And then?" he managed to inquire, lightly.

"Oh, nothing. It was cool inside. I remember that."

"So what happened?"

"Nothing. He just made me feel—"

"Feel what?"

"I can't explain it."

"Touching, kissing maybe, saying . . . ?"

She looked away, then back, bit her lip. He felt seasick. She raised her eyes to him, the father—an old look. "It was all right," she insisted. "It was all okay!"

Lex touched his face and found it cold, got up but could not go, sat down.

"Oh, Daddy! What's it all about? It's not about anything —he's so much older!"

"I know, but you love him."

"What if I do . . . what if I did?" He was finally going out, her vexed cry followed him.

So they were never to move there or anywhere near. He called his lawyer that very day to say that he had changed his mind about the Coast property. The house, definitely, was over.

2

Still in the Mercedes, the perpetual wandering planet, he drove there once more, to the house that they had meant to buy. He went up the curved driveway, he sat before it in his glistening beige car. He let all feeling in. He thought of his dream self moving within it, the rooms all decorated, upholstered, furnished, painted, tiled, with framed oil paintings, watercolors, hunting prints from England, engravings: the Mall, Piccadilly, Regent's Park, and in the den between the windows, a huge Piranesi, "The Arch of Constantine," some thing like that, suggesting triumph. Fragonard and Boucher for boudoir and dressing room—his ladies filed away in basement quiet, as before. (Maybe he would give them up. For he was fated perhaps to become a tender and successful lover in this place.)

And gently at twilight, as he would sit reading a new literary journal on one of the comfortable white lounge chairs in the glassed-in sun-room which looked out on the garden, with its camellias, azaleas, birdbath fountain, rock garden, and flagstone walks, Dorothy—gentle, sober, and smiling—would come shyly fresh from her bath in a loose printed robe, sit near him on a hassock, lay her head gently on his knee. Not looking up from his reading, he would caress her hair while from the kitchen in the other wing, the chatter of Lucinda with her young friends, just in from sailing or tennis, would come wafting for a comfortable moment, then fade away. Thousands had this, or something like it. He had not come into billions, was no Vanderbilt or Rockefeller . . . only well off for a change. So what was wrong he couldn't have what he dreamed of? All they had come to was a glimpse of an ordinary American paradise. Then it had been denied him. Who had done it? What had worked against him? The name was there, everywhere, he gripped the wheel till his knuckles turned white, squinted through tear-glazed eyes at the white unobtainable vision. "Mrs. Graham will have to continue therapy indefinitely, perhaps for the rest of her life . . . long periods away from home, for observation . . . few responsibilities." The sun was strong that day, waxing, as hot as it would seem in more powerful July. Things are not given to me, he thought, and a sob overtook him, but turned into a dry cough. In a wavering glaze, he saw a blue corona of light appear behind the house, a halo drawn around it, across which the ridgepole of the apron roof rested as straight as a dissecting line.

She might have been all right . . . if only.

The corona, as he watched it, pulsed once. He rubbed across his eyes, blinked, looked again. It had vanished. But it had all but said the name, possibly aloud: Carrington.

Dorothy had met Carrington, of course, that last night on the Coast; he had known it all along. He was in the hospital, she out in the night as wild as a vixen, brush tossing, in heat under a full moon. She even told him about it finally, outright, late one night—why she had vanished from them on the highway coming home. It was Carrington first and somebody else to follow up with, and he saying, "Hush, you'll wake Lucinda. Hush, not now." And she, "Then when? Is there a good time? Make an appointment for me. Write it down."

Well, all done now. New buyers found, papers signed, earnest money partially reimbursed. Write off the rest . . . from the meaning of it, there is no adequate release. But he would feel harmony, not despair. So ran his resolve.

He eased forward onto the highway. The day rang clear and strong with sun, fresh as polished glass.

At a turning between the two halves of the divided highway, the car's front wheel dipped into a long troughlike rut, filled with water, a drainage pipe leaking, perhaps. He accelerated to miss it, almost rammed a passing truck whose driver shouted at him and, swerving with a clatter, drove on. He wound up in the opposite lane, paused in a parking bay, on the seawall, hands trembling on the wheel. But he would be all right in a minute. Then he felt calm. He got out to wipe a splash of dirty water from the winged curve of one enameled fender. Then he re-entered the factory-bright haven, the discreet clunk of one door closing behind him, the smell of leather as enveloping as incense.

Calm, bright, harmonious, he would not return to despair. . . .

Ordering a harmonious meal in a restaurant whose split-level elevation, swelling outward like a ship's lounge, overlooked the water. A man who looked familiar, who walked with the air of a proprietor, came to his table. "Everything all right, Mr. Graham?" "You're from Carrington," Lex said at once. "No. Wait. Against Carrington. But still, in a way, from him. It's the same."

The reply was a laugh—defensive? professional? "Glad to see you well again."

"You must remember. He killed his wife. You told me that. Then got blackmailed by a doctor."

"Fever like you had—gives you some bad dream." He moved as smoothly as a machine might have, resuming with a usual smile the normal task, the average speed. The exchange had not occurred.

Later, Lex checked on the existence of the hospital and, having parked there, walked to the lighthouse. The door to it was locked, set mysteriously deep and slanting, fitted into a slanted wall. My baby went in there, he thought, and shuddered. Six feet through or maybe eight, to the other side, it might as well have been the earth's deepest, darkest castle. Bluebeard. He could hear the door shut with a soft almost animal cry to its iron hinges; the cool within such a small enclosure might still hold something of herself: a little fallen comb. His head throbbed; he went back to his car in the net of a cast spell.

Down street by shady street, Notchaki unfolded itself to Lex Graham. On one he spied a row of small houses like stores lined up in back of a giant spreading oak. The storm had tilted this tree, but had not brought it down. Its roots were holding, though on one side exposed. There he saw the people who were working, students mainly, up on ladders, mixing paint, carrying freshly framed windows; he heard the bang of hammers, the grate of a saw. He thought of Breughel, motion and distance. Arnie Carrington was out there, of course, holding the foot of a tall extension ladder where a boy was mounting (he recalled the water tower) and there on the porch, setting out a basket full of plants in a long box, was a woman he had seen before: the day of the island trip, she had brought sandwiches to the boat. He had the sense of a busy, oblivious happiness here and knew he had to hurry on, though certainly forever invisible to their eyes, another order.

He had one more errand. The bronze smile he once had seen: he needed it. He would let its harmony meet his own in one quick Oriental look, enough to last. So he came to the scavenged house.

The yard was still the same, though thick now with summer growth, and through it, the flagstone walk still wound whitely past the stone Great Danes and the urns to the front door. He came to the backyard, parked, and walked past the corner of the house, but the Buddha was gone. There was only a bare spot in the earth. Even its platform had been taken away.

Without purpose for a moment, he leaned against the fence and looked at the ducks. Everything was still. A man came silently out of the path that led through some thick growth around the clump of pines. He had a broad face with jet-black hair irregularly cut, and mahogany-colored skin. He wore a cheap tweed coat and jeans, and Lex realized he was an Indian. He would have known he was an Indian even if he had never seen an Indian, known the way Americans always know Indians, by some imprint taken long ago. The Indian said nothing. Lex said hello. He wanted to be answered but was not. The Indian walked past as though he did not exist. He leaned his head against the fence. The absence of the Indian was terrible to experience. Nothing was ever fair.

Across their compound, the white ducks had huddled together in a far corner. Their beaks were turned on him and their eyes as well. Emerging behind one commonly understood as leader, they now stepped forward on yellow feet, straight along a line that could be drawn from them to him, and as they slowly came they began to quack. They were solemn, ludicrous, and, it would seem, relentless. The quacking rose above their solemn processional chant.

He was alone with a flock of ducks.

He was alone with a hostile flock of white ducks.

He was alone in an uncaring universe with a hostile flock of white ducks.

3

The two checks for five thousand dollars which Carrington had received went as quickly into the bloodstream of his debt as two slugs of bourbon into an alcoholic's. It helped only in that it put a new complexion on things. During summer holidays at the school, he went back to work on his Byron book. Some new publications had arrived at the library by special order from the Library of Congress. They had to be looked into. He had gotten Byron as far as Albania on his way to Greece. He fell to thinking of Albania, a country, a name that had vanished from the earth. No one any longer mentioned it. It was, he supposed, lost. Yet it had been there, a European country, with kings and dukes and princesses, somewhat exotic, backward, maybe, but people did arrive to visit and fell in love and others moved there to live, learn the language, meet the nobility, gossip about the royal family. Carrington quartered himself upstairs with mountains of manuscript, stacks of notes, ranks of books.

The room where he worked was a bare study—desk, chair, and lamp at the far left corner: it looked out one window toward the Gulf. His tower. Property was the farthest thing from his mind.

So it was when his son Kelly showed up from Houston. Arnie scarcely seemed to notice. Yet the house had filled up suddenly, and so had his heart. "What do you know about Albania?" he called downstairs. "I was once in Turkey," Kelly sang helpfully back.

Helpful in other ways, Kelly exploited old acquaintances, spread himself about, sold four lots for his father in three days. He got somebody to remove all the rubble from the old hotel foundation in exchange for the bricks, also to grade it, roll it, plant grass, and set out shrubs.

After dinner on the fourth night, they talked till late, drinking red wine in the living room, and the truth came out: Kelly was bankrupt. The chemical processes which his partner was using to make paper from oil by-products did not pass required government standards and certain harmful effects were not, without additional equipment, some not yet patented, removable. For example, one stationery sample was shown to contain formaldehyde, poisonous when swallowed. "But who wants to eat it?" Arnie asked. "Some people might; it takes all kinds." On conclusion of the business, Kelly collected a portion of his capital (actually, he had more cash than he'd ever had before) and so had given his father five thousand dollars. This drop in the bucket brought teardrops to fatherly eyes and he refrained from asking too many questions. No doubt they could have been answered promptly. Kelly was always, indefatigably, plausible. Muzzy-headed from the wine, they found appropriate gear—the torches, nets, and spears—and went floundering at two A.M., wading calf-deep in the Gulf glowing under full moonlight.

The next morning near the city hall, Arnie ran into Yates. "I am convinced," he said, "that Mattco is nowhere near any central position in any crime outfit." "That's what I've been trying to say," said Yates, "and so has Mavis, and so has everybody." "Including Frank himself," said Arnie. "Sure," said Yates, "Frank, too." "I have got to stay afloat somehow," said

Arnie. "They use the island anyway," said Yates. "We know that already." They had this exchange in passing.

Kelly gave some thought to moving to the Coast to set up a boat supplies and rental business. He could, in the beginning, till a place near the water opened up, take over one of Arnie's little shops. He had met and liked Mavis, now comfortably running her art and sewing business in one, and had shaken hands, at least, with Joe Yates, whose architect's address was now the one next door. And in passing he had even seen Barbra K., a pleasant black who baby-sat. The oak tree itself, tilted by the storm, belonged, he was told, to an association of live oaks, to whom Arnie was appealing for aid to put it upright. Given half a chance, it would be in its old position once more. Arnie said he would think about the boat supplies business; so should Kelly think about it. Then he went back to Byron. When he left him, it was to walk alone along the beach. Someone was sitting on a bench near a small marina.

Her head was turned, but he knew her at once: Evelyn.

He sat down quietly beside her. She did not turn her head but continued to look out to sea. She once said: "There is nothing else you can look out on but the sea. Mountains stop you, plains wear you out—they're tiresome as deserts—but not the sea."

The saucer-cut hair, like a thick pelt set down on her crown, ruffled slightly in the wind. There in profile was the definite strong nose, the full mouth. She had gotten a bit heavier, that was all. Ought to diet.

"What was Byron doing counting on the Albanians? For helping out with the Greeks."

"You've forgotten the countess," she said.

"But that was long ago, when he was just a boy, taking the Grand Tour."

"What's that matter? All the more reason."

"You might have something."

"Take it from me." Then, "Kelly—" she began, and stopped.

So by a marina, that's why. His heart twinged. If she came back at all, it would be about Kelly. Childless, she had loved that boy. But then she would say, if asked, that she was always around for Arnie. That was true. Only he didn't often see her so plainly.

He kept his gaze religiously outward, but finally he dared at last, unable to stand it, to turn, creakily, like somebody with a crick in his neck. No one was beside him.

He turned all the way around then and saw a large woman in white slacks and a slick yellow raincoat, billowed out in the wind, moving toward the seawall. What had he been about to say? Had somebody bothered her grave?

He kept on talking rapidly, in his head. I've made sure you're okay. Frank never asked for details, just promised. I was crazy the night I took you there. Snatched you from the coffin at the funeral home. I couldn't stand them, would have wiped them out in another five minutes. All that fuss and bother. "The Great Funeral Home Massacre." Swiggart got me out of it; said I'd decided on cremation. Oh, what a help he was! He even found somebody's body to cremate. You had liked him . . . Swiggart. You said, "Funny names don't matter." He had been a hero of the Coast, a rescuer, a catcher in the rye, provided what you mean by "rye" is a charcoal-black sky pouring out a hundred-and-fifty-mile-an-hour wind with tornadoes whirling in and out like a mad chorus line. Swiggart had been out in all that—fearless. Finding here a stranded couple, there a stray dog, once a toddler in coveralls snatched from his mother's arms by wind and blown along like a tumbleweed. Oh, Swiggart was a hero. He would do anything, even ferry a stout dead woman (granted, the cancer had already shaved off thirty pounds) out to an island, dig down six feet by the dark of the moon, you wrapped around with sail-cloth, planks of driftwood for a coffin, ease you down. Me—I was possessed, doing the work of five, of ten. I've seen dogs like that, snarling even at some beloved master from over the carcass of a rabbit—what you kill is double-times your own. And so madness; no limit but the sky, the earth being mine. How else but madness for measuring up to what the gods do to you? It was just another kind of caring. Caring, don't you know? That's all.

So about Matteo, tell me quick. Was it right to deal with a crook? How could it ever be right? I've thought it over too long.

She had come back, one way or another, to answer. "Isn't he worth the chance?" Was a question an answer? He felt bet-ter just the same.

4

"And the next thing is . . ." said Frank Matteo these days, with the deed to an island stuffed casually in his pocket. He swung the combination often on his own secret-door entrance to the windowless black-lined gambling room, where bald heads and gray and brown bent, sometimes in ten-hour mara-thons of unbroken attention, above a table cluttered with chips and cards. And through another door the click of rou-lette and the call of cards forever turning. The girl who served drinks in the early evening was a special friend, whose shift included a visit upstairs, after hours. He tallied up the number of times on a bridge scoring pad while tucking in his shirt. Her bonuses were regular; she seldom conversed. He had asked her up more often recently (though he hadn't noticed it so much until she actually spoke up: "Jesus, I'm turning out bowlegged" was what she said). The reason was that something was bugging him, in spite of the island he had finally talked Carrington into parting with. Something was bugging hell out of him.

The trouble was he wasn't quite sure exactly what. He only knew its area; he could draw a circle around the names and situations. Blood was what it added up to; the name of it was blood.

For instance, that nephew of his, Toni, whom he could bare-handed strangle, and whom he often wished to blindfold like an unwanted stray dog, drive a hundred miles north, east, or west, and dump by the side of the road; yes, this Toni, still, was his blood kin. While in the womb of Mavis Henley, who had come after him like another stray, his own flesh and blood lay curled and peaceful, waiting. For a long time, he had been satisfied to say, "It's probably Carrington's doing," but more recently he had discarded that entirely. He knew it wasn't Carrington's. He knew it was his own.

As though she were two people, one to whom this had occurred while locked in his arms in bed, and the other an old girl friend he could still talk things over with, he went by and talked to Mavis, but what he talked about was not her but that gang, the Weasels.

"I'd get rid of them like that," he said, "but there's Toni. I wish to hell he'd got ahead in one of the jobs I landed him."

"Why didn't he?" She was mainly in the shop these days and he had to stop talking when she had a customer. While she sold knitting thread and some kind of patterns, he paced around the back of the store, then he came back.

"Either he can't make it, or he's trying to spite me. A third thing: he likes that damn gang." And since there were no customers there for the moment, he called them a number of names. "I could get rid of them like that, except for him."

"How would you do it?" Mavis asked. She was curious.

"I could set them up, let the law take over."

"If you leave them alone long enough, won't they do that for themselves?"

"Don't be crazy. The law's busy thinking they're tied to *me.*"

"I guess they're right, in a way." She resumed her knitting. He was about to get angry with her.

Well, at least he was there, thought Mavis, though she was only too aware of being two people to him, the one a listener, wife-mother-mistress-lover-friend, the other forlorn and abandoned, waiting to be lifted up out of darkness, taken out of solitary, summoned out of the tomb. When she thought of that Mavis, she wanted to bend her head and weep over the poor woman. What could she do for that Mavis? Nothing. Nobody could do anything except Frank Matteo, and he, far from being absent, was standing there right before her, laying (doubtless) some girl at the restaurant, and coming to Mavis to worry (not about her but something else). Mavis threw down her knitting.

"What am I putting up with you for?"

Frank was astonished, not to say hurt. But in a split second more he would get angry and, not wanting that, she said, "Why don't you go and talk to the Weasels? You never have, I bet. What are you, chicken or something?" So she cut his anger off—*snick*—as if with scissors.

"They're dirty," he said, more to himself than her. But he would do it now. He thought awhile and walked out on her.

It made him almost sick, in fact, to think of them; he

thought of dirty fingernails that held spoons which reached into cans. He, with the same impulse that prompted Aunt Gianna in Montreal and the girl who had found him in Philadelphia and got him out to parties and such and taught him to dress, wanted to lift Toni Stallone right out of that bunch like a rabbit by the ears or a puppy by the scruff of the neck—to clean him up and set him down, straight up and right, even sharp-looking, in some qualified place. The purple car started with a snort which meant muffler trouble but adequately expressed his feelings.

Frank Matteo, who now had an island in his pocket, couldn't be expected to behave as if he didn't know it. Another trip to Florida was his next move, but since actually seeing her again he had gotten Mavis on his mind, and he brooded a good deal.

Blood. He thought about it in the abstract. Those boys had dared to spill it, Mavis was daring to keep it unspilled— that was worth thinking of. He had seen a lot of blood in the general order of things—that was different, beside the point.

Maybe he would go to Philadelphia, find the all-but-lost wife, maybe take a new look at things. Changing a whole idea about his life—it might or might not work for him. Not that he would have to hang around indefinitely after he'd done it. But a boy of his deserved a name. The world would think that. He had respect toward the world. He looked out windows, wandered in and out of the restaurant, conversed at the bar, sat empty-faced on the corners of desks, wondered whom he meant to telephone. In New Orleans, he looked up a Tarot reader, but she was black and assumed some pattern having to do with an exchange of houses. Giving up a house, finding a new way to live. . . . It was strange. For houses, he might or might not read wives; he longed for the Mavis he had known in Palm Beach. Class. She used to have it; could she get it back? "You'll give up this house you got for a new pick; you know the property already, it's just you hadn't thought about it like that, but you will." Give up Tarot, I got no house. He didn't say it. Those damn ducks.

Those damn assholes, the Weasels. You couldn't even call them boys. Three or four, somebody actually said, were girls. Oh sure, he'd answer, they sex-change each other day and night—it's as easy as swapping bluejeans. He had recently missed two cases of California red wine from the back of the restaurant. Who would know where it was but somebody who'd seen it? Another reason for going to Miami, to make it clear that just get this nephew out from among them, out and away, and he was ready to strike and scatter the rest. Why not the boy, too? Well, he couldn't. A nephew, after all. A family tie. Still, who cared where he wound up—Tijuana, Reno, Atlantic City, who cared? Nothing wrong with a guitar, provided you could strum it well, but Toni wasn't even good at that. The thing Frank couldn't shake off was suspecting it wasn't just Arnie they'd hit at, slaughtering ducks, it was Mavis, and through Mavis to him. Her broken up like that, and he thought of the other time, the abortion, what it had done. Blood layers, layers of blood. His face in the mirror scowled. Look out for age—he resumed a blank mask, and went to find Carrington.

There he encountered a son of Carrington's he had heard reports on, but never seen. People tried to keep their lives secret. Carrington came down from working on a book. They talked in the kitchen. "I don't know what to do with them," Matteo confided. "What would you do, if your nephew was involved?"

"I imagine your nephew being involved might be a little different from the average nephew, just any old nephew."

"You think that," said Matteo, "because you are not thinking through what we have stated already."

"No, I guess I'm not. What was it?"

"The world is one. A nephew is a nephew. Property is property. We had this out. We are in one world together."

"Playboy and playgirl, rich man and poor, beggar and thief, champagne and rotgut . . ." He broke off with a laugh.

"You're getting out of bounds," Frank said. "I was serious, or we wouldn't have traded. I thought you were."

"I was serious," said Arnie. "Look. Go find your nephew, warn him. Get him out because soon I may decide to hurt them. Anywhere, just out."

"You don't understand families," said Matteo with a sigh.

"Meaning what?"

"If I ask him, he won't go. In families, it's like that."

Arnie quit work to call up Yates. He was so astonished he could hardly explain. "This guy might be from some Italian emigrant district somewhere up in New Jersey or Philadelphia, but he's sounding more like Mississippi every day. 'You don't understand families!' It's what he said. Don't we have a patent on all that family stuff? I gather not. He and the nephew have got the family grudge script. It must play the same everywhere."

"Mine are mostly underground, buried," said Yates. "I thought yours were the same. Back to Matteo—you want my opinion?"

"Sure."

"He's bought that island and paid cash for it. Let them all kill each other. What do we care?"

Arnie, never trained for coldness, retreated into his manuscript. What would happen? he sat wondering between pages. It was too late to learn unfeeling ways—for rats or crooks, ducks or waifs or wives. Too late even to try.

5

"You got to learn principles," said Frank Matteo to his nephew, Toni Stallone. "You got at least to go to that much trouble. You got to bother to get yourself up right and meet the world eye to eye. If you got some superior to refer to, like for instance me—I'm your natural superior down here—then open up your thinking. Tell me what your aims might be. There's not nobody would force you against a natural desire, unless you've committed a grave offense. You got a friend, okay, it's up to somebody else to converse with him in any critical way, you're clear. You got a girl friend, it's okay, a wife, too—there's respect involved. Find an opening in just anyplace—you got the same measure, exactly the same measure. You got to look good, meet eye with eye. The way you are, somebody looks at you they've got to look away. You don't respond."

"I responded to you," said the dark slight boy in jeans and muddy cowboy boots, shirt open down the front. "I left off fishing in the bayou off Back Bay to see what the hell you wanted. I thought you had a job for me."

"We needed to talk," said Matteo, who had asked him all the way upstairs for the first time. Had played music. Had offered a drink of Jack Daniel's—Toni wanted beer. "I got no job for you till I can get through to you."

"You don't like me," the boy said. He was fidgeting in the comfortable chair.

"Like you!" Matteo put his drink aside. It was morning and he never drank in the morning. It went to his head.

"Toni, boy! You could be like a son to me, if you'd listen. More than kin!"

The eyes, dark, had a lot of white around the pupils. It was that that flashed. Sheer hatefulness. "Can I go?"

Matteo got up and looked out the window. "Come, go. What's the difference?" He spoke so low he had to repeat it and, when he turned again, the boy was gone. The beer can, overturned, was left on the rug.

The next day a truck shipment of supplies for the restaurant got rocked at dusk on the highway and, coming into a downpour with a busted window, had to turn back. The next day the late order was mixed up; he got Chinese egg rolls instead of soufflé potatoes, and the trucker left word he was getting scared of this route.

Frank called in Dancey. "Just where do those punks hang out? They got to have a roof over their heads. There's been too much rain lately for them to live outside. Where is it?"

"Hit's just a old house, if you mean them boys plays gittars and such, hangs around. Back t'other side the railroad, before you gits to the air base."

"Gits there from this side," Frank mocked Dancey, "or gits there from the other side?"

"Over this away, in between Notchaki and Biloxi. Back in some piney woods. They keeps a fire for the gnats, cooks ever night, all time singing."

"If they'd just taken the damn ducks and eaten them, nobody would have known." Disappearance was better than murder: it was a rule.

"Suh?"

"Nothing."

But then he wrote a letter, just a note on a memo pad. "Stop bothering Carrington. Knock it off, or take bad medicine. —F.M." He dispatched Dancey with it one afternoon to wherever the hangout was. The heat had gotten overbearing and he had given up working on his boat to go up and get stripped off in an air-conditioned room when Dancey returned with a message, written on the back of his own. "Don't take nothing off you. Take your own fucking medicine." So he knew what made things stop, monkey wrench in the works; hurt pride. Families hurt the kids, the kids wound up in life like this—eating french fries, barbecued chicken torn out of a foil bag, wieners on a cracked plate, cheap glare of orange mustard, beer or wine swilled right out of the bottle, and dirt stuck to thin blankets. Smells to everything, none pleasant. He did not want near it, not even to see it.

You got to get it over with, he said to himself. But why?

Running a restaurant was enough for any one man to handle; in addition, he had the gambling to preside over, paying his hush money and dampening down the brawls. Just last week, his shipper had had the highway trouble. Two waiters had gotten in a fight over the receptionist who, though sexy as hell and last year's runner-up for Miss Pascagoula, came from a leading doctor's family in Ocean Springs—he had prided himself on "looking after her." He would never ask such as her upstairs. No sooner had he gotten the island than somebody had vandalized it, kicked the old sand dune apart, apparently looking for fishing or galley equipment, whatever they could find—maybe treasure. Stories lured people on. True, the Weasels had not been seen in boats. But the island worried him, now that he had it. He was fair game, the way Arnie had never been. There was the end with the grave, for instance. "Don't really bother anything down there," Arnie had begged. And Frank had said, "Anything that's resting there can go on resting." "Oh, thanks. Oh, thank you," Arnie had said, with bright eyes, tears. Remembering maybe a bad night, wind tossing high, small boat, a corpse. But why do it?

People's craziness was what made them. Their craziness was their fate. The Weasels had to act up at Matteo; Matteo had to track them down. If he waited much longer, they would laugh when he came.

Just a loose jacket, a flashlight, gun in the car, then that big lumbering purple piece of Detroit was getting him out there over roads it covered completely, out among the softly whispering pines. He passed hurricane ruins, blasted houses, barred fences around them, warning signs (CONDEMNED PROPERTY) in what used to be yards, then piles of junk, mountains of useless trash—people had had to make these piles in order to move again at all. Then there would be just pines again, a sense of lostness among pines, a forever lostness—how to get out: no way—but Dancey's directions took him onward, and he found it. How did Dancey know everything he knew? Friend of Arnie's woman, Barbra K. If you had all those two knew between them, no need to worry. And sure enough, at a turn, the house was there, like Dancey said.

He cut his lights, and let out a long weary breath, just looking at it. Downstairs gutted, yard overgrown, shaded heavily, abandoned. The broad steps from ground level proceeded up to the second floor where some lights were burning, but when he neared the steps he saw they were nothing but substructure, the part to walk on torn away, sometimes a nail left sticking up, sometimes half of a planking. How did the Weasels get up there, out of a tree? There must be another way. He circled, the flashlight leading with its oval of light. Some steps ahead, on the north side, looked sound. Were protected there. Gingerly, he let them take his weight, mounted. The jacket he wore was a suede import from France, loose and luxurious, bought in New Orleans; he mounted slowly, feeling the shudder in the wood, hearing it creak. There was a door above and he heard the sound of voices.

At first, all he thought was: They're nothing but babies; because they did look overly small, maybe like another sort of human, just landed out of the space ocean. In a bunch together. They hadn't seen him yet. White pygmies out in a jungle by a fire. It was burning in the old fireplace. He was the big cat, the tiger creeping out of the forest: fire-drawn, circling, padding closer.

"Watch out!"

The cry came from what seemed a girl's throat, screechy, and he started back, wondering if a rattler was coiled down on the shadowy floor in front of him, but no, it was a ragged hole in the planking. He stood looking straight down into darkness, stopped just in time. When he raised his head, a face had come up, lighted by the fire, rags and tags of hair strung around the ears. Girls with that crew weren't what he thought of as being girls, sex with anybody they happened to be lying next to, all in a bunch, why not? He had contempt for stuff like that. Yet somebody had spoken up to save him.

They were all looking up at him, out of the fire's glow into the yawn of the dark room where he stood. "Is Toni here? Toni Stallone." He didn't say the last *e*, not wanting to come on too Italian, kin.

"Hey! Toni!" Over past the firelight, a single form detached from a tangle of what looked like coats, blankets, old clothes. Then stood. He wore no shirt, just a blanket wrapped around his shoulders, his hair plastered to his head. A smell of pot washed up stronger, out of the stir of the blankets. He looked to have wet hair, maybe from swimming, cooling off in some swampy swimming hole in afternoon heat, now in the cool night drying by the fire. No way to live. Frank's mother's sister, Ciara, married Rudy Stallone, never showed good sense, had this excuse for a son. Fit for nothing but trailing around uninvited after Uncle Frank. Matteo stood in silent judgment—big, expensive, arrogant.

Around the fire, they were all rising slowly and facing him, the way Toni had. Twelve or fifteen of them was all. Another girl's face with jagged dark hair around it was suddenly illuminated in a burst of firelight. They all seemed like one creature, connected flesh like Siamese twins multiplied, born in a chain.

He was active now, the shark gliding in free depths: he felt his own nature. "Who was it told me to watch out? Tell me who." Nobody answered. Had to try. "Toni, you come with me. Come go for a ride, have a nice steak on me, good baked potatoes, lots of salad and beer. You're in need of that, is my opinion."

"Fuck off."

Who said it wasn't the point. Just that he knew it for his answer. They had one mouth was all. He picked up a broken-in chair from the floor near him. "So you know how you want it. All right. So who's been slaughtering ducks? Whose bright idea to kill somebody's poultry?" He flung the chair into the middle of them, like trying to scatter a flock of buzzards at a carcass.

Fright and yowling. Mainly words, the kind they talked in, jumbled, jumping out at him. "You crazy or something? What about ducks?" That was Toni.

"You know better. You're setting me up over here like some kind of cheap operator. It's got to stop here and now. It's going to. One warning's all. Don't push your luck."

"Jesus, all he's got's a fucking flashlight" . . . "Big deal" . . . "You're no fucking kin to me. . . ."

They sounded like a quacking lot of ducks themselves. He had picked up the cushion seat from an old sofa, spilling off it some magazines, a pack of potato chips, beer empties, and hurled it over their heads at the fireplace. It smothered out the light almost at once, then the fire grabbed at it, couldn't make it, dampened down to smoldering, a gush of black smoke. When hands snatched it off, he stepped over the hole in the floor and waded in among them, pulling them back by the ears and hair like so many squabbling puppies, flung aside, and flung again, the same ones twice and three times over, as often as they scrambled back. The half-burning cushion went back on the fire. There were teeth in his leg. He gave a kick, breaking into the pain, and saw the fire gush up around the upholstery, a mildewed green. Done.

He coughed out smoke, squinting a way toward the door, and outside, shining the flashlight before him, went down the wobbly stairs. A rush of all their words, curdling, shrilled over him, like birds screaming out in the Gulf. Then he gained the ground, without the stair falling—Jesumaria, a miracle for the day—but as an afterthought, turning back, he yanked twice at the banister and the whole structure moaned and swayed out, finally letting go, falling outward in an arc like a tree.

He was not in the habit of looking back. Already, he was thinking ahead. All that echoed as he drove away was the sound behind, the steps crashing down. It did not seem like much of anything he had done. He wiped at the soot on his brow—slightly gritty, distasteful. In the light, he would check over his jacket.

Days later, he got the end of the affair from various people: from Dancey, from a passing gossip at the bar, from Mavis, who had no idea of his part in it, while if Dancey guessed he didn't say.

The Weasels had slaved at trying to put the fire out, like a family wild to save a beautiful home. They had some plumbing still working upstairs; they ran it dry fetching water. They smothered fire with old blankets and wet clothes, beat at it with pillows, stamped on it, chased runners of flame like cats after mice.

Two anonymous Weasels had been hurt badly just from that over-devotion, not leaving in time. One had a fall out where the steps were gone from the side, but he was just broken up a little. Another wouldn't get out at all, but kept calling about trying to help somebody, though nobody was left up there to be helped. He had been hopped up on something already, acid maybe, and then there he was up in the fire, yelling. He was still talking about getting somebody out, up to the last, in the hospital. There was a girl who tried to go back for him. She, not anonymous, confessing out of bandages, turned out to be the daughter of a fine old family in Delaware, who came down for her in such distress they did not wish to hear the details of anything at all, but whisked her away by special car, the family physician, an old friend, attending her. It was said they had paid a visit to Arnie Carrington in the little time they spent there.

Toni Stallone was out of it. Simply removed. Like a pulled tooth. A story went around that said he had been given something a good deal stronger than pot, driven six ways for Sunday around the local roads and byways, put on a plane in New Orleans or Mobile or Jackson, and flown to New York, Miami, Philadelphia, or Chicago.

That was all.

Silence.

6

"Mr. Arnie, he workin' on a book."

"He readin' on a book?"

"No, he *writin'* on a book."

"Oh."

The voices came comfortably floating up at Yates, who was strolling in the cool of the evening, down to the end of the street of shops, down to where Barbra K. ran her day-care nursery center, modern in the front, but an old-fashioned two-room dwelling in the back, fixed up much like it had been, he guessed, before any hurricane was heard of. He stood in twilight, alone, puffing on his pipe. He assumed the voice he heard was that of Barbra K.'s husband Reuben, who showed up from time to time, but moments later it was the boy who worked for Frank Matteo's restaurant who came out of the alley, walking by. A pleasant woman, Joe Yates noted, would always have men around to talk to.

What he overheard was true. Arnie was buried in his book, earnestly at work, sending Kelly on runs to the library, letting Kelly see after the property business, listening to Kelly's ideas, Kelly's exploits, Kelly's confidences over wine in the late hours.

The face of Lord Byron was floating among them all. Mavis felt out of things. She had understood the Buddha better than all this study and talk over a dead poet. "Just call him George," Arnie advised, "that might help." "Why George?" she inquired. "Because that was his name. George

Gordon, Lord Byron." That's how he could make her feel silly. She didn't like it.

"The Greek enterprise," Arnie held forth to Joe Yates and his wife. "Well, you can see it only if you consider it a continuation of his personal affront, lifelong (yes, with his own person, and yes, existential is the word waiting there), against whatever constricted, held prisoner, the choosing, deciding spirit. It's the reason back of all the many women, the reason for leaving England, the reason for leaving in Italy the one woman he might ever have been said to love. She, too, was finally doomed to be seen as a jailer, and love itself as a barred window. He left for Greece with core comrades, a band of brothers, free spirits of an inner circle. Then, irony. It was they at the last who hemmed him in. Ill, he had to be bled, or so the doctors told him, and his friends gave in to urge it on him. Right or wrong, he didn't want to. Lancet in the vein: he weakened and died, the conflict never ended. . . ."

It would be at the Yateses' that he sat talking like this, Kelly there, too. The taste of their house, quiet and classical. Ellen's antiques, restored after the hurricane, glowed in lamplight, and her splinted-together spirit shone with pride at having him as her guest. Yates smoked contentedly, but Kelly could sit still for just so long. He said to Yates, together with him in the kitchen:

"He sure better bring that book off soon. He needs to swing something."

"He's swung quite a lot," Yates said, "what with the property saved and moving again."

"Dealing with a hood," said Kelly. "Not much in that to brag on."

"What he's really trying to swing," Yates said, "isn't property or books, either, come right down to it."

"Then what is it?"

"He's got bigger goals. You must know that. Things I wouldn't believe in, hold out for, but he does."

He spoke with some sharpness, correcting Kelly. Childless, he hated it when children grudged stature to their parents.

"But what's he doing?" Kelly pursued. "What actually is he doing?"

"If the idea is there," Yates told him, speaking with more conviction than he had suspected of himself, "what the idea is about may be there, too. Think about it. Closer I can't get." He turned and glasses in hand, walked back into the room. "Ellen and I keep talking about your book," he told Arnie. "We think it's going to be great."

They gave him praise.

Mavis knew he was over with the Yateses. She had seen the small superior house, its one wind-damaged wing repaired to match the other, both just alike, regular in style. She could not even guess at the kind of furniture and stuff people like this would have inside, but knew it was the right kind whatever it was and that Yates's wife was a congressman's sister, somebody up in the Delta. That woman had been through the works—first drinking, and after that goofballs, then something stronger yet till they caught her at it and broke her. "Everybody's into something," Frank had said, "from the highest to the lowest." He came hanging around her now, tall in the shop, careless. What he hadn't liked he was rid of—the Weasels; what he had wanted he had gotten—the island. He didn't say any of this: he stood it, he walked it, he wore it like a cape slung over a shoulder.

Mavis sat knitting, a still center in the middle of her fear.

Anything could happen and usually did; anything could happen to her.

Though very little had gotten into the papers, she knew the Weasels had been crushed in the blow of one powerful fist (Frank's), and that one had died. Could you make an omelet without breaking eggs? She thought that young boy was still in flames somewhere in the back of Frank's head, but she couldn't prove it, and didn't ask. Better not to meddle.

Frank ranged where he pleased. There were rumors that a wealthy divorcée had invited him to one of her more elegant dinners and later talked business with him—controlling interest in a condominium was what she might have to offer. But just now he was watching Mavis knit, like looking down on something minuscule, in motion, from the top of a mountain.

"What is it?" he said.

"A sweater." But her hands with the two long steel needles slowed, then stopped their motion, and fell quiet into her lap. She didn't look up. "You got your island. So that's enough for a while. You ought to go slow. You ought to think. If it wasn't for me—"

"Yeah, I know. You made a bridge. I thought of it that way, more than once. You kept in with Arnie, kept a balance between me and what's here. I knew it was needed, but couldn't do it. I go around feeling like president of the Kiwanis Club. Arnie suggested cub scouts! But you're better at it, even than me. You've got everybody from Waveland to Ocean Springs hooking rugs and painting pictures."

"You think I did all that for you, you're crazy. I felt like I had to keep going. You saw the papers, didn't you?"

"What papers?" The very mention recalled his feeling that the light treatment he had gotten about that house half-burnt, the gang scattered, was too fortunate to be true. He felt a pair of small furred inner ears prick up.

"Another boy from that gang. He got shot. You didn't see it?"

"*See* it?"

"I mean the article."

"No. Where?"

"One of the boys in that gang, a leftover, I guess, he was hanging around with some man's daughter up just to the north of here and they were always getting into pot smoking, late nights, and such, and this man didn't want his daughter with anybody like that, so he warned him away, but when he came back, her father took a shot in that direction just to scare him, but it must have hit him by mistake."

"Or maybe he said it was a mistake."

"Maybe so."

Another Weasel gone. "What's his name?"

"No kin to you."

"Couldn't be. That one's gone."

Matteo then said he was going to Florida, that it was what he'd come by to tell her.

"For good?" she asked at once, not meaning to—her core of fear had spoken, and it just fell out. When he didn't answer, she looked up. Their eyes met.

"Back in a day or so."

"You have to report, I guess. To people wanting to know about things—the island, getting rid of that gang. You wouldn't like rumors to get there before you did."

"Think you got it figured out, don't you? Anything else I'm going to do?"

"Anybody could figure out that. Nothing to it."

"That sweater's blue," he remarked, looking at her handiwork.

"Boys."

"What?"

"Blue's for boys."

Warm winds had sprung up around her. The day was sunny, hot, still. No one came into the shop. The police chief had said to Frank: "You're under better control here than you know about, but at the same time we're going easy on this fire thing; it was something we could never have got done ourselves, so however you thought of it, don't tell me about it, just let's forget it." He was alone with Mavis now, and she with him.

He almost took her hand. "Let your hair back the way it was." He got up and walked around her. "Florida will be hot as hell. But there's always a pool."

"A pool and some girl."

He stopped still, looked at her, laughed. "You bitch. Tell you one thing. Any relative of mine shows up and starts cadging around—well, I'm off relatives."

"Them fooling around me is unlikely."

"You can't tell. You're—"

"I'm what?"

She thought he might have answered, but her bell jangled and two ladies came in. They were gray-haired, dressed in bright slacks suits, blue and yellow, and had the eager, bird-hunting look of women about to do something for the house.

Frank Matteo, leaving, wondered who could do more harm than some churchgoing Baptist shooting a boy down in cold blood because his daughter had a little healthy curiosity about pot and the usual hot pants. Too self-righteous to feel any guilt, people like that. And for that sort of thing to rub off on Matteo, now that the sky was clearing over the fire. "Going to Florida," he said to Dancey, and to the girl who kept the books, and to the bar girl who came upstairs for him, and to the nice doctor's daughter from Ocean Springs, who worked in the restaurant and admired him, it might be, a little too much.

7

"Go back to Texas," said Arnie to Kelly, who at first had torn up the pea patch with eager plans and talkathons, but who now was bored and wilting like a banner in windless noonday heat. "Your girl's out there; she can get you a job." From once to twice a week, this girl and Kelly were now on the phone at least once a day. Arnie gave him his five thousand dollars back. Kelly had sunk the rest of his capital (How do you get capital? You go bankrupt.) in boating supplies and found too late that an outlet on any marina would not be possible to rent—two national firms had bought up the franchises and concessions: he would have to go inland, remain tied to Arnie's street. Arnie said that at least he could advertise and sell out the stock on hand. Probably make a profit, which might pay the phone bill to the girl in Texas.

The man in Florida whose life Arnie had saved in Korea wrote to ask him to rent some land along the beach for putting in a miniature golf course. The motif was to be dinosaurs: you could play golf in the shadow of prehistoric monsters, shooting the balls along their thorny spines and into their yawning gullets. Arnie sent the five thousand dollars back with a considerate and grateful letter. Some crimes, he thought, by nature seem worse than others. A golf course of dinosaurs along his precious Coast really did seem worse than murder.

His pockets now were lined with Frank's unholy money. A reason for getting Kelly away was because of that farmer who had taken a shot at one of the former Weasels and killed him. The police were up and excited again, just when the business of the fire was calming down. Kelly had a record in Texas. Nobody mentioned this as they drove to New Orleans together to say goodbye.

August.

Oh, blessed good miraculous summer that had brought his boy home to him, out of luck, to lick the wounds of a failed business, hear him out about Lord Byron's final years, sip nightly wine, take up flambeaux for flounder, grant fellowship to an aging father, do little harm, return encouraged, back to source. He understood Kelly's visit now. His money gift was a means of saying: I don't come to you like a defeated prodigal but in order to help. And yes, he had helped. Before Matteo had actually laid down the cash, Kelly had footed the bill for back taxes. He had restrained himself from talking too much about Evelyn (no use to claw at the wound), had not pried into matters about Barbra K., had been kind to Mavis. It was respect he had earned and a dinner at Antoine's.

In the afternoon, they sat around the French Quarter, in a well-known patio, sipping rum poured over crushed ice.

"Everything I do," Kelly said suddenly, breaking a silence, "it looks like it turns out wrong."

That had to come out, Arnie realized, sooner or later. The father on a tightrope. "Sometimes I feel that too, son—about myself, I mean." Silence. He knew how critical Kelly had been. Smart-ass was the word. He held his breath. "You've got the winning card, though: youth."

"But if I never—!"

"Never what?"

"Never *amount* to anything!"

Oh God. The American anguish.

"Evelyn had a list of phrases she hated. 'Amount to anything' was up near the top."

Kelly smiled, but he was still falling. Soon he would land and bounce. It was time to speak of the Buddha and Arnie did so. The Buddha was in the city museum, stored, so far, not yet displayed, though soon. Arnie might have been speaking of a mutual friend. Kelly, who had forgotten about the Buddha, heard him out with a shrinking look which meant he thought his father was nuts. Kelly, at least not that, bounced.

Over the table at Antoine's, they talked of general things. The oysters arrived; the wine, crushing ice in the bucket nearby, laved and beaded with chill, quickly wrapped in white linen, filled their glasses. What more to do for a son than this? A dinner of quiet pomp, amid white napery, dark chairs, under a dusky high ceiling—these things had been here forever, one reason for preserving the world.

"Write or call me how it all turns out about the Weasels. Who they were—the ones that got killed. Could have been Kennedys . . . Rockefellers."

"Or just ordinary people. Kids like that, mixed up with the world in the worst connection—" He stopped.

"The way I used to be," Kelly amiably finished. "What outside people don't know is you don't think about drugs so much, in the general run of things. They're just part of the way you live, and that's the only way you can live because it's the only way there is."

"Or used to be." Arnie hadn't wanted to say that. Coming on fatherly. He could have bit his tongue.

"Or used to be," Kelly echoed, with genuine eyes, and made him thankful, for the next thousand years.

Alone in the city the next day, Arnie went to the museum. He talked his way into the storage department on the ground of being a former custodian of what he wanted to see, nothing to be gained by keeping him out, nothing to be lost by letting him in. The curator, a sensitive, worried young man who went about constantly with a clipboard under his arm, let him into the storage area, where paintings in their heavy frames rested in large racks and some plywood packing cases as big as elephant crates were ranked along the walls. The Buddha, like other statues, had been covered with sheets of heavy cloth. It could be reached along a plank walk set above the cement floor. This high up in the museum, attic-level, the windows looked small and low. The Buddha was near the windows. The curator slid back the cloth.

There he sat, Arnie's old companion.

He had told the curator the story on the way up, some of it, about the hurricane, the mud in the ears, the memory of the pleasure of keeping a great work. "Just take your time," the curator said. "It's not at all orthodox to do this. But I think it's worth the chance." He went away. Arnie heard the door close. He found something covered up but solid, and sat on it.

"I thought I ought to come and tell you— No, wait. Let's start over. I *wanted* to come and tell you what's happened, what I did. I sold the island, after all. Maybe I sold my soul: Evelyn there, and who's that crook to take—" He stopped. He was looking at the blank smiling mouth, looking and feeling nothing about what had gone on that he had come to tell. The words just ended, wouldn't come. The organizing principle was not there. Something was missing. Starting again, he rambled.

"I took a big chance, I know. About property, well, I scarcely care that much, though I do care how things are done. Good people are coming on. They're buying in. They see through clearer air, how to restore, control, give back to nature. My weakness is for the nearest ones, the longest there.

I mean by that Mavis, the baby, even Matteo—yes, it's getting some notion of him, a growing notion of him, that's what's getting to me. To pass my notion on to him, how can I? Especially when Joe Yates—the weak point in this kind of thinking —denies anything good can touch Matteo. Sees him cold. Now do you understand my fears? Yates, for instance, has a relative in Congress. He's working on something about that island. How can I tell just what it is unless I talk about it? I've been holding off any mention of it. Mention would be folly, show support for Matteo, all his corrupt web. You can come to a balance so fine you might as well vanish. Or rise above it all, like you once managed to do. Once and for all.

"Oh, I know you suffered a lot once. No god without suffering. Show me a really happy god. You understand I was just making it all up that time about your smile having conquered all. I've known all along that it hasn't, it never did, it doesn't."

He scratched his ankle, thought it was getting hot up there in spite of air conditioning. The sun was coming in from the park outside, and beyond lay the low roofs of the Metairie District.

"Something's the matter, isn't it? I wish I could figure out what it is. Are you so lonely here? Did you get used to us? We were like a family to you, I guess, like friends who took you in."

He sat reviewing the salient words. Suffering . . . lonely . . . friends . . . family. . . . Then, suddenly, he knew. The ducks. The Buddha wanted something on the ducks. "They're dead," he said aloud, "the ducks, I mean. Somebody killed them, those boys got on the loose. My fault, in a round about way. I enraged them and they took it out on me. Not on me so much, it was Mavis who grieved the most, unless now you will. You felt for them, didn't you, being Oriental, possibly Chinese in origin, or so the experts agree. Poor old Bud."

He got up slowly. His joints all but creaked; they were aching, he got that more and more, in the winter had put it down to the damp, but of late knew the spring then should have healed and warmed him, but still there was that cold persistent ache like old iron must feel, deep in its hinges, though the sun beat down. Age. And the thought of Evelyn, she too with cold joints, stiff from lying still, though he had just seen her in sunlight, hadn't he? Last Wednesday, by the beach. "I'll come again," he told the Buddha. "Two ducks are left. It's why I came, to tell you about it. And ask: How can we gather everything up? Everything we know? Everyone we know? And preferably not as corpses." His sign at this was profound, occurring on the moment of rising. He bent to touch the bronze knee and a tear fell for everything from wives to ducks to poets dead in Greece. It landed on the Buddha's slippered foot and he wiped it off with the end of his tie, patted the solemn knee, and went away.

8

The Florida that Frank Matteo went to was hotter than before, full of rich green, and subject to sudden summer storms. He drove out of curiosity up through Tallahassee, where that doctor who called himself Swayze or Swiggart had by rumor been said to settle in and stopping for gas at a filling station went to a phone book and looked the names up and there it was: "Swayze, E. H., M.D." So the story fit. He closed the book shut, paid for the gas. He would have what he needed if he needed it. But what was that? Arnie broke laws—what use would that be to Frank Matteo? He had a feeling of not being able to think it through, and that meant there was no target area in it. Still, knowing was knowing. It was better to know.

He was going to Eddie. Conversations with Eddie hummed through his head like a tape on a neat Japanese recorder. He rejoiced in the compactness of machines like that, saw small encasing nests for recording devices nestled under the tops of strong desks, built by design into the woodwork. It was a fascination. Soon people's brains would be wired with such a thing, something that started the memory cells working, playing them straight through, nothing missing or dropped. Hell for you when the law got you. But a way to smash it, turn it back human again, that would have to be part of the invention. He checked into the resort hotel in midafternoon.

The room was, he thought, going up, the same number as before. He had a moment after tipping the boy who had brought up his bag and after switching on the air conditioning and the TV, of growing dizzy, empty, in the center of the room, before he could reassure himself it was the same room, the same sort of trip, and that he would be treated in the same way as before. He checked his appointment with Eddie and went down for a swim.

But the pool was empty, cracked, and dry, with a line of weeds growing up along the cracks, and no chairs were outside to lie in. So he came back in, feeling awkward and remembering now what he had not dared to register before, that the room smelled of cigar ashes and a sour mattress, and the curtains were torn from the hooks in two unmended places, left hanging. Well, it was summer, he thought; maybe renovations were being planned. He flopped down on the

bed, first having turned up the air conditioner which had a
rasp in the mechanism, missed something and then knew what
it was, the face that leaned down and smiled above the mini-
mal scraps of white bikini, so easy to shed when the perfect
curtains swished shut and the air conditioner did its job with
a soothing purr. What was her name? Not the real one, but he
couldn't even remember what she'd said the fake one was,
but only lay with a hand over his eyes trying to keep from uneasy movement, trying to lie still.

Eddie's office, though, was the same.

"You cutting back here," Frank asked, "or just taking time
out for hot weather?"

"What you mean?"

"Run-down room, dry pool, night life shut." For he had
noticed, when he came through the lobby, that the No Questions Bar and Club was shut up tight.

"Permanent cool down—the money's pulling out. We sold
in April—thought you'd heard."

"How would I hear? I don't see nobody."

"Keep your ear to the wall. Even over yonder on the
Coast. Why don't you?"

"I try to," said Frank, but within now he was feeling li'
the closed doors to the night spot and the dry swimming
cracks like the grins of dead alligators. "I try. Am I r
something?"

"Missing a nephew, ain't you? Or so I heard."

"Oh." His laugh was real relief. "It's not
hurt. I got him out to the East, up to Dino
ought to be straight, though. It's balance h
thing. I gave it a good deal of thought."
rette. "Considering his mother."

"Somebody did get hurt, though."

"Whoever got hurt, it was their

Eddie looked speculative. He began to play with a large clear paperweight in which some heavy liquid moved dreamily around. "So what about the island?"

"I told you. By phone. The night it happened. Mission completed. And no rift. I got capital of goodwill, some to spare. Don't think it wasn't tricky."

"So what about the island?" Eddie asked again.

"You hear me. Can't you credit it? Project complete. I'm ordering up some plans for the Island Wharf Harbor Club, a fishing paradise."

Eddie paced around, looked out the window, came back, leaned back in his chair, stared at the ceiling. He was small, like another race, compared to Matteo. He spoke very low. "You know who that island belongs to, or will in two months?"

Frank's "Who?" was almost a whisper, and Eddie's answer was low also, but he repeated it one turn louder so that it was clear both times: "The fed-er-al gov-ern-ment." Then he looked like nothing, a vacuum, while both color and breath drained out of Frank to fill it.

So they'd done it. Not only done it but done it to him, for Carrington must have known, letting go of ideals like that, actually dealing with somebody (like him) connected. "I told you, Eddie. I warned you. Telephone call back there in April, I said, 'Look, Eddie, the rumor is out that the government is buying up more of this offshore island property than anybody foresaw.' You said, 'I got nothing on it, but I'll give it a looksee.' I got no line to Washington, Eddie. You know that. Who has? You have."

"You sitting there trying to tell me I'm the solitary soul in the solar system. You could have found yourself a line to Washington."

"Eddie. I had you. You told me not to worry, Eddie."

"I don't recall no such conversation."

Silence.

So the score was plain. Eddie was throwing the blame back to Frank. That island was now included in a new government survey or a revision of an old one, and Frank hadn't known. Yates, he thought. Those trips to Washington. Not once, not twice, but often. And his wife's connection, open door to an office that did things. But Carrington, too, must have known, yet he took the money. And Mavis, too? It would go grinding down to Dancey knowing; that mulatto woman of Carrington's would have told him. Left for Frank was swimming five miles out to drown—shark food, a large toothpick. But he didn't believe it. That is, he believed it about Yates—a mystery, one of those high-toned Southerners went around any way he liked, being of such a good connection—but not Arnie, whom he knew at heart, not Mavis; no, never. She'd wade through her own blood to tell him. He got up suddenly, turning Eddie to a dwarf, the fine office to hole-in-the-wall. For Frank Matteo was the guy who threw a sofa cushion big as a camp bed on the fire, and pulled whole staircases off the walls of houses when they bothered him—one pull and down it crashed. From great heights, he had looked far down on the woman who held his child within her. She might have been filling a bucket from a well, cooking, washing clothes. Instead, she was sewing. But betrayal? The forked stick. It had happened before. He couldn't set the idea aside. Why not betray a crook? He knew whose thinking that was—Yates—but then there was mystery.

Eddie, who had been perusing a portfolio, closed it. "You got some black marks, Matteo."

Frank's mouth was dry inside. He sat down and swallowed. He might not leave here. He had contempt for Eddie, a short guy whose trousers always looked too long, crumpling about the suede shoes he wore, barely missing the floor when he walked. Frank could have picked him up like a dog taking care of a rat, even wagging his tail at the kill. He could have hung him on a hook and departed. Frank felt some renewal of what he had felt when he stood before the gang of Weasels by the light of their sad hell fire. He was great. Eddie was not great. But Eddie was a link in that all-important chain that wound its heavy way from point to point over a map as big as the world. It probably even went to the moon, every time anybody went up there at all.

"So what's our planning to go for now, Eddie?"

"I wouldn't be the one to say. You got your restaurant, ain't you?"

"I can raise money—the forty thou down gone to Carrington for the island—pay you back cash. It will mean a mortgage till the government buys me out, but I—"

"It wasn't so much the money. That's not the top issue."

"I don't dig."

"Coming to the surface, nothing to show. Outflanked. Looking sick."

They sat silently. Eddie sighed. Frank sighed. Both, in separate ways, for the moment, looked like Italian villagers, life saddened, sitting in some village square drinking weak beer, thin winter sunshine.

Frank did not stay the night. He started back in the afternoon, under a troubled, changeable sky that ran through a lot of color, burst out in wind and lightning at times, at others grew dead still. Along a road in the Florida Panhandle, driving a lonely highway, in such a stillness and with a light around everything that couldn't be called morning or evening, he saw ahead of him how the world had broken in two like a plate. Say that the outer show, what you looked at and called the world you were passing through, was a plate stood on its rim but it was broken; and say that the two pieces, each painted with trees below, sky above, were sitting apart and that the break was proceeding as irregular as a river from top to bottom of the two halves which were standing up straight both of them against a black velvet ground. That black was, oddly, right in the run of the road ahead, and as he was just first seeing it, it swayed, moved, a slow forward writhing: then he knew.

He had had the radio on since leaving the resort, and not consciously listening, still had heard the warning, "Tornado watch in . . . counties . . . travelers cautioned . . . all residents alerted. . . ." Now the roar. A thousand freight trains barreling down a grade. There it was. Danger was not where he had first thought of it, back there behind him; they had sent it to overtake, turn, and confront, and if necessary split the world half in two. But by then, he was down in the roadside ditch where he dived out the side door to roll into, and felt the wind like hands already grabbing at his thighs, had thrust head and both shoulders into a drainage culvert, confronting mud and a few odd sticks and, yes, something that scuttled or ambled or crawled away, hasty, and he thrust farther in. Suddenly, it was dinning about his ears, a great battering and echoing of a passage so powerful and deliberate you could think the noise was a dropped bomb. The culvert banged with sound like a cannon fired in a cathedral, a flock of maniacs beating it with sticks. Then a vibrating silence.

He crept out backward with ringing ears, into a stillness that seemed to extend through the whole earth. The thing had left the road just to the east, plunging through a heavy growth of timber, leaving a path like a herd of elephants, then lifted. He turned, searching for his car. Not seeing it, he crossed the road, but heaven and earth were empty of it. All he saw was what had scuttled out of the culvert: a small alligator lay at the base of a small tree, dead. Blood trickled from the side of its ugly mouth. Broken branches lay every which way. The break in the world had mended. His car was nowhere.

He thumbed a ride. Only after he got into a pickup which was going into Jacksonville did he notice that his shoes had been taken clean off his feet along with one sock and one trouser leg had been torn away at the knee. For some reason, he had grabbed his jacket when he leaped from the car and within, neatly in their accustomed place, were the credit cards, the insurance, registration, driver's license, and health insurance cards, all links to the world held in place, good spars on a boat. He thought for a while of vanishing. The car found, without him in it, who would know but that he had been blown out of the culvert like the little alligator, dropped somewhere in the swamp? This was wild country, desolate. Buying new shoes, socks, trousers, in a Jacksonville shopping center, he paid cash, and cash, too, brought him home in the small hours by way of the bus. However, when he reached his apartment, he found, the last of several, a message on the answering machine from Dancey: "Mr. Frank, Mr. Eddie done called, he say he glad you got out okay because yo' car done been foun' in the top of a pecan tree. He say hit split the tree trunk, and the car ain't no good either, 'cording to what Mr. Eddie say."

Frank cut off the tape and, weary to the bone, almost fell down, landing on the carpet. His brief freedom, the first he had felt since the days before his long-ago Philadelphia father-in-law had smoked him out of hiding, was just a dream. They had known about him, possibly every minute. In superstition, it persisted: the idea of the tornado dispatched like a hit man, "Matteo's coming. Stop him." He woke where he had slept, on the wall-to-wall, on the floor. He sat up, cross-legged, and rubbed his eyes, his head.

But what his body was in memory still doing was throwing that sofa mattress on the fire, was pulling a whole staircase off the wall, was looking down on her while she sewed . . . that was it, he thought . . . myself . . . me. Who could have also shoved the whole fucking damn house down with one shoulder. He rose suddenly, at once, lightly, knowing to have told himself something true, but then stood able and marvelous in the middle of the room, with nowhere to go.

9

What could people out of Arnie's past matter to Mavis Henley? Nothing, she thought, absolutely nothing. But they were all over the place, matter or not; all at once, they were everywhere.

First there were only snatches of appearances, so quickly gone, you could pretend you didn't think much about them, and believe they were gone for good.

Mavis in her shop, fair game for anybody seeking Arnie, found herself puzzling over them, feeling that going was something they'd never do. She minded this, quite a lot. She minded because life, no matter what tensions were waiting elsewhere, had gotten peaceful along the street. Maybe the baby would never be born; she would just be always knowing about it, at six months going on seven, feeling its soft nudges and shiftings, awakened at night by kicks and nudges, calls from inner space. She knew that houses were going up—

four in number—on the hotel property, and she'd seen the designs, the conical roofs—"hip-roofed," Yates's oft-heard phrase, copied from the old Jefferson Davis's offices in the yard of Beauvoir just to the east—"in keeping," Arnie boasted. But maybe they, too, would never be finished. She lived at a still center, neighbor to Barbra K., with her day-care nursery next door, the sound of children's voices, lulling, like music boxes sometimes (her grandmother had had one), but again, screaming and yelling, accusing one another. Her child might play there.

The people who came seemed like flesh and blood, solid enough, but she saw them as merely shadows. There was that Dorothy Graham, a hyped-up woman from New Orleans now, though she used to be up at a college. Now she was in a "rest home" or something like that, and crazy to see Arnie, even if she had this young stud with her, driving her, somebody in a Mexican shirt with a silver-studded belt, she would sit in the store, saying, "But of course you'd know where he is. You're his girl friend. Aren't you married yet? Won't he even marry you?"

"That's none of your business," Mavis said, and stabbed into the needlepoint.

It seemed a shame, a good-looking woman ought to be happy, but this one couldn't be, she guessed. She wanted to say, Mrs. Graham, if I had had half the breaks you have had, I'd be at home counting my blessings. But she guessed that wasn't true either; she could say it, but that wouldn't make it true. Arnie said, "Possessions don't mean a thing. Happiness is within." It came from what was in you. She thought this and the baby kicked. Arnie was up working on his book at the house and never came to the door, and he especially would not come for Mrs. Graham. She made a note of it that a man never likes his own past. But Mrs. Graham's present was the dark silent boy in the Mexican belt, who slouched around, looking at things, more amiably than not, and occasionally remarked that they ought to get going if they were going to get to Navarre Beach. So finally she went. God alone knew where they'd wind up—a drug weekend?—but then before she knew it, though it was actually some hours later, the husband, that professor named Lex, showed up, looking for her. He evidently had made the connection that his wife would see Arnie if she could, and he lingered, not having been let into the house either, having sought out Mavis, whom he remembered. He sat in a straight chair in front of Mavis, his arms folded, looking amused, faintly detached, though his Mercedes, glossy out front, was never far from him, wasn't to be thought of as ever separate from him, might be his true love.

"I know you know why I'm here; she's got out again. I used to care if I found her, but now I don't, not very much." It was like a remark on the weather. "I used to love her, but now even liking her is hard to do. She's just a dark place, something shut off in a house."

Like my ex-husband, Mavis almost said, but figured that would take some explaining. What she did say was, "Arnie is working at trying to finish a book. He doesn't want to be bothered."

She was knitting, hands up and resting on her conveniently expanded stomach, fingers moving rhythmically. She jerked a length of wool up from the knitting basket at her feet. Her class in crewel work was coming soon. When she looked up again, the professor was gone, melted into air. She had heard no door close, but it must have. The class was arriving.

She did little these days that made her stand. Her designs, her threads, her hanks of wool and yarn, her paints and dyes. She sat under a high ceiling, in a rocking chair, her long robes around her sandals. Whatever she worked with she could reach, leaning forward. At times she rocked; at times she dozed. Only occasionally did she let herself be afraid. What of? Arnie had helped and would again. Suppose something happened to Arnie? Then was there no one? So what? Would she starve, go on relief, give the baby up for adoption? No, never that! For the rest, the Lord knew, according to Barbra K. Mavis did not believe in the Lord. ("He there anyway," said Barbra K.) Even if He is there, she thought, what does He know about me? Or about anybody? She rocked and the chair squeaked. The baby wasn't due till November. They had gotten through August without a hurricane, only a couple of warnings, way out in the Gulf. Most people assumed the baby was Arnie's. Some thought they had gotten married. The shop was earning money, but how could she keep it going once the baby came? There would be alimony, sooner or later, wouldn't there? Yes, but when was alimony ever enough? She needed to think, plan everything. Instead, she sat and rocked and when she got to thinking this way, her hands fell to her vanished lap, and her needle and crochet work still resting there, she would sleep. Or the door would jangle for a customer and she would rise laboriously and go to meet them. She had attached a pull to the door, with a small bell at the end, to make a silvery sound.

But what came in was never Frank.

Sometimes she looked up at the ceiling. In bad weather, the gulls flew in from the Gulf. They gathered, clumsy on the roof slope, their claws scratching the tin. The roof was high as a cathedral. But it was safe. Joe Yates, who knew architecture, said it was. On the other side of it toward the south, Yates himself might be sitting on his high stool, answering the phone, pecking out letters or statements on his old-timey upright typewriter, cooled by a great big electric fan that turned from side to side. None of them had gotten air conditioning yet, but the high ceiling and the old brick kept the heat down. Students came. Customers came. Barbra K. came in every so often to borrow something—"borry," she called it. It struck Mavis as odd that Barbra K. had no children, so one day she called her back and asked her. "Yes'm, I've had two churn. One died and my daughter married over in N'Orleans. I go to visit, every week or so." Why didn't I know that? Mavis wondered. She thought she would mention it to Arnie, but Arnie, when he came, brought her a kitten. "Oh, he'll get in the wool," she cried, "I'll have to cover everything. No, I can't!" He was in her lap already, kneading and purring. Claws sharp as needles. Frank didn't come.

When Arnie went off somewhere—Texas, maybe—giving himself a break from the book, then Frank came.

He stood around looking older, lines between his brows. His nephew, Toni Stallone, was now into a job up in the Finger Lakes, New York State. They'd wanted to give him a shaking up before he left the Coast, but Frank wouldn't let them. He'd been through all that, and he knew. He sat on a table Mavis had, swinging his foot, looking anywhere but at her. Yes, been through it himself, and she, yes, remembered that story, too, the one he meant now, not just the knife scars, thin and white, crossed above the heart, but the hole (more than a scar, deeper) in the tender part of his groin, a burn. Cigarettes? It was like a navel, the cord that tied, and as evidence of certain lengths gone to, tied still. She knew about it, and more—she knew with love, loved with knowing. But he left, and she never once noticed him looking at her, and she dozed, thinking of his business, how what made him restless, she could only suppose, was the government about to take that island over, his own schemes shot to hell, how he'd had to mortgage the restaurant to pay back what some guy in Florida had loaned him to pay Arnie for the island. She had gotten this one way or another, in fragments, out of Barbra K. (They had somehow gotten in cahoots over men.) She speculated that Arnie certainly had not known about this, but she thought that Yates had. Yates had been to Washington on some kind of business; his wife was kin to a congressman. Locking up the shop after work, she heard Barbra K. out under the hurricane-slanted live oak, leaning comfortably against it with one hand, talking to Dancey. Everything would be in what they said, but she couldn't hear the words. Thunder out on the misty Gulf. Heavy weather coming in. Labor Day weekend. Gulls close to shore, close to ground, squalling.

Was it true that Frank had leaned to kiss her when he left? How to remember that when she wanted so much more? But arguing got her nowhere. It ran him away. Her mind was tangled up like wool.

Men. Three of them and they were always rotating. Whose time was it now? She dozed and opened her eyes when the bell tinkled and there he was again, Lex Graham, the one she disliked. She always knew him, but what was he after? "Arnie's away," she said, though it wasn't true. He'd called that morning to say he was back.

"It's all right," he said. He sat down. "Why do you have so many chairs?"

"I have students. I give classes in handwork, artwork. They come here from all over. Some are my students from the junior college. I'm not teaching now, but some come here."

"Life goes on," he said. He was sitting exactly the way he had before, and in the same chair and wearing the same clothes, with the Mercedes parked at exactly the same place outside, so perhaps it was just illusion that he'd ever left.

"My wife will never be all right again. Perhaps she never

was entirely all right. There has to be some way to explain why she wanted me. But life goes on." He was half smiling, speaking in an inflectionless voice. "I sent my daughter away to college, late in the spring. I had to get her out of the house, so as not to witness the daily parental debacle. She's pretty, a pretty girl. You'd say so, wouldn't you?"

"I would if I ever saw her," Mavis said.

"I thought you had. So now what's she done but meet somebody in summer school with her, staying on to visit his family, wants to marry him, whoever it is. From Maine, a long way off."

"That's good news to go with bad," Mavis said.

"Everything changed. Since I came down here last fall. Not even a year ago. I can't get through to you. I've tried before. Just sitting here now, trying again, I think part of me will always be sitting here, trying all my life, the rest of my days, to tell, to tell you. (Why you? I don't know. You were in on it, so you ought to be able to see it, to see what I mean.) To have you understand. What's your name?"

"Mavis."

"Not Carrington. You didn't marry him?"

"No."

"That first weekend, the time I saw you near the boat. It all came out of that—all of it. Going out to the island with the one person I should have stayed away from—forever. I went because of a private vow to be rational, a private conviction that I had gone beyond all that. You won't believe me, but listen. I knew, but I denied what I knew. I denied it because it was not reasonable to believe it. You've stuck here yourself where Carrington is, you see. Oh, don't tell me it's not his child. I can't see that that's the point. I really cannot. Your hereness—that's the point. Wouldn't you say he has some sort of power?"

She felt in school, in a classroom, agreeing where expected; but she did agree. "It's true."

Lex Graham sat for a time, judicious, meditative. "Arnie Carrington had the power to destroy me. Why? It's a question I cannot answer. I don't know why. I simply know that he has done it."

"In one weekend."

"That's right."

"Listen," said Mavis, "do you know why I'm here? My husband—the man I was married to—over-reacted to an affair I was having. I needed the affair, but if he'd just kept his head, shown he loved me, why, I would have stayed. I cared about his children. When they acted right. So I wouldn't have gone. But all of them—they had some kind of devil. I brought it out. That was over in Palm Beach. When I saw it, I left. Oh yes, for good and all. Do you know why they were that way? I could go back and ask till doomsday. It wouldn't matter. You just have to take some things and go on. Go on somewhere else, I mean. It's no use hanging around."

The voice that had no expression, no rise and fall, but was still professionally full of a manner of speaking rich and lecturelike, had not interrupted, but had waited neatly till she finished before going on.

"You mustn't think I am unhappy because of the things perpetrated. Not at all. I worry about this sometimes. My lack of unhappiness. Lucinda would have to go sometime, but alone in the house without her, I feel her presence still. She told us—her mother and me—some time ago, that she was 'born again,' converted to Jesus Christ. We were very ashamed of this, it seemed almost indecent. We kept it as quiet as possible. She's let up on all that now.

"It was after she came back from the Coast with me, the time I nearly died; if she was different then, I thought—I dared to think—it was because of me. Her mother at that time had got wild to the point of no return. What I dreamed of, had hoped for, seemed to be mine. Off Jesus, on to me. We were holding the fort, she and I, two together while her mother roved like a mad gypsy. A real daughter. Then it came out. Carrington. He had taken her into the lighthouse. What did he do? Who knows? Nothing, he would say. 'Absolutely nothing, poor old Lex. That lovely child? The idea!' But she thought of him. He was with her. Through all her mother's turmoil, she stayed serene. But she had to leave. Not a healthy atmosphere, they said. All that line of thought. I asked myself: How can I endure to see her leave? But I could. Knowing she was gone already. Carrington. He'd robbed me.

"The curious thing is I can stand it. I can even like it. I have greatly enhanced the house. I have a taste for beautiful objects, strange to find in an ordinary faculty-type residence in Hartsville. Chinese porcelains, English prints, framed portraits of eighteenth-century ladies, reproductions, of course. My new dinner service is impeccable. I've installed an upstairs bar. Someday I will begin to entertain.

"A lady came recently to call. She had been given the news to bring: I had been made chairman of the department. In the years ahead, I can see, some high administrative post will also be offered. But for now, the chairmanship will do. The lady was the dean's assistant. Unmarried, smooth black hair, excellent looks and manners. I saw the pattern of her hopes for coming, of theirs for sending her. I responded, flirted, took her out a time or so. Then I dropped her. She was puzzled, but now when I see her I find some way of recalling to her an episode concerning a young man, a student she was rumored to have had some affair with several years ago, during the campus troubles. She can't defend herself, but the reference wounds her. So I keep my distance, my freedom. Letting women in control . . . the danger can mount quickly. I may never be quite ready for that again. Dorothy, you see— well, there was such wildness in her . . . ! Who let out the beast? It couldn't be trapped again."

If he doesn't leave soon, thought Mavis, I'll scream.

"When I got the final word from the fifth psychiatric inquiry into her condition, that she'd have to go into a 'controlled environment' for an 'indefinite period,' I came down here. What did I want? I wanted to walk by the marina and find an old notebook, dropped by a fence, see inside a series of entries, a diary: 'Take Graham to the island. Get money out of him, or punish him—definitively punish—not only him but the whole lot of them. Lure the wife down, renew a fatal sexual tie. Seduce his daughter if possible, she's virginal, possibly even devoted. Drive them all away.' I wanted to go to the same motel as before, find the desk clerk, bribe out of him what I already knew: that my wife, having asked that night for another room because of a 'headache,' sneaked out, tore blood from her breast under the moon, lurked in shadows lusting, forced entry into his house, found him. But not before he had got my daughter with him to the inside of a lighthouse. . . ."

"Is this still Arnie you're talking about?" Mavis had to ask it, though she was convinced he was crazy. What's he doing with a job, a professor? Maybe up there they think he's sane. She remembered her husband and the whooping children. To the voice, she was simply an annoyance.

". . . and after that everything changed—for me, for them. We were (I grant you) delicate. Can you see us? Understand? Our family base was fragile, but it might have strengthened. Our footing on that fragile base was at least, for the time being, secure. With Carrington (I, so simply desiring, from the first, friendship), how trusting I was, entering a web, a trap, a spell, a viper's den. Not even metaphor. I was bitten literally, stung almost to death. Oh, I can rage! And I have raged.

"Listen. The day they told me about her, and I finally believed them, do you know what I did? I came here and saw him, and you, too, I suppose, working on these houses here . . . he *would* get help from friends, students, never money of his own to spend, only loyalties, and they are, for him, inexhaustible. I went looking further, since nobody had once looked up and seen me there, looking for what I'd seen once, something I thought might help me. It was the Buddha he had. It had something—a sense of peace maybe, maybe a sense of knowing there were things before Carrington and beyond him. And maybe he, I thought, will give me a sense that he knows me, too. So that I may know, too, myself.

"But the Buddha was gone, a bare place in the yard. It was like a note to me, that bare spot. Not from Carrington this time, but from the world. 'Seek,' it said, 'but you shall never find. Knock, but no one is there.' It was then the ducks started for me. You had some ducks there, didn't you? I found the door to the kitchen open, a knife was easy. I destroyed them."

Mavis dropped her sewing and walked out of the shop. She was uncertain where to go but going was what she had to do. The Graham man was still sitting just where he had been, in the chair, eyes fixed. He might have been lecturing a class. She saw the children leaving the door of Barbra K.'s house, and she walked through them as they, each holding a little lunch box by the handle, began to run toward their mothers, each in a waiting car. She ran toward her own car. The door handle was red-hot to the touch. She wrenched open the door. But where to go? Actually, she had not moved. This man—so civilized, so quiet, so elegant—was worse than the Weasels, whom Frank had so injured: one dead, one damaged by fire, and another (though for different reasons) shot in the woods. "You fool," said Mavis in a low voice. And then she hit him with her large wooden knitting needles. "Fool!" She was trembling.

Lex scarcely noticed her. He put his hand to his brow where the blow had fallen. "Everyone is right, except me." He said this sadly, and she did not at once take it in. Then she did.

"I'm sorry for you if you feel that way."

"I want to pay for them," he continued, "but it's hard to find Arnie. Can you tell him? It's been rather on my conscience. I can mail him a check if I knew how much."

"He's working on a book," said Mavis, now struggling, as one trapped in nightmare, only to wake. Get him out of here.

"Yes," said Lex Graham dreamily, "and it will be published one day. Front page of the New York *Times Book Review*. He will be known as the definitive U.S. authority on Byron, perhaps the leading scholar of our time. It sounds impossible. But it will happen."

Another word and she would suffocate. She got up slowly, teetered, and, feeling heavy and slightly sick, bent to pick up the needles from where they'd dropped. Lex, under no obligation, sat looking at her.

"You're really a marvelous woman, aren't you?"

She closed her eyes to wish his absence, to unwish his existence from the universe, but within her shaded pupils the image was caught forever: the slaughtered flock, white as snow, lying along the shady bank, blood trickling in timorous rivulets toward the pond.

Customers entering did not find her and went away, but finally one, a boy ashamed of liking needlework but liking it anyway, ventured back of the counter and saw her lying in a heap of colored Indian fabric, on the floor. He ran next door and found Barbra K. who called Arnie Carrington, who called an ambulance.

So it happened that, straight from the phone, Arnie was running to his car, had to get there with the car, in case the ambulance was out or late. In driving onto the highway, he had to stop for traffic, and there, poking behind a diesel truck, was that inevitable beige Mercedes. It had to be Lex Graham. Oh, Lex! Lex! He had almost hit him. That would be the day, a bang on the sacred fenders. But later, he wondered if he would have hit anything, if either Graham or that thing he drove had ever known any real existence. He might have driven his old Chevy straight through machine and driver, like a plane through cloud. Then why was he sticking his head out the window to call, "Lex! Lex!"? For a moment, he thought of stopping just long enough to say something human, for the stiffly held, distinguished head did turn, as though it had caught something, its own name called, perhaps. It turned against a blank distance of Gulf water, decided it was hearing things, turned back again.

Arnie had to get to Mavis; of course, he did. Just at the entrance to his cherished street, he saw the ambulance approaching down the highway and heard the muted claxon, how it elevated slightly, sank back to nothing. He paused to gesture. "Here!" he shouted. He led it on.

Barbra K. had been positive from the first minute she saw her what was happening. Now, what with one thing following another, here they were in the back of a ambulance, she and Mr. Arnie, both holding on to Mavis's hands. "Jesus," said Barbra K., "I just pray it ain't too soon for this birth." The young doctor closed the doors. He kept saying to Mavis to relax, lie still, try not to move, we'll get you there, it's all right, we got you in time, it's all all right. He went on like that, while she kept saying, "Frank, where's Frank?" Then she came out with a lopsided yell, and in one great contraction her legs flew wide. There was darkness for them all to see and blobs of blood, darkness within, a burst of fluid, a life on its thundering way to light. Early or not, it's here, thought Arnie, and watched where her nails were biting his arm, he watched the blood well. That damned kitten of hers, the one he'd given her, he'd kicked it through the shop door and slammed the door shut, but it went on mewing in his head. Shut up! he all but said aloud, not meaning Mavis.

Arnie had been interrupted just at the place in his manuscript where his own will, along with Byron's, was fighting back the bleeders, the leeches, those people in their sound mind who had so sensibly wanted a poet's blood. He, too, had been believing in the freedom of Greece, a people's proud resurgence. So there was blood before his eyes, here and now. Let this child live, he prayed, to God, to Buddha, to whatever there was, to the power within. "Call on Jesus," he said to Barbra K. "What you think I'm doing?" she asked, right back. Let his father come and claim him, claim her, claim himself, claim us all. For "Call Matteo!" was what he'd shouted out the door to Joe Yates, who had come butting out into the street with a pencil behind his ear, just as the ambulance wail was awakening again and the doors were closing to.

It was hope, only that, they were riding with, swift as a charged cloud, ready to gather strength and speed, to break with hurricane force into the bright redemption of love.

10

Who could describe the inefficient bureaucracy of hospitals? Of anywhere, this day and age, Arnie thought, but especially of hospitals? In hospitals, you sit for hours waiting in an emergency room while skin swells and purples above a fracture, blood oozes from the cut of a broken bottle, the eye with the splinter in it weeps a quart of tears. But in the case of unexpected birth (or rather in the case of Mavis's baby's unexpected birth), doors swung open as if a President had been gunned, and the patient, still yelping out not so much at this point from pain or anguish or shock or joy, as from life's many wild surprises, glided on rubber wheels into antiseptic, air-cooled mysteries, leaving her followers behind to wait.

So back to the waiting room with Barbra K. Arnie sat silent, cap in hand, waiting raw-eyed, knowing the strain of what the keystone of the world's arch knows constantly—that everything has only the one chance in infinity of going right, but those there are who are always taking it. He saw Joe Yates appear with Frank Matteo. They stood near the door, wordless.

"Mr. Frank," said Barbra K., "yo' wife been having this child."

No one else spoke. In Arnie's head, the kitten mewed again.

It was a waiting room different from the one Arnie knew so well, on another floor, the second, while his waiting and anguish had dragged itself out on the first. Still, he could see the window and he remembered the girl, Lucinda, and all that curious sex-charged day, the emotions dark and light, light and dark again, hastening. He remembered the precise cool-dark smell of the lighthouse within. Cool dust, so quiet. Tomb-cool dust. And resurrection.

This waiting room was better decorated, doubtless to soothe the nerves, keep cheerful and optimistic those countless waiting fathers, one of whom, anonymous, was now fidgeting over in the corner, going for short walks to the water cooler and the men's room, and returning. When a nurse appeared, in the green gown of the delivery theater, her mask pulled down, they all looked up. She went to the man in the corner and whispered, and he jumped up to hurry after her.

"Let's all sit down," Yates suggested. His crumpled seersucker, his straw hat; the gentleman uptown. Of the best family, dressed like anybody else. Just ran an errand he didn't care much for. Slightly intellectual. Had his own ideas. Not easily swayed. Snobbishness not quite visible. Disdain.

"Yates," said Arnie, "it isn't just every day—" His voice broke.

Yates looked around him. "No, it isn't," he finally said. He wet his lips. His understanding was there, present. It raised its walls around them, as if that in itself ought to be enough, as, for the moment, it was.

But it was not enough. It couldn't be. No walls can be designed to hold our need, thought Arnie.

There was a rumble of thunder, a darkened sky. Regular phenomenon of the Coast afternoons. The light, turned poignant and golden for September, darkened. Frank Matteo looked at no one. He walked outside, but remained in shadow form visible through the beveled glass of the door. He came back in, restless. The things that had happened, who knew them all? Proud, he watched over them in his own way, alone.

A little rain came on, lashed for a moment at the windows. It passed on.

Barbra K. put her face in her hands. She looked like Evelyn. The same amplitude. Arnie had never noticed it so strongly as now. When had he first seen it? Perhaps down where nothing got actually told, down where the knowing started, beyond where the words began and ended. We can go to the island one day, he thought, surprising himself. But no need to go there, really, with her here, ashore.

A nurse appeared. She looked like the other one, and perhaps was the same.

She surveyed them all, a group, obviously known to one another. "It was premature, we all know that. Just under seven months. But we think . . . we can only hope . . . we even believe that it's going to be all right. It's in the incubator."

"Thank you, Lord," said Barbra K., as though speaking casually to someone constantly around, who might have brought her something fresh from the garden. (No Buddhas for her. She had once said to Arnie, "What you want with that thing?")

"Phew!" said Yates, and fanned with his hat, but Arnie was holding yet.

The nurse looked at them all, then walked over and stopped in front of Frank Matteo. "You must be the father. Well, you can see them soon. See her, I mean . . . and him, too."

Ah, thought Arnie, and though waiting still, he moved, out of sheer exhaustion, to sink back into a chair, which, out of exhaustion also, he missed, and fell over, on to the floor. Perhaps he blanked out.

"What do you think you're doing?" It was Frank, pulling him upright, supporting him who had himself supported, Arnie recalled, many others. This damned crook, this dark projection in their lives. Would he change? Probably, but how much, how little? You never know. He was holding Arnie up. I've got old, thought Carrington. Ancient. I feel it in my bones. Frank was helping him sit down.

"Frank," said Arnie, not knowing how long he'd blanked out, "go to her. For God's sake."

"The minute they'll let me," said Matteo. He raised his voice. "You think I don't want to? Seeing my son. Why, that's all there is!"

Like something for the moment leashed, but about to be cast, he turned to look at the others. Had they trapped, betrayed, deceived him? He had to defy what threatened, to fend off what was always ready to strike.

"You think that's not everything there is?" he challenged. "You think for a minute that's not all?"